Runner 13

Amy McCulloch is the Chinese-White author of *Breathless*, an international bestseller and Waterstones Thriller of the Month selection. She has also written eight novels for children and young adults. She has climbed two of the world's highest mountains, completed an ultra-marathon in the Sahara Desert, and visited all seven continents, including Antarctica. *Runner 13* is her third thriller.

Runner 13

AMY McCULLOCH

MICHAEL JOSEPH

PENGUIN MICHAEL JOSEPH

UK | USA | Canada | Ireland | Australia
India | New Zealand | South Africa

Penguin Michael Joseph is part of the Penguin Random House group of companies
whose addresses can be found at global.penguinrandomhouse.com

Penguin Random House UK,
One Embassy Gardens, 8 Viaduct Gardens, London SW11 7BW

penguin.co.uk

Penguin
Random House
UK

First published 2025

001

Set in 13.5/16pt Garamond MT Std
Typeset by Jouve (UK), Milton Keynes
Printed and bound in Great Britain by Clays Ltd, Elcograf S.p.A.

The authorized representative in the EEA is Penguin Random House Ireland,
Morrison Chambers, 32 Nassau Street, Dublin D02 YH68

A CIP catalogue record for this book is available from the British Library

HARDBACK ISBN: 978-0-241-64139-2
TRADE PAPERBACK ISBN: 978-0-241-64140-8

MIX
Paper | Supporting
responsible forestry
FSC® C018179

For Sophie — next time, you're going to have to run it with me.

Prologue

Adrienne

Faster, Adri.

I will myself to dig deeper, even though I'm right at the edge of my limit.

He's gaining on me. For the last few miles of this hundred-mile race, it's been a game of cat and mouse. I want this win, more than anything. But *want* doesn't win ultramarathons. Resilience does.

Planning helps too. The Yorkshire 100 is not only my local race but it's renowned as one of the UK's toughest, cutting right through the heart of the vast, remote Yorkshire Dales in the dead of winter. The route winds its way through boggy moorlands, down snow-covered trails, and over so many rugged peaks that our elevation gain will be akin to climbing Mount Everest, all the while facing brutal fierce cold winds, driving rain – and that's if the weather gods are kind. But I know I'm ready. I've been training for months, learning every twist and turn of the route, knowing I'll have to navigate while sleep-deprived and in pain.

I'd managed to stick diligently to my plan – right up until the sixty-mile checkpoint. I'd allotted myself thirty minutes to rest and refuel, then I had to move on. I'd been looking forward to this one. My ex-husband, Pete, was bringing our three-year-old son so I could hug him before his bedtime. But as I'd staggered into the freezing church hall, I couldn't see them amongst the small group of hardy volunteers. I'd waited, downing ramen noodles laden with cheddar and salami, as many calories as I could stomach, one eye on the door. My phone messages went unread. Time ticked by, my thirty-minute break turning into an hour, eating into my narrow lead. I knew if I had any chance of winning I had to leave. So I left.

But my closest opponent hadn't spent long at the checkpoint either. He'd sped through it, not even eating a hot meal, and with the rest of the pack several hours off the pace, from then on it had only been the two of us in contention.

Now there are only five miles left. My heart and lungs protest more than my muscles, screaming at me that they can't go on. I ignore them. Slowing down is not an option. I dare not waste any energy even looking over my shoulder. Maybe he's fallen back. But I doubt it. A course record is on the line. He came here to win. Unfortunately for him, so did I.

I'm deep into what we ultrarunners call the 'pain cave'. For me it's the place my mind goes when it's convinced I've hit my limit – but somehow I have to keep going. This pain cave is well earned. I've endured hours of torrential rain in the pitch-darkness, falling over in the mud and slush, one hundred miles of eye-stinging wind, muscle cramps and blisters. Thankfully, the sun has risen on a dry morning – though my hands are still frozen into claws inside my gloves, my eyelashes coated in frost. My vision is tunnelled down so all I can see is a few feet in front of me. Still, I know this route so well, every pebble, blade of grass, dip and climb of the trail burned into my memory.

That knowledge is the padding of my pain cave, the way I keep myself comfortable. I settle in and keep putting one foot in front of the other.

The cross-country track I've been following ends and, for the first time in twenty-four hours, I'm running on tarmac, on the undulating country road that leads to the village hosting the finishing line. A marker nailed to a telephone pole indicates the final mile. I stretch and wake everything up to find another gear. I stick my head out of the cave. I need to feel the pain now. This is *grit my teeth and somehow bear it* time. A dream of hot tea and crumbly ginger biscuits floats through my mind. My mouth salivates at the thought.

After hours of silence and isolation, suddenly there are people *everywhere*. Lining the route, shouting and waving, holding up hand-painted signs. Are they surprised to see it's me? I can't tell.

Tears well up in my eyes, but I need to hold them back. I can't let myself get overwhelmed with emotion yet. The lead-up to this race has been the most difficult of my life, so much so that I almost didn't make the start. The temptation to take back my accusation, to do anything to make the trolls go away, is so strong. But I'm not taking anything back. And I'm not going to let it stop me from competing.

Racing has always been my sanctuary. The time I feel most myself, no matter what is going on – good or bad. It's my mindfulness. My meditation. My *salvation*. I'm not about to let Coach Glenn take that away from me too.

Only a few hundred yards left now. My eyes clear, I lift my head and even chance a smile. It's not just the run. It's this, the competition, the push and pull, that makes me feel alive.

Before I know it, I'm grinning from ear to ear. And I'm still running. No, more than that, I'm flying. I'm filled with a sudden, absolute certainty that I'm going to win. I don't relax, though. I dare to push that little bit more, and my body responds.

The finishing line comes into view, a huge banner stretching across the high street with a digital clock underneath, the red numbers ticking up. The time it displays shocks even me. If my running maths is correct, I've smashed the previous course record by over five hours. I had no idea I was moving that quickly.

Two volunteers hold a stream of white tape across the path and I think instantly of Ethan, my son: how proud he's going to be of me, when he sees that medal round my neck. Where is he? Pete normally brings him in front of the finishing line so he can watch me cross it. He dresses him in a bright yellow coat so he's unmissable. But I haven't spotted them yet. *Where could they be?*

There's a burst of applause, but it's not for me. It's from behind me. Is the other runner making a push for the finish? I can't get complacent. The win isn't mine yet. Runners can lose a race in the final steps. I surge forward, sprinting those last few feet. The tape snaps across my chest.

I've done it. I've won.

Cheers crash over me like a wave, and I wait a beat – arms raised, eyes closed – for the euphoria of the moment to hit. But then a voice rises above the crowd, louder than all the rest.

'LIAR!'

I stumble, my foot slipping as I spin round, searching for the source.

I just about manage to stay upright – but not before I hear the voice again: 'MURDERER.'

The crowd noise becomes more hesitant, hushed. Between the cameras flashing, banners waving, I can't see who it is.

Murderer? What the hell?

I take a step forward, but that's when my legs give out, the adrenaline flooding my system, overwhelming me. My knees bash against the ground and I wince with pain.

Someone steps forward to help me. Heavy black boots, the toes polished. Uniform trousers. A high-viz vest over an all-climate shirt, a radio on their shoulder.

Police.

'Adrienne Wendell?' the officer asks, but he doesn't need an answer. He knows who I am. It's written on my race bib above my number. 'You need to come with me. It's about your son. There's been an accident.'

Seven Years Later

The Ultra Bros Podcast

Hot & Sandy Edition

Jason: Welcome, trailblazers, to this very special edition of the Ultra Bros, as we start our coverage of Boones's newest race, Hot & Sandy.

Mac: Hmm, kind of sounds like a weather report to me. Hot & Sandy.

Jason: That's part of his trademark – why his races are nicknamed 'the Ampersands'. There's Big & Dark through the Blue Ridge Mountains and Long & Windy in Denali National Park. But this one is a two-hundred-and-fifty-mile self-sufficient stage race through the Sahara Desert in Morocco and it sounds totally bonkers. Boones is back, baby!

Mac: OK, OK, back up a second – we already have the Barkley, the Ultra X races, Badwater, UTMB. Heck, the Marathon des Sables has held the title of 'the world's toughest foot race' for years, to the point that even finishing is a badge of honour – and it kinda has a lock on the Sahara. So what's got you so amped up about this race in particular? Fill our listeners in on why this is different – and why they should be glued to this coverage.

Jason:	With pleasure, mate. Look, the difference between those races and this one? Boones. This guy doesn't just blaze the trail, he fucking razes it to the ground. His mission has always been to push the boundaries of what is humanly possible. How far will you go? That's the question he asks all his runners.
	Next, you don't 'enter' a Boones race. He handpicks you. Exclusive invite through the post, all very hush-hush. Then there's always a twist during the race itself – in Big & Dark, Boones makes you fill containers with different soil to prove you've been in the right places, so you have all these runners on their hands and knees basically pushing dirt into these tiny vials in the middle of the trail.
Mac:	Oh, so he's a sadist.
Jason:	More like a scientist – and we're his lab rats. When he launched Long & Windy – we didn't know if it was 'windy', as in referring to strong winds, or 'windy' because of the million switchbacks. Turns out, it was both. Only one person ended up finishing Long & Windy – our mate and frequent podcast guest Rupert Azzario – and since then he's ended up with sponsorships out the wazoo, brand deals, a Netflix documentary – a professional ultrarunner's wet dream. He's the King of the Ampersands.
Mac:	Yeah, and didn't someone die?
Jason:	RIP Steve Parsons, lost in his prime. He was the race leader, real competitive guy, but the

high winds and narrow trails got the better of him and he was blown off the route. They never even found his body.

Mac: Jesus.

Jason: Look, Steve was not the first elite – and he won't be the last – to die doing one of these races. They're inherently risky – but that's where you can practically see these elite athletes salivating at the idea of rising to the challenge. It sounds mad, but these guys want to be pushed. Whether they admit it or not, they want to find their limit. Sure, for any other race director, an incident like that would shut them down for good. But if anything, it only added to Boones's mystique. He got even more mainstream publicity after that. The next Big & Darks were covered by major media outlets, posts went viral on social media, the whole shebang. He has this group of fans online – the Booneshounds – who obsess over his every move. Boones's star was rising and every elite runner wanted a chance to tackle his races. And then, two years ago, he stopped. No Big & Dark. No Long & Windy. Speculation was rife – maybe he was scouting for an even better location for a new race, maybe he was on a running pilgrimage down the length of the Americas – there were supposed sightings of him in Mexico and Argentina! There were even some rumours that he'd died, and

	questions about who was going to take over the races – or whether they were done for good. But now he's back, and you'd best believe he's got something extra in the bag to really set this next race apart. It's a true game changer. Can you guess what it is?
Mac:	The money.
Jason:	Damn right, the money. Five hundred thousand bucks. Two thousand dollars per mile. Ever heard anything like that in ultrarunning?
Mac:	Never.
Jason:	So that's twist number one.
Mac:	Kind of out of Boones's typical ethos, isn't it? I thought he was a less-is-more kind of guy.
Jason:	Except the question is always the same: how far will you go? I bet he's going to make us runners work for that cash. Yep, that's right – the next surprise for our listeners is that I'm going to be on the starting line!
Mac:	What? How'd a joker like you end up getting an invite?
Jason:	Your guess is as good as mine! As soon as the race was announced I've been shouting about how much I want to run in it, so maybe Boones took pity on me. Got my invite three months ago. Barely enough time to tweak my training plan and squeeze in some heat acclimatization, but I'll be there.
Mac:	Any idea how many other nutters will be joining you on the starting line?

Jason:	No clue. But the prize money and the invites are for the 'elite' race. Boones also released five hundred 'fun runner' places – if you can call a race of this type 'fun' – for people who want to pay a hefty admission fee for the privilege of running in the desert. They're not there to compete, just to have the experience – mad sods. But that's probably how he's managed to raise the dough.
Mac:	What if one of the fun runners wins?
Jason:	I'm sure Boones has a plan for that. But I can tell you, the elites will be as motivated as hell.
Mac:	Who do you think you'll be up against?
Jason:	Rupert, of course. I assume the top Moroccan runners will be there. Farouk Lazaar and Nabil Alami. They've dominated desert races in the past. Then there's people like Pete Wendell, Alexander Schmidt, Mariam Hussein . . . but who knows? There are some wild rumours flying around.
	But what I'm truly interested in this year, is who is going to be Boones's runner thirteen?
Mac:	Runner thirteen – that mean something?
Jason:	It's Boones's pick. His 'runner to watch'. Whoever gets the number-thirteen bib is the runner he thinks is going to win – or, sometimes, the runner he thinks is going to flame out spectacularly.
Mac:	So if you're number thirteen, you gonna give me a share of that cool half a mil?

Jason: I'm going for the shits and giggles, you know
           that. I'm not gonna win. But I want my place in
           the history books. Mark my words, Mac. This is
           going to be a race to remember.

*The Ultra Bros Podcast is brought to
you by Blixt Energy.
For when 'One foot in front of the other' just isn't
enough. Blixt. Beyond endurance.*

I

Adrienne

The plane door opens and I step out into a furnace. The blast of heat is intense and immediate, accompanied by a fierce wind that forces me to hold on to my cap to stop it from being blown away. The same winds had almost diverted the plane to a different airport – much to the consternation of everyone on board. We're all in Morocco for the same reason, after all.

The Hot & Sandy race. I still can't quite believe I'm going through with it. Up until the moment I boarded the chartered plane at London Gatwick, I thought about turning back. The reasons not to run felt so much more important than why I've come out here.

For one, there's Ethan. I've never left him for this long before. Even though he's ten, he's still my baby. And the last time I raced . . . I can't even finish the thought without shuddering. The horror of it still has a lock round my heart, a cage I can't break free from.

Then there's Pete. He also got an invite. Running my first race in seven years against my ex doesn't seem like the smartest plan. Pete is surprisingly relaxed about it, but I think it's because he doesn't see me as competition. I don't even see me as competition. Showing up at the start feels brave enough for me.

Last – but definitely not least – Boones. The mysterious

race director of one-name-only notoriety, the Madonna of the running world. I've never wanted to run in one of his races. Only Boones made sure this was an invitation I couldn't refuse.

Ethan, for his part, is delighted to have both his parents racing. He'll be tracking us on the website, watching our every step. He looked up Boones online and put together a booklet of facts, like it was some kind of school project. Boones lives deep in the forest of North Carolina. He launched his first race – Big & Dark – over thirty years ago. Only ten people have finished his races in their history. No woman has *ever* finished.

'You're going to be the first, Mum,' he says, filled with the kind of innate confidence I wish I had in myself.

But focusing on the facts helps me too. I like to visualize the challenge ahead, mentally prepare for the pain – putting some padding in my pain cave, so that when I enter it during the race (and it's inevitable that I will), I have something to bounce off to stop it from hurting so much. It's what I did when I broke the course record at the Yorkshire 100, and when I podiumed at UTMB. It's what I try to do now.

The lack of information about the race has made that task difficult, though. All I know is what I've gleaned from the website, loaded from a QR code on the invitation: a two-hundred-and-fifty-mile five-day stage marathon across dunes, dried-up riverbeds, and the rock-strewn mountains (known locally as jebels) of the infamous Sahara Desert. The first two stages are twenty-five miles. The third and fourth are fifty miles each. Then the fifth day is the big one – one hundred miles – already nicknamed the 'long day'. Each stage will be timed and must be completed within a strict limit – bringing up the rear will be two Berber volunteers and their camel to sweep up any stragglers. Temperatures might range from freezing cold in the night to over fifty degrees centigrade in the day. Sandstorms are likely, as are venomous creatures. We are expected to navigate the route using only a copy of a map hand-drawn by Boones and a compass. And every runner must carry their own food, sleeping bags and survival gear for the length of the race. All we will be provided with is water every ten miles or so and an open-air tent each night set up in traditional style by the Berbers in a miniature city known as a 'bivouac'. There will also be medics and photographers along the route, and we will be wearing GPS tracking devices.

So far, so manageable. But I know there will be curve balls to come. Boones is famous for them.

The invite itself had been the first surprise. When it arrived on my doorstep, I thought it was a prank. I was going to put it straight in the bin. Then I turned it over.

On the back was a handwritten note.

COME AND FIND ANSWERS. It read. Then, underneath, a licence plate: *LK1X XFG*.

My heart pounded so hard, I could hear it ringing in my ears. *It couldn't be.*

Seven years ago, I'd had one of the worst nights of my life. Yes, I'd won my race. But at the finishing line, the police had met me with the awful news: Ethan had been in a hit-and-run accident.

They never found the driver.

Who did it? That became the question that dominated my life. Who had tried to hurt my baby?

I'd gone straight to my laptop, opened the vehicle enquiry page on the government website and typed in the plate number.

IS THIS THE VEHICLE YOU ARE LOOKING FOR?

The question seemed to taunt me. It's the one I'd asked myself every day for seven years.

RANGE ROVER.

BLACK.

The same make and model as the vehicle involved.

I'd dropped the invite then, the paper searing my fingers. It had to be a sick joke from one of the trolls who still hated me for what I did. I kicked it beneath the counter, not wanting to look at it, think about it. Then Ethan had come home, buzzing about the fact that his dad had been invited to some exclusive new race: Hot & Sandy. He'd even taken a photo of the invitation. They were the same.

It wasn't a prank.

Boones knew something about the accident. I'd tried to email him, write him a letter, even sent direct messages to the Ampersand race social media accounts. But they all went unanswered.

He wanted to tell me at the launch of his new race.

I knew then that I'd be entering. I had to find out.

Never mind that I'd spent seven years out of the ring. Seven years not racing, hiding away so as not to draw attention to myself.

The moment I boarded the plane, amongst hordes of other runners, the word was out. I try to stay off social media, but still, I couldn't help but open the apps to glance at what people were saying. Some were curious, some were neutral – but most were horrible. Variations on *how dare she?* and *what the fuck does she think she's doing?* And a couple even worse than that: *Oh great, the lying bitch is back. Who is she going to bring down this time?*

I glance over my shoulder before descending the stairs to the runway, the tarmac steaming through the soles of my trainers (of course I'd worn my running shoes on the plane – I wasn't going to risk those getting lost in transit). As I walk to the single-storey terminal emblazed with large letters reading 'ERRACHIDIA' – the name of the closest town to where the race begins – I'm soon overtaken by other eager runners. Do they know the race hasn't started yet? Each one has a small backpack slung on their shoulders, similar to the one I've got. We're carrying everything we need to survive for the next few days.

I hardly recognize anyone. A decade ago, I would have known almost everyone participating in a race like this. But the plane was packed with fresh-faced newcomers. I recognize Rupert Azzario, wearing a dozen brand patches on his clothing from top-of-the-line sponsors. He's like a walking billboard. My snide thoughts are accompanied by a spike of jealousy. At my peak I'd beaten him at the Yorkshire 100, the Dragon's Back and the Lake District Ultra, but he's the one making a living from his running, chasing races and records across the world. He has hundreds of thousands of followers. One of the privileged few living the dream. On the surface he's mild-mannered, humble, quiet – everyone likes him, looks up to him. Ultrarunning's golden boy. But beneath that genial persona there's a fierce competitor – one with a ruthless desire to win. It's served him well.

Rupert dodges eye contact, but I expected that. I'm sure

I'll experience worse. I feel on high alert, goosebumps rising on my skin despite the heat.

Liar. Murderer.

Those words still haunt me.

I try to shake them from my mind. I need to focus on getting to the bivouac, then finding Pete. That brings a smile to my face. It's nice to think of Pete as an ally instead of an enemy for once.

Pete's been in Morocco for a week already. He wanted to spend some time acclimatizing to the heat. Smart – it's something I would have done if I could have afforded the time off. He's much more used to these big races, having spent almost two decades on the circuit. His goal was always the prestigious American races – Western States, Badwater, Hardrock – or to podium at Comrades in South Africa. In my time I'd preferred to stay closer to home, focusing on races in the UK and Europe. As I board the coach for the next leg of the journey, I feel a flutter of butterflies in my stomach. Anticipation for the race, or fear? I find it hard to tell any more.

I choose a seat towards the back, turning my body to face the window, hoping I look like someone who doesn't want to be disturbed. I'm grateful when no one sits down next to me, and I spread my belongings across the empty seat for good measure. We have a six-hour coach journey to the bivouac, then our medical and equipment checks, and the registration to pick up our race numbers.

'Excited?' A man stops next to me, so I have to turn towards the aisle. He lifts his sunglasses on to his forehead. He's so tall he stoops and he's young – late twenties maybe – with soft brown eyes and a buzz cut.

I know the polite thing would be to remove my sunglasses too, but I keep them on. 'Mm-hmm,' I reply, shifting even closer to the window, hoping the man gets the hint and takes a different seat.

He doesn't.

'You're Adrienne Wendell, right?'

I stiffen. There's something irritatingly familiar about his voice; it grates on my nerves like sandpaper. I can't put my finger on why I recognize him. Has he come into the shop?

'I'm Jason.' He extends his hand, expecting me to shake it. I don't. Because now I know who he is. He's one of the presenters of *The Ultra Bros Podcast*. I spent years avoiding their questions. I'm not about to answer them now. 'Wow, you came! The "rock goat" returns . . .' He points to the empty spot next to me. 'Can I sit here?'

'No!' I blurt a little too loudly. I don't want to be interrogated for the next six hours. I scramble around for a reasonable excuse, my hand protectively guarding the seat.

'Because you're saving it for me, *n'est-ce pas?*' A slight woman with burnished brown skin and cropped silvery hair pushes her way past Jason, forcing him backwards. I hadn't seen her because she'd been hidden by his bulk.

'Mariam!' I don't think I've ever been so happy to see someone. I quickly clear the seat for her, and she slides in.

She reaches over and pats my knee, then looks up at Jason. 'Sorry, mate,' she says. It sounds hilariously casual in her lightly accented English, her third language after Arabic and French.

Jason fumbles in his pocket. 'I'm in tent sixteen. Adrienne, please come find me. A few minutes of your time is all I need.' He passes me an Ultra Bros business card with his tent number scribbled on the back. I take it but put it in the front pocket of the seat. There's no way I'll be seeking him out.

'Thank you for saving me,' I say, once he's moved out of earshot. I notice that other eyes have turned towards us, some people craning their necks to get a glimpse of me. At least that's what it feels like. I swallow my paranoia, shrink down and force a smile for Mariam. 'How have you been? I am so glad to see you.'

'Me? I feel the same way about you! It has been far too long.'

'You look well,' I say, and I mean it. She looks lean and strong, her dark brown eyes sparkling beneath her thick lashes, spidery laugh lines spreading from the corners. She must be over fifty but she's in peak physical condition, and she's been on the podium of several desert races over the past year. This is her home terrain, as she was born in Morocco, although I met her after she'd been living in Paris. We'd run in several races together across Europe and I'd always admired the way she'd balanced racing with raising her family.

When everything kicked off seven years ago, I thought she might stand up for me, vouch for me. But she stayed silent. I don't blame her. Not many people wanted to stick their head above the parapet.

'Ah, you're too kind. Every time I travel to a race, I think, it's finally happened! I am too old for this. But then I hear the word "go" and I'm off.'

I laugh, but Mariam doesn't join in. Her eyes search my face, curiosity bubbling under the surface. She might have saved me an interrogation from Jason, but he's not the only one with questions.

Thankfully, she seems to think better of asking any, instead wriggling around in her seat. She whistles through her teeth. 'Long journey ahead. I am going to try to get some rest. You should too.'

I nod, and she pats my knee again. Then she whips out an eye mask and pulls it down low.

Tears spring up in my eyes; I'm not used to such kindness. I turn back to the view to disguise it. The warm beauty of Morocco flashes by – clay buildings blending seamlessly into the dusky orange desert terrain beyond, interspersed with pale green foliage from olive trees. Everything seems suffused with soft light, like the place exists in a permanent golden hour. Yet there's evidence of damage from sand and wind everywhere too, tattered window coverings and blown-in glass, walls rough and crumbling. If the climate can do that to rock and stone, what can it do to the human body?

The six hours pass all too quickly for me. When we arrive, Mariam is straight off the coach – she'd spent most of the final hour crossing her legs and fidgeting – but it won't be long before I see her again, since we are sharing a tent in the bivouac. As the other runners rush towards the registration tent, I linger a bit longer, waiting for the aisle to empty.

Now that I'm here, the reality hits me. I'm about to face the community that worked so hard to shun me. It's going to require bravery, confidence, pride. I'm not sure I have any of that left.

My phone buzzes and I fish it out of my pocket. The camp is one of the last places we'll have signal.

It's Ethan. *Meep meep!* He accompanies the text with an animated cartoon gif of road runner.

That's why I'm doing this. I grab my pack down from the overhead compartment and swing it over my shoulders.

For Ethan. For me. To get the answers I need and get home.

It's time to put myself back in the arena.

2

Stella

Camera? Check.

Volunteer badge? Check.

Sanity? Back in California, where I left it with the rest of my boxed-up belongings. I'm here following my ultrarunning-obsessed boyfriend deep into the Sahara. The things you do for love.

Fiancé, I correct myself. Not boyfriend any more.

I lift my camera and snap a photo of him standing in front of a huge Hot & Sandy banner. He flexes his biceps and raises his leg into the running-man pose. It makes me laugh.

'There, much better,' he says, coming forward to kiss my cheek. 'I know you're worried, but look — look at this place.'

'It's pretty impressive,' I concede. I don't share that the sight of the bustling bivouac beyond the banner is only adding to the feeling of dread in my stomach.

'Meet you at my tent after my medical?' he asks.

I nod.

He gives my hand a squeeze. 'It will be OK. You'll see. And then we can start planning the wedding.'

I flash him a smile. The novelty hasn't worn off. The ring on my left hand still feels like a foreign object — after all, he only popped the question yesterday. I should be floating on cloud nine. Instead, I'm weighted down by a sense of impending doom, like a storm is coming.

He jogs towards the medical bays for his check-up. He's been preparing for this for months, ever since he received that damn invitation. It's consumed him. Technically, no family, friends or spectators are allowed at the race, but there was no way I was going to wait at home, watching his progress from my laptop. I managed to convince the charity he's running for – Runners for Hope – to hire me as an official race photographer. That way I have a reason to be here on my own terms. It's the only way I could think of to keep him safe.

So now, despite vowing I'd never be involved with an Ampersand race, I'm here in the very thick of it. And I have a job to do. I take a deep breath and try to get my bearings.

Straight ahead of me is a semicircle of open-sided black camel-hair tents pitched with wooden poles and lined with rugs in traditional Bedouin style. More modern white marquees sit to one side – the hubs for admin, comms and the medics – a queue of people snaking out of the front, patiently waiting in the glaring sunshine for their packs to be checked and to receive their race numbers. In the gaps between the tents, further from the runners, I spot cars, trucks, caravans, even a helicopter – accommodation and transport for the hundreds of volunteers and staff – the cogs that keep this operation running. Finally, burly guards patrol the perimeter, making sure no one unconnected to the race enters the bivouac.

Between the security, the runners, the volunteers, the medics, the press, the admin staff and the Berbers in charge

26

of maintaining the bivouac, there must be upwards of a thousand people here. It's impossible to tell the elite runners from the 'fun' right now, but I'm struck by how *clean* everyone looks. Bright white shirts and perfect running shoes, freshly shaved faces and neat braids. It won't take long for that to change.

I flick the dial on my camera. Staring at the screen, I focus on a pair of runners who walk into my frame, the perfect 'before' shot. I snap. I always see things better, clearer, through the lens. It calms me.

As for this race, it's a miracle it's even happening. It's a logistical feat that requires an army to put together. I'm shocked Boones pulled it off.

The Boones I knew shouldn't have been capable of it.

But then I haven't come to expect much from my dad.

I haven't told Boones I was coming, but I have no doubt that he knows I'm here. He's always had this uncanny ability, this *way* of knowing things. For someone who lived most of his life as a recluse, he's exceptional at reading people.

A memory strikes me, of being on the starting line of a Big & Dark race. The start was only a couple of miles from our house, a little cabin on the edge of the woods in the Blue Ridge Mountains. Six years old, sitting on his knee, watching as runners in torn T-shirts and grubby running shoes emerged from their tents, most of them puffing on a final cigarette before the race. There'd been no polish, nothing fancy about the race or the people who ran in it. Just a tough trail and a few folks mental enough to test themselves against it. Even the start was casual. He hadn't looked at the runners. He'd only inhaled deeply, spoken the words 'Well, all right then,' clicked his fingers, and off they'd gone. As one man went by, Dad had given me a nudge. 'That guy,' he'd said. I'd written down the race number of the person he'd pointed out in a little Polly Pocket notebook. Number thirteen.

'That guy' had been the only one to finish that year. Dad just seemed to know.

The races were always the good times, when Dad seemed most alive. Most present. The rest of the time? Mom and I might as well not exist. He would disappear on his own madcap expeditions, sometimes not contacting us for months.

Mom packed us up and left not long after that. We moved halfway across the world to the south of France to get away. She remarried, had another child – my half-sister, Yasmin.

Once I asked her why she never spoke about Dad. 'The thing about Boones is that he treats people like his little experiments,' she'd said. 'And it's never long before some-one gets hurt.'

The message was clear: we were better off without him. She'd been right, of course. But there was something dif-ferent about race day. That was the time I missed him the most. So Mom let me go back once a year, to be there at the starting line. To give Boones and me a chance to main-tain some sort of connection.

That lasted until I was seventeen. I'd flown in as normal, and Dad had put me straight to work – again, not unu-sual, and I used to love getting swept up in the excitement of race day. Already things had been changing back then. More cameras. More runners. More publicity.

More women on the starting line too. I was pumped by that. I wanted to see a woman cross the finishing line, and one woman – Nina Carter – looked like she had the chops to do it.

The weather had other plans. That year it was dire – so much rain that the trails turned into mudslides. Strong winds threatened to bring trees down on the route, endangering the lives of the runners. I (and a good many others) pleaded with Dad to cancel the race.

He refused. We begged him to at least let them wear GPS trackers so we could find them if they became lost. He refused. Those were the terms of his race.

None of the runners finished that day. A few – including Nina – still hadn't showed up twelve hours after the time limit. I helped to coordinate volunteers for search parties, and we finally found them huddled at the bottom of a gully, unconscious and suffering from hypothermia.

Dad's response? They just weren't good enough. And that's when I saw him for who he truly was: a sadistic punisher who only wanted to cause pain, not celebrate human achievement, or whatever pompous justification he gave for putting people through actual mental and physical torture. He was lucky nobody died that year. He didn't get as lucky later on.

I stopped my annual visits to Big & Dark after that. He didn't seem to miss me.

I couldn't get away from running completely, though. It became Yasmin's passion. She would drag me out on rocky coastal paths near our home in Marseilles, running for miles with the sea breeze in our hair. I tolerated it so long as I could take a dip in the azure blue waters of the calanques along the way. When she started racing seriously, I became her biggest support. I crewed her races, took photos for her social media, helped her attract sponsors – whatever she needed.

She used to pester me about the Ampersands, but I never had much to tell her. She said it was her dream to be the first woman to finish one.

My biggest regret is that I didn't dissuade her. If I had, maybe she would still be alive.

'Are you here with Runners for Hope?' A young woman, copper hair in two braids lying neatly on her Hot & Sandy vest, approaches me. She taps her clipboard. 'Stella Mamoud, is it?'

'Yes, that's right.' I took my mom's last name a long time ago. Not that it matters – no one seems to know Boones's real name anyway.

'Great. I can show you to your tent.'

'Lead on. I was wondering how to find my way round this place.'

She smiles. 'It can be a maze. But you'll soon learn.'

She introduces herself as Camille, one of Boones's administrative staff (he has staff? That's news to me), and she takes the time to show me the dining tent, where the Berber chefs are already laying out the provisions for a monster buffet, with all the Moroccan specialities – a huge tagine of vegetable couscous, grilled chicken and lamb, plus a variety of carbs that I know the runners will love: mountains of bread rolls and vats full of pasta. It's the only time the runners will be fed the entire race. Otherwise they have to eat the food they've brought themselves.

'And this is the comms tent, where we have the

all-important Wi-Fi. So if you need to upload your images, you can do it from here. Just remember, you can't share the password with anyone else on the race.'

'Got it.'

A moment later, she stops in front of an open-sided tent – similar to the ones set up for the runners – with several people inside. 'This is where you'll be sleeping. Any issues, let me know. And here.' She hands me some sheets of paper stapled together in the corner. 'This is the final-ized list of runners, their race numbers and tent allocation. So you can get your interviews done for social media.'

'OK, thanks,' I reply, glancing at the paper.

A man steps out of the tent, stooping to duck beneath the edge of the black camel-hair cloth. 'Camille, hi!' he says. He glances over at me, rubbing at the thin line of beard running along his jawline. 'This our missing tentmate?'

'That's right. Dale, meet Stella. He's another race pho-tographer. You'll be paired up in the Jeep tomorrow.'

'Nice to meet you.' He extends his hand to me. 'I was just about to get some pre-race shots. Soak up the atmos-phere. Want to come with?'

But I don't have time for that. 'Is this a joke?' I ask.

She frowns. 'Excuse me?'

'This list.' I can see from Camille's face that she thinks I've lost my mind.

'Problem?' Dale asks.

Damn right there is. On the first sheet of paper is a list of the elite runners. And right at the top? A name I never expected to see.

Adrienne Wendell.

Fuck. How did I not know she'd be here?

'Boones,' I manage to spit out. 'Where is he?'

But Camille isn't listening. Her hand flies to her ear – an earpiece connected to a radio. 'Sorry, bivouac emergency,' she says, her hands flapping. 'I have to go.' She darts away before I can stop her. I can't exactly play the *don't you know who I am* card. I don't want anyone to know I'm related to him if I can help it.

'You're looking for Boones?' Dale asks. He's tying a bandana round his forehead, keeping the sun off his bald scalp. A DSLR camera hangs on a strap off his shoulder.

I nod.

'Then come with me,' he says. 'I know how to find him.'

3

Adrienne

The queue to register stretches out in front of me, thirty-odd people deep. Under the glare of the bright sun, my skin tightens and my eyes prickle, as all the moisture seems to be baked from my body. I wonder if others are feeling as uncomfortable as I am, but most of the elite athletes would have acclimatized to the soaring temperatures using fancy heat chambers, some of them with built-in treadmills so they could really get their bodies used to exerting themselves in the heat. All I'd managed to do is convince Debbie at the PureSpa in town to let me use the sauna for a few hours as a thanks for sending so many clients her way from the shop. If it gets much hotter, I'm not sure that's going to cut it.

I dig out my water bottle, use some of it to soak my cap, then take a big swig. I pop a salt tablet too. It's not only about hydration; I must also replace the electrolytes that I'll be losing through sweat. The thing about the dry Moroccan heat is that the sweat evaporates almost instantly, so it's easy to get dehydrated without being aware of it.

Some people have failed in desert races purely by forgetting to take their salt. I'm not going to be one of them.

With my cap and sunglasses, dressed in a long-sleeve moisture-wicking white shirt and black running shorts, I blend seamlessly into the crowd. For the first time I

33

don't feel eyes on my back. I'm just another runner, like everyone else. All around me, excited chatter fills the air, the atmosphere electric. The buzz of athletes about to embark on a challenge they've been training their minds and bodies to achieve for months. They are either ready or not. But can you ever truly be ready for a two-hundred-and-fifty-mile race? Ultimately it's going to come down to grit.

And that's why I love it. I hadn't realized how much I missed it.

That turned out to be the cost of speaking out. If I'd known, would I have made a different decision?

Never, I think, shuddering, but then it's my turn at the desk. I approach a frazzled-looking man with a clipboard and show him my invitation.

'Oh, you're an elite?' he asks.

I nod, even though hearing it out loud makes me feel like a fraud.

He waves me away with his hand. 'Over that way.'

'Aren't you going to weigh my pack?'

He tuts. 'All the elite checks are taking place in a different marquee. You didn't need to stand in this line.'

'Oh,' I say. I'd been in with the fun runners. No wonder the atmosphere had felt so much more relaxed.

He eyes my pack. 'That thing does look a little heavy.'

'You can tell by sight?'

'When you've seen as many runner packs as I have, you start to make a good guess! The ideal is around six kilos in my opinion. Any more and your form will suffer – any less and you probably don't have enough nutrition.'

'I'll worry about my form and nutrition, thanks.'

He tilts his head in deference, and I wander over to the correct tent.

I'm shown straight in. Even with fans blowing, it's stuffy inside the marquee – and surprisingly dark. I remove my glasses and cap before greeting the two women sat behind the desk. 'Um, Ms Wendell signing in,' I say.

The two exchange a look, and then one of them gets on the radio, speaking in rapid-fire French, too quick for me to understand. The other one gestures for me to open my backpack. I swing it round off my shoulders and place it on the desk.

'We're checking to make sure you have all the mandatory equipment. If you add anything later – or have someone else carry food for you – that is also grounds for dismissal from the race.'

I nod, watching as the woman examines my fastidiously packed gear. I double- and triple-checked the mandatory kit list, so I'm not worried about missing anything. I've got packages of food (marked with the number of calories for each day), spare socks, sleeping bag and mat. A small foldable stove and fuel cubes for boiling water. A first-aid kit, compass, pocket mirror (for signalling, not vanity), whistle – and some slightly more unusual pieces of equipment: a snake bite and antivenom kit. My phone and a solar-powered battery charger. I've included a couple of personal extras – a little lion teddy and a small digital camera. Surplus to requirement, but I wouldn't travel anywhere without them.

She then puts it all back and hangs it above a scale. Eight kilograms. Two over the minimum. She raises an eyebrow, but I shrug. There's no maximum weight – but in a race like this, every gram counts. It could be the difference between finishing and not. For me, though, the boost those items give me is worth it.

'OK, all is fine with your gear. I'm going to attach a tracker to your bag.' She clips a bright orange tag to the strap of my backpack. I almost stop her, hoping that she hasn't placed it somewhere that's going to dig into me as I run. I've trained with the bag – as is. Even the slightest change could cause a hotspot that ends my race. But I swallow down my protest. I can't control everything. And I'd much rather have the GPS tracker than not.

'This will also serve as your emergency beacon,' she continues. 'If you need help, you press down both these two buttons on the top here. You need to press *both*,' she repeats, 'to activate the beacon. Then stay where you are and we'll send someone to your location as quickly as possible. Do not use it if it is not a true life-threatening emergency – pressing it will result in your immediate exit from the race. Your race bib should be here any – Ah! Here he is.'

The back of the marquee flies open, and for a moment I'm blinded by the bright white sunshine flooding in. I lift my hand to shield my eyes and hold my breath. This is it. I get to meet the man who claims to have the answers I've been waiting for.

'You made it!'

My heart sinks and I exhale. It's not Boones. It's a young guy – tall, lanky like a string bean and with a mop of wavy hair – with a posh Home Counties accent. He's wearing a crisp white shirt beneath his Hot & Sandy vest and pressed trousers, in stark contrast to everyone else in athletic wear.

'I'm Henry, race logistics. It's very nice to meet you.'

'Thanks for inviting me,' I reply.

'We had our doubts you would come. You were the final runner to register.'

'I thought it was a hoax at first. Or a mistake, at least.'

'As you can see, no hoax.' He stops on the other side of the table. 'I've got your race number here, personally assigned by Boones.' He places it face down.

'When do I meet Boones?' I ask, trying to sound nonchalant.

'Plenty of time for that – don't you worry,' says Henry with a smile. It doesn't do much to reassure me.

A doctor wearing a red cross on his breast pocket, a stethoscope round his neck and a nameplate that reads 'Dr Emilio', stops by our table. He looks like he's far more used to spending time in the Moroccan sun than I am – his skin evenly tanned – and he has thick dark, almost black hair. Mediterranean heritage is my guess – and a heavy Italian accent confirms it. Boones has assembled an international team.

'This is the next elite?' he asks, gesturing at me.

'Yes, meet Adrienne Wendell,' Henry says.

The doctor frowns. 'Oh, any relation to . . . ?'

'Pete Wendell?' I finish for him. 'He's my ex-husband.'

Dr Emilio quirks his upper lip as he exchanges a look with Henry. I feel like there's a conversation happening that I'm not a part of. 'Is, uh, everything OK with Pete?' I ask.

He doesn't answer me. 'Your medical documents, please,' he says instead.

I hand him my up-to-date resting electrocardiogram and a letter certifying my good health from my GP. He examines it with a critical eye. 'This all looks good. Strong heart. May I listen?' He lifts his stethoscope.

I nod, breathing deeply to keep my heart rate normal – and to keep from blushing. It's been a while since I've been in such close proximity to a handsome man. I open the top button of my shirt and he leans forward, pressing the cool metal face of the stethoscope against my chest. He doesn't say much, but he writes a few notes, which I take to mean everything is OK. 'I need to take some bloods and a urine sample, then you can go.'

'Bloods?' My stomach flips, this time having nothing to do with the doctor's rich brown eyes. I hate needles.

'For a drug test. We will take them at the end as well. Nervous?'

'That obvious?'

He laughs as he begins the process of wrapping elastic round my bicep. 'I'll be quick. So you haven't met Boones?'

The way he pronounces 'Boones' makes it sound more like 'Bones'. I know he's trying to get me to chat, to distract me, but I just want to shut my eyes and pretend there's no needle.

'Not yet,' I say.

'He's not so scary in person, I assure you.'

'Maybe when you're not running in one of his races,' I say through gritted teeth.

'You have a point,' he replies. He's good this doctor – I know he's moving quick and the process so far has been painless. But it's not the actual pain that I'm afraid of. It's the needle, the blood being forced from my body . . . It sends me into instant fight or flight.

I don't want to faint now. I don't want to give them a single reason to doubt my ability to run.

'Look, is there something I should know about Pete?' I ask, still curious about the way the doctor had reacted to his name.

'Do you know his tent number?' he asks.

I nod. Of course I do. Ethan made sure I had it memorized. It's sweet that he wants us to look out for each other. And for his sake I will. There's something in the doctor's tone that has me worried.

'Then I suggest you make that your next stop.' He caps the blood vial and releases my tourniquet. 'All done,' he says. 'We'll get this processed and if there are any issues, we'll find you in your tent.'

I stand, resisting the urge to place my hand over the spot where the needle went in. I gather my backpack. 'Thank you, doctor.'

'It's Emilio, please.'

I smile. 'Emilio, then.'

'Oh, don't forget your bib,' Henry says, as I'm almost through the door.

He hands it to me, and I do a double-take as I realize what race number I've been given.

I've always been told Boones has a sense of humour. Or maybe this is the start of one of his infamous games I've heard so much about. I think about protesting. Offering to take any other number. Maybe some runners have dropped out – there must be a different one available.

No. This is a test. It must be.

Runner 13.

4

Stella

Dale walks me directly to Boones's trailer, but he's not there. Evidence of him is all over the place, though. A packet of Marlboros resting on the windowsill. A pocket watch dangling from the rear-view mirror of the Jeep outside and a tin of moustache tamer on the passenger seat. He was meticulous about some things. Parenthood just wasn't one of them.

'He was here half an hour ago,' Dale says. His palm is grubby where he used it to peer into the window. He wipes it against his shirt.

'Damn it,' I mutter under my breath. The bivouac is far larger than I imagined. He could be hiding anywhere.

Dale cocks his head. 'Everything OK? Do you know Boones or something?'

My jaw clicks as I bite down my back teeth. I take a breath. 'It's fine. I'll catch him later.'

'Well, duty calls.' Dale pats his camera. 'If I see Boones, I'll tell him you're looking for him. It's . . . Stella, right?' He stares at me like he's seeing me for the first time. Then he leans his head back and shouts 'Stella!'

'Please, no *Streetcar* references.'

'Couldn't resist,' he says with a grin. Then he waves and wanders back towards the centre of the bivouac.

No way I'm waiting around for Boones to show. Even

if I am desperate; he doesn't need to know that. 'Hold up, I'll tag along,' I say. I do have a job to do while I'm out here. Finding the people signed up with Runners for Hope and documenting their journey. Whatever my opinion of Boones, the runners deserve respect. These people have prepared for months, their thoughts consumed by the race, every spare moment of free time eaten up by training. Family life, social life, hobbies – all sacrificed in the name of following a strict regime. 'Can you help me find these people?' I show him the list of people who are running in support of Runners for Hope. I need to take photographs and record interviews for all of them.

Dale glances at it and nods. 'Sure.'

'You seem to know your way around,' I say, as we walk towards the circle of runner tents.

'I've been here a couple of days already. I came early to help set up. You should see those Berber guys at work – they can whip up these tents faster than you can blink. Boones has been rushing around, waving his arms at everyone like the conductor of the world's most insane orchestra. But the race is going to be something else.' His tone borders on reverential.

I resist the urge to roll my eyes. I'm used to people talking about my dad like he's not a man but instead some kind of ultrarunning god. Doesn't mean I'm comfortable with it. 'Are you part of Boones's team then?'

Dale barks a laugh. 'Not exactly! Just a fan. If it weren't for my leg, I'd have a race number on, rather than this.' He gestures to his camera.

'What happened?'

'Busted my ankle, never properly recovered. Not enough to run two hundred and fifty miles anyway. I'll have to be satisfied watching through the lens.'

We pass a tent with a number '38' hanging off it. 'Hang on, this is on my list,' I say to him.

'Oh, I figured you'd want to go to the elites first. That's where the real stories are.'

'No, I'm good here,' I say, waving him off. I hope he doesn't catch the grimace on my face. The last place I want to go right now is to the elite tents. Not when I might run into *her*.

Dale lopes off, fiddling with his GoPro. I duck under the canopy of tent thirty-eight. A man with curly hair pulled back into a ponytail is diligently fastening strips of electric blue kinesiology tape to his toes, prepping his feet against blisters. At his side is a bib with the race number 124.

I glance at my list, matching his number to a name. 'Hugo?' I kneel so my face is in the shade. 'I'm Stella – photographer for Runners for Hope. Mind if I take a few snaps?'

'Only if you get my good side!'

I laugh. 'Don't mind me, carry on as you were.' After photographing his feet, I document the contents of his backpack, which spill out on to the woven carpet covering the tent floor: the foam egg box-like mattress laid out behind him, feather-light sleeping bag on top, the toothbrush with half its handle sawn off. Anything to save a few grams. Been there, done that.

I put the lens cap back, sliding the body of the camera round to my side, then take out my phone so I can film in vertical for social media. 'Do you mind telling me your story? Why have you come to run Hot & Sandy?'

'Of course.' He faces the camera, holding up a Polaroid of a beautiful young girl, her head wrapped up in a butterfly-print headscarf. 'Hi, I'm Hugo Pritchard – race number 124 – and I'm here with Runners for Hope in aid of my daughter. She was diagnosed with leukaemia at the end of last year and my wish was to raise five thousand pounds for the charity that helped our family through this incredibly tough time. I'm already at an amazing four thousand, six hundred, but every little bit helps, so please keep donating.'

Once he's finished telling his story, I turn off the video. 'I'm so sorry to hear about your daughter,' I say.

'I just want to make her proud. I know she'll be watching that tracker, and that will keep me going when it gets tough out there.'

I write down his GoFundMe address and promise to make a pledge. Hugo's video ends up being the first of many incredible, moving personal stories that I record. By the end of the day I'm going to be broke. My phone is full of them.

Runner 650 – running to show support for women who have experienced pregnancy loss.

Runner 501 – running in memory of his father, who lost his life far too young.

Runner 444 – raising money for a local child carer, to give them a much-deserved holiday.

So many worthy stories. So many people with 'whys' bigger than themselves, willing to endure physical hell to shine a light on a cause that means something to them.

Listening to them makes me nervous. I know how much this race already means to people. Boones did that. But he can't be trusted to keep them safe.

My phone buzzes with a text. *Medical tent. SOS.*

Fuck. It's already beginning.

5

Adrienne

Seven years earlier
Yorkshire

'It's about your son. There's been an accident,' the police-
man says.

I struggle to my feet and follow the uniformed officers
to their car, my whole body shaking. Someone – the race
director maybe – throws a Mylar blanket over my shoulders and I hug it tight round me.

Everything – the win, the pain, the horrid shouts at the
end of the race – is shoved from my mind. I feel like I've
been plunged through a hole in ice. 'What's happened to
Ethan?' I ask, my words coming out in a stutter as I'm ush-
ered into the back seat. I've barely spoken in thirty hours
and my voice sounds unnatural in my own head.

The officer in the passenger seat turns round. 'Your son
is in hospital. His father is with him.'

A moan, involuntary and primal, escapes my lips. When
I didn't see them at the checkpoint I should have waited. I
should have known something was wrong. The last call I
made had gone to voicemail . . .

That's when it hits me. My phone. When I take it out
of my pocket, I see the screen is smashed. I press the 'on'
button but it doesn't come to life. I might as well have

been carrying a brick for all the use it gives me. It must have broken beneath my weight when I slipped and fell on the frozen ground at mile eighty-two.

The officer is speaking, but only a certain amount slips through my fog of fear and worry. I get the gist, though: Ethan had been riding his trike back from the park when a car mounted the kerb at speed and knocked him down. They were looking for the vehicle and driver now.

'But . . . but he's OK?' I ask, my throat constricted.

'He's stable. I don't have any other updates.'

'Can you drive any faster?'

At the hospital I leave the officers in my dust, racing up to the paediatric unit. In the waiting room I catch sight of Pete talking to a nurse in scrubs.

'How is he?' I blurt out.

'He's OK,' Pete says. 'He's sleeping right now.' He looks ashen, shaken.

'I need to see him. Where is he?'

'Room fifty-five,' says the nurse.

I don't waste another second, rushing down the hallway to find the room. I take a breath before opening the door. I don't want Ethan to see my panic.

He's lying in the bed, so small and fragile. He looks beaten up – a bandage across his head and his arm in a sling, his cheek red raw and grazed. I sit on the bed next to him. At the movement he curls towards me.

I choke, my heart breaking at the thought of him being in pain. At the fact that I hadn't been there for him. I reach out and stroke his cheek, feeling his soft breath on my fingers.

After a few moments, a doctor knocks and asks me to

46

follow him outside. I'm reluctant to leave Ethan's sleeping form, but I need answers. He leads me to a small room, where Pete is waiting – and he's no longer alone. The police officers are back, and they've been joined by a woman in a dark grey trouser suit. She flashes a badge at me, introducing herself as DS Flintock.

Her eyes narrow as she takes me in, but my mind is too scrambled to interpret her expression. I'm only looking at the doctor.

'Your son has suffered a fracture to his arm and took a bad bump to the head – we're going to keep him overnight for observation, but he should be fine,' he says.

'Oh, thank God,' I say. 'What happened?' I direct the question to Pete.

He rubs the bridge of his nose, shaking his head. 'It's such a fucking blur . . .'

I give him a moment as he takes a deep breath.

'We were on our way back from the park, getting ready to meet you at the checkpoint like we planned. Ethan insisted on riding his tricycle. Then this maniac driving a massive black Range Rover comes careering round the corner. Mounts the kerb near to where Ethan was. I swear, it was like it was aiming right for him. I ran but I couldn't get there.' His voice breaks, and I can hear all Pete's fear and worry and anger welling up. 'Ethan managed to swerve away, tumbling into someone's front garden, then they drove off.'

'Did you get a look at the driver? Or a number plate?' I ask.

He shakes his head. 'I was too worried about Ethan; I wasn't thinking . . .'

'We're going to check the traffic cameras in the area,' says one of the officers. 'We'll find the vehicle that way.'

'Thank you,' I say. The adrenaline that had flooded my system and kept me upright is leaking away, and my head feels fuzzy.

'There's something else.' DS Flintock steps forward now, clearing her throat. 'Can you confirm your whereabouts yesterday, between the hours of eleven a.m. and three p.m.?'

'That's easy. I was running.'

'You never left the course for any reason?'

'Of course not. They should have a GPS log of my route. What's this about?'

'You recently made an accusation of sexual assault against your coach, Glenn Knight, didn't you?'

Immediately I stiffen. It's not really a question, and the detective doesn't wait for an answer.

'The police over there didn't exactly find you credible, did they? They didn't pursue any charges,' she continues. Again, not really a question. Just a statement of fact.

'Wait – do you think that has something to do with why Ethan got hurt?' I shift on my feet. I think of the vitriol I've received online, the comments that had graduated to doxing, letters shoved through my door. Demands that I stop racing. Calls for me to be prosecuted for slander.

Then there were those shouts at the finishing line.

Liar.

Murderer.

The detective shakes her head. 'Mr Knight was found dead at his home early this morning.'

'What?' My jaw drops. 'How?'

Pete looks equally aghast. 'You can't be serious?'

'Have you seen or spoken to Mr Knight recently?'

I pause. 'Not since . . .' Then I realize why they are asking me about my whereabouts. 'You can't think I had anything to do with his death?!' I exclaim.

But if they think that, maybe others do too.

My hand shoots out and I grab Pete's wrist. 'What if it was because of me?'

'What, Glenn's death?'

'No, Ethan's accident. The driver . . . what if I caused this? Someone angry at me about the accusation?' *And the lies*, I think but don't dare say out loud. I turn to the detective. 'It could be, couldn't it?'

'We'll look into it,' she replies, but the way she snaps her notebook shut doesn't give me much confidence. Ethan is OK, that's the main thing. But it's likely the reason the police won't give it any more thought. 'And we'll be looking into that GPS log too.' With a sharp nod of her head, she gestures to the other officers that she's ready to go.

Pete and I sit in silence until we're alone. My fingers are still round his wrist.

I let go. 'It's my fault,' I say, dropping my head into my hands.

'Don't say that,' says Pete, shaking his head. 'You know what people are like on the roads. It was school run time too; it's always mayhem on that street. I should have kept him closer. If anyone should be blaming themselves, it's me.'

I nod. 'I've tried to slow him on that tricycle before – it's impossible. It's going in the bin.'

'You can try – Ethan loves that thing. Come on now.

Let's not jump to any conclusions,' he says, and the words hang like dead weights over my shoulders. They seem pointed. He's biting his tongue, and I appreciate it – even though I can hear what he wants to say as loudly as if he'd actually spoken. *You've got a reputation for false accusations. Don't make it worse.* 'Let the police sort it out.' His legs are twitching and he gets up. Pete is such a doer, a man who always wants to be on the move. 'Can you believe it about Glenn?'

I shake my head.

'I wonder what happened.' He pulls out his phone, glancing at it and frowning. 'I've got to . . .' He points at the screen.

'Go. I'll be fine here.'

He nods, already dialling.

Glenn is dead. *Good. At least he can't hurt anyone any more.* That's the first thought that pops into my head. Then the righteous anger turns to guilt. *But the people he hurt won't get justice now either.* He's died as a victim of false accusations, his precious reputation upheld. *And that's your fault.*

It's too much of a coincidence. I speak out about Glenn. Glenn dies. My son is put in the hospital.

My stomach clenches and I retch acidic bile on to the floor.

6

Adrienne

I take the long way back to my tent from registration, trying to avoid running into anyone I know. Although I want to find Pete, I'm in no hurry to bump into other elites. I prefer the anonymity of being amongst the fun runners. Most people are already wearing their race numbers, bibs pinned proudly to the front of their moisture-wicking tops. But I've buried mine deep in my backpack.

That number: *13*. I can't wear it. It marks me out as Boones's pick, and I don't want *any* special attention. The doubts I had about coming here all resurface at once, bubbling up inside me. I already felt like there was a target on my back. The number '13' makes the bullseye even more prominent.

Even more reason to find Pete. He'll know what to do.

I hope he's OK. The doctor, with his concerned frown, has me worried.

This is the first race we've started together since we split up almost a decade ago. Despite my nerves about competing against him, I'm glad we're here together. It feels right somehow. After all, racing was how our relationship had begun. Supporting each other. Driving to remote trailheads in the early hours of the morning. At checkpoints he'd be waiting for me with a bowlful of reheated spag bol, a steaming-hot coffee and a Cadbury's Fruit & Nut bar. I'd slump into a chair, stuffing my face, and he would tend to whatever needed attention – blisters on my feet, chafing on my back, tightness in my shoulders. I'd do the same for him on his races, ready to cheer him up if he came into the checkpoint feeling down or to give him a detailed update on his competitor's timings and his splits. Sometimes I'd have to spoon-feed him his macro-balanced fuel, force him to drink electrolytes, anticipate his needs like a toddler. We'd both got so good at reading each other.

Until we weren't any more. After Ethan, it became harder to feel like a team. I still wanted to compete, but he wanted me to take a step back. My coaching became more intense, required more time away. Pete couldn't understand how becoming a parent made me a more ambitious runner, not less. When we couldn't resolve things, we went our separate ways. We divorced when Ethan was barely a year old.

Ironic that only a couple of years later, I did stop racing. But that had been a choice born out of fear. Pete saw what not racing did to me, and later he encouraged me to get back into it. So when I confided in him that I'd not only been invited to Hot & Sandy, but that I would be running in it, he'd surprised me by giving me a big hug. He told me how proud he was of me, talked excitedly about how we could look out for each other on the course. It felt like we had turned a corner in our relationship.

The fun runner tents are bustling with activity – some people have lit fires outside and are boiling water for hot coffee and rehydrating meals, but most are busy organizing their gear and getting to know their tentmates. We elites have our own section clustered at the far end of the bivouac. I must be getting close since I spot two of the Moroccan runners – Nabil and Farouk. There's a crowd of journalists round them, taking photographs and asking them questions in French and Arabic. They're in tent number one.

I pass my own assigned tent, number six, and see Mariam but I don't stop. I don't even drop in my backpack. Twelve, thirteen, fourteen . . .

Finally, I've found the right place. There's a photographer in front of this tent too. I pause. With the camera up to her eye and a dark mass of curls cascading down her back, it's hard to make out her face. But there's something familiar in her profile – her stance – that stops me in my tracks. *It can't be.* She lowers the camera and I take a cautious step forward.

Is this what Boones meant about finding answers? We haven't spoken since that terrible night – and it's not from lack of trying on my side. Every attempt at contact I made had been blocked. Eventually, I gave up.

It was actually easier for me that way. Leave her in the past, along with the rest of it. Move on – or at least try.

She leans forward, helping pull someone to their feet. A man. Now this is a face I'd recognize from any angle. And he's wearing an expression I've seen a few times before as well: anger, disappointment, frustration. My instinct is to go to him, to comfort him – even though we've been divorced for ten years.

Do they know each other? How is that possible?

He looks at her and she cups his cheeks with her hands. It's such a close intimate gesture that it takes my breath away. Not as close as what they do next, of course, which is kiss. His shoulders relax; she is the one taking his sadness away now.

My stomach twists in pain; it feels like betrayal, even though it shouldn't. My intake of breath must have made a sound, because Pete's eyes slide over and catch mine.

Shit. I wish the desert would up and swallow me whole. I spin round and power-walk away – even though there's nowhere for me to go.

I hear Pete calling after me. 'Adri, wait!'

I slow down. We're about to spend the next five days together. It's time to be a grown-up. I spin round and hold my head up. But my eyes don't land on him. They land on her.

Stella.

She trails behind Pete by a few steps. She doesn't look shy, though. She's jutting out her chin – a bit too much, in fact. Maybe it's an effort for her like it is for me. To show that we're not bothered about seeing each other again.

'Something terrible has happened,' Pete starts.

That grabs my attention. 'What? With Ethan?' My pulse races.

'No, no, nothing like that. No – it's me.' His shoulders slump. 'The mandatory drug test. I've failed it. They're sending me home.'

I blink back my surprise. 'Oh my God, Pete! Are they sure? Did you ask them to check it again?'

'Yup. But they won't change their decision. Rules are rules.'

'But you didn't . . . ?'

'Of course not. It's a fucking outrage. Some kind of fix. I don't know if it's because I'm engaged to his daughter but . . .' Realization dawns on his face as he takes in my expression. My face stings like I've been slapped. 'Oh God, Adri, I'm not thinking. This is –'

'Stella,' I say, cutting him off. I swallow, unable to catch my breath, trying to hold on to my dignity.

By contrast, Stella is the picture of composure. She hasn't changed much over the years – still stunning, tall and willowy like a model. Physically so like her sister. But their personalities couldn't be more different. Yasmin would never look down on me the way Stella does. She makes me feel small – and not because of our height difference.

'Adrienne, hi.'

Pete stares between us. 'You know each other?'

'From a long time ago,' Stella says.

'So you two are –' I gesture between them – 'engaged?'

'Yeah. I'm sorry, Adri, I didn't want you to find out like this.' He intertwines his fingers with hers. 'I asked her to marry me yesterday.'

My mouth feels bone dry, my tongue thick. 'Wow. Congratulations. I had no idea you were even seeing someone, Pete. How long have you been together?'

'On and off – what's it been?' He looks at Stella. 'Years?'

'Years,' she repeats.

'Long distance most of the time. Stella lives in California.'

Every sentence feels like a little kick to my gut. But at least all the times Pete begged me to switch weeks with Ethan so he could go and run in America make sense. 'But I've finally been able to get her to settle down.' He lifts her hand, where – sure enough – a diamond catches the sunlight, and kisses it.

Questions flood my brain. How did I not even know he was dating, let alone in a relationship this serious? Have I been that wrapped up in my own issues? Has Stella told him how she and I met? Was she already dating him when she met me in Ibiza? But one question stands up above the rest. 'Does Ethan know?'

Stella answers before Pete can. 'We wanted to wait until we took this step.' She strokes Pete's arm. 'But I've heard so much about him. I can't wait to meet him.'

I bite my lip. How can they be planning a life together when she doesn't even know Pete's son? But Pete has that puppy-dog look in his eyes. He is smitten.

'This isn't how I wanted this introduction to go, but maybe it's for the best,' Pete says. 'Maybe now we can leave together.'

I stiffen. 'Leave?'

'You can't stay here on your own, Adri.'

'Why not?'

'Come on. Who's going to look out for you?'

Pete's audacity shocks me. That he still thinks he has a say. I think of the handsome doctor who treated me. Maybe I should go and get his number. 'I can take care of myself.'

Stella turns to Pete. 'I'm not leaving either.'

'What?' Pete looks like he's about to explode. This is a lovers' quarrel I don't need to be in the middle of. He's not going to be any help to me. He's not even going to be at the race any more.

'I'll leave you to it,' I mutter, and I notice that neither one of them protests.

Pete is furious. Stella defiant.

As I slip away, my mind is still reeling. Pete and Stella. Stella and Pete.

'Adrienne?' Someone shouts my name from the next tent over.

I glance back. Jason – the podcast guy – runs up beside me.

I stiffen, my shoulders tight by my ears. 'Not now.'

He holds his hands up. 'I know, I hear you. I get it. I'd leave you alone if I felt like I could. Just five minutes . . .'

'I'm here to race, that's it. I don't have five minutes.' A crowd of photographers and media have gathered by tent number two, where Rupert holds court, and a man carrying a huge video camera on his shoulder blocks my path. I dodge out of the way, but Jason still follows me.

'Please, it's important. I have something to show you. You'll want to see it.'

I sigh. 'What?'

He glances over at the documentary crew. In his hands he's got a red spiral-bound notebook, which he grips tight. 'Not here. Come with me.'

'No, I can't right now.' I want to be alone.

'After dinner, meet me?'

'OK!' I say, exasperated, desperate to get this guy to leave me alone.

'Promise?' He wipes away a few beads of sweat from above his eyebrow.

I walk away without answering. I don't want to be dragged into Jason's podcast; it took everything I had to get them to leave me alone the first time. It was hard enough getting up the courage to come here. I want to concentrate on my why: the answers promised by Boones.

Jason reaches out, grabbing my arm. I twist away, but he only holds on more forcefully. I almost scream, but the look in his eyes stop me.

'It's about Ethan, OK?'

I feel the blood drain from my face, my insides turning to liquid. There's no trace of a lie that I can see. No trickery.

'You were right all along. It wasn't a random accident. And I can help you prove it.'

'Show me,' I say, my previous reticence forgotten.

But then the camera I dodged earlier is suddenly right in my face. 'Adrienne Wendell?' a young woman asks, standing behind the cameraman's shoulder. 'I'm Jackie Henman from OutRun Productions – we're doing a documentary on the race. How does it feel to be Boones's runner thirteen?'

'Excuse me, I was in the middle of –'

Jason sneaks behind the camera and mouths 'Later' at me. He lifts his notebook, pointing to it.

I nod, following him with my eyes as he retreats. Then Jackie asks me another question, and, just like that, I'm sucked back into the vortex of being in the public eye.

The Ultra Bros Podcast

Hot & Sandy Edition

Mac: Bros, you're in for a treat. We promised and now we're delivering a LIVE update from the Sahara, the night before the race start. Now, I'm sure you can tell that I am not out in the desert. I'm still here in boring old Newcastle, because someone needs to be the bloody tech support, GPS dot watcher and all-round 'keeper of conversation flow' in case our UK-to-desert communication ends up going tits up. But for the moment we have our man on the ground, Jason Lowry, on the satellite phone. Jason, how's it going down there?

Jason: Mate, the race hasn't even begun and I'm telling you it's been a wild ride already. This is a race unlike any I've seen before. It's so impressive. When Boones decides to go big, he goes BIG.

Mac: I wish I could be there! How you feeling?

Jason: Pretty good, pretty good. Passed all the medical checks and gear screening. They're being extra strict with the elites, probably because there's so much money at stake. I've also seen a few big corporate sponsors on the hunt for new talent. But it's not been smooth sailing for everyone. There's been drama already.

Mac:	C'mon, do tell . . .
Jason:	Well, some people have been sent home before the race start. Some big-name elites. One shocker is Pete Wendell. Apparently he failed his tox screen and he's now on his way back home.
Mac:	Whoa. You're joking!
Jason:	Nope. Didn't expect that of him myself. And then the Finnish runner Henne Hinsta had an issue with her ECG and they won't let her race either. In addition to the two elites, thirty-odd 'fun' runners have dropped out.
Mac:	Jesus. That's like . . . ten per cent of the participants out before the start. OK, so of the people who will be on the starting line, any surprises?
Jason:	Not to brag, but I was spot on with all my guesses. Rupert, Nabil, Farouk, Mariam – they're all here. There is one massive wild card that NO ONE guessed: Pete's ex-wife, Adrienne Wendell.
Mac:	You've got to be shitting me?
Jason:	You heard me right. The 'most hated woman in ultrarunning' is back. If you want to know why I call her that, we did a five-episode series about it.
Mac:	Of course – 'The Glenn Affair'. If you haven't heard it, dear listeners, check it out in the archive.
Jason:	It's a story that had everything. Sun, sea and scandal. Coach Glenn was one of the most

sought-after ultrarunning coaches in the world, and places at his legendary running camps came by invitation only. When Adrienne joined his roster, she started smashing all the records, racking up podium finishes and generally making a name for herself on the European ultrarunning circuit. His all-female Ibiza camp was set to launch some young up-and-comers on to the scene. Rumour had it that he was looking to train the first female finisher of a Boones race – and Adrienne looked like she was primed to be the One. But it all ended in disaster. After the camp finished, Adrienne posted on her social media, accusing Glenn of sexual assault. Glenn always maintained his innocence. And the Spanish police seemed to agree with him – at least they didn't hold him on any charges and let him return to the UK.

Mac: Any smoke without fire?

Jason: Well, that's just it, isn't it? The whole situation totally divided the running community. And when Glenn let it slip that Adrienne had been dropped from his roster during the camp . . . well, you know what they say about women scorned.

Mac: She made it up?

Jason: It's her word against his. But that wasn't the end of the story. Despite being in the eye of the storm, Adrienne continued to run, breaking the course record at the Yorkshire 100 only a couple of weeks later. But you know what's spooky? That same day Glenn was found dead in his home, not far from the starting line of that very race. After a short police investigation, the coroner ruled that he died of natural causes. A heart attack.

Mac: Bullshit. A guy that fit?

Jason: Right? But with the stress of the accusations, the threat of losing his top clients, his business ... a lot of people believed Adrienne had a lot to answer for. She gave up running after that, and there were plenty who were happy to see her go.

Mac: So she's got balls entering a race again.

Jason: And you'll never guess what else ... she's Boones's runner thirteen.

Mac: OK, now you're really having me on! How can she be the top contender when she hasn't competed in years?

Jason: Who knows what goes through that man's mind?

Mac: Speaking of, have you seen the big man himself?

Jason: Not yet. There is, like, tension, in the air. Everyone is wondering what Boones's next surprise is going to be.

Mac: Is it still a shock if you know there's more in the works? Feels like being told there's a 'big twist' in an M. Night Shyamalan movie or something.

Jason: Trust me, when you're the one running, even though you know they're coming, you get nervous. Remember our interview with Rupert Azzario? He's won the most Ampersand races out of anyone, like he's specially adapted to Boones's brand of wacky racing. He told us about what he calls 'the Spike' – that jolt of fear he gets when confronted with a Boones surprise. It's the Spike that keeps things interesting, he says. Most ultramarathons you end up sort of shutting down as the miles drag on, going on autopilot – but that's not possible here. You need endurance in your legs and in your mind. It's why so many incredible runners, who might easily conquer the distance, fail to complete an Ampersand race.

Mac: Where does it come from, do you think? Boones's drive to test people, push the boundaries?

Jason: Boredom? Curiosity? Boones isn't exactly out here giving in-depth interviews, no matter how many times we've asked.

Mac: And you've asked a lot.

Jason: Yup.

Mac: Anyone might say you're a bit obsessed.

Jason: Me? I'm nothing compared to Booneshounds. They spend hours unpicking every detail about the Ampersand races, trying to anticipate Boones's next move. For Hot & Sandy they're wondering if –

[The podcast is interrupted by a strong gust of wind.]

Mac: Whoa – Jason, are you still there? Apologies to those listening live who got their eardrums blasted.

Jason: I – I'm still here, mate. I know I'm banging on
            about what Boones has in store for us, but the
            desert itself has a mind of its own! The wind
            has been something else.

Mac: We'll let you go then and we'll chat tomorrow
            after the first stage. Good luck, man. We're all
            rooting for you. Seems like the Sahara Desert is
            conspiring with Boones to make it one hell of
            a race.

Jason: 'Hell' is about the perfect way to describe it.
            See you on the other side.

Jason: Mac, you still there?
Mac: Course.
Jason: We're not live any more, right?
Mac: Nope. What's going on?
Jason: You're going to think I'm crazy, but I think
            I've seen a ghost . . .

7

Stella

A gust of wind whistles down the gap between the tents, shaking the wooden posts, and I shield my face from the sudden influx of dust and sand. The sky darkens, the sun covered by a thick grey veil of cloud.

I bite at the edge of my thumbnail, only stopping when I taste the iron tang of blood.

I force my hand to my side, balling it into a fist.

DNS.

Did Not Start.

It's worse than a DNF – a *Did Not Finish.*

At least, that's how Pete sees it. Denied even the chance to compete. His reputation on the line. If he can't somehow clear his name, he's going to have to do a lot of damage control after this. He's got a plan to do an independent drug test in Ouarzazate, but that means leaving the bivouac straight away.

After seeing Adrienne, Pete and I had the biggest blowout of our relationship. Pretty sure the entire bivouac heard us. He thinks I should forget about my obligation to Runners for Hope and leave with him. But that would be letting people down. That's my dad's role – not mine. The end result is that he's on the bus back to Ouarzazate, along with some of the other DNS-ers. And I'm still here.

I rub the engagement ring once again, spinning the diamond round so it digs into my palm. I can't believe he didn't tell me she would be here. He obviously knew. But I can't even bring myself to be that pissed off. Because there are things I haven't told him either. Another reason I need to stay at Hot & Sandy.

Later. Later will be the time for truth. Now I need to turn my focus to Boones.

He can't avoid me any longer. I know he's here somewhere.

Where are you hiding?

I wander around the bivouac, through the aisles of tents. With Pete gone I can finally concentrate. Dad loves to be with the runners. I wouldn't be surprised if he's here somewhere, bumming a cigarette off one of the Berbers or sharing a cup of coffee with one of the elites. If anyone looks like they're about to engage me in conversation, I lift my camera and take a photo, and they leave me alone. The camera makes me part of the set. Background noise. No one even gives me a second glance.

In a gap between tents I think I spot him. He's leaning down, chatting to a runner – race number 501 – who is flowing through some yoga stretches. He's one of the people I interviewed earlier for Runners for Hope. Matteo.

Matteo moves into downward dog as I walk towards them.

Yet by the time he completes his vinyasa, Boones is gone. 'Shit,' I mutter under my breath. This is just like him. Testing me. Toying with me. Probably enjoying my desperation. *Fuck, I'm playing right into his hands.*

'Two hundred and fifty miles,' Matteo says, lifting his arms over his head and bringing his hands back down in prayer. 'This is ludicrous, isn't it?'

The blunt statement makes me laugh. 'Hey, you're the one who signed up for this, not me,' I reply.

He shakes his head. 'Like I said, ludicrous.'

I think back to the interview. 'You're doing this for your father.'

'That's right. He was my idol. And now he's my reason to keep going when the going gets tough.'

'You're lucky to have that.'

He takes a deep breath, staring out at the darkening sky. 'And it helps that we're in such a beautiful place. I never dreamed I'd get to see something like this.'

I follow his gaze, past the line of tents to the tops of the jebels visible on the horizon. I'm not sure *beautiful* is the way I would describe it right now – it's alien and hostile, a contrast to the welcoming oasis town where my mother's family is from, in the foothills of the Atlas Mountains. There, a tributary of the River Todra feeds an explosion of date palms, olive trees and ferns – it's so lush and green it's hard to believe the Sahara is on its doorstep. It's enchanting.

A bell rings out, calling the runners for dinner.

'Are you coming?' he asks.

'No, you go ahead.' Then I second-guess myself. Boones might make an appearance at the meal. Give a speech, like a proud father offering a toast at a wedding.

The thought of my dad giving a speech at my wedding to Pete makes me chuckle and Matteo gives me a strange look. No way. The only place he's gregarious is at the starting line of his precious races. Sometimes not even then.

'Good luck tomorrow,' I say.

He gives me a wave as I turn away.

I'm not alone, though. A tall man stands behind me, mirrored sunglasses covering his eyes. He's wearing a race number – 21 – and above it reads 'Jason – GBR'. My stomach flips.

'Excuse me, aren't you Stella Mamoud?'

'Who's asking?'

He extends his hand. 'I'm Jason, from *The Ultra Bros Podcast*,' he says, confirming my suspicion. 'I was wondering if you had a few minutes? I'd love to ask you some questions?'

I recoil from his touch. 'I don't think so.'

'Off the record then?'

I duck my head and walk away, in the opposite direction to the crowd heading to the dining tent, hoping that he'll ignore me, give up. But I also know that's wishful thinking. He's nothing if not persistent.

'Are you going to take over when Boones is gone?' Jason shouts at my back.

I stiffen but keep walking. With my head still down, I almost bump straight into Dale, the photographer I'd met earlier.

'You OK? That guy's a prick.'

I let out a snort of laughter – that happened to be exactly what I was thinking. I unclench my fists; I'd been ready to knock that guy out if he'd come near me again.

The sky darkens above us. Clouds of dust obscure the sun, casting the bivouac in a mustard haze. Tent doors flap furiously all around us, and Dale and I exchange a look.

Something is brewing that even Boones won't have control over.

And we don't want to be exposed when it hits.

8

Adrienne

A strong breeze rattles the tent posts, adding to my nerves. I'd managed to avoid answering too many questions on camera to that journalist – my bland responses not making for great content. Jason is nowhere to be found – not in his tent or near the dining area. Watching everyone tuck into their food makes my stomach rumble, but I don't want to eat something I haven't prepared myself. Gastric issues can spell the end for any runner's race; it's just not worth the risk. I head back to my tent, where Mariam is sitting on her foam mattress, headphones in, frowning.

She spots me and her eyes open wide. 'Have you heard this?' she asks.

'Heard what?'

She doesn't reply. She just takes her headphones out, puts them in my ears and presses 'play'. It's the latest *Ultra Bros Podcast*.

'What are you going to do?' she asks, when I've finished.

'I have to find him.'

'Why? He is no friend to you. He has made sure every-one knows who you are.'

She's right. Now I won't be safe, even amongst the fun runners.

'He says he wants to tell me something about . . .' I can't say Ethan. Mariam doesn't know that side of the story, or about my suspicions that someone had tried to hurt him deliberately. 'Something important he found out about that time.'

She scoffs. 'He is probably making it up to get you to talk to him.'

'Maybe. But you heard him on the podcast – he was obsessed with the case. He had a whole notebook full of his research and there's a chance he can answer a question I have.'

Mariam shrugs. I'm not surprised she's a sceptic. I have no reason to trust Jason, and it's far more likely he wants to somehow manipulate me into an interview. I am the missing factor from his vast 'Glenn Affair' equation.

My phone beeps. I glance down to see a message from Pete wondering if I've heard the podcast and telling me it's not too late to leave the race. I swipe it away.

I still can't believe he failed his drug test. Pete is meticulous about his health and what he puts in his body – he eats a vegan diet, scrutinizes his supplements, tracks every macronutrient. No matter how bad he wants it, he wouldn't resort to performance-enhancing substances. Would he? Maybe he felt the pressure to perform in light of who his future father-in-law might be.

I entertain the thought for about a microsecond before dismissing it outright. It must be a mistake. Mixed up blood vials – I don't know. I do know how gutted he must be feeling to be out of the race, though. He'd been training for this for months. Made it his entire life.

He's not alone on that. Earlier, I'd listened to my two other tentmates – a Canadian guy named Alex and a Japanese runner called Hiroko – discussing their plan for the run. Biding their time over the first stage, trying not to go out too quick. Keeping an eye on the Moroccan runners, not letting them get too far ahead. Working together to keep a good position until the very last leg. In a stage race strategy is important. The time is cumulative, and you can't fall too far behind or else there will be too much of a gap to close.

I wonder if I should be planning too. There's been nothing conventional about the way I've prepared for this race. In the years since my last race, I've become a more intuitive runner, choosing not to adhere to a strict training schedule but instead just listening to my body and going with the flow. And of course I don't have the time I used to, pre-Ethan, to be that regimented. The time, oh, the time! How I wish I could send a message back to pre-parenthood-Adrienne, to tell her to luxuriate in all the free hours she had. Hours that had been hers and hers alone, to do with what she wished. The number of times I'd hop in the car and drive to some remote trail, carrying a bivvy on my back and running until my legs gave out. Or at the last-minute I'd sign up for a run along the Jurassic coast and spend the night kipping in the back seat of our car. Even casual mid-afternoon sessions on a track were out, unless they were carefully negotiated around after-school clubs and play dates.

Motherhood altered every aspect of my life – but especially my running. I had to learn how to move in my new body, one that had grown another human, stretching and changing almost beyond recognition. I had to knit together muscles in my stomach that had been ripped apart, gaps in my abdominals so large I could almost put my fist through.

I figured out how to pump at the side of the trail, bottles of breast milk sloshing in my backpack until I could get home to Ethan. Training squeezed into times I could find childcare. Pete's life changed too, sure, but not in such a visceral, primal way. Becoming a mother both ruined and remade me.

And I wouldn't change it for a second.

The urge to talk to my son is suddenly all-consuming. I don't know what the signal will be like deeper into the race. So I call him.

'Mum!' he says. 'What's it like? Have you seen the camel yet?'

I laugh. 'Not yet, but then I don't want to catch his attention!' It was one of Ethan's favourite Hot & Sandy facts that if you got caught by the camel, you were out of the race. I try to describe the tent and my companions to him, but he doesn't seem to hear. The connection fails as the wind outside picks up.

'Sorry, honey, I don't think we'll be able to chat long,' I say, once the connection is back.

I hear his sigh. 'OK,' he replies, dejected. My heart aches with the sudden urge to be with him. It's missing so fierce it's as piercing as an arrow. 'Don't worry, Mum. You know the way,' he says. Our phrase. A show of confidence. It's the thing I say before every one of his tennis matches. To remind him that all he needs he already knows.

And now he's reminding me.

'I love you!' I almost shout it, as the connection begins to break up again.

'Love you too,' he says.

I click off. Anxiety builds in my stomach. What if Jason

73

is going to tell me that something else is going to happen to Ethan? I remind myself that he's with Pete's parents. They'll protect him. And so will Pete now that he's headed home. I can't help but feel a tiny bit grateful for that, even though I know Pete will be devastated.

But it's not enough. I'll never forgive myself if I let my pride get in the way of finding out what information Jason has. I grab my backpack and jump to my feet.

'Wait!' Mariam says. 'Have you not seen outside? The storm has arrived.'

To punctuate her words, dust and stones are blown into the tent, swirling round our ankles. I jump on Alex's sleeping mat to stop it flying away. The tent sides billow, straining against the guy ropes, and Mariam clings to the centre post to stop it falling over. We're not the only ones struggling. Outside the Berbers who helped set up the bivouac are scrambling to secure the sides of each tent with heavy rocks.

With a quick nod to each other, we decide not to wait for help. We crouch down low, but even so we're almost knocked off our feet by another gust.

I read about this phenomenon. A Saharan sandstorm. If we're lucky, it will blow through in a few minutes. But that's enough time for any loose gear inside our tents to be swept away, so we follow the Berbers' lead and grab as many heavy rocks as we can, layering them on the edges of the black fabric.

'Where are the others?' I shout over the wind, thinking of Hiroko and Alex.

'At dinner, I think?'

'What about their things?'

'Securing the tent is the best way to keep them in.'

I nod, though I doubt our efforts will be enough if the storm gets much worse; already some of the tents on the outer edge of the semicircle are coming apart in the strong winds. I hear shouts as people rush to keep their tent posts upright. There's debris flying everywhere and I spot a running shoe rolling away like tumbleweed in the wind. Someone's going to find it difficult to run without that.

'It's not safe to be out here!' Mariam shouts over the wind.

I nod, unable to speak without getting a mouthful of sand. I pull my neck buff over my nose and mouth.

We rush back inside and lower the centre pole, so there's less fabric for the wind to take hold of, and we close the front flaps to stop sand and rocks from getting inside. It quickly goes dark.

I lie back on the carpet, my hands gripping the straps of my backpack and hugging them tight. Mariam huddles next to me. The wind buffets the tent, howling around us.

All we can do is wait for the storm to pass.

9

Stella

Being a photographer in the desert is a goddamn nightmare. Keeping your gear sand-free? Impossible. Lugging it around in the heat? Unbearable. And the charity's checklist is a mile long. They want racer profiles, landscape shots, behind-the-scenes life, pain, beauty, relief, elation – the whole spectrum of emotions and scenarios to choose from.

But I could never have anticipated what happened last night. My plan to finally track down my dad thwarted. Dale and I barely made it back to the tent after being blasted by wind loaded with fine granules of sand, scraping against my skin and making it difficult to open my eyes more than a squint. At about one a.m. one side of the tent was ripped up by the storm, heavy metal tent pegs flying everywhere. I managed to grab a handful of the loose fabric and spent the rest of the night weighting it down with my body.

At around three a.m. the wooden pole in the centre collapsed, bringing the black material down on our heads. I kept thinking that *surely* the storm would die, but it had the energy of a rabid animal, clawing at us, defying us to get any rest at all.

According to my watch, it's now barely gone five a.m. My other tentmates are still wrapped up in their sleeping bags, trying to rest now that it's calm, but I can't. I feel suffocated.

I roll off the tent edges and crawl outside. It's a fucking mess. Stuff is strewn everywhere. I reach out for a half-filled bottle of water – not sure if it's even mine – and pour some on to my hands to wash my face. I don't even dare to look at my camera. What a state.

At least the skies are clear, leaving an eerily still morning. My skin and hair are covered in a layer of sand, gritty to the touch.

As I'm wondering if the winds will return, I notice Camille – the administrator who'd shown me around the day before – running, sprinting, in the direction of the runners' tents.

Without thinking I spring after her, clutching my camera. I'm still fully dressed – I'd barely been able to move, let alone change, last night.

Camille isn't the only one heading in that direction. The doctor from yesterday, the Italian one – what was his name, Emilio? – is running over there too, his medical bag in hand. It doesn't take me long to catch up.

Camille comes to stop outside one of the elite tents, letting out a strangled cry. She spins round, burying her face in her hands.

A man is curled up on the ground outside tent sixteen, the side of his face covered in blood. There's a deep wound visible above his ear, sand matted into his short close-cropped brown hair. Rupert is crouched at the man's side, gripping his hand.

'What happened?' I ask, unable to tear my eyes away.

'The storm. It was insane. Things flying everywhere. We

thought the tent was going to rip apart. We all grabbed a side and tried to hold on. I heard a thud but I couldn't move to check . . .' His voice chokes. 'Fuck, Jason, don't be dead.'

The doctor kneels by Jason's head. He places two fingers against his neck, his mouth set in a firm line. He looks up at Camille. 'Tell Boones we need a heli-evac, asap.' She nods, backing away, her face white. Then he focuses on me. 'Help me with this.' He takes a thick roll of gauze out of his bag.

I drop down beside the doctor. 'Tell me what you need.'

'Hold his head still,' he replies.

I place my palms gently round Jason's skull, trying not to think about how worryingly cold he feels.

'Is he going to be OK?' Rupert asks Emilio.

'I need to wrap this first. We don't want it getting more contaminated.' He places a wad of gauze over the wound on the guy's forehead, the reason he must have bled so profusely. Then he winds a bandage round it to keep it in place. Jason's face is swollen and bruised, his hands and knuckles scraped too. He looks like he's been in a war. His bib has been torn off his running top, gaping holes where the safety pins used to be. 'This is a pretty serious head wound. His pulse is thready. He needs to get to a hospital now. What's his name?'

'Jason Lowry,' says Rupert.

I swallow. The podcast guy. It shouldn't be my first thought but I wonder how my dad's going to handle it. Maybe I'll get my wish and the race will be cancelled.

Two other medics come running to the man's side, replacing me. They lift Jason on to a stretcher and carry him towards the helipad.

78

'Shit, Emilio, look.' I point to an iron tent spike –
bloodied at one end, where it would have hooked into the
ground. It looks like the culprit.

Emilio grabs it, turning it over in his hands. 'That would
do it.'

'Should you be touching that?'

'Why not?' he asks me.

And I don't have an answer for him. It's not like the
wound is suspicious. Just God-awful luck.

'You're right,' I say. 'We should show Boones, though.
Maybe someone can learn from it.'

He nods. 'He is with the Berbers.'

'I'll find him.'

I want to throw up. I should have never stopped looking for Dad. I could have said something. Stopped this
idiocy. Because that's the thing about my dad's races.

People die.

As the helicopter lifts, it kicks up a cloud of dust. That's
when I see him. Standing, watching the chaos – but not
interfering. There is a slight frown on his brow, but his
moustache obscures his expression. His piercing blue eyes
aren't watching the chopper.

He's looking only at me.

10

Adrienne

'Adrienne, you must hurry.'

I wake up to Mariam's concerned face, her hand shaking my shoulder.

For a second I don't remember where I am. My back is sore, my eyes gritty, my tongue bone dry as it runs over my sandpaper lips. I'm a husk, all moisture sucked from my body by the wind. I sit up, open my eyes, then immediately have to shut them again against the brightness. The tent has been resurrected, sunlight streaming in.

The desert. The race. The storm. I don't think I've had more than a couple of hours sleep. I feel like death. I can't believe anyone is fit to run twenty-five miles today.

Mariam shakes me again. 'Come.'

My voice is croaky as I attempt to speak. 'What happened? Is everyone OK?'

She doesn't answer me, just gestures with her arm and then starts moving. I scramble to follow her past the sleeping forms of Hiroko and Alex. They made it back. Mariam doesn't wake them, though. She only wants me.

Even though the sun is up, I'm thankful for my jacket. There's a chill in the air, or maybe it's the state of the bivouac that's leaving me shivering. It's been decimated. There are going to be a lot more DNSs than even Boones could have anticipated once everyone wakes up and realizes that their belongings have been scattered to the wind.

Mariam slides her sunglasses on and adjusts the bandana holding back the short spikes of her silver hair, such a contrast against her dark skin. She takes me to where I can see a small crowd has gathered in front of a tent. She stops a little way back and puts a hand on my arm to stop me too. I realize we're at tent number sixteen. 'You said you needed to speak to Jason, right?'

'Yes, urgently.' My eyes scan her face; her expression is pained. 'Why? Is he OK?'

She shakes her head. 'He's been taken away by helicopter.'

'What?!'

'He was covered in blood, unconscious . . . Struck in the head, apparently.'

A wave of nausea hits me. 'My God,' I say, breathlessly. 'By who?'

I can't help but think: *Was it because of what he wanted to tell me?*

Why did we have to get interrupted?

Mariam shakes her head. 'Not by anyone. Apparently one of the tent pegs came unstuck in the storm and flew about like a weapon,' Mariam says. 'So unlucky. His belongings are strewn everywhere.'

Some of the tightness in my chest releases – an accident. Bad luck, not malice.

A coincidence.

I don't believe in those.

Mariam brings me back to the present by tightening her grip on my arm. 'You said he had a notebook? We have a few minutes before we need to start getting ready – we can search.'

I stare at her for a moment, finding it hard to compute what she's saying. Then I realize she's right. 'Yes, yes. It was a red spiral-bound book.'

I pick up a packet of food, still in its plastic bag, neatly labelled with a calorie count. The letters 'JL' are written neatly in Sharpie ink in the top right-hand corner. So he was a fastidious labeller too. That will help. I gesture to Mariam and show her the mark. She nods.

We're not the only people sorting through the detritus. There are other runners out here, combing for their missing items. There doesn't seem to be much logic to the way the wind has scattered things, and the search field is massive – as large as the desert itself. I find myself following items out past the toilet tents, towards the tufts of bushes that have caught things in their spiked branches.

I feel like a vulture, picking through the bits and pieces of people's racing lives, discarding anything that doesn't have that neat 'JL' written somewhere. I shed my jacket, wrapping it round my waist – the air is so hot and still that it's impossible to think this is the same place where the storm happened. More and more racers appear, emerging from their tents bleary-eyed and pale from lack of sleep, preparing for the start of the race. I'm going to have to go back and do that too if I want to make the starting line on time.

But I feel desperate now. I need to find out if Jason knew anything. And that's when I spot it. Tucked under a bush, half buried in sand. A bright splash of red cover, spiral-bound. 'JL' inscribed on the corner.

I reach through to get it, wincing as a thorn scratches my skin and blood beads on the surface. I flick it open, but some of the pages are torn and missing. Still, it's enough for me to see what he was working on – the Ibiza case, not a surprise.

'You found something?' Mariam shouts to me.

I nod, lifting the notebook.

She jogs over. 'Any clues?'

'I . . . I'm not sure.' It's hard to read Jason's tight scrawl, but I recognize the dates that he has circled – the start of the training camp and when various people left. I chew my bottom lip. As far as I can see, he has some pieces of the puzzle but there are still glaring omissions. Stella's name, for example, is conspicuously absent from the list of people at the Ibiza camp. She's managed to keep that a secret. No wonder he was finding it so hard to put the picture together.

I turn the pages, taking in the information as quickly as I can.

Finally, I see something that stops me in my tracks.

A note, circled. *BLAMES AW FOR GK'S DEATH??*

Then the Range Rover licence plate. The same one that had been written on my invitation.

STILL WANTS REVENGE.

But there's no name. I slam the notebook shut, my heart pounding.

Mariam jerks back. 'What did it say? I can't read upside down.'

'I —' But I quickly shut my mouth as I see a volunteer wearing a Hot & Sandy vest striding in our direction. It's Henry, the man who checked me in.

'I'll stall him,' says Mariam, going over to intercept him.

I grab my digital camera from my bag, snapping a few pictures. But I'm running out of time. I turn my body to shield my actions from view and tear out a handful of pages, stuffing them in my pocket.

'Thank you for searching for his things,' Henry says as he approaches.

'No problem,' I reply, awkwardly dropping the notebook into a plastic garbage bag that he is using to collect anything that belongs to Jason. 'Any word on how he is?'

'Not yet. You had better go get ready. The race is going to start in half an hour.'

'So the race is still happening?' Mariam asks.

'Boones is making an announcement in about ten minutes,' he replies.

'Boones. Can I speak with him?' I ask Henry.

He glances at his watch. 'You don't have much time. Look out for a dark green Jeep. That's his.'

'Got it,' I reply with a tight smile. Henry twirls the bag handles so it shuts tight, the notebook gone forever. Then he marches off in the direction of other runners doing their own searches.

'What did you find?' Mariam whispers to me as we walk back towards the bivouac.

My words come out all in a rush. 'Mariam, I don't think I can do this. What Jason was going to tell me — it had to do with Ethan. The same day Glenn died, when I was running the Yorkshire 100, Ethan was hit by a car.'

'*Mon dieu*, Adrienne!'

'He was OK, luckily, but I have always been sure it was connected. Maybe someone who blamed me for Glenn's death. Jason agreed. Look at this.' I pull out the pages of the notebook, smoothing them so she can read it. 'Someone out there wants revenge. What if they're going to target Ethan again? I need to go back home. Protect him.'

'You think they are after your son? Or after you?'

I pause. 'Well, me,' I say. 'For what I did.'

'And you are here.' She grabs my wrist. 'The Adrienne I used to know wouldn't hide away. Remember your petition?'

I cringe, thinking about how brazen I used to be. A few years before the Ibiza camp, I'd found out that a friend had been refused permission to defer her place in a race because of pregnancy. Outraged by the injustice, I'd launched a full-blown boycott campaign until the race directors changed the rules, which — thankfully — they did. But that was fighting for someone else. That's always come easier to me.

But Mariam's right — I'm here now. I'm in the running for the first time in seven years. I've come to face my demons. And one of those demons might just be the psychopath who targeted my son.

Maybe I should let them come. If I retreat now, I'll always be looking over my shoulder. Always worried. I want to show whoever it is that I'm not going to run away any more. I won't be made to feel afraid.

A feeling of inevitability settles in my stomach. I need to focus on my mission: to get my answers from Boones.

I think about that race number. That number thirteen. I can let it be a curse. Or I can let it change my life forever.

Mariam seems to see the decision in my face. She links her arm with mine, patting my bicep. 'Come on. Let's get back to the tent. This race is going to be full of surprises. We need to be ready.'

II

Adrienne

Seven years earlier
Yorkshire

A few weeks after the accident, Pete and I are called in for a meeting with DS Flintock. Confirming my alibi for Glenn's death wasn't hard – the GPS tracker recorded that I'd been miles away – and the coroner had ruled Glenn's death had been from natural causes. A heart attack. This meeting is about something else: my theory that Ethan had been targeted by someone who blamed me for Glenn's death. I know how I must seem. The paranoid mother. The lying 'victim' who cried wolf and is now suffering the consequences.

I hand her printouts of some of the vitriol I've received online – the threads about me, the horrific emails exclaiming how I've ruined lives and careers. There's also the letter: *STOP RACING OR SUFFER.*

'You see? It can't be a coincidence,' I insist.

Pete sits next to me, his knee bouncing underneath the table. I want to give him a kick, but I don't think that would look good.

The detective sighs. 'We're looking into it. But I brought you in here because we located the vehicle involved in your son's accident,' she says.

My breath hitches. This is it. My time to find out who was responsible.

'The black Range Rover was rented,' she continues. 'Reported stolen that morning.'

'Reported by who?'

'An American tourist. We've done a thorough interview and he has no connection to you or Mr Knight, and we have him on CCTV at his hotel at the time your son was hit. We've looked closely into Mr Knight's family and friends – anyone who might have had a motive, as you say, to hurt you. We can't find any correlation. Our conclusion is that your son was the victim of a joyride gone wrong.'

Every sentence hits me like a blow. I can see it in the detective's eyes. She's done pursuing any other avenues.

'Can you tell me the name of the tourist? Maybe I can spot a connection you've missed?'

She shakes her head. A no – but also she's fed up with me. 'Did you speak to Glenn's ex-wife?' I press.

'She's in Sardinia,' the detective says. 'Hasn't been back to England in years. As I said, we've cleared the family.'

'Adri, this is good news,' says Pete. 'It was an accident. The simplest solution is often the correct one, right? Some kids joyriding – that makes way more sense than some kind of planned attack.'

'But the letter ...' I hate how whiny I sound. How pathetic.

'Are you *sure* there's nothing else you can say about Ibiza that might be helpful?' Pete asks, reaching over and squeezing my knee in what he thinks is a reassuring manner.

It only makes me retreat further into myself. I wish I

could tell Pete everything that happened on that island. But it's too late. 'There's nothing,' I say.

The detective's eyes flick to the clock on the wall behind me. She's probably got other, more pressing cases to work on. 'If anything else comes up, Mrs Wendell, you know how to reach us.'

Pete stiffens beside me.

'It's Ms,' I say through gritted teeth.

The detective bows her head, gesturing us towards the door, ushering us out. We drive back to my flat in silence. Pete wants to check in on Ethan, so he comes in with me. I allow him to do bedtime after we collect him from nursery, then wait for him to come back downstairs.

He's staring intently at his phone when he walks into the living room, a small smile on his face. A smile? After all we've gone through? That's when it hits me: I've been the one living through the nightmare. As far as Pete is concerned, Ethan had a knock but he's made a full recovery. A massive shock for sure, but the sense of danger has passed. He's even running again.

For me the danger still feels so very present.

'I've decided Ethan and I can't stay here,' I tell him.

I brace for a protest but surprisingly Pete nods, as if he's seen it coming. Well, that's hardly a surprise. I've barely slept since Ethan's accident, terrified of who might know my address.

He slips his phone into his pocket. 'Where will you go?'

'Um, my old university landlady has an annex in the Lake District, Ambleside. She's offered me and Ethan the place. There's an outdoor shop there hiring a running consultant.'

'What about your training? Are you still doing UTMB this year?'

I shake my head. 'No more. I'm not going to race.' *Ever again*, I think to myself.

Emotions war across Pete's face. 'Are you sure?'

I nod. My running career was over the moment I went to that training camp. The police can tell me all they want that what happened to Ethan wasn't connected. But I am always going to blame myself for not being there.

STOP RACING OR SUFFER.

So I'll stop.

'Yes, I'm sure,' I say. It hurts me more than I realize too. A tear rolls down my cheek. I take a deep breath and box up the sadness.

He reflexively reaches out to wipe the tear away, but I pull back. He sighs. 'Adri, help me understand. What happened in Ibiza, really?'

I almost melt. I feel the truth lying thickly on my tongue. He was once my husband. He is my son's father. It might not have worked between us, but I once trusted him with my life. I should be able to trust him now, shouldn't I?

But – like in the police station – the story sticks there, refusing to come out.

Maybe the facts don't even matter now. Justice can never come. I will forever be the Runner who Lied. But I can take that. At least no one else is going to get hurt by him ever again.

He watches my face. He knows me. He knows I'm not going to break – not now, not ever.

He pulls his hand away. 'If you insist on keeping secrets, Adri, how can anyone help you?'

He strides towards the front door. But I have one more question for him.

'Wait – what the detective said, it bugged me.'

Pete turns, one hand on the handle. 'What do you mean?'

'*We cleared the family.* That implies Glenn had one, don't you think? I mean, I obviously know the ex-wife. His parents died a long time ago . . . Who else could they clear?'

'I think you need to drop this.'

'But you knew him too. Did he talk to you about other family? Kids, siblings, cousins?'

Pete, infuriatingly, just shakes his head. 'I think moving is a good idea. Get away from all this. Leave it behind you. Because, as far as I'm concerned, Adri, if you keep stirring up trouble, then the only person who is putting our son in danger is you.'

12

Stella

We don't hug. This is no big emotional reunion. In fact, seeing Boones brings long dormant insecurities bubbling to the surface, as I wonder what his opinion is of me now. I hate that that's my first reaction, but he has the infuriating knack of making people yearn for his approval, even if he's done nothing to deserve it. He sets high bars, and people strive for years to reach them. If they do, he only pushes them higher. Moves the goalposts. It's what makes the Ampersand races so addictive. It appeals to that extreme-athlete mindset: *what is possible if I'm given the chance? What am I capable of?*

Dad makes a small gesture with his head – a slight tilt to ask me if I'll come. He's giving us a chance to talk.

When was the last time we spoke properly? Seven years ago? That had ended badly. I'm a whole new person now. With a whole new life. A fiancé. A job I love. I've never been able to fully escape the world of running, but I didn't want to. I wanted to carve my own place in it. Not to be overshadowed by him.

I follow him, leaving the chaos of the bivouac for a different sort: the inside of Boones's trailer. Almost every available surface is covered in paper – maps of the Sahara, wind and weather charts, lists of participants, medical and emergency numbers. Boxes of supplies teeter in every corner. Bottles of water, first-aid kits, flare guns, radios – and that's just what I take in at first glance.

His eyes dance – his version of a smile, even though his lips don't move. To my shock it sends a thrill through me. I check myself: this is the man who chose organizing his races over a relationship with me, who wilfully endangers lives despite repeated warnings. He is not my family.

He clears his throat. 'You look good. Happy to see you here. I wasn't sure if you would come.'

'I'm not here for you,' I say, hating how petulant I sound.

'Oh?'

'My fiancé is one of the elite runners. Well, he was . . .'

'Ah yes, Mr Wendell. He's been dying for an invitation to one of my races. *Please, Boones, it would be the honour of my life to run in an Ampersand.*' He raises an eyebrow. 'I presume he knows who you are?'

'What, that I'm your daughter? Of course he knows. We're getting married; he knows everything about me.'

That makes Boones laugh, and my cheeks burn.

'Well, he got an invite – surely you should be saying "Gee, thanks, Pa."?'

I grit my teeth. So Dad did know about my relationship. Yet another way to manipulate me. He wanted me to be here, to witness this, but didn't have the guts to invite me directly. Or maybe this was his way of giving me the choice. He didn't know if I still cared. By making all this effort, I proved to him that I did.

Shit. I've played right into his hands.

And Pete doesn't even get to run any more.

I blink. 'Oh my God, Pete's test results?' I say, speaking

my realization out loud. It's not really a question. I know the answer.

He doesn't deny it. 'It's better this way.'

Anger flares up the back of my neck, a flash of fire. 'That's my fiancé you're talking about. Do you know what this could do to his reputation in the running community to have a DNS for performance-enhancing drugs? And inviting his ex – was that for my *benefit* too?'

'I invited those who I thought were worthy.'

'Bullshit. You got me here, like you wanted. Tell me why I should stay, or I'm getting on the first plane home.'

'You've been at the bivouac for, what, twenty-four hours? Twenty-four hours you waited to find me. You've seen those faces out there. You've heard the stories. What people are running for. *Why* they're running. Don't you want to see them do it? Just like we used to . . .'

'I was a child, then, Dad. I trusted you. I don't trust you now, and I don't want to be part of whatever diabolical plan you've got in store.'

He shakes his head. 'Please – stay for one stage. This is my ultimate race. The one I've been working towards.' He gestures at his trailer, at the mountains of paper littering every surface. The detail and the planning. His master-work. How anyone could be so diligent and so relaxed at the same time, I'll never know. But it's his madness and his obsession. His impossible dream. The one he's dedicated his entire life to.

'Did it have to be here?' I ask.

He chuckles – he sounds almost like a child, and that grates on my already shredded nerves. 'You think there's anywhere else I can hold the ultimate challenge than the largest desert in the world?'

'What about Yasmin?' I cry out, kicking the leg of the table, sending papers flying. 'Did that promise mean nothing?'

He's not laughing now. 'It means everything.'

'And yet you're here,' I say in a voice barely loudly than a whisper. 'Staging a race in Morocco. Just like I asked you not to.'

'Unless it was the last thing I did,' he finishes.

He seems all of a sudden unsteady on his feet, rocking back and catching himself on the table with his hand. He doesn't sit, but he leans his bodyweight against his palm, his knuckles turning white as his fingers dig into the wood.

I don't know why I didn't see it before. In my memory and in every photo or video I've seen of him, he's always been as lean as a rake. He's still that, with his curling moustache and full beard, eyebrows with a mind of their own and long grey wiry hair pulled back into a low ponytail. But there's a sunkenness to his cheeks, the inward curve of his body more pronounced.

So this is what it's all been about. He's sick.

I swallow, hard. 'Is it bad?' My voice has a tremor.

'Not hiding it as good as I thought, I guess.' He coughs into his sleeve. 'This is it for me, *ma petite lapine*. My last hurrah.'

'Cancer?'

He doesn't reply but pats his chest. His heart. He's always had issues with it. He's taken medication for as long as I can remember. But this must be different. My anger dissipates into worry and fear that grips me by the throat. I'd gotten used to feeling like I didn't want Dad in my world. But actually I realize I can't imagine a world without him.

Anarchic, chaotic, infuriating as he is, there's brilliance there too. I see that.

We stand there, staring at each other. I don't know what to do. Affection doesn't come naturally to either one of us.

'So, no more after this?' I ask.

'This is it from me, baby.'

Eventually, I nod.

'You're always welcome to help me with running the race, like the good old times . . .'

'Don't push it,' I say. 'I'll stay and do the job I signed up to do. But it's not for you. What you did to Pete was cruel. You could have given him a chance. I won't forget that.'

'I understand. But if you don't want to join us on the inside, then you'd better wait for my announcement like everyone else,' he says, waving me towards the door of his trailer.

As I leave, my eye catches on something pinned to the wall. It's an old photograph of people standing in three rows, like a class or sports team photo. There's a logo in the corner that does look familiar, though – a sword – and names along the bottom, too small for me to read. I reach out and snap it from its pin. 'Dad, what is this?'

He plucks it from my fingers, dropping it on to the table. 'History,' he says.

I catch his eyes as he passes me, opening the door and stepping down the stairs. In that split second I see the hunger there, the anticipation. Even in the hundred-degree heat, it turns my blood to ice. I use my phone to take a photo of the image and follow him back out into the desert.

13

Adrienne

Mariam and I stand shoulder to shoulder in a crowd of other runners, waiting to hear Boones's announcement. It's only now that I really feel the scale of the race. I can't move without a runner's backpack smacking me in the face, each stuffed to the brim, everyone in hats and wraparound sunglasses, sand gaiters attached to Velcro on shoes, feet twitching with nervous energy. Yet it's also not as jubilant as other race starts I've been on. The storm put paid to that, and news of Jason's injury has spread like wildfire throughout the camp. My nails are bitten to shreds, and not just because the pages that I took from Jason's notebook are burning a hole in the bottom of my bag, waiting until I can take a closer look at them.

I take a sip of water from a straw poking out of the bottle tucked into the shoulder straps of my backpack. I don't know what it is I want Boones to say – if he's going to cancel the race or not. If he does, I won't get my answers. I'll always be looking over my shoulder, wondering when this attacker is going to show up again. Wondering who is out for revenge.

Hiroko, standing on the other side of Mariam, is discussing that very possibility. 'He didn't cancel Long & Windy when poor Steve Parsons was blown off a cliff. I don't think a sandstorm is going to put him off launching

Hot & Sandy.' His eyes drop to my race number. He grimaces and takes a step back, as if the number thirteen was something you could catch. If he'd been Catholic, I think he might have crossed himself. 'You OK wearing that?'

I shrug. 'It's just a race number.'

His mirrored sunglasses make his eyes unreadable, but his lips quirk. 'When Rupert had it, he wore his bib upside down, like they do in the Tour de France.'

'I'm fine with how it is,' I say through gritted teeth.

The crowd hushes, and Hiroko lifts on his tiptoes to see over the heads of the other runners. I, on the other hand, look up at the sky. The weather couldn't be more different from last night. Now the sun radiates down on us, the air still. There's not a breath of wind, nor a single cloud in the sky. Just miles of endless blue.

The crowd murmurs, as a Jeep drives slowly into the centre of the bivouac. We all stare expectantly at the doors, waiting for whoever is going to emerge.

But no one does.

There's a clap. One loud smack of hands.

Then silence.

Another clap.

A man steps out from amongst the runners, walking right up to the car and clambering on to its roof, nimble and light-footed. He sheds his hat and glasses, revealing the person we've all been waiting for.

Boones.

He grins. Then he claps again.

The sound reverberates through the crowd. Even though he's only one man in a crowd of almost a thousand, I hear him as loud as if he is right next to me. It's like a camp counsellor's attempt to gain rowdy teenagers' attention.

But it works.

He does it again. Except this time, others join in. The claps sound louder than ever. As one, the beat continues, speeding up, spreading from person to person until it seems like the entire desert is applauding, then cheering and yelling, all the pent-up energy from the night before released, the whole mood of the bivouac changing.

If anyone else had tried it, I'm certain it would have flopped. But it's like Boones has been able to alter our collective brain chemistry. There's a frenzy, a fervour that takes hold. People stamp their feet and shout loud whoops. In front of me, Hiroko bounces up and down, Alex beside him, arms round each other. Even I'm clapping so hard my palms sting. A woman nearby starts crying – tears of joy. Or at the very least they're a release.

Boones raises his hands again. It takes a little time but the crowd calms. There's no dejection now in the shoulders around us. Chins are up. Heads held high. Mine too.

He lifts a microphone from his pocket. He speaks directly into it, his characteristic rasp somehow still crystal clear. 'Well, I promised you hot and sandy,' he says in his American drawl.

The crowd roars with laughter.

'That was quite the night. Some of you have been hurt. Some of you have quit. The desert is testing us, even before the race has begun. But those of you who are still here – bravo. As you're experiencing right now, you're facing the toughest challenge of your life. It will be hard. It will be beautiful. Maybe you will be pushed to breaking point. You will come face to face with your demons, duke it out on those sands. But, my God, it will be worth it. And I for one can't wait to see who manages it.'

The crowd roars again.

'This is an experience like no other. And I want you to live every moment of it. So new rule: no electronic devices.'

My heart drops, my fingers automatically going to my phone. I grip it tight. I'd promised to message Ethan whenever I had signal. But, more than that, the last time I'd raced without a phone, the worst had happened. If he needed to reach me and couldn't . . . I would never forgive myself.

'No phones, cameras, music players, chargers, any watches with a function other than basic time. You get it. We're going pure. We're going simple. If you get into trouble, there's no faster way to get help than to use your emergency beacons. Henry will run through the logistics. If you don't want to comply, you can join the thirty-four others who have left already. No shame in admitting this isn't for you. It's not going to be for most of you. Only the brave can handle what's coming. See you on the starting line. You have fifteen minutes.'

He clambers down from the Jeep as the murmurs grow.

He's cutting us off from the outside world. Henry takes the microphone and is saying something about how volunteers will be coming round to collect the devices.

Mariam shrugs. 'I didn't even bring my phone.'

'This is brilliant,' says Hiroko. 'I spend enough time on my devices at home. I can fully unplug and blame Boones.'

Volunteers in Hot & Sandy vests are moving through

the crowd with what look like dry bags with roll-top lids. 'I have to go,' I reply. Mariam calls after me but I'm already on my way.

Most people hand them over without fuss. It's not as if there's much signal out here, and having that purity of experience – cut off from technology – has its appeal, as Hiroko said. But I cling on to mine like a life raft, dodging runners and volunteers alike in my urge to get to the edge of the bivouac.

I dial Nancy, Pete's mother. I know it's six a.m. in the UK, but she's an early bird, up to walk their pair of over-excited black Labradors. But for some reason today she chooses not to answer. Same with Pete's dad, his number ringing out. *Where on earth are they?* I feel panicky now, as I see Henry has spotted me. He's approaching with an open dry bag like a threat.

I keep walking, dialling the numbers. It crosses my mind to call Pete, but I push that thought away. He won't be with Ethan yet and he can hear the news about the race from Stella. I wonder if they're taking away phones from the photographers too.

I glance behind me and see Henry is busy with another runner. I stop to record a video, taking a couple of deep breaths, trying to rearrange my face into someone who is calm and in control. Not wildly panicked and flailing. 'Ethan! It's Mum. This is just a message to say that Boones is taking our phones away so we can concentrate on running. Didn't you tell me that he hates technology? So there you go. You were right. But please don't worry – remember you can follow my dot to see how I'm doing. Know I'm always thinking about you. Know I love you very much. Be good to Nanny and Grandad. Good luck in your matches. You know the way. And remember – I do too. See you very, very soon.'

I watch the message swirl around and around, the signal strength wavering as it attempts to send the video. I beg it to go. When I lower the screen, there is Henry.

'Ready?' he asks, holding out the open bag.

'Can I make sure this sends?'

Henry glances down at his watch, sucking in his bottom lip. 'I don't know . . . OK, well, I also see here you have a digital camera and charger on your inventory – they need to go in too.'

I nod, feeling sick. I hadn't had a moment spare to look at the pictures I'd taken of Jason's notebook on that camera. Now that information is going to be locked away. The charger is in an easily accessible side pocket, but I take my time searching for it. I finally see the double tick to show the video has been sent, and I drop both the phone, charger and camera in the bag. He rolls the top and seals it, marking it with my race number. The bag is slightly padded, made of heavy-duty black material.

'It's a Faraday pouch. Blocks any signal,' he explains. 'You'll be able to pick it up at the end of the race.'

'You must have had all these prepared. Why didn't you tell us earlier?'

Henry laughs. 'It's all part of the race, to keep you on your toes. We volunteers are giving up our phones too. The only person with one is Boones – otherwise we're running on radios.'

I frown. 'That doesn't seem safe.'

'Don't worry, there's a laptop in the admin tent that

will be manned twenty-four seven. There'll always be someone watching your GPS trackers. We'll know if any emergency beacons are activated and get help to that location straight away.'

'So the photographers don't have phones either?'

'No one. They'll have their cameras and will be able to send their images from the comms tent. Good luck, runner thirteen,' he says, before walking away.

Without my phone I feel naked. Cut off. Alone. I'm still not sure that I can go through with this.

Then I see the dark green Jeep. This is my chance.

I start running. 'Boones!' I shout. Thankfully the vehicle moves at a crawl through the busy bivouac, and I am faster. The car stops as I bang on the window.

He lowers it, then examines me from head to toe, his eyes lingering on my race number. 'Adrienne.'

My words come out in a breathless rush. 'What you wrote on the invitation. I need to know. Who was driving the car?'

He raises both eyebrows at me. 'Aw, come on now. You're here. You're wearing the number. We're minutes from the start.'

'Right. That's why you have to tell me what you know.'

'Answers at the *end* of the race.'

'There could be someone here who's trying to hurt me.'

'It seems to me like someone has been trying to hurt you for a long time.' He leans over to the glovebox and pulls out a folded piece of paper. I hold my breath as he hands it to me. I unfold it – it's a black-and-white still from what looks like CCTV footage. The logo for the camera brand is in the left-hand corner. In view is the Ranger Rover. I recognize the street it's on as well. Just round the corner from my house. But the driver's face is blurred.

'You have this video?'

'I do. I'll show it to you. After the race.'

I crumple the paper. 'How long have you had this?' My mind is racing. All this time he's known. 'The driver . . . are they here? Am I in danger?'

'Honey, you're in the middle of the Sahara Desert. There's danger everywhere.'

14

Adrienne

A foghorn sounds around the bivouac as Boones drives away, signalling five minutes until the start of the first stage of the race. My heart pounds in my chest. I close my eyes, tilting my head back, letting the sun warm my face and calm my racing adrenaline. It doesn't work. Searing-hot rage rises instead, feeding on the undercurrent of fear.

At least Boones wasn't bluffing. He knows who was driving the car. I just have to play his game, run in his race, and then he'll tell me. Boones might like surprises, but I hope he's a man of his word.

The river of fear works its way deeper. The challenges of the race I can handle – the heat, the miles, the pain. But what if someone is out there, wanting to hurt me? The one other person who might have told me the answer has already been seriously wounded, and Boones couldn't stop it.

Anything can happen.

I focus on the first stage. Twenty-five miles. A little less than a marathon. There will be other runners, photographers, medics, volunteers lining the race route. I'm wearing a GPS dot that tracks my location at all times. Maybe the safest place for me is to be out on the course.

I walk towards the starting line. Now I need to focus

on what I can control: when I eat, when I sleep, whether I stop to fix a hot spot, how much I drink, when I stop for the toilet – all of it a vast algorithm I must carry in my head, constantly doing the mental calculations of how far I have to go and how fast I can push the pace. This is what I used to be good at.

The rest is a mental game. Even without the threat Jason brought to the front of my mind, this is a Boones race. I'm not going to be able to switch off my brain and just run, like I might in a road marathon or on a trail I've done a million times. I'm going to need to keep my wits about me. The more the miles drag on, the harder it's going to be.

The storm might have caused chaos in the night, but it's covered everything in a thin layer of sand, disguising the myriad footprints and car tracks that had marred the desert surface before. It looks pristine, like fresh-fallen snow – except golden instead of white. The mountains in the near distance look clearer now too, lit up by the morning sun. Even from here I can see what look like waterfalls of sand pouring down the side of the jebels. We won't have to face those today. That's a challenge for the second day. I push it to the back of my mind.

As I make my way into the starting zone, people whisper behind their hands. Most of them have heard the podcast, igniting the old flames of scandal that had turned my running career to ash. They see my race number – that thirteen on my front – and they wonder why am I Boones's pick. What's so special about me?

And in turn I wonder about them. *Are you the one? Did you try to hurt my son and are you back for more?*

I don't breathe normally until I'm with the other elites. Amongst them I feel the muscle memory returning, my old self emerging from her stasis. The starting zone is marked out with two huge flags set on top of trucks. It's not as elaborate – or as professional – as the starting line for UTMB. It's more rugged, more simplistic. But what was it that Boones had said in his speech? He was aiming for Pure & Simple. Maybe this is part of it, despite the obscene amount of prize money on offer.

I glance down at my watch – only two minutes until the starting gun. I've missed my opportunity for a proper warm-up. I can see the two front runners, Nabil and Farouk, jogging together, looking so relaxed and free. Whoever wants to challenge them for the title is going to have to keep them close. A fun runner approaches – I can tell, because their race numbers have a blue background, not white like ours – and asks them for a photo before their phone is taken away. Nabil agrees, graciously, while Farouk stops to tie a loose shoelace. The two talk for a short time, and I wonder if Nabil is giving the runner tips.

'I thought you'd quit,' says Mariam, who has snuck up next to me, making me jump. When I glance back at Nabil, the fun runner has melted back into the crowd.

'Not yet,' I say. 'Had to send a message to my son before they nicked my phone.'

She nods, bending at the waist and swinging her arms, loosening up.

I readjust the shoulder straps of my backpack, then reach down and pull up my socks. I start to strategize. I can't help myself. It's not in me to run a race and not

wonder what it would be like to win. *One stage at a time,*
I remind myself. But if I want to leave myself a chance,
I'm going to have to race smart. There's no way I'll be
able to match Nabil and Farouk for pace out of the gate.
But over this sort of incredible distance, anything can
happen. It's uncharted territory for most of us. There
is no training you can do to guarantee you are ready for
two hundred and fifty miles. All you can do is take care
of yourself, try not to get too injured, too sleepy, too
dehydrated or too delirious, and let the rest of the race
fall into place.

To the side of the starting line there is a bank of
photographers, their lenses panning the crowd. I don't
see Stella amongst them. Maybe she did go home with
Pete. A frisson of anticipation slides down my spine
and I stand straight, holding my head high. This might
be the only image that Ethan is able to see of me if he
is checking online. I want him to be proud of his mum.
To see me as I struggle to see myself: someone strong,
someone to be proud of. The last thing I want is for
him to see someone who is scared. So I try my best to
look relaxed.

I think of all I've risked to get here. I think of what I
have on the line. I think about Ethan. The life I'll be able
to give him if I can free myself from the fear that's kept
me rooted in one spot.

There's a healthy chatter amongst the crowd, but it dies
down as Boones pulls up to the starting line. He gets out
of the car, surveying the runners.

I'm holding my breath and that's not going to help
me run. I take a deliberate deep inhale, followed by an

extra-long exhale. I see Rupert staring at Boones with laser-like intensity. Is there going to be another big speech?

'Well, all right then,' Boones says. And he clicks his fingers.

So we run.

15

Stella

And they're off.

Boones got his way, as usual.

The race is on. I'm kneeling in the dirt, a few steps ahead of the starting line, my camera pointed at the line of runners. The sun's rays beat down on the back of my neck. Fierce. Prickly. *Why am I not sitting by a pool like Pete is?* The question has crossed my mind several times. Just find a driver to get me back to Ouarzazate. Leave Boones to his final shebang.

But I can't bring myself to go.

So if I'm still here, and the race is going ahead, then I might as well do my job while I keep an eye on things. I start with several shots of the elites – Nabil, the front runner, tall and strong, long-limbed. His lips are set in a firm line, his eyes looking out to the horizon, hardly blinking. Next to him, Farouk, shorter and stockier, keeps his expression a little less serious. He reminds me of my cousins, always with a small smile playing on their lips, like they're in on an inside joke. At the signal from Boones they leap off the starting line, powering ahead of the pack.

A helicopter flies overhead, swooping low and sending up clouds of dust that I shield my lens from. I squint up at the sky and think I catch sight of Boones in the chopper, leaning out of the open door behind a cameraman.

He must have jumped in straight away, wanting a bird's-eye view of his creation. The fun runners jog past me next, and I continue taking photos until the last runner is off the line. Already some people are walking. Do they really imagine they can go the entire way without breaking into a run? Conserving their energy, perhaps. It could be a strategy. I fear that they will be the first ones Boones will weed out.

After the last runner is away, a camel follows, two men walking beside it. I snap a photo – it might work for the charity's social media. A funny anecdote. And, with that, my first job is done. I stand, stretch and wander back towards the bivouac. There's still plenty of activity, even though the runners are gone. The tents are almost all broken down, and the equipment is being loaded on to the backs of trucks ready to be moved and set up at the next location.

'Stella!'

I look up. It's Dale, waving me over to one of the Jeeps.

'This is our driver, Ali,' Dale says, once I reach them.

Ali puts his left hand over his heart and extends his right to me. I shake it. '*As-Salaam-Alaikum*,' I say.

Ali smiles. '*Wa-Alaikum-Salaam*,' he replies. 'Welcome, sister, it is nice to meet you.'

'And you,' I reply.

He looks young – maybe only eighteen or nineteen – his dark hair covered by an NYC-branded baseball cap. He's wearing a traditional moss-green thobe overtop of his jeans.

'You're sure you're qualified to do this?' Dale asks, looking Ali up and down.

Ali seems to take his scepticism in stride. 'My uncle has

been running tours in the desert for many years. I do much of the driving in my time off from university. You're in safe hands, trust me. Five stars on Tripadvisor,' he adds.

'I want to be first to get the best shots, so that means we're going to have to be fast and flexible, ready to move at a moment's notice. Can you do that?'

Ali stands straight, like he's receiving a military order. I can't tell if he's mocking Dale, or if he's on board. 'Whatever you need,' he says, and he gives me a wink.

I suppress a smile behind my hand.

'Let's go then. What are we waiting for? I need to catch up with the elites.' Dale clambers in the back of the Jeep. 'You coming?' he asks me out of the open window.

I hesitate, staring out at the bivouac, marvelling at how it's returning to its original state. Our existence being wiped away, as if we had never been there. Even the starting flags have been taken down, ready to move to the next camp. Boones's trailer is gone. I don't even know how I would arrange a car back to Ouarzazate anyway at this point.

I get in the car but I take the front seat next to Ali. 'I'm ready,' I say.

Ali waits until he sees me clip in my seat belt, then he's off, driving out into the sands.

We don't follow the runners directly but instead trace the edge of a large dried-up riverbed, keeping a high vantage point. Ali drives for about half an hour, one ear to a radio, before pulling to a stop next to a large boulder, its pitted and cratered surface tempting us to climb it. Clambering up with our equipment isn't easy, but from the top we get an incredible view, looking down on the cracked-earth ground of the wadi. It's like we've driven to Mars.

'Look, there!' says Dale. He thrusts his arm out and I follow his pointed finger. The first runner appears on the horizon at the head of a thin line of mostly white shirts bobbing up and down. They shimmer ever so slightly in the heat haze reflecting up from the ground, like moving mirages. I'm amazed at how quickly they're able to run in such intense heat and on such little sleep from the storm. They're superhuman.

Dale starts snapping away as Nabil – the current leader – steams past us far below. Dale doesn't even stop to adjust the settings on his camera, whereas I'm slower, more deliberate.

I'm not worried about photographing the elites anyway. My charity clients will be nowhere close to them – they're probably hours away – so I focus on getting images of the landscape, showing off the vastness of the desert they're running through, the remote nature of the challenge.

Dale finishes before I do and he jumps off the boulder. I stay a bit longer, relishing in the grandeur of the vista in front of me. I've got to hand it to my dad. He knows how to choose a location.

'Are you much of a runner?' Dale asks me as I climb down.

'Not really,' I say. 'I leave that to my fiancé.' I don't share with him who my father is. That's none of his business. 'What about you?'

'Before my injury I couldn't get enough. My family were all runners. My mother even competed in the Olympics.'

'Really? That's incredible.'

'I had to take up ultrarunning just to get out of her shadow!' He laughs. 'No, she inspired me. It was running with her that made me realize; it takes me a marathon distance before I *really* start to love it. Ultras, man. They're an addiction.'

'I knew someone who felt like that,' I say.

'At least he gets to be out there, in the running,' Dale mutters.

I don't correct him, but I wasn't referring to Pete. For him, running is a sport – a hobby. For my sister, Yasmin, it had been a lifestyle. A passion.

Dale pulls his cap off, wiping his hand across his brow. His whole face is covered in a thin layer of sand, darkening his sparse beard.

Ali holds out bottles of water for us both, which I take gratefully. It's blazing hot, and I wonder how the runners are handling it. It's not even that I'm drenched in sweat, because the sweat evaporates the moment it appears, leaving behind a salty, grainy residue that mingles with the sand.

I'm not the only one suffering. Dale staggers as he opens the car door.

'Are you OK?' Ali asks Dale.

'Fine, fine. How the heck do you handle this heat?'

Ali smiles. Then he squints as he looks up into the sky. 'The temperature is going to climb even higher today.'

'Is it normal for this time of year?' I ask.

'It gets hotter every summer. More sandstorms. More heat.'

'Christ,' Dale mutters.

'Where to next?' Ali asks us.

'The second checkpoint,' Dale says, quickly, not letting me get a word in. But I'm happy for him to take the lead.

'I want to make sure I catch the elites coming in. I doubt they'll spend long there.'

Ali nods, consulting the map, and drives away in the direction of the second checkpoint. We're quite far from the runners but we catch a glimpse every now and then. I spot medical personnel on the route too, parked in their Jeeps, ready to jump into action in case any of the emergency beacons are activated.

'What do you think of all this?' I ask Ali, gesturing at the map of Hot & Sandy pasted up on the dashboard.

He laughs, considering his answer. 'It's impressive!'

'Oh, come on,' says Dale. 'You don't have to be all PC on us. You think we're all crazy white people, don't you?'

Speak for yourself, I think.

'Coming to your desert and running until we die.'

'You do know some of the top runners out there are Moroccan, right?' I say.

Dale rolls his eyes. 'It's got to be the money, though, in this case. Five hundred thousand dollars.' He lets out a low whistle. 'People will do crazy things for that kind of cash.'

'It's a fortune,' says Ali.

'That Boones guy – do you know much about him?' Dale asks me.

I shoot him a look from the front seat. 'Not really,' I say. It's not even a lie.

'This doesn't really seem like his kind of race. Everything else he's done has been so raw, pared back. He calls this "Pure & Simple" but it's anything but. All those medics, the corporate sponsors – heck, even all of us with our cameras and drones. He says he wants to see how far people are willing to go. But will he *really* put people to the test if it comes down to it? Seems to me like Boones has had his teeth removed.'

'I wouldn't underestimate him,' I say. I don't elaborate further.

We arrive at the second checkpoint, which is only manned by a couple of volunteers. Their task is mammoth, too big for the two of them: setting up shelter, unloading hundreds of bottles of water ready to pour into the runners' containers.

'They look like they're struggling,' says Dale. 'Hey, can we help?' he asks the nearest one.

I sigh. Somehow, despite what I said to Boones, I'm roped into helping with the race, after all. I hammer stakes at the corner of the tent shelters so that runners can rest if they want and hang plastic bags from a post to collect any rubbish, trying to keep the desert as clean as possible.

As I move to the tables, ripping open huge packs of bottled water and setting them out in neat rows, I hear a shout.

The first runner – it's now Farouk – has appeared already. He's setting a storming pace, but the other elites aren't far behind. I instinctively grab my camera, taking photos of him coming up over the rise and towards the checkpoint. A whole series of cars arrive now – the medical teams and the rest of the volunteers. 'Where's Nabil?' I ask Dale, who's at the next table. When we'd last seen them, Nabil had been ahead.

'No clue. Maybe something happened?'

Farouk enters the checkpoint via my table and I photograph the volunteer topping up his water bottles – although it appears he hasn't drunk that much over the course of ten miles. His acclimatization to running in this kind of heat means he's more efficient with his hydration intake. The next person to appear is Rupert, his dark hair peeking out beneath a bright red cap. Then, finally, Nabil strides into view, along with the first of the women: to my surprise it's Adrienne, looking strong.

My throat catches, as I strangle down tears. Watching her run – it's like the events of seven years ago never happened.

If I had my choice, I'd never have seen or spoken to Adrienne again. I'd blocked her after Ibiza and dodged her approaches until she finally got the message and gave up. Yet life weaved a tangled web that kept us connected – not least because I couldn't help falling in love with her ex-husband.

I'd met Pete a few months before Ibiza, at a race – naturally. I was crewing for Yasmin during a fifty-mile race in northern California, waiting around for hours at the halfway checkpoint for her to pass through. The conditions had been atrocious that year, and some of the support teams were held up when the main road to the trail flooded. Pete had hobbled into the checkpoint, injured, and with no crew in sight. I'd taken pity on him and offered him one of my homemade flapjacks as a pick-me-up. We got to chatting and he DNF'd the race to continue the conversation. He always says it was the luckiest twisted ankle he'd ever had.

After the race and her incredible performance, Yasmin and I were asked to join Coach Glenn's training camp in Ibiza. And Pete had asked me out on a date.

Seven years since everything changed.

16

Stella

Seven years earlier
Ibiza

When Yasmin runs, the sun's rays follow her like a spotlight.
Her skin lights up, suffused with gold, so it's impossible to
take your eyes off her. Her smile might have something to
do with that too. Even after an eighteen-mile training run
in the intense Spanish heat her smile is broad, like she's
won the lottery. I told her that once. She'd laughed and
agreed with me. 'But I have won the lottery, Stella. Look at
what my life is!'

On a day like today I can almost see what she means.
She's running along a cliff edge, the ozonic, salty sea air
scented with orange blossom, to a background track of
waves crashing against the white-sand beach far below.
Through my lens she casts a navy silhouette against a dusky
blue sky, her arms pumping, legs pounding the earth, the
tail of her signature pink hijab streaming out behind her. I
still don't fully understand it, the desire to push your body
and mind to endure silly amounts of pain and suffering
for the sake of a race. Yet watching Yasmin makes it seem
beautiful. Natural. She was born to do this. She would run
forever if given the chance.

I can see why she's come here. For a week she's been

intensively training under the guidance of the legendary ultrarunning coach Glenn Knight, alongside four of his top performers. There's Adrienne, Yasmin's idol. The mountain-loving phenom, who's been beating men and women alike in impossibly long races in the most brutal conditions. The 'rock goat', they call her, because she's the greatest of all time on the skyrunning courses. She's the physical opposite of Yasmin in so many ways – fair-haired, shorter, slight, like a stiff breeze might blow her over – but the rock goat is as stubborn as she is fast. She doesn't give up, and, as a result, she's a champion.

Then there's Keri and Ivanka, university students and best friends from Ireland and Poland respectively, on the running team at Manchester University, where Glenn lectures. They are both sub-2:45 marathoners – but with a burning desire to make their names out on the trails. As if 26.2 miles isn't long enough – some people are nuts.

Winona is another relative newcomer, spotted by Glenn at an ultra in Colorado. She'd come from nowhere and ended up on the podium, with two broken bones in her foot and a dislocated shoulder from a fall. Grit personified.

And finally there's Yasmin herself. My half-sister. The nineteen-year-old with talent bursting from every pore. The one who set up her own backyard ultra in the garden of her south London studio flat and ran over a hundred miles in twenty-four hours, documenting every moment of it online, going viral.

I'm the only non-runner here. Glenn hadn't wanted me to come. He harped on about the sanctity of the camp, how they needed to feel like they were cut off from the rest of the world, totally devoted to their craft. No family or support crew permitted.

He only changed his tune when Yasmin told him who my father was.

Because this training camp has only one mission: to get a woman to win an Ampersand race. The ultimate ultra-marathon test. And he's gathered only the best of the best to the island.

To that end, I'm the secret weapon. Emphasis on secret. No one outside the camp is to know that I'm here. I don't even tell Pete, which has the added benefit of not having to reveal to Adrienne that I've started dating her ex.

But the truth is, I hardly know anything about my dad's races, not really. The last time I'd been to one, I was seventeen. That didn't stop Glenn from grilling me for every detail over dinner.

'They say he likes to push the boundaries of what humans are capable of – what we're willing to endure. Would you say he's a sadist?'

'Probably,' I reply with a grim laugh. Then I shake my head. 'Not a sadist. More like . . . a scientist,' I say, paraphrasing my mom's words. 'It's not that he enjoys watching people in pain. But he wants to know how far someone will go. Each race is an experiment. He tweaks the variables every year, then sits back and watches the result.'

'So his runners are like rats in a maze.'

'Rats who volunteer,' I counter. 'He doesn't force anyone to run.'

'He pushes others – but has he ever pushed himself?'

'All the time. He devises challenges for himself – things like crossing the US on foot. Walking to Alaska from

Mexico. His own pilgrimage through the Sahara. He doesn't do it for records or acclaim, though. Sometimes he doesn't tell anyone what he's doing. Just comes back with the stories.'

'So why, then?'

'Same reason he put on the Ampersands, I suppose. Curiosity. But he's a better race director than runner.'

'What about when he's not directing races? What does he do then? When is "Boones" not actually "Boones"?'

I pause. Of course 'Boones' is a nickname. A play on words. A boon is meant to be a good thing. When he's not in that character, he's an ordinary man, with an ordinary job – a bookkeeper for a couple of local businesses. Truth is, he works as little as he can get away with. He's never been massively rich or ambitious in any other avenue other than racing.

His notoriety is what's worth millions. People fall over themselves to impress him. But his ordinariness might be part of it. Because ultrarunning doesn't attract flashy attention-seeking people – it's too long, too arduous, too painful for that. Boones wants to elevate the ordinary to extraordinary.

And, in his mind, diamonds are only made under extreme pressure. Otherwise they remain part of the dirt.

The information I give Glenn seems to satisfy him – at least for a bit – and he lets me stick around. When I'd arrived here a week ago, I'd been so tense, my back in knots with anxiety. Despite her talent, I didn't want Yasmin to run in one of my dad's races. Not only were his trails dangerous – *he* was dangerous. Everyone applauded him, but I know the risks.

Watching Yasmin thrive under Glenn's instruction has gone a long way to making me feel more at ease, though. She's in her element on the trails, navigates with ease, manages to stay relaxed. With time she'll be a contender. For now I'm counting down until the camp is over, when Yasmin and I have planned a backpacking trip around Spain. Sangria in Barcelona, tapas in Granada, and lots of lounging on sun-drenched beaches after all this high-intensity running. Since I moved to California and she lives in London, we hardly ever get to spend quality sister time with each other. I cannot wait.

Yasmin runs past me, and I snap photos of her finishing. She raises her arms high in the air, sweat gluing rogue strands of hair that have come loose from her headscarf to her forehead.

'Great job!' Glenn high-fives her as she crosses the imaginary finishing line. He throws a towel round her shoulders and offers her a bottle of fresh ice-cold water, which she accepts gratefully. He's a whirlwind of advice after that. 'Beautiful action on those uphills. You'll just want to watch your form – don't be afraid of dropping to a fast walk to keep your footing. Remember that nose breathing: in, in, in, out. Can I see your watch? I need to note your stats. Knowledge is king.'

Yasmin holds her wrist out as he takes down all the metrics recorded on the fancy GPS running watch. Glenn is as bald as a cue ball but wears it well, with a strong, chiselled jaw and unique amber-flecked brown eyes that don't seem to miss a moment.

'Get any good pics?' Yasmin asks me in between gulps of water.

'Loads. I'll pick a few for your Insta and drop them to you. How are you feeling?'

'*Épuisée*,' she replies. 'And I'm still way behind Adri's time. I don't know how she does it.'

'You'll get there,' says Glenn. 'Now, drink this.' He takes her water away and gives her a different bottle filled with a murky brown liquid.

Yasmin grimaces. 'This that recovery blend again?' She spins the top off. 'So gross.' She throws her head back and takes a deep swig.

'It's good for you. Why don't you head back to the resort?' Glenn says to me. 'I want to run through a few cool-down drills with Yasmin and some boring performance-review stuff.'

'Are you sure?' I direct the question to Yasmin.

She nods. 'Yeah, definitely. I'll see you back in the room to get ready for dinner.'

I wander back down the hill towards the lavish sports resort Glenn uses as a base for his camps. Someone in a light blue visor is jogging in the opposite direction. 'All finished?' she asks as she looks up, and I realize it's Adrienne.

'Yeah.'

'Where's Yasmin?'

'Oh, she's with Glenn. They're doing a cool down or something.'

Her eyes flash. 'Just the two of them?'

'Yep.'

She drops her head back down and powers past me. I stop, watching as she sprints the hill. I think about that look in her eyes. Anger? Jealousy? I wonder. It wouldn't surprise me if she and Coach Glenn had a thing going on. There had been rumours about him – creepy behaviour, some negative comments from other runners not invited to his special camp – but Adrienne had been the one to assure Yasmin he was the best. Told her how her career could be transformed through Glenn's coaching.

The light is so beautiful on the island. The sun is setting, casting everything in a purple haze – a built-in Instagram filter. I take a photo looking out to sea, then check the result in the viewfinder. I flick through the images on my camera.

There is Yasmin. Except not Yasmin.

I see Atalanta, goddess of running. The one who challenged any man who wanted her to a race and beat them all.

I only hoped that whoever would eventually catch up with her would be worthy.

17

Adrienne

At last, I'm running again.

The tension of the bivouac is behind me, along with the snide comments and side-eyes, the storm-battered weariness. Now I can say all I need to with my feet, and that's how I like it.

I'm amazed by how quickly the first few miles disappear. I keep pace with Mariam, matching her stride for stride. We push hard in the early morning, trying to cover as much ground as possible while the sun is not at full strength. Navigating is easier than I imagined too, despite the crude hand-drawn map. Every so often we pass a rock that has been spray-painted bright blue, marking the route. They're easy to spot amidst the otherwise monochrome shades of brown landscape.

I'm not fully able to relax into my stride, though. My nerves are frayed, stinging like they're exposed to the air. Pete's disqualification, Jason's injury, the note in his journal – it's all put me on edge. I keep looking over my shoulder, waiting for . . . I don't even know what.

Knowledge is king, Addy.

Hearing Glenn's voice in my head makes me recoil, despite the fact that he is right. He's the only person to ever call me 'Addy', as if renaming me was part of the control he could exert.

It almost makes me stop in my tracks. But I grit my teeth. I'm not going to let him – or his memory – distract me. This is part of the reason I stopped running. Because I couldn't dissociate it from *him*.

From what he did.

I focus on the other voice in my head. Ethan's. *Mum, you know the way.*

I wonder if he's at the tennis courts right now. He normally goes first thing in the morning, whether he's staying with me, Pete or his grandparents. At our local court the net hangs half off, but we still hit a ball around until it's time to walk to school. I've never been the best player – even at ten, he can run circles around me – but I've got better thanks to the sheer number of hours we've practised. I'm so proud of his discipline – maybe because I recognize it in myself.

It's not the only thing he's got from me. At his last tournament he got suspended from the team. The night it happened, Pete had dropped him off with me, absolutely furious.

'Tell your mum what happened,' he'd said.

'It wasn't fair,' Ethan had replied, his arms folded across his chest. 'Finn's ball was in. The umpire was wrong. He should have won his game.'

'And you thought yelling at the umpire was going to help?'

Ethan had stormed off to his room.

Pete had sighed. 'Can you talk to him?'

'Was the umpire wrong?' I'd asked.

'Not the issue. His outburst was, and the coach says he's not to play again until he understands that.'

I'd winced. He was right. Ethan needed to learn to control his temper. Losing it was something he'd inherited from me.

'The ball was in,' Pete had conceded, eventually.

And that's when I knew. Ethan was more like me than I had realized – the good and the bad. His fierce sense of justice. That strain between the truth and the reality. What's fair about a ball being in and the umpire calling it out? One is the truth, but the other sometimes needs to be accepted as real to be a good sportsperson.

Sport, like life, doesn't always abide by the rules.

Ethan's never known me as an athlete. Certainly not as a champion. And I've never told him. My boxes of medals are stuffed under my bed. I don't compete at his sports day. It's easier that way. To pretend that my life began when we moved to Ambleside and I started working in the outdoor shop. That I'm just his plain, boring mum.

Maybe now he'll see a different side to me.

The further we run, the more spread out the pack becomes. I lose the front runners but I'm not worried at this point. The race is long and these are literally the very first few miles. As long as I keep a good pace, I'll be able to make up the time.

Still, when I reach the next checkpoint, I'm grateful. I've been playing it close to the line with water, and my bottles are nearly running dry. In my long-sleeved-top, shorts and compression socks, most of my skin is protected from the force of the sun's rays, but I feel like I'm cooking from the inside out. Sweat beads on my forehead and upper lip, the suncream I lathered on my face now dripping into my eyes, making them sting – a rookie error. And we're not even at the peak of the day yet. As I pass through, one of the volunteers hands me my water. I need to transfer it to the reusable bottles lodged in the straps of my pack, the straws at a convenient height so I can sip without removing them, so I step into the shade of one of the shelters. I could also do with putting some sachets of rehydration salts in with my water, to help me as we're about to enter the dunes.

Taking a break makes me feel agitated about my time, but I tell myself it will just be for a few minutes.

A groan sounds from the back of the tent. I peer into the darkness, my eyes having trouble adjusting from the searing bright light outside.

I step closer. 'Nabil? Are you OK? *Tout vas bien?*' I ask in halting French.

'*J'ai besoin d'eau.*' He gestures to his water bottles. The ground is wet by his feet; I wonder if he accidentally tipped them over.

'Let me get one of the volunteers,' I say.

'They say no more,' he replies, shaking his head.

'That's ridiculous.' He looks worryingly unsteady, swaying on his feet. I reach out to help him, but he waves me off. 'Here,' I say, spinning the lid off one of my bottles and pouring the fresh water into his. There's no rule against sharing water. It's not food or any other gear. It's part of my ration. If that means that my race suffers later on, that's my choice to make.

'*Merci,*' he says. He fumbles in his pack and pulls out a small bag of tablets, pops one and then takes a swig. Salt, I assume.

'Are you OK to run? Do you want me to get a doctor?' I

don't want to leave him like this. But he seems to recover as he takes in the water, standing straighter, his eyes brighter.

'I will continue. Thank you again. You have saved my race.'

'You're welcome. I've watched some of your race videos. You're an inspiration to me.'

'Not today,' he says, bitterly.

'Every day,' I say.

He laughs. 'OK,' he says. 'I am fine now. Thank you.'

I back out of the tent and into the daylight. I hesitate. There's a medical tent right next door, and the handsome Italian doctor from yesterday is inside. I debate calling him over. But then Nabil emerges from the rest tent and sets off at a jog. A fast jog.

It reminds me that this is a race. I set off after him, not wanting to lose sight of his heels. A competitive spark ignites within me, one I thought had been long extinguished. If I can stay with him for the rest of the stage, then maybe I'll have a good enough time to remain in contention. I think about Ethan logging in to see how well his mum is doing. I'll make him proud.

I keep my head down, watching the ground changing beneath my feet. No longer is it cracked, dry and littered with tiny stones. Instead, it's fine sand, like I'm back running on the beach in South Wales, where I took Ethan on our last holiday. We stayed in a caravan right on the edge of one of the largest sand dunes in the UK.

But these dunes are different. For one, the sand is much more bronze here, and the heat reflecting off it is intense – so much so that it threatens to melt the soles of my shoes.

Here there are decisions to be made. Nabil has gone off

in one direction, following the ridge line of the dunes. But if I follow him now, I'll be running on sand already broken by his footsteps. The surface will be unstable. With every step I take the sand will send me back by two.

If I choose my own line through the dunes, running along an unspoilt ridge, following Nabil's idea but not his actual footsteps, I might be able to keep up a good pace. So I choose a different dune.

Immediately, I regret my decision. I'm no good at picking out the firmer patches of sand – every step I take, the ground seems to sink beneath me, causing me to slip and lose balance. My head is spinning, my vision becoming blurred. I can barely keep my eyes open against the glare; even through my category-four sunglasses everything is too bright.

This doesn't feel right. I look around and I feel myself sliding down the side of a dune, tall mountains of sand looming. But hadn't I set a course to run along the ridge line? How did I end up here?

I give my head a shake, but that makes me drop to my knees. One of my bottles falls out of its shoulder pocket, leeching water into the sand through the straw. A sound comes out of my mouth that barely seems human, a groan, as I try to get my hands to work to pick up the bottle. My fingers fumble with it, making things worse.

'Hey! Hey!'

I hear shouts but can't find the source. I squint into the sun and spot a shadow on the top of the dune, waving.

I try to lift an arm to wave back but I can't.

I just need to drink something. I try the next bottle, which only has a few sips left. That's when I remember – I gave some of my water to Nabil. Now I've spilled what little I had. This could be it. My race over.

'Need any help?'

My head pounds and I feel a flutter of panic. I haven't come this far only to fail. This isn't even the biggest dune field I'm going to face. I can do this. I force myself to my knees, then to my feet. I manage to raise my hand. 'I'm OK,' I say, my voice croaking.

'Sure? We've got an emergency over here but I can come back for you . . .'

'I'm OK!' I say, louder.

To prove it – to him and to myself – I take a step. Then another and another. I'm slow but I'm moving.

My head swims and I think I'm about to faint. I pinch myself, hard, on the inside of my arm, the pain sharpening the rest of my senses. I don't know what's come over me. The doubt that accompanies the light-headedness is overwhelming. Am I really cut out for this? Maybe throwing myself into the world's toughest race as my 'comeback' after seven years away wasn't the best idea.

No. There's no way I'm going to stop on the first day. I think of the answers I've been promised if I finish. That's enough to get my feet moving.

Then there's the competitive fire that's been lit now. That's enough to quiet down the voices in my head. There's no going back. Only forward.

I keep my focus on that flame all the way to the end of the first stage.

18

Stella

We bundle back into the Jeep after the last elite is through the checkpoint, Dale still keen to stay ahead of the pack. Our next stop is the dunes, and this is where I want to wait to get photographs of the charity fun runners on my list. This will be the money shot. The stereotypical vision of a desert: golden sands rippling in waves, arcing left and right as far as the eye can see. A perfect snapshot of their adventure.

Driving over them is an adventure in itself. I have one hand tightly gripping my camera, the other one holding on to the handle above my head, my knuckles white. The car seems to take off – almost fly – as Ali navigates us into prime position. We pull to a stop in a valley between two monstrous sand mountains, and Dale jumps out straight away, powering up one of the dunes.

I take my time, switching my lens and reapplying suncream. Even though I tan easily, I need to take care.

'How come you speak Arabic?' Ali asks me.

I smile. 'My mother was Moroccan, from the Todra Valley, although spent most of her life in either the US or France. She died a few years back.'

'Oh, I am so sorry to hear that.'

'Thank you. What about you? What part of Morocco are you from?'

'I am from Tafran, a tiny village in the mountains. Although I studied in London. Business school.'

'Oh, that explains the British accent!'

He winks. 'You will have to come to Tafran after this. See what all of this is helping.'

'What do you mean?'

'Oh, I shouldn't have said anything.'

'It's OK, you can tell me.'

'My aunt – she is one of the elite runners. Boones promised that if she finished the race, he would donate money towards rebuilding the school in our village.'

'I didn't know that,' I say, blinking back my surprise. 'That . . . that's great news.'

'I hope so. We desperately need it.'

I nod, a sinking feeling filling my stomach. Boones offered one of the runners an incentive to run in his race? That doesn't seem right. My father is up to something. He's playing games with people's lives.

There's a shout from Dale at the top of the dune. He's waving his arms. 'I'd better go up and see what that's about.'

Ali nods, still appraising me with his deep brown eyes.

'Come with us? If you point your aunt out to me, I'll get some photos of her,' I say. He smiles again, and follows behind me as I start to climb the dune.

For every step I take, my feet slip back. I'm almost brought to my knees, like I'm crawling. I look up at how far I have to go, when I'm struck by the image in front of me. Of Dale standing at the top of the dune, his hands on his hips, looking out at the horizon. I fumble with my camera to take the shot. It also gives me the chance to catch my breath. When I eventually get to the top, I slump to a seat on the crest. I pick up a handful of sand, allowing the grains to fall through my fingers like rivulets of water.

It's beautiful, but it's searing hot. I rub my hands together, shaking off any loose grains. I can't imagine running through this place. Simply existing is hard enough.

'You made it,' says Dale. 'Look, over there.'

Farouk has appeared at the edge of the dune field. He doesn't hesitate in choosing his line. Rather than travelling as the crow flies, he makes a left, following the curve of one of the dunes. His feet barely seem to make an impression on the sand at all – it's as if he floats above it.

'I might try flying the drone,' Dale says. He opens the backpack at his feet and takes out a small black device with little blades like a helicopter. The thing buzzes like a bumblebee, leaping up from the palm of his hand. He manoeuvres it using a video-screen controller – or tries to, at least. It seems to have a mind of its own. Eventually, he seems to gain a modicum of control and sends it high over the dunes.

I lean over his shoulder to watch the screen. It's incredible to see the runners from this angle, putting into perspective how tiny they are compared to the immensity of the dunes. A true ocean of sand.

Dale follows the leader – Farouk – for some time, then pans back towards the entrance of the dunes, making sure to capture Rupert and then Mariam in the frame. It's difficult now that the runners are more spread out, but it looks truly incredible on video. I can already see how this will come together for social media.

The next two into the dunes are Nabil, followed by – I have to squint to make out who it is. But there's her race number, 13; it's Adrienne. She's still running well.

Dale tracks her with the drone. I wonder if he's got a memo to keep tabs on the magic 'runner 13'. An uncomfortable feeling rises inside me. A fiery anger I thought I'd extinguished a long time ago. But then Dale pans back to Nabil. By contrast to Adrienne, he *does* look like he's suffering. He's staggering left and right, then sliding down the face of one of the dunes, as if he's lost control of his legs.

'Ali?' He comes over to view the screen. He watches for a moment. 'Should we go to him?' I ask.

'I thought that was not allowed.'

Of the rules that Boones gave us, interacting with the runners is high on the list of forbidden items. We're not allowed to give water, allow them to use the car as shade or offer any food or assistance of any kind. If we do, it's an immediate disqualification for the runner.

'It's not allowed. But –' I don't need to say more. On the screen, we watch as Nabil stumbles, then falls almost flat on his face, tumbling down the sand. He doesn't seem to make any attempt to stop himself.

We jump in the car and Ali guns it to where the drone is hovering. When we get to Nabil, he doesn't respond to us. I reach up to his shoulder and activate his emergency beacon. I want to drive him to medical care, but the doctors will be able to reach us quicker this way. Plus, if we move him then we might cause further injury. The way he's fallen, he might have hurt himself badly.

Ali is beside himself, panicked, flustered, trying to rouse Nabil.

But I take a step back, my entire body falling still. I clench my back teeth, closing my eyes. It might not be worth driving him anywhere. Because I'm fairly certain Nabil has dropped dead.

The Ultra Bros Podcast

Hot & Sandy Edition

Mac: Hello, bros and bro-ettes, it's Mac here. Yup, just me. I know there have been a lot of rumours and speculation flying around about my co-host and friend Jason, so I want to address that right away.

I received a message before Boones took everyone's phones away: Jason has been injured and taken to hospital. He suffered some kind of freak accident because of a massive sandstorm that hit the bivouac last night. I'm still waiting on an update on his status, so I'll keep you posted. As for the race itself, it's hard getting information out of the desert and things appear to be changing all the time.

We know, of course, that the first stage of the race is now underway – the tracking beacons are on and the Hot & Sandy official account is providing some sparse updates. The runners are out there. And we are the Ultra Bros. You know we plan for every contingency. So even though Jason is out of commission, we have a secret squirrel on the ground, reporting LIVE to us. As part of our agreement, we've had to disguise the sound of their voice, but trust me on this – it's a real source.

So welcome, Anon, to the podcast.

Anon: Thanks for having me.

Mac: Well, you're the one risking your position at the race to speak to us. Hopefully you've been able to hide from watching eyes.

Anon: You understand if I have to hang up quickly.

Mac: No problem. Let's not waste any more time. It's been quite an eventful twenty-four hours to say the least. Drug test fails. Injuries. Dropouts. The sandstorm of the century ... And now what's this we hear about Nabil? Social media is all in a tizz about this. We were following his dot; he was with the front runners as expected. He hit the dunes and then ... what happened? The official feed is being very quiet about this.

Anon: [nondescript sounds]

Mac: Sorry, Anon, we can't hear you.

Anon: My fault. Had to move as someone was coming. Look, as far as I know, Nabil collapsed and his emergency beacon was activated. The doctors arrived as quickly as they could.

Mac: Shit, is he OK?

Anon: He's been driven to Ouarzazate hospital. Apparently we're going to hear from Boones at seven p.m. He's waiting for the last runner to finish and then he'll gather the entire bivouac for an announcement.

Mac: That doesn't sound good.

Anon: I know. I'll let you know what he says. But honestly, it was carnage out there today, especially amongst the fun runners. Everyone knows that a desert race is going to be hot. But this was hotter than any forecast predicted. Scorching. Once the main pack of runners hit the dunes, people were dropping like flies. I've never seen so many people needing IV drips. I don't know exactly how many runners are out, but I assume we'll hear about that from Boones too.

Mac: That's nuts. Seems like one thing after another with this race.

Anon: That's putting it mildly. I'll tell you the truth: it's not safe out here. All the runners are in danger.

Mac: OK, mate, we hear you. It sounds tough out there – you take care of yourself. Call us back when you've heard the announcement? I know our listeners will be desperate to know what's going on. Mac out, for now.

19

Adrienne

When I cross the line of the first stage, I raise my arms to the sky and pump my fists in the air. I think of Ethan watching the live feed at home, and I want him to see his mum cross the line fierce – not like every step over the last mile had made me want to be sick, which is how I really feel.

Hiroko and Alex finish seconds after me. They seem to be running as a team, helping each other keep pace and navigate the route. A race volunteer steps forward, handing out cups of hot, sugary mint tea, and giving us our water allotment for the rest of the night – all we'll have to cook with, clean with and drink until the start of the second stage.

I'm parched, starving, exhausted and in pain – but I can't keep the grin off my face. Runner's high.

God, how I've missed this feeling.

But my smile is not returned by the volunteer. I take in her frown, her drooping shoulders. 'Everything OK?'

'We don't know,' she replies. 'Something's happened to Nabil . . .'

I don't hesitate. I head straight to tent number one, where I spot Mariam sitting next to Farouk, who has his head in his hands.

'I just heard. How is he?' I ask, gulping down breath.

'We don't know,' she replies. 'We thought you might have been with him.'

'I saw him at the checkpoint, then we ran together until the dune field. From there we went our separate ways. I didn't want to follow his line.'

'And how did he seem?'

'At the checkpoint he didn't look well. He'd run out of water so I gave him some of mine. But when we were running he seemed normal again. I thought maybe he'd been a bit dehydrated.'

Mariam shook her head. 'Nabil wouldn't make mistakes like that.'

'I should have stayed with him,' says Farouk, slapping his palm against the carpet.

'It's not your fault,' says Mariam. 'You couldn't have known.'

'I'll go to the medical tent, see if I can get an update,' I say.

Mariam nods, settling back inside the tent with Farouk, offering him what comfort she can.

I drop my backpack and water off in our tent, pouring some recovery shake into one of my bottles before walking over to the medical tent.

To my surprise, it's almost empty – Emilio is the only doctor there, leaning against a tall tower of supplies. He runs his hands through his hair, looking sweaty, sandy and tired – almost as if he's the one who ran a marathon today.

His head darts up as I walk in, as if he's expecting someone else. But his face doesn't fall when he sees me. In fact, it lights up. 'Adrienne, you're OK? Let me check you over. I was worried about you.'

I'm too tired to protest. He shines a penlight into my eyes and checks my pulse. 'No dizziness or wooziness?'

'A bit. Just didn't drink enough. Trying to get on top of it now.' I shake my drink for emphasis.

'Of course. When I saw you in the dunes, you looked pretty rough. I was worried for a moment there.'

'That was you? So you must have seen Nabil?' I ask.

He exhales, slowly.

We lock eyes and my heart drops into my stomach. I almost throw up my recovery shake then and there. 'No!' I whisper.

He raises his hands to shush me, looking around, though there's no one here but us. 'We got him into the car as quickly as we could. They will have a much greater chance of saving him in Ouarzazate.'

I lean against one of the chairs, my legs suddenly feel unstable. 'What happened?'

Now Emilio shakes his head. 'It's my fault. It's all my fault.'

'What? How?'

'I shouldn't have cleared him to run. His resting ECG showed evidence of pre-excitation – an abnormality that I was concerned about. I sent him for a new one but he was so affronted that I even asked. He's one of Morocco's top runners! He trains out here all the time; he's won the Marathon des Sables Legendary six times – I was delighted when the second ECG seemed fine. I gave him the go-ahead. But I should have trusted my instincts.'

'You think it was his heart?'

'What else could it be? But we will find out from the

hospital soon enough – if those photographers hadn't found him using the drone, we may have been too late.'

I think about the dunes, how easy it would be for one man to be missed. If he was alone, with no ability to activate his beacon . . . he could have simply died without anyone knowing. The thought sends a shiver through my body.

'He seemed dehydrated at the checkpoint,' I say. 'I had to give him some of my water. I debated alerting one of the doctors, but, like you said, Nabil is a legend and I . . . well, I didn't want to ruin his race.'

Emilio nods, distracted now, his radio crackling. The bright screen of a laptop catches my eye from behind him and I wonder if he'll let me send a quick 'I love you' message to Ethan. I know it's against the rules. But two runners have come close to death already on this race. I try to ignore my gut screaming at me that I could be next.

'And Jason, do you know how he's doing?' I ask.

'Sorry, I have to go. Another emergency beacon has been activated.'

'You're kidding?'

'I wish I was. It's too hot, and people aren't prepared.'

'And this is day one.'

'This is day one,' he repeats, his eyes looking dark. 'Take care of yourself, Adrienne.'

He gestures for me to follow him out of the medical tent, clearly not wanting to leave me in there on my own.

Back in my tent, I take my time inspecting my gear after the first stage. Word spreads that Boones's announcement will happen at seven p.m., just before the sun sets – and about half an hour after the cut-off time for the fun runners. Anyone who finishes after that will be disqualified. I wonder how many people will be on the starting line tomorrow.

I finally have a moment to look at Jason's pages. It feels like a lifetime ago that I ripped them from the notebook, but it's only been a few hours. His scribble is almost illegible, impossible for me to decipher.

But a few things stand out: *Booneshounds*. The community of Boones superfans. I guess Glenn might have been one of them back in the day, given how obsessive he had become about Boones's races. Maybe it was one of Glenn's online friends who wanted to avenge him?

RR BLACK. I assume that stands for Range Rover. The car that struck my son.

And those words – *STILL WANTS REVENGE* – which sends another set of shivers down my spine.

None of this helps me without context. I need him to explain. I'm furious with myself for not listening to him when I had the chance.

It's an anxious wait, but before I know it it's almost seven. I walk with Mariam and Farouk to the centre of the bivouac, where – once again – Boones is sat inside his vehicle, waiting for the crowd to gather.

Farouk is hardly able to keep still, his hands opening and closing into fists.

'I don't like this at all,' says Mariam.

Boones is punctual, my analogue watch showing exactly seven p.m. when he clambers on to the roof of his car.

'Friends,' he says. 'I have news we all didn't want to hear. We have lost one of our family. I had to wait to tell you all until his loved ones had been informed, but it's true. Nabil

145

Muhammad Alami passed this afternoon. He suffered a heart attack in the dunes and unfortunately could not be resuscitated.'

The reaction is immediate – the entire bivouac rippling with collective shock, sadness, disbelief. Mariam and I turn to Farouk, who buries his face in his hands.

Boones waits for the wave to hit the very outer edges of the circle. When he speaks, his voice is soft. 'I personally am devastated by this loss. He might have been Hot & Sandy's first winner. But alas, it was not meant to be. We will have a minute of silence to remember our comrade.' He holds his hands up.

Silence has never felt more difficult. I want to shout out, to ask questions, to cry. It seems so unjust. I think back to what the doctor said, about the abnormality on his ECG. His reluctance to disqualify one of the front runners. Then there's how he looked at the checkpoint: tired. Wrung out. I should have spoken up. Expressed my concern.

Farouk spins on his heels, striding back in the direction of the tents. I move to follow but Mariam grabs my hand, giving a small shake of her head. She interlaces her fingers with mine and squeezes them tight. She looks on the edge of tears too; she knew Nabil much better than I did, so I clasp my other hand over top and stay strong – for her.

When the minute is up, Boones speaks again. 'I know this is hard to process. Take time this evening. The race will continue tomorrow as planned – as I know Nabil would have wanted.'

I don't know what emotion is more powerful for me:

revulsion or relief. I don't want to race knowing a man has died. But at the same time I'm surprised to feel glad I have the chance to run again. That tiny spark of competitive fire is burning brightly.

Boones has made the decision for us all. And he's not done yet.

'Nabil wasn't the only medical emergency out there. In total, two hundred and three people pulled out today, including seven elites. That brings our number to around two hundred and fifty continuing to stage two. That's almost a fifty per cent dropout on day one. Tomorrow's stage is another twenty-five miles, and it needs to be completed in eight hours. Miss the cut-off and you're out.'

He climbs down from the car, apparently finished.

Mariam and I drop our hands and I rub at my wrists, where sweat has gathered the sand into small clumps. As the sun goes down, I feel a chill too.

'Fuck,' says Mariam.

I agree with her.

'Farouk must be heartbroken.'

'Everything broken. He was like a brother to Nabil. An uncle to his children.'

'Nabil had kids?'

'Three.'

My hand flies to my mouth, tears springing up in my eyes.

As we walk to our tent, Mariam grips my upper bicep. There's a crowd of people round tent number one. I flash-back to what happened to Jason – surely there can't have been another accident? We can hear Farouk yelling and there's a scuffle, a cloud of dust as a volunteer stumbles out of the tent holding a backpack. Then Farouk appears, his face thunderous with rage.

'What's happening?' Mariam asks, as she rushes forward.

Except it's no volunteer. It's the main Blixt guy himself.

'Henry? What's going on?' I ask.

Henry pulls himself up, pushing his floppy hair off his forehead. 'As Farouk is the current leader, we're doing a gear check.' He sets the backpack down on the ground, as someone else holds Farouk back from protesting.

I vaguely remember being told that we could be subject to random bag checks – to make sure we're still carrying all the mandatory items and haven't ditched anything for the sake of weight. But to choose Farouk seems exceedingly insensitive.

Henry has a checklist of items that had been in Farouk's bag at the start. He opens every single pocket, diligently taking things out and checking them against the list. In one of the drinks pockets, stuffed underneath the water bottles, are a few energy bars.

He consults his list, frowning, then asks another volunteer to double-check. She shakes her head after reviewing it. I glance at Mariam, whose mouth is set in a firm line. Farouk's nostrils are flaring, his hurt barely concealed.

'These weren't in your bag at the start of the race,' Henry says.

'Those are not mine,' he says. Then he switches to rapid French, gesticulating wildly.

'He doesn't know how those got in his bag,' says Mariam, translating in case Henry is lost. 'He's never seen them before in his life. They don't even sell that brand in Morocco.'

'OK, well, he needs to come with me,' says Henry.

'What? Where are you taking him?' asks Mariam.

'To see Boones.'

Farouk follows without protest, still muttering.

'Do you want us to come with you?' I ask him as he passes.

He shakes his head. 'It's a mistake.' He leaps forward, grabs Mariam's hand. He says something to her, too fast for me to understand, and his eyes flick to me as well. She reaches up and touches his cheek, nodding. Then he lets her go and follows Henry, his posture hunched, resigned.

I exchange a look with Mariam. 'What was that?'

'He says we must continue to run if he is kicked out. That he wants someone with honour to win.'

I suck in my bottom lip. I'm both touched that he included me in that sentence and horrified that it's come to that. 'This is all too much. First Pete's weird tox report, then Jason and Nabil, now Farouk might be disqualified . . . what is going on?'

'I am not sure. But we should keep our gear close in case anyone is tampering with the race.'

I clutch my bag to my chest. It's a terrifying thought but Mariam is right.

'Let's get some rest,' she continues. 'Tomorrow we have to climb the jebel. If we are not prepared for it, it could be a killer.' Mariam walks off, not realizing how unsettling I find her words.

In twenty-four hours the fabric of the race has completely changed. If Farouk really is out, then the race will have a new leader. Rupert is now in pole position. He's standing in the awning of his tent, watching the action but not participating – not protesting. His eyes catch mine and I'm shocked by the intensity of his glare.

'It should have been you,' he mouths at me.

20

Stella

Once the sun sets in the bivouac, the atmosphere shifts. Most of the runners pass out in their tents not long after dark, the effort of the day catching up with them. The other photographers, the medics, the volunteers – they're all exhausted too.

But I feel wired. I take a seat on a log outside, sipping lukewarm coffee I made over a tiny stove, waiting until I'm certain Dale is asleep. I need his drone. I want to see for myself what happened out in the dunes.

Another race, another death. Somehow I'd known this was going to happen, and yet I hadn't spoken up. No more. I'd gone straight to Boone's trailer straight after his announcement.

But Dad wasn't there. Henry told me he'd driven off to the city to meet Nabil's family. At least that was a decent thing to do – so decent it made me doubt whether he had actually done it.

I peer inside the darkness of our tent, listening to the steady breathing of its occupants. Dale left his drone in the middle, so I sneak in and carefully lift it out. I choose a spot behind a bush, where the artificial brightness of the remote viewing screen won't be so noticeable, then rewind back to when it starts hovering over Nabil. I don't know what I expect a heart attack to look like. But to me it seems like Nabil is suffering long before he collapses. Wouldn't it be instant? Or had his heart been slowly failing him from long before he entered the dunes?

Then the drone hovers a little while longer, as we rush to reach him. I see myself pressing his emergency beacon. Then the video goes dark.

I remember the moments after that. The agonizing wait for the doctors to arrive. Ali's panic. Dale stock-still, unable to tear his eyes away. The sour taste on my tongue. Trouble catching my breath.

The dark-haired doctor Emilio was next on the scene. After that, things happened quickly. He'd administered first aid, then bundled him in the car to Ouarzazate. We'd returned to our vehicle and driven back to the bivouac in silence.

The video is just as upsetting to watch as it was to witness. Like a reflex, I reach into my pocket for my phone before remembering it's gone. Fuck. I want to call Pete. Ask him to go to the hospital in Ouarzazate and see if he can find out what exactly happened to Nabil.

Maybe the doctor will speak to me. Something doesn't feel right, and I need to know if my instincts are correct.

The medical tent is manned through the night in case of emergencies, so there's a chance he's still awake. I tuck the drone back into Dale's backpack before crossing the bivouac.

As I enter, a young woman is packing something away in plastic boxes, ready to be moved in the morning.

'Excuse me,' I ask her. 'Is Dr Emilio still here?'

She jumps, spilling one of the boxes. Rolls of tape, a few needles and small bottles of iodine tumble out on to the rough rattan flooring.

'Oh shit!' I say, bending down. 'Let me help with that.'

She shakes her head, glancing behind her. 'My fault. I wasn't expecting anyone.'

'Rough day, huh?'

'Horrible. So many people we had to help. If tomorrow is the same, we will be in real trouble. I can't even think about the hundred-mile day . . .'

'Nightmare.'

'Um, the doctor is with a patient. If you wait a little bit, I'm sure he'll be out soon.'

'Thanks,' I say.

She lifts the boxes and carries them out of the tent, as I wander towards the back. A sign requesting privacy is hung across a canvas door, but we're in a marquee set up in the middle of the desert – it's a bit unreasonable to expect much privacy in this environment.

I cough, loud enough to let him know there's someone waiting. I hear what sounds like the snap of gloves and a low murmur of voices. Some tapping, fingers on a keyboard. I wonder if there's a computer in there I can use to send a message to Pete. Then the flap flies open.

'Can I help you?' the doctor asks.

I sneak a look over his shoulder, but if there's a device in there I don't spot it in that split second.

'Yes. I was with Nabil this afternoon.'

The doctor stares at me for a second, then nods. He rubs his temple. '*Scusa*, I recognize you now. One of the photographers. Stella, right?'

'I can't believe he's dead.'

'I know. It's a shock to us all. But he had a heart condition that he failed to tell us about.'

I pause, studying the doctor's face. There's a grim shadow across it, the faintest hint of some warring emotion – guilt? 'I was reviewing some of the video footage and it looks like he was in trouble long before he actually went down. Stumbling around. Kind of woozy. Wouldn't a heart attack be more sudden?'

The doctor keeps his features very still. 'It's hard to say.'

'But in your opinion . . .'

'My opinion doesn't matter very much – it is for the examiner in Ouarzazate to determine what happened.'

He's a closed book. I grit my teeth. There's something else that's been playing on my mind. 'Have you worked at many ultramarathons?'

He shakes his head. 'This is my first one. And last, I think.'

'Oh really? How did you come to be in Boones's orbit, then?'

'That is private information.' The doctor's mouth is set in a firm line.

'I can't help being intrigued. You know, since I'm his daughter and all.'

'You are?'

'Yes. And I know he's very sick. He's suffered with his heart his whole life. But if you know anything about my dad at all, you'll know that getting any information out of him is impossible. How worried should I really be?'

The doctor's expression softens, the guarded look in his eyes turning to pity. 'I cannot divulge that. But if you are his family, it is good you are here. Is there anything else I can do for you, Stella?'

'Oh, yes. Do you have any painkillers? An aspirin

or something? In all the madness I forgot to bring any with me.'

He sighs. 'Everything has been packed away. They'll be in the trucks already.'

'Are you sure?'

'Give me one second and I will see if I can catch Wendy before she puts the last box away.'

'Thank you.'

As he leaves the tent, I push through to the private area he'd been in before. There's a desk set up covered in files. I push them aside, searching for a laptop.

No such luck. But there is a black bag on the floor. I recognize it as the one Emilio had been carrying all day. Maybe he has a phone I can use.

I open it, rifling through the contents as quickly as I can. There are all the normal things I would expect in a doctor's bag: bandages, stethoscope, syringes sealed in sterile packaging. But there's something I don't expect. An empty, crumpled water bottle, like the hundreds of bottles we handed out at the checkpoints throughout the race.

Except this one has writing on it. A number half erased by sweat. It's one of the runner's bottles.

I take it out and hold it up to the light. A dribble of water remains. But in the water there's a residue of powder, leaving a trace all along the bottom of plastic.

It could be nothing. Maybe he's just a conscientious doctor picking up the trash. But it sets my heart racing.

I dive back into the bag, my search taking on a different urgency. My fingers snag on a flap of material, and when I pull, the bottom of the bag lifts.

Underneath is an assortment of pill bottles held down

by elastic. I'm no doctor, but I recognize the drug name. Ketamine. Why is a running race doctor walking around carrying sedatives? And is it for a patient or for his own personal use?

I hear Emilio's footsteps returning. I grab one of the bottles, slipping it into my pocket, replacing the bag's contents as best I can.

I'm back in the main part of the medical tent when Emilio emerges with a blister pack of aspirin. I mutter my thanks, rushing to get out of there. My breath catches in my throat as Emilio calls out my name.

I spin round slowly, the bottle burning a hole in my pocket. 'Yes?'

'Your father,' he says. 'He needs you. Spend as much time with him as you can.'

I nod, and slip out into the dark.

2 I

Adrienne

I wake in the middle of the night, still haunted by Rupert's words.

It should have been you.

It sends me right back to those awful memories from seven years ago. My racing family abandoned me once the charges against Glenn were dropped. Most people wouldn't pick up my calls, left my messages on 'read'. The ones who did answer were sometimes worse. I had to face their confusion, their outrage and betrayal.

How could you do that to Glenn?

They were right to ask. As a coach, he'd taken me from a lump of directionless talent and shaped me into a contender. Goals that had seemed impossible were suddenly in my reach: sponsors, prize money, a chance to turn my running hobby into a proper sporting career. But what I couldn't tell anyone was how wrong I was to ever trust him. And no one *will* ever know, because of a promise I made, and the rash, impulsive decision I made to tell a lie in the heat of the moment.

Yet no matter how many times I relive those events in my head, I always come to the same conclusion: that if it happened all over again, I'd do the same thing.

I slip out of the sleeping bag, careful not to disturb my tentmates.

Outside, there's a reward for my restless mind: the night sky in the middle of the Sahara. It takes my breath away. I'm not sure I've ever seen such a concentration of stars, even though it's one of my favourite things about ultrarunning: being out in the wilderness in the middle of the night, taking the time to look up and appreciate the window to the rest of the universe. Here there's so little light pollution that it's like that window has been polished to a crystal-clear shine, and the overwhelming silence – no buzz of electronics or roar of distant vehicles – makes the experience even more immersive. The otherworldly cloud of the Milky Way hangs in the air, like a veil caught in a breeze, so much colour and movement. I feel like I've been given a front-row seat to the most spectacular night-time ballet, and I wish I could just sit and watch for hours.

Most of the other runners are sensibly asleep, giving their bodies the rest needed to be ready for another stage. Normally sleep isn't a problem for me. I've been known to catch five or ten minutes on a chair mid-race, able to drop off even if there's hustle and bustle around me. When Ethan was a newborn, I'd had no problem following that old adage of 'sleep when the baby sleeps'. I wasn't sure if ultrarunning had prepped me for motherhood or if the broken post-partum sleep was added training for ultrarunning. Regardless, Pete called it my 'superpower'.

If I had it, the power's abandoned me now.

It's why when I spot someone else walking through the bivouac at this hour, it grabs my attention. They're moving quickly, almost breaking into a jog. It's only when they pass beneath a small light hanging outside an administration tent that I catch a glimpse of the person's face.

'Stella!' I've called out her name before I can stop myself. I wish I could take it back, but she's turned now; she's seen me.

Now it's my turn to jog. I want to talk to her. I don't want her to run away from me again.

'Hi,' she says, when I'm close.

'Um, listen. I'm happy for you and Pete. Really. It's . . . it's good to see you.'

She wraps her arms round her waist, then drops them, shifting in her stance. 'Sorry you had to find out that way. That wasn't our intention. I didn't even know you'd be here. Presumably Pete knew?'

'He knew.'

She shakes her head. 'Probably didn't tell me as I wouldn't have come if I'd known.'

That stings. 'Well, you're going to be part of the family now. Part of Ethan's family. So I'm glad you're here. We need to talk. I tried to reach out after what happened.'

'I know,' Stella replies.

'And I don't blame you for –'

'Blame me? Excuse me?'

I hold up my hands. 'No, that's not what I meant. I know you didn't do anything wrong. You didn't owe me anything. I know that. I get that. This is coming out all wrong. When I heard about Yasmin, I . . .'

A bolt of pain flashes in her eyes when I say her name, and she almost crumbles.

'This was a bad idea,' she mutters.

'No, wait, Stella, please.'

She spins round on me. 'Why did you come here? I thought you'd stopped racing for good.'

159

'I wouldn't have come, but your dad –'

'My dad? What's he got to do with this?'

'On the invitation he told me to come and "find answers". He promised to tell me something important if I finished the race. But it's probably just a big game, right? I mean, how could he know anything about what happened that night when the police didn't even know?'

'The police? What are you talking about?'

'Surely Pete must have told you. When Ethan was three, he was hit by a car. It was right after all the . . . well, what happened in Ibiza. He survived, and the police closed the investigation. Joyriders, they said. But I was convinced it was connected to Glenn. Your dad knows who was driving the car, and he'll tell me if I finish the race.'

Her lips purse, but she remains quiet.

'If you get him to tell me now, then I'll quit the race,' I say.

She sighs. 'He's not here. He's gone to Ouarzazate to talk with Nabil's family.'

I shake my head. 'I still can't believe he is dead. It doesn't feel real.'

Stella doesn't reply.

My shoulders slump. It's too late. The gulf is too wide to build a bridge between us.

'For what it's worth, I am sorry. Yasmin deserved so much better. If I had known what she would do . . .'

'Nobody could have stopped her,' Stella says, her voice tight. Her body stiffens, and I can see the grief still buried there, so close to the surface.

I feel an old simmering rage return to boil within me. The same emotion that bubbled up when I heard that scream seven years ago and realized what Glenn had done. He'd extinguished one of the brightest lights I'd ever known. I close my hands into fists to stop them from shaking with anger.

Stella coughs and my eyes snap back to her. She looks me up and down. 'Don't quit, Adri. You should run. You look strong out there. She would be proud of you.'

Then she walks away.

22

Stella

Seven years earlier
Ibiza

For the duration of the training camp every minute of Yasmin's time is scheduled. Since the goal is to win an Ampersand race, Glenn throws in (what he considers) creative twists, like an hour-long speed-work session turning into a surprise overnight wild camping run. No one told me, so I showed up for our group dinner only to end up alone.

That ground my gears. I have to keep reminding myself I'm here for Yasmin. To support her. To take photos when she needs. When she's off running, I'm supposed to hang at the resort. But there's only so much lounging around a pool that I can do. I spend a lot of the time researching for our backpacking trip or entertaining myself by teasing Pete with bikini pics. He thinks I'm away on a work assignment, photographing a new luxury hotel opening.

And it means I cherish the time I do get to see her. Like during breakfast. Breakfast is our time. Every morning we'd grab coffee and smoothie bowls from the resort buffet and take them to go, finding a spot out on the hotel terrace in the sunshine.

Except this morning is different. Everyone else – Glenn,

Adrienne, the other female runners – shows up to the buffet, but Yasmin is nowhere to be seen. I storm up to her room, banging on the door until she lets me in. When I finally see her, I stifle a laugh. Hair dishevelled. Eyes bleary. 'Wow. You look like crap.'

She crawls back into bed, pulling the covers up over her head and groaning.

'Everything OK?' I ask.

She re-emerges and shakes her head. 'I feel awful.'

'No shit. You've been running an insane number of miles in this killer heat.'

'I'm not cut out for this.'

'Of course you are. But he needs to let you relax and let loose a little.' Lined up on the TV stand are several empty bottles of recovery fluid. I pick one up and take a sniff, wrinkling my nose. 'God, this is what he makes you drink? No wonder you feel sick. In a few days we're going to get on that ferry and before you know it we'll be sipping delicious sangria outside in a beautiful courtyard in Barcelona. Not this garbage.' I toss the bottle in the trash.

She smiles weakly. 'Sounds dreamy. Except, Stellz . . .'

'You should see the itinerary I've put together. Got us last-minute tickets to Parc Güell and then we'll get a train to Granada to see the Alhambra. And yes, don't worry, I've researched some of the top trails in case you feel desperate for another run . . . What the fuck?' An internal door opens, almost giving me a heart attack until Glenn sticks his head round the door.

'Almost ready, Yasmin?'

'Five minutes,' she says, injecting more brightness into her tone.

'You can't make it up,' he replies, tapping at his sports watch.

'I know, Glenn. I'll be there.' Yasmin sighs as Glenn disappears.

'Uh, is that normal?' I ask. 'Him just popping in your room like that?'

Yasmin shrugs.

'And *"you can't make it up"*?'

'It's one of his sayings. It means, like, you can't get the time back. You've either put in the work or you haven't.'

The internal door opens again, but this time it's Adrienne. I try to catch Yasmin's eye. I wonder if the 'rock goat' and Glenn have been sharing a hotel room.

'Morning, you two. Glenn told me the good news. I'm glad you're staying on with us,' she says.

I turn to Yasmin. 'Staying on?'

'That's what I've been trying to tell you. Glenn asked me to stay a few more days for some extra training sessions. Really hone my technique.'

'It's a great opportunity,' says Adrienne. 'I'll be here too.'

To my relief Yasmin shakes her head. 'I don't know. I'm just . . . I don't think this is for me.'

'Is he tough? Sure. Unconventional? Definitely. But he's changed my life. You have to stick with it when it gets hard. Push through.'

'That's the thing. I don't think I can.'

'I've seen it in you. It's like the pain cave. You have to find some way to endure the dark times and then on the other side there's the glory.'

'Or you could *not* worry about winning one of my dad's races,' I interject. 'Change your focus to something else.'

Adrienne glances at me. 'It's up to you, of course. See you downstairs, Yasmin?'

'See you soon.'

As soon as Adrienne is out of the room, Yasmin sighs, before dragging herself out of bed and grabbing her running clothes from the beside drawer. 'I wanted to tell you. But I think I'm going to do it.'

'So . . . what about me?'

'I'm sorry, Stellz. This is important. Adrienne says this never happens. Glenn sees real promise in me.'

'But this trip –'

'It's only a few more days.'

A few days when we'll miss our hotel bookings, sightseeing dates, flights . . . everything. Our bonding time cut short. It might be months until we see each other again. But I know what this means to her. This is her passion. If she takes the next step, she could make it her career.

'Don't worry about it,' I mutter, turning away.

'But you'll stay too, right? I need you here.'

'Yeah, no. Doesn't seem like you do. Make Adrienne your photographer monkey.' Already my mind is spinning. I can go to California early, spend some time hunting for a new apartment. Maybe I'll stop off in Manchester. Surprise Pete. Meet his son, like I've always wanted. It will be easier without any risk of running into Adrienne, since she'll still be in Ibiza.

'Stella, please.' Her voice is small.

'What? You got what you wanted. Private coaching. One-on-one attention. Screw me and our time together, right?'

She launches into a stream of curses in French as I storm

165

towards the door. We're like this. Fight. Make up. Fight again. When she's in the wrong, she cooks for me. I wondered what baked goods I'm going to get. I'm hoping for madeleines. When it's my fault, I get her flowers. Orchids if I've been a real dick.

'You'd better get ready for your session,' I say. 'Can't deny Glenn, can we?'

23

Stella

I don't know what to do with the bottle of pills now that the sun is up. It was stupid to take it. Emilio is a doctor – I'm sure he has a legit reason to have the drugs. But then he also had that water bottle filled with residue. Why did he keep that? Thoughts ricochet around my brain, giving me a headache. I need to find a way to get a message to Pete. He can find out if Nabil's death is at all suspicious. If it is, then I can go to the police with the pills. For now, the best thing I can do is stay with the race – and keep an eye on my dad.

In the meantime, all I can picture is Emilio tapping my shoulder and demanding I give him back what I stole. So when someone touches my arm, I leap out of my skin.

'Wow, jumpy much?' It's only Dale. He doesn't wait to hear my answer; he just rubs his hands together, practically vibrating with excitement. 'Second day, ready to do it all again? The runners are going up the jebel, where the cars can't reach, so I'm thinking we leave really early – like, right now – and we'll have time to climb and set up before the elites get there.'

'Go for it. I'm staying here.'

He frowns. 'What?'

'I'm staying in the bivouac. I'll find another driver.'

'Are you kidding? But you'll miss all the action.'

I grimace. 'I've seen enough, thanks. I'm going to stick to following my fun runners.'

'Honestly, I kind of expected more . . .' He trails off, but I don't miss his pointed look.

'What the fuck's that supposed to mean?'

He leans forward. 'It means, I know who you are, Stella. I've studied my Boones history – and you were a feature at his early races. I figured Boones's daughter might have a bit more ambition.'

'Screw you.'

He holds his hands up. 'Just saying.'

Ali drives up in the Jeep before I can throw my camera at Dale's head. When he hears I'm not coming with them, Ali is also concerned. 'Are you certain? We can wait for you – my instructions are to take you both.'

'No, really. I'm OK.' I glance around, but Dale is distracted by loading his belongings into the trunk. He's out of earshot. I lean in close to Ali. 'Hey, do you know where I can get hold of a phone?'

He blinks, then shakes his head. 'No, sorry. They made me hand mine in.'

'Same with me. OK – well, if you hear of anyone who has one . . .'

'Right, dude, let's get this show on the road,' says Dale, jumping in the passenger seat. 'We only care about winners in this car.'

I fold my arms across my chest. When they're gone, my thoughts return to the previous night: not only the pills I found in Emilio's bag and the bottle of water with the powdery residue but the conversation with Adrienne. My mind has snagged on the snippet she dropped about

Boones – his vow to provide her with information if she finishes the race.

It reminds me of what Ali had told me in the dunes. That his aunt has been offered funds towards the rebuilding of the village school. Was that a coincidence? Or are the promises somehow part of the make-up of this Ampersand race? What has he said to other runners?

And, even more unlikely, can he keep those promises if they fulfil their end of the bargain? It strikes me as more of a trick. One of his cruel games.

I march towards his trailer. If there are answers, they'll be there, amidst the mountain of paper. I need to get there before they pack up and move it from the bivouac.

But when I enter, I've been beaten to it.

'Stella! Good morning.' Boones smiles at me, unfazed by my unplanned arrival.

'Dad.' I suck in a deep breath. Might as well ask him outright. 'I spoke to Adrienne last night.'

'Oh?'

'She told me what you promised her at the end of the race.'

'And what was that?'

'Don't play dumb. It's messed up to make promises you can't keep. I know the police thought it was random joy-riders who hit Ethan. How can you have evidence they don't have?'

Boones taps the side of his nose. 'I have my ways. It's all here.' He opens a drawer, where there's a metal box locked with a combination. He spins the code, opens it up and removes a memory stick from a pile, marked with the number '13'.

I stiffen. 'That means nothing. It could be blank for all I know. Give it to me.'

'I don't think so,' he replies, before dropping it back in and closing the lid. There's a click as it locks.

'So you'll tell her? Just like that?'

'She has to finish first. Them's the rules.'

I swallow. 'And Mariam . . . you promised her a donation?'

He nods.

'Jesus, Dad. You've gone too far. You don't know what someone will do to finish the race and earn your sick rewards. The lengths they might go to.'

'That, my dear, is exactly what I'm hoping to find out.' There's that damn twinkle in his eye.

I think about the other memory sticks in the box. The other secrets they might hold. Or is he bluffing? There's a good chance he has nothing at all. 'What else have you promised?'

'Have you changed your mind then, about helping me with this race?'

'What? No. A man died yesterday. One of your elites. Surely that changes things?'

To my surprise the blow registers. He shuts his eyes and presses down on his eyelids like he's holding back tears. Then he shakes it off. 'An unfortunate heart issue.'

'Is that what the doctors in Ouarzazate say? Or this "doctor" Emilio? How well do you know that guy anyway?'

'He's been my personal physician for the past two years. I trust him with my life.'

His personal physician? So maybe the sedatives are for him. Pain relief. And now my suspicions have been proven – Boones has offered incentives to some of the elite runners, adding extra fuel to their fire. Could some of those promises be worth killing for?

The thought makes my skin crawl. I can't help but think that by staying, by supporting even the fun runners, he's making me complicit in his games. I'm getting pulled into his whirlpool of pain without the strength to swim away. The only way to escape it is to leave now. But I can't – not now I know what's in that box. I have to find a way to stop him.

'Now, excuse me, I have a race to oversee. I think today is going to be very interesting.'

He ushers me out of the trailer, climbs into his four-by-four and leaves me in the dust. Now I need to send a message to Pete even more urgently than ever. If I can prove something more happened to Nabil than a 'heart issue' – something nefarious – then the police will come and stop the race.

A different car stops in front of me, blocking my path.

'What the fuck?' I yell, but the words die in my mouth when I see who it is. Ali. He gestures for me to get in. 'Where's Dale?' I ask.

'He got a lift in one of the helicopters. He was much happier with that.'

I climb into the passenger seat.

'I couldn't say anything before, in case Dale overheard me. I have a phone.'

My eyes open wide. 'You do?'

He leans over and opens the glovebox with a flourish. 'I handed in my Moroccan phone, but kept my UK one hidden in the car. It's ancient but it works well enough.'

'Oh, thank God. And smart not telling Dale. He's a superfan of my dad and would have ratted you out straight away.'

But when I look into the compartment, it's empty. 'Um, Ali?'

'What?' He pats around the box, as if the phone might be there – but invisible. 'I put it in last night.' He looks genuinely stricken.

'Maybe someone saw and confiscated it?'

'I was very careful,' says Ali. His eyes are wide. I wonder if he's thinking the same thing I am: if the phone had been found by someone official at the race, he would have been sent away from the bivouac. But someone's stolen it and not mentioned it.

That can't be good.

'Wait,' I say. 'If you managed to keep a phone, there must be others who did too.'

Ali nods. 'I can ask around.'

'Let's meet by the administration tent when they hand out the map to the next bivouac. And, Ali, please be careful. Someone took your phone. They might be watching.'

Knowing Boones, he has eyes everywhere.

But all I need is a split second to get a message out. Because if my suspicions are right, I have to be quick. Before another runner gets hurt.

24

Adrienne

Lining up at the start of stage two feels very different. We're down to fourteen of the original twenty elites. There's no smiles, no excited chatter. No Boones on his truck ready to try another slow clap. Thank God – that would have been completely inappropriate.

I sway from foot to foot, unable to keep still. I still can't believe Nabil is dead. He's not going to be returning to his children after the race ends. It's a stark reminder of just how much I am risking. People die in these races, even without a target on their back. The only thing keeping me on the line and not finding a car to take me back to the city is Boones's promise. This unshakeable feeling that if I can put that chapter of my life to bed, I will be able to move on.

Not that finishing is a given. Far from it. The environment itself seems to be doing its best to be intimidating. The skies are clear, the sun is bright – we're destined for another scorcher. And we're going to face our biggest challenge yet: Jebel Tilelli.

In the tent I'd studied the map in detail, trying to picture it in my head. I've always done well over difficult terrain – it's one of my specialities. One of the reasons why I thought this race might suit me. If a race is too flat, the course too monotonous, I lose concentration too quickly. But give me a bit of technical running – over boulders or on perilous ridges – anything with a bit of exposure and an incline, and I come alive. I never loved being known as the 'rock goat', but I could see why it suited me.

The jebel is where I'm going to make my move. Today, though, is less about being first over the top and more about getting to know the landscape, so that when I cross it again on the long day, I have that knowledge padding my pain cave. Today is about learning.

But it's not Boones who steps out of the Jeep at the sidelines. It's Henry. He's still in his Hot & Sandy vest, but as he strolls down the starting line, walking past me, I can see it now has the words 'RACE DIRECTOR' on the back.

I frown. A promotion?

He has a megaphone in his hands, which he brings to his mouth. 'Attention, runners. My name is Henry Roth and I'm the CEO of Blixt Energy. I'm thrilled that I have the immense privilege of starting today's stage.'

My jaw drops. I'm not the only one. I don't know what kind of reception Henry was expecting, but judging by the look on his face it wasn't stunned silence.

'You what?' shouts someone from the crowd.

That breaks the tension, and now everyone is talking.

'Where is Boones?' Mariam mutters from beside me.

I'm not sure how Henry could have heard her, but he answers the question anyway. He shouts into the megaphone to be heard. 'Don't worry – Boones will return to the race this afternoon. But we at Blixt are proud to be the principal sponsors of Hot & Sandy. We know each one of you needs more than just a mantra to get you through a race like this. That's why at each of the checkpoints today, you'll be offered one of our Blixt Energy drinks in addition to water.'

'This doesn't sound like Boones at all to me,' says Mariam. 'Something is wrong.'

A creeping, prickly form of dread creeps its way up my spine. Mariam's right. This doesn't feel good. Some trick is coming our way, and there's nothing I can do to prepare for it. All I can do is run my own race.

Focus on your own feet. I bet Blixt would be delighted to know it's a mantra that's going to see me through.

'Anyway, without further ado . . . what is it that Boones says again?' He looks down, consulting a notebook he has in his hand. Then he looks back up to the runners. 'Well, all right then,' he says.

And the race is on once more.

Mariam is off like a shot. Farouk's words – that he wants someone with honour to win – must have inspired her as she seems more determined than ever. I keep my pace more in check, remaining well within my capabilities. If Boones does have surprises for us, then I need to have some energy stored to draw from when they come.

The first few miles take us across a wide desert plain, but it's far from the barren, lifeless habitat I thought it would be. Little blooms cover the ground, tufts of purple and white flowers sprouting from the parched earth, hardy tendrils searching out the sun. There are larger bushes too, clumps of low twiggy branches with tiny leaves and spikes that risk penetrating the soles of our shoes. I know some people use the bushes as a bit of cover for a bathroom break – but it is a risk. There are living creatures in the desert, many of them venomous, and they're drawn to the shade.

Running makes the world seem so big and yet so small. It allows me to see things I would never be able to otherwise, go to places unreachable by any other means – my feet taking me deeper into a landscape than a car – or any form of transport – ever could.

It's a way for me to mark the passage of time. When I'm running, no day is the same. I feel more present, more aware of my surroundings, more focused on the changing of the seasons. Running means I see more sunrises and sunsets, means I notice when lambs are born, and when the first leaves turn from green to auburn and gold.

The jebels are just smudges on the horizon but they are the perfect example. Remote, intimidating. Inaccessible by car. Not even helicopters can land up there. But with a bit of leg power I can climb to the summit. If we get into trouble, the only way down is on our feet.

What happened to Nabil is another reminder that ultrarunning can be dangerous. Deadly. But the past few years have made me redefine what is 'safe' and what is 'dangerous'.

I used to think that my home was safe. The threatening notes proved that wrong.

That the walk to the park was safe. Ethan's accident went against that.

That my running club – presided over by a coach I'd known and trusted most of my life – was safe. But it ended up being more dangerous than I could ever imagine.

I fly through the first checkpoint. I feel unleashed. The mountains loom even closer on the horizon, so I run through a mental checklist of how I'm feeling. I sense a tiny bit of weakness in my legs, a gnawing in my stomach, so I dig out a packet of dried mango to give me a burst of energy before the climb.

The terrain starts to become more undulating, large boulders that have crumbled from the mountainside littering the ground. There's no defined route up the mountain – we can pick our own – so I chose the most direct path I can. As the way becomes steeper, I'm forced into switchbacks, slowing my pace to a fast walk so I don't lose my footing.

I glance back at the view, taking a moment to appreciate where we've come from. I spot Hiroko and Alex – still running as a pair – tackling the jebel using a different path. But there's someone else coming up the trail, following my line. A man. I squint, but I don't recognize him. Only . . . something feels oddly familiar about his gait.

My heart starts racing.

Who could it be? He's wearing one of the fun runner numbers – I can see the blue background even from this distance. That means he must be experienced enough to somehow catch up with the elites. Shit. One of Glenn's friends?

Still wants revenge.

This could be it. The person who tried to hurt my son all those years ago, who is angry I'm making my return to the sport, hunting me down.

I stop lingering, disturbed by how quickly the man is moving. I turn back to the jebel, scanning for the best route to the top. There's a difficult steep, sandy climb ahead. If I divert to the cliff wall, I can make use of a rope, strung up as an aid for the treacherous terrain. But using the rope will slow me down.

I grit my teeth and power directly up the slope, trying to remain light on my feet while fighting the unstable ground. With the sun beating on my back, I regret not choosing the rope, which would have kept me closer to the cliff face and the shade. But I keep my head down and carry on moving, using my hands to propel me, until I finally reach where the sand becomes stone and a gulley is cut into the jebel itself. Rock the colour of burnt sienna rises on either side of me, cradling the route and offering welcome shade. It's tightly enclosed, the path hidden from view. I glance over my shoulder before I disappear into the mountain and watch as the runner reaches out to the rope and tests its strength. He's gaining on me, but I'll be able to move much faster than him now.

My footsteps echo, and I become acutely aware of the sound of my own breathing. It's a little laboured, the closeness of the rock – and the man behind – stressing me out. I need to get up to the top and the open air.

Yet the path seems endless. Looking at it on the map and experiencing it in person are very different propositions. My visualization has failed me. My palms get clammy, my footing no longer so assured.

When my quads start twitching, like a violinist playing pizzicato on my muscles, I know I've made a mistake. I was so worried about the man, I forgot to drink. When was the last time I took a salt tablet? Ate some food? Went to the bathroom? Cursing myself, I wonder if I've put enough of a gap between myself and the man that I can refuel.

My legs are really shaking now. If I *don't* stop, I could get in a bad way. The path is narrow and there's almost nowhere to get some privacy – or to hide. That's when I spot a boulder, just a bit higher up where the route opens out a touch. It looks like there's a cavity on the other side of it, big enough to conceal me. I scramble my way over, picking each foothold with care. I place both palms on the rock, feeling the heat radiating from it. I take a few deep breaths and squeeze my way round to the small opening – tighter than I'd hoped. I fumble in my waist pack for a salt tablet, pop it on my tongue and take a swig of water.

Movement by my feet catches my eye.

Something curled up, tense, and unravelling rapidly.

My mouth goes dry. I realize how stupid I've been.

A viper, its body in perfect camouflage with the rock behind, its head raised. It's blocking my path back; I must have stepped over it in my haste to hide myself from the other runner. Suddenly that venom pump in my bag doesn't seem so useless. I still hope I don't have to use it.

I wish I had poles with me. Or anything to distract the snake. It begins to sway, focused on me.

We're locked in a stand-off, and it feels like time drags out – seconds becoming minutes.

And then: it lunges.

I jump, my palms catching the rock, feet desperate to find a hold. But the snake is more scared of me than I am of it, if only marginally, and it slithers away, disappearing into the mountain.

I don't waste any time darting back on the trail. My adrenaline is really pumping now, and it powers me up; I move faster than I thought possible.

The breeze at the top of the jebel cools my heated blood. It also sweeps away my fear and anxiety. On the ridge I feel more in control. This is where I come into my element – on pathways that are barely as wide as my foot, with over a thousand-feet drop on either side. It's from this vantage point that it becomes clear just how remote we are – vast desert, as far as the eye can see. No sign of human civilization anywhere. The heat casts a haze over the ground, an almost unearthly shimmer. The colour palette of red, orange and brown clashing with the bright blue sky. There's almost no green to be seen.

I leap from rock to rock, my speed part of my ability to stay safe. If I overthink, question every movement, hesitate rather than haste, I'd likely lose my footing. Some of the rocks are more stable than others. One wobbles precariously beneath my foot but I'm not balanced on it long enough to allow it to alter my stride. I spring on to the next, a jolt of fear the only damage.

This is good. This is exactly what I came here for. We're going to be crossing a jebel on the final day. I'll be even more confident when I tackle it now that I know what to expect.

I almost don't see the photographer lift the camera and snap my picture. He comes out of nowhere, hidden in the shade of a tower of rocks. Even though I feel alone up here, I'm not. And when I steal a look behind me, I see the mystery runner burst out on to the ridge. The chase isn't over yet.

Damn. I don't want to be followed by this guy the entire way. Even if he's just a fun runner on an amazing charge, having him mere minutes behind me and gaining is sending my stress levels through the roof. If the photographer managed to hide from me, maybe I can get out of sight of this guy too. I veer off the route – checking for snakes – and tuck myself down, hoping I'm no longer visible.

My legs shake as I crouch. I need a distraction. I take my backpack off, enabling me to sit down even lower, and chew on a piece of dried jerky I pull from a side pocket, adjusting my position to avoid cramping. I realize how stupid this would look to any other racer on the course. Like I'm throwing away any advantage that I might have had. But I'm not even thinking about winning at this point. I need to find out who is behind me.

I don't have to wait long. I hear his feet pounding on the rock, then his breathing – deliberate sharp breaths, as if he's trying to keep a lid on his fear and adrenaline. He's not as comfortable with exposure as I am. Good. That gives me an upper hand.

He passes by too quickly for me to read the name on his race bib, but I see the number again: 501. I was right. He's not one of the elites. He's got thick dark hair and a stubbly beard – but it's that gait, that stride, which I can't stop watching. It's the way he carries himself, head held high, shoulders back, hips driving forward, that really reminds me of someone. Add in the staccato tempo of his breath . . .

I give it a while longer, waiting for him to drop off the ridge and allowing the distance between us to grow. I know that my chance at the prize money is likely gone, the time gap too big to make up. Some 'runner 13' I am. But I'm OK with that. Boones only said I had to finish, not that I had to win.

It strikes me then that maybe *this* is the real reason he

wanted me to run in his race. Not that I had any true shot at winning. Not because of his belief in my talent. But because he wanted to see how I would do being chased by people who hate me. The ultimate test of my limitations.

I flash back to a training run with Coach Glenn in the Ibizan hills, when he gave a tip to Yasmin about maintaining speed while scared. God, I haven't thought about that in so long. Yasmin could have beaten me easily with her long strides; it should be considered cheating to be that tall and strong. But she would freeze on the exposed high ascents, and ultrarunning was full of those. Coach Glenn taught her to nose-breathe to maximize airflow and oxygen intake, to calm her heart rate and focus on her goal. Three quick inhales through the nose, then a long exhale. The same pattern that runner 501 had been using.

But Glenn hadn't trained any male runners that I knew of – what a major red flag that should have been. He'd written books about his technique, though. Maybe 501 was an avid fan, angry that I'd returned to the circuit.

Angry enough to want to hurt me?

There's nothing I can do about it on top of a jebel. I start running again, confident that I've left a long enough gap. The way down is much faster – and more fun – than the way up. The huge hill of sand gives way under my feet; it feels almost like skiing rather than running, clouds of sand flying up behind me. Once I reach the bottom, there's only a few flat riverbed miles until the finishing line for the day. I need to catch up with Mariam. See if she can help me figure out who runner 501 is.

I settle into my rhythm, listening to the pounding of my

feet against the sand, regulating my breathing. This is my happy place. My time.

Yet I catch a flash of white out of the corner of my eye, emerging from behind one of the shrubs, and hear footsteps rapidly catching up with my own.

Runner 501 has been waiting.

25

Stella

Ali meets me back at the car, just as the convoy carrying all the tents, supplies and volunteers starts making a move to the next destination. The second stage of the race has started and, strangest of all, Boones wasn't the one who launched it.

It sets my teeth on edge. I don't think too hard about how that might signal the end of the Ampersands. Maybe bequeathing them to Blixt and this Henry guy is his succession plan. I can't imagine him handing it over to a corporation. But then again, I've never thought like my father.

Ali has good news. 'A friend of mine has a phone.'

I could almost kiss him. 'You're a lifesaver. Where is it?'

'Come. I will drive you to him.'

Ali and I pass the line-up of cars until we catch up with his friend Rachid, owner of the precious phone. With a couple of toots of his horn, we signal for him to pull over. We wait for the other cars to proceed until we're certain that we're alone. Rachid looks furtive when we approach his car window. He and Ali speak in Arabic, which I can just about follow: he's worried that we'll be caught.

'I won't be long,' I say.

He nods, so I jump into the back seat, taking the phone with a grateful smile as he passes it to me, and I dial Pete's number as fast as I can.

It rings several times before he answers. 'Hello?'

'Pete, it's me – Stella. I'm calling from someone else's phone and I don't have much time.'

'Babe, thank God. It's so good to hear your voice. It's been chaos here, since the news about Nabil hit. I can't believe it.'

'That's what I'm calling about. I need you to get to the hospital. Find out what you can about what really happened to him. If you find out anything, send a message to this phone. It will get to me.'

'What? Why? Do you know something?'

'Just – please. Do this for me. Find out if there's anything suspicious about the way he died.'

Ali taps on the window. He gestures to a car in the distance that has turned and broken away from the convoy, which is now driving in our direction.

'I gotta go. I'll check in later.'

'But –'

I hang up before he can say anything more, then hand the phone back to Rachid, who quickly slips it into a compartment between the driver and passenger seat.

'Thank you,' I say. '*Chokran.*'

Ali and I walk back to our Jeep, trying to keep our movements casual.

The random car pulls up. It's Henry.

'Everything OK here?' he asks, leaning out of his window.

'Yes, my fault,' I say. 'I thought I'd left my shot list in the back of Rachid's car. But I must've been mistaken.'

He nods. 'And now? I'm driving to the first checkpoint if you want to get some images of the fun runners passing through.'

My breath catches when I see Emilio in the passenger seat. He leans across Henry to talk to me. 'Feeling any better?' he asks.

It takes me a moment to realize what he's talking about. The painkillers he gave me last night. The legitimate ones.

I force a smile. 'Yes, much, thanks.'

He sits back, satisfied, which helps me relax. If he's noticed the missing ketamine, he doesn't suspect me. Though the same can't be said for me, about him.

'Sure. We'll follow you,' I say.

While I wait to hear back from Pete, this is my opportunity to keep an eye on this doctor. And if he is responsible, to make sure that no one else gets hurt.

Once we're driving, Ali explains why Rachid was acting so nervous. 'One of the medics was caught with a cell phone by the Blixt staff. They sent him straight home with no further pay. They said he violated the agreement. But Rachid took a gamble to keep his phone, because his wife is ill and he will face the wrath of his daughter if she cannot reach him.'

'If they find it, I won't let them fire Rachid,' I say.

'And how would you do that?'

'Boones is my father. And my wrath is something to be feared as well.'

Ali can't hide his surprise. It makes me smile, despite all that's going on. Owning it. Taking back some power.

'I didn't realize Boones had a family. When he visited our village, he has always been alone.'

'I wouldn't exactly call us a family. He's my biological father, but he was barely involved with me growing up.'

'I am sorry to hear that.'

186

'My parents got divorced when I was five. I only ever saw him once a year, during race season. Then I quit visiting when I was seventeen, and that was it. He didn't make any attempt to see me again.'

'I can't imagine that.'

'It's true. His races were his children, not me.'

'But you never wanted to run?'

I shake my head, almost shiver. 'No way. I can't seem to escape it, though. My baby sister – half-sister – she wanted more than anything to be the first female winner of an Ampersand race. I tried to tell her what Boones was really like – that he was a twisted old man who liked to play mind games, not someone to worry about impressing – but she didn't care. The Ampersand races were already a legend, dad was the mastermind and my sister wanted to be the hero.' I sigh. My whole life I've watched from the sidelines as the world seemed to worship my deadbeat dad. 'I've only seen him a handful of times in the past decade. Most recent was seven years ago, at my sister's funeral. He didn't even come to my mom's.'

'I am sorry – that is so much loss.'

I give myself a shake. 'It means that Boones owes me. So don't worry.' Yet, my confidence waivers. Boones might have orchestrated my arrival here, but he's been absent most of my life. He's already shown me how little I mean to him. And I don't want to be another one of his experiments. I spent my childhood trying to live up to his expectations, hoping I would pass whatever imaginary test my dad had set for me that would mean we could have a relationship.

But there was never a test. Not for me.

I wasn't worth that.

'Tell me about your family. I'm sure it's much more interesting than mine. Your aunt is Mariam, right?'

'That's right. You must come and visit Tafran when the race is over.'

'I will, with pleasure.'

'She inspired me – she left our village and chased her dreams around the world. When I was old enough, I decided I wanted to study business in London. I return in the holidays to help my uncle with his tourism business. But most foreigners want to travel so quickly, dashing from Marrakesh to the dunes and back in two days – it's madness. Boom, boom, boom, barely stopping for tea! You can't really experience a country like that.'

'What about by running through it?'

'That is very difficult. I respect all the runners out there. I wouldn't attempt it.'

'It takes a special kind of madness, that's for sure.'

We arrive at the checkpoint and I spend the day in Dr Emilio's shadow, taking photos, portraits that capture key moments and emotions in the race: the agony, the despair, the determination. Amongst the fun runners, I see people at the edge of their limits, working harder than they've ever worked before. It's inspiring. It's terrifying. And I watch Boones as he greets people coming through the check-point, slapping them on the back, handing out water. This is him in his element. Not just the overlord of the race but down amongst the rabble. The spike of resentment I feel hits harder than I realized. I thought I was over expecting that kind of affection from him. But seeing that he is capable of it? Seeing that others are making him proud, when I never could?

It fucking hurts.

And it's an illusion. None of these runners, staring at him in awe, drawing strength from his presence, none of them know him. They know 'Boones' the persona. Not the man.

His legacy is wrapped up in the Ampersands. But are the races bigger than him now? If they somehow continue – if Blixt take over, for example, although I can hardly imagine it – will they still attract the same attention?

Whatever happens, the races and my dad will be inextricably linked. Maybe this is his experiment. Maybe he's found a way to live forever.

I wish my sister could have too. But she never had the chance.

The Ultra Bros Podcast

Hot & Sandy Edition

Mac: Hello, bros and bro-lasses! Mac here for a quickie, because guess what? I finally get to leave the confines of this podcast booth – all right, all right, the cupboard under the stairs I've converted for the cause – and head to Morocco myself.

First of all, I want to say ta very much to everyone who's been getting in touch since our last live podcast. Especially huge thanks for all the messages of support and well wishes for Jason. I've got them lined up and ready to show him when he wakes up. I know how chuffed he'll be. Things were a bit touch and go – classic Jason, bringing the drama – but the latest report is that he's turned a corner and is on the mend.

A reminder that if you want to connect with other listeners, leave a message for Jason or send in a burning question you want me to ask our mystery guest, you can join the chatter on our Ultra Bros forum. It's pretty lively over there. For Ampersand noobs like me, I'm learning a lot. Like, did you know that Boones had a daughter? Someone who ran in Big & Dark back in the nineties posted an image of

Boones with a little girl at the starting line. Imagine having Boones for a da. Doesn't strike me as a warm and friendly hug-a-minute type. I wonder if she's a runner?

In addition to learning some new trivia and bonding with other Boones-race obsessives – excuse me, Booneshounds – you can contribute to the book of condolences we've set up for Nabil's family. There's a fundraising page too, should you feel inclined. There's been an outpouring of messages and support already and it warms my normally feckin' freezing cockles to see the racing community rally round like this. Keep donating and keep writing.

But the race must go on . . . and speaking of, day two of the Hot & Sandy has taken another unexpected turn.

Our man on the ground texted in – it's too difficult for him to speak on the phone, since Boones and his security team is on high alert after the last podcast release. Still, his message delivered a shocker: that Boones didn't actually start the second stage of the race. Some chap named Henry did. Now, I'm not the sleuth Jason is, but if we're talking about Henry Roth, then he's the CEO of Blixt Energy, the same guys who sponsor our podcast. I swear we had nothing to do with it! So is Blixt running the show now? Have they taken over the Ampersand races? Have we seen the end of the Boones era?

While you chew on that, how about an update on the race itself? The GPS tracker shows that without Nabil and Farouk, the front runner is now Rupert Azzario. He's had the lead for almost the entire stage, so I doubt if he's going to let it go now. If he can establish a good time in these early stages, then it is going to be very difficult for the other elites to catch him over the long day. He's got the strategy down pat – no matter what Boones seems to throw at him, he overcomes it. Looks like he's about to do the same for this one and come out of it a lot richer.

There's also another dot to keep an eye on. One of the fun runners seems to be making their way through the field. Isn't that interesting? They've been keeping up with the elites, even passing some of them. I wonder what Boones will do about that. Or maybe it's not up to him any more and Blixt is calling all the shots?

Let me know your thoughts on the forum. I need you all to be sleuth-Jason to my ignoramus-Mac.

Back with another live after the second stage has finished.

The Ultra Bros Podcast *is brought to you by Blixt Energy.*
For when 'I can do hard things' just isn't enough.
Blixt. Fire up your fortitude.

26

Adrienne

I trip over my own feet, hitting the ground with a thud. I feel sand between my teeth and taste the metallic tang of blood on my tongue.

'Oh shit, are you OK?' Runner 501 comes over and offers me a hand. 'I didn't mean to scare you.'

I don't take his hand. I scramble to my feet and dust myself off. 'You jump out at me from behind a bush and don't think I'll be scared?'

I don't wait for him to reply, just start walking. The adrenaline rush messes with my stomach and makes my hands shaky. I want to throw up and collapse at the same time. Instead, I spit the blood out of my mouth and pick up into a jog. As long as I'm moving forward, towards my goal, then I'll be OK.

Although it frustrates me, he falls into step behind me. 'I just – I'm completely lost. I panicked when I came down the jebel and couldn't see you.'

'Don't you have a compass?'

'I do but I don't know how to use it. I've been lucky so far, I guess. Always had someone in sight.'

'You're not one of the elites.'

'Nope. But I've been training hard. Guess it's paying off.'

I don't reply to that. I don't like that he wants to follow me all the way to the finish of this stage, even though there's absolutely nothing that I can do about it. It's not like I can ask him to stop and wait – it's the middle of the Sahara Desert. Instead, I decide to simply not talk to him. I have enough to concentrate on anyway. If I'm lucky, he'll get the hint.

I suck on my straw and keep my head down. We're probably less than an hour from the finish. If I keep up my pace, maybe he'll drop behind me naturally. But he seems determined to stick to my heels.

And determined to talk to me. 'I know who you are,' he says.

'Oh?' I clench my fists at my side, grinding my back teeth. The man's tone sets me on edge. *Focus on your own feet*, I repeat to myself over and over. I watch the white of the gaiters covering my trainers cycling against the dark brown of the ground. *Just run, Adri. Just run. Keep going.*

'I heard the podcast. You're a brave woman.'

Is he trying to goad me? I can't tell. But I don't have the will for conversation. I don't have brain space for anything other than running.

The bivouac has appeared on the horizon now, the flags of the stage's finishing line fluttering in the breeze. I can't concentrate on that, though. I can't get ahead of myself, or else I'll speed up prematurely and run out of steam before the end. Keeping a steady pace is so important.

The thought of finishing also brings up twinges of pain in my body, things that I had been blissfully unaware of until I had dared to dream about finally getting to sit down. Things like pressure under one of my toenails, probably a blister, and chafing along my lower back from where the backpack bounces against my body with each stride. My

194

right quad throbs with pain – I think I aggravated an old injury when I fell – and my eyes sting where the salt from my sweat has dripped on to my lashes. There's intense pressure in my bladder too; I hadn't had the chance to relieve myself on the jebel. If I stop now, this runner 501 will probably wait for me. If I was on my own, I'd just let it go on the run – the sun is so hot, the liquid would probably evaporate on contact with my skin. No one said ultrarunning was glamorous. But with him in tow I feel I need to hold it.

His breathing bothers me too. That rhythm.

He's wormed his way into my head and I can't focus. I can't get into the zone. It's the most frustrating way for me to run, and I resent him for every moment he has stolen from me. It's not the attitude that I want to carry with me while running. I drop my pace by the tiniest amount, so we end up running side by side, rather than him being in my wake.

'It's impressive you caught up with us,' I say.

'I've been pushing hard since yesterday. You think Boones will let me join the elites tomorrow officially? Be in with a chance at the prize money?'

'He likes a trier, so I bet you have a good shot.'

'When I was a kid, all my dad talked about was the Ampersand races. That's why I've come here. To see what all the fuss is about.'

'And?'

'I think I get it. Boones provides the arena. But it's up to the individual whether to push their limits or not.'

'I bet your dad is really proud of you.'

'Hard to be proud from the grave.'

195

We run in silence for the next few minutes, as I berate myself for my lack of tact.

'I never gave him much to be proud of when he was alive,' 501 continues, after a while. 'But he didn't give me much to be proud of either.'

'So really you're doing this for you.'

He looks over at me as I say that, cocking his head like a curious child. 'And you? Why've you come back, after so long away, like that podcast said?'

'Because I have to know.'

'Know what?'

I think of Boones's promise. The answers he's going to give me. But I realize that now there's a different question I've wanted to ask myself. *Am I capable?*

I can't escape the feeling that this is where I'm meant to be. This is me in my element. And I'd forgotten how much joy I got out of it, even under these circumstances. I run because I love to run. I run because of where it can take me. I run because that's what it feels like my body is made to do.

'I'll let you know when I find out,' I reply.

It's cryptic, even for me, but to my surprise he nods – as if he understands perfectly.

'Same for me.' He pauses. 'You think you deserve to know?'

I falter – in thought and in my step. The question is so unexpected. 'No, I don't. But I'm not going to let that stop me.'

We run a few more steps, our feet pounding in sync against the dry earth, cracked into almost perfect hexagonal patterns. Nature's geometry. If I'd stayed at home, ignored Boones's summons, suppressed my curiosity, I wouldn't be here, seeing this. If I hadn't lied, would Yasmin and Glenn still be alive? Would we have found some other way to reveal the truth? Would I have avoided making my son a target?

So do I deserve answers? No, I don't think so. But I've been offered them. And I'm going to take advantage, give it my all. Finishing is far from a given. I could have come all this way for nothing.

'By the way, I'm Matt,' he says. He sounds more breathless now, his pattern thrown out of whack, and his footsteps are dragging.

Meanwhile, I feel like I could go on forever. By my judgement we're less than a mile to the bivouac, so I can finally engage that extra gear. Sure enough, as I push that tiny bit harder, he begins to fall behind. Before he gets too far, I look back over my shoulder one more time. 'Good luck with the rest of your race, Matt,' I say, before taking off.

27

Adrienne

Matt gives it his best shot, launching himself forward to keep up with me, but he is spent. He's used up so much of his energy catching up with me and the other elites and not left enough in the tank for the final mile. I don't feel bad about leaving him behind. There's no way he will get lost – not with the flags so prominent and visible on the horizon.

I cross the finishing line of the stage, but don't linger in the end zone. Instead, I head to the tent. Mariam is already there, fast asleep and curled up in the far corner. Keeping the focus on my own feet, I try to run through all my post-race rituals: drink my recovery shake, do my stretches, tend to my blisters and sore spots, look over the course for tomorrow. I want to rest, but I also feel wired.

My muscles are beginning to stiffen so I make the decision to walk the bivouac.

All the elites are in now. There are so few of us left, the field having been depleted by the events of the last forty-eight hours.

Outside tent number one, Rupert is being interviewed again by the documentary crew. My instinct is to give him a wide berth. But something about running the second stage – taking on that jebel and feeling strong – has empowered me. I forgot how running can do that.

'The ultra community is small, and we're all friends here,' Rupert says to the woman with the microphone.

'All of you?' she asks.

'The ones who matter,' he replies. Do his eyes flick to me in that moment?

I've had enough. I wait for them to finish and until Rupert is alone.

I might be outrun. I might be threatened. But there's no way I'm going to be intimidated off the race.

I stride towards him. 'Rupert? I was hoping we could talk,' I say, ducking inside his tent. He scowls in response, but doesn't ask me to leave. I take that as an opening. 'What did you mean yesterday: "It should have been you"?'

At least he has the grace to look awkward about it, rubbing his hand against the back of his neck. 'Nabil was the best of us. If anyone deserved this win, it's him. But you — you ruined a good man's life. Glenn was a brilliant coach. One of the best. Why did you do it? Because he dropped you from his roster?'

'How do you know that?' I say, unable to hide my shock.

'Keri, my girlfriend, she was at your little camp. She told me Glenn fired you for refusing to race in an Ampersand. So why the fuck are you here now?'

'Same reason as you, Rupert.'

'I highly doubt that,' he mutters, darkly. 'I didn't want to be here.'

I frown. 'Then why are you?'

He shakes his head. 'Look, just stay out of my way.'

'Why, are you threatened? Is it because last time we raced against each other, I won?'

He stares at me dead in the eyes. 'It's not you I'm worried about. Now leave me alone.'

I swallow hard, backing out of his tent. My hands are shaking, and I clench them to stop. I didn't think many people knew about Glenn dropping me. Rupert's animosity makes more sense now. He thinks I made up the lie to get back at Glenn. The urge to scream the truth is so strong.

But it would be my word against that of a dead legend. Without proof I've already lost.

I'm distracted by a loud cheer rising from near the finishing line. Fun runners are crossing over, and they'll keep coming in over the next few hours. My heart lifts to see the camaraderie and the support offered by the other runners. This is part of what I always loved about race days. Even though running is such an individual event, the way runners come together to support each other makes it feel more like a team sport. It's inspiring.

It's also testament to the hard work each person is putting in each day. As I approach the medical tent, I can see another – a line of almost fifty runners is waiting to be seen by a doctor. Foot issues are the most common problem. The tent will be packed with people piercing blisters, slathering them in iodine, wrapping them in tape. I've learned to take care of all that myself, even if the offer of professional help is there. During races I like to be self-sufficient. In control.

I wander out of the circle of tents, past where the toilets are set up. I wish I had a camera with me, to take a photo for Ethan. He would love these mundane details, the everyday facts like how do you even go to the loo in the desert. I hope one day I can be in a position to bring him to Morocco and the Sahara Desert – to sleep under the immense canopy of stars and see the magnificent dunes for himself.

Five hundred thousand dollars would go a long way to achieving that. The thought creeps in. What would it be like to win? There are only ten of us left now. My odds are increasing.

Without realizing it I've walked almost halfway round the perimeter of the bivouac, towards the admin trailers. They look surprisingly cosy in the darkening sky, lights illuminating their windows. The bit of black fabric over my head and the egg-carton foam serving as my mattress is just not cutting it when it comes to comfort.

Suddenly someone storms out of one of them, the trailer door slamming out on its hinges. They rush down the stairs, almost pushing me over in their haste. It's Emilio.

He swears loudly in Italian, then he spins round. 'He's a madman,' he says to me, pointing back at the trailer. 'You shouldn't race any more. Please, Adri. It's not worth it. It's not worth your life.'

He seems almost mad himself, his eyes so wide I can see their whites, his hair in disarray from where he's run his hands through it.

'What happened in there?' I ask.

He shakes his head. 'I don't understand. You know he doesn't *actually want* anyone to win, right?'

His earnestness makes me laugh, even in the face of his anger. 'Of course. That's the whole point of entering a Boones race. He wants "can they even finish?" to be the main question, not "who won?".'

'But that's crazy!'

'You didn't know?'

'I'm his doctor, not an ultrarunner. I had never heard of Boones or these races before he came to me.'

I frown. 'So you're not a doctor for Hot & Sandy?'

'I am. I'm also treating Boones for . . . well, I *was* treating him, for all the good that's done him. What a waste of time. He'll be lucky to even see the end of the race.'

'Boones is that ill?' I feel panic start to rise.

He waves his hands. 'Ah, I'm exaggerating. He's got time. Well, as long as he doesn't try to run the last leg himself or something equally idiotic.' Emilio seems to have calmed over the course of our conversation, his breathing becoming more regular, his features less lined with anger and worry. Behind him, the sun is setting, bursting with colours that seem too vibrant to be natural. The Sahara seems to bring its drama and scale to everything – not just the sand but even the sky.

I'm so distracted by it that I miss that Emilio has been staring at me, his eyes scanning my face. His scrutiny makes me blush.

'Only nine left,' he says so softly that I can hardly hear. 'Nine out of twenty. One poisoned. One nearly brained to death. Not to mention the ones who have dropped out from severe dehydration, skeletal injuries, dysentery . . .'

'Wait, poisoned? You're talking about Nabil?' I think back to how I felt in the dunes. Woozy. Unable to stay focused. Hardly able to stay upright.

I'd shared my water with Nabil.

What if I had been poisoned too?

Still wants revenge.

I could have been the target.

202

'You mean to tell me his death wasn't natural?' I press again, when his lips remain tightly shut.

'I shouldn't have said anything. Adrienne, I'm worried about you.' He takes a step forward, lifting his hand to my cheek. The boldness of it stills me. His fingers are warm to the touch, and his eyes – when I stare into them – are filled with kindness, worry and maybe a hint of desire too. I place my hand over his, leaning into his touch just the tiniest bit. But it's not butterflies in my stomach, not right now. It's fear. 'Do you really want to be next?' he whispers, and the fluttering gets even worse.

When he puts it that way, my plan to put my life at risk and run hundreds of miles for Boones's promised answers sounds ridiculous. Taking the advice of this handsome kind doctor seems like a much better plan, quite frankly. Fifty miles are already in the tank, but there are still two hundred to go. Poor, poor Nabil.

I wonder if Emilio takes my silence as agreement, because he breaks out into a smile – and I'll be damned if it isn't as breathtaking as the sunset. I teeter on the edge of the decision. When he lowers his hand from my face, our fingers are intertwined.

But the moment is broken when Boones's trailer door opens again, and he steps out. After what Emilio said, I had expected to see a frail, fragile figure – but Boones looks full of vigour. It's like the drama of the race energizes him rather than depletes him. His moustache is sharp, his eyes bright. And when they land on me, I know I'm going to give it my everything. I'm not going to let this opportunity slip away.

'You'll want to come and hear my announcement,' says

Boones. 'It's a doozy.' He doesn't wait for my answer, just strides off in the direction of the bivouac.

I break out of Emilio's grip and follow, my feet moving of their own accord.

Emilio's interest in me is flattering. But I haven't come here for that. I'm here for answers. And the news about Nabil's death only cements my decision. If someone is trying to scare me off, then that means they're here – and not after my son.

I'll do anything to protect him.

And I've come too far to turn back now.

28

Stella

Where is Rachid?

Ali has gone to look for him, while I stand inside the finishing zone, capturing images of exhausted fun runners dragging themselves over the line. Normally Boones would be there to greet them, but it's Henry doing it this time. Strange.

At least today's stage seems to have passed without incident. I hardly left Dr Emilio alone for a moment and I got used to his scowl in my direction.

The biggest news of the race is a fun runner who'd kept up with the elites. Runner 501. One of the guys on my Runners for Hope list. Matteo Poddighe. He had moved through the checkpoints so fast I didn't even see him. Doubtful if he can keep it up for three more days but impressive nonetheless. The most anticipated stage is the fifth day – nicknamed the 'long day' – where the runners will have to complete one hundred miles in one go. Most of these fun runners will be running through the night, in total darkness. It's the challenge within the challenge. As if it wasn't already hard enough.

But this is what the people who signed up *want*.

They want to be pushed.

They want to be tested.

That's what my dad is counting on.

I hope Pete can find out information about Nabil's death before then. I won't be able to stay on Dr Emilio's tail all that time. I hope my suspicion is wrong. But I can't take that risk.

Through my lens I catch sight of Ali gesturing for me to come over. I don't waste a minute. I jog over straight away.

'Any news from Pete?' I ask.

'Yes. He is on his way to the bivouac.'

'Wow, OK. He must have found something out. Did he tell you?'

Ali shakes his head. 'Only that he must speak to you in person. But – there is a problem.'

'What?'

'The security in the camp. It's so tight – they won't have any chance of sneaking in until it's dark.'

I glance down at my watch. 'Still got a few hours then.' I bite the edge of my thumbnail, my mind whirring, wondering what Pete knows.

That he's coming at all is a big part of why I love him. That the moment I need him, he leaps to my aid – no debate. No rejection. No ridicule. No expectation that I should figure it out on my own. No secret tests.

Maybe I should have told Pete about Yasmin when it happened. Given him the whole story about Ibiza. We'd been a couple, after all, and I know he would have been so supportive. But I was too consumed by my grief to think about bringing him into it – not to mention how complicated Adrienne had made things by inserting herself into the story. Instead, I'd reached out to Boones. I don't even know why. I guess I needed my dad in that moment.

Fat lot of good it did me.

He'd let me down, just like he always did.

Henry waves me over, so I say a quick goodbye to Ali, agreeing to meet him at sunset. Then I jog over.

'Can you get some photos of runner 501?' he asks me. 'He's one of your "Runners for Hope" guys who absolutely killed it this stage. I know they'll want his story documented.'

'Sure,' I say. I might as well do something while I'm waiting for Pete. I already feel useless, rattling around the bivouac like a spare part.

I find runner 501 sitting outside his tent, apart from the rest of his fellow runners. He's shovelling food into his mouth out of a bag – one of those meals you hydrate with hot water. With his sunglasses still on I can't get a good read on how he's feeling. But he looks tense. Like he's still in the zone.

'Hey, congrats on your run today.'

He looks up sharply at the sound of my voice.

'Mind if I take a few pics?' I continue.

'Who are you again?'

'Oh, I'm Stella. I'm with Runners for Hope.' I fumble for my security pass.

'Stella . . .' He lifts his sunglasses, his eyes searching my face. 'Have we met before?'

'Yeah, I took a video of you on our first day in the bivouac.'

'No, I mean, before this race?'

'I don't think so.' But I frown. There is something familiar about him. I can't place it.

'Oh, OK. Well, go ahead.' He gestures to my camera.

I don't get him to pose or position him in anyway. I just wait for him to get back to his food and take pictures of him going about his business.

If Yasmin were here, if she was still alive, she would be the one I was taking pictures of. If she hadn't received an invitation on her own merit, she would have bought a place at the race. Maybe she would have done what Matteo did. Run so fast and so hard that Boones couldn't deny her a place with his elites. 'You think you can keep this up?' I ask, tucking my camera to one side.

'I want this more than anyone else out there. I want a chance to compete against the elites officially. To chase them down one by one until it's only me out there. But that's up to Boones.'

'You deserve it. You've earned it.'

He snaps his fingers. 'I like the way you think. Guess we'll find out soon enough.'

'Think I've got everything. Good luck in the race.' If he gets promoted, at least that would be one elite not running to fulfil my dad's agenda.

It's almost dark and I wave as I walk away.

'Hang on a second,' he says and I turn back towards him. 'Do you have a sister?'

The question hits me, closing my throat. It takes every-thing in my power not to cry.

'Not any more,' I reply.

I can't stay a moment longer. I power away, keeping my head down. As I move through the bivouac back to my tent, I see Adrienne deep in conversation with Dr Emilio. Goosebumps rise on my skin. I think about going to her.

Warning her about the drugs I found on him – about what I suspect he did to Nabil.

Warning her that anyone connected to my dad is not to be trusted.

But I don't know anything yet. Not really.

I need Pete to get here. And somehow we can put an end to this nightmare together.

29

Adrienne

Darkness descends on the camp in a snap, so when Boones clambers up on his Jeep, he faces a sea of head torches. I don't have mine, so I linger near a group who do. The tips of my fingers tingle with anticipation. Three more stages to go.

'Well, congratulations to those of you still running,' says Boones. 'Day two and that jebel – brutal stuff.'

A murmur of agreement spreads through the crowd.

'I apologize for not being there to start the race this morning. I know my Blixt friend took over. They're keen, those guys. Keen beans.'

As always, Boones's irreverent tone sets me on edge. Despite his almost childlike wonder, it's like the more jovial he is, the more sadistic the next twist will be. I wonder what he's come up with.

'Well, I'm sure you've heard the rumours flying around the camp about the infiltrator in our race. The one who snuck in under the radar, with ideas above his station.' Boones chuckles. 'Runner 501. Thanks to your performance, I'm promoting you to the level of elite, bringing the number of elites to ten. Ten of you all competing for my grand prize. How does that sound?'

There's a burst of applause from the crowd, a chant starting of 'one of us' amongst the fun runners. But I don't raise my hands to clap.

So Matt will be joining us on the elite starting line. Unease churns in my stomach, a gnawing anxiety about who he is. I wonder if my gut knows more than I realize. It told me to get away from him. Now he's going to be on my heels.

Boones continues. 'Just don't think I'm going to make things easy on you. I'd suggest y'all get some rest. Not long to go now, folks.'

The crowd disperses.

Mariam finds me as we walk back to the tent.

'What did you think of the announcement?' I ask her.

'I was expecting more,' she says, rubbing her chin.

'What do you mean?'

'Don't you think everything has been a bit too easy so far? Yes, OK, the no-phones thing – but to be honest I rarely bring my phone to a race. I prefer to stay in the moment. It is not some great surprise.'

'Don't you worry about your kids not being able to contact you? I just feel overwhelming mum guilt, worrying that Ethan needs me.'

'He can get hold of Pete, no?'

'I should hope so.'

'And you've left him with people you trust?'

'Of course. With my life.'

'Then remind yourself that good mums also need to do things for themselves. I know you say you came here searching for answers from Boones. But I think there is something else you have been seeking. The Adrienne from before. The one who chased after her passion. The one who gave herself permission to excel, who didn't hold back. The "rock goat". Remember her?'

'Vaguely,' I say, laughing. But Mariam's words are a gut punch. It's true. Motherhood was the excuse I used to shut the door on the running chapter of my life. When the real reason was fear.

'You need to show Ethan this side of you too. He'd want to know it. No matter what happens here – whether you find the answers you are looking for or not – he should know this Adrienne too. And he will be proud of you.'

Her words bring tears to my eyes.

She smiles at me, continuing while I compose myself. 'Then this other runner – OK, it's one thing to be promoted, but he is already so far behind most of the times, I am sure he is not threatening for the money.'

'That's true,' I say, not adding that he might be threatening for *other* reasons.

'Either Boones has lost his bite or there is something else still in store for us. That makes me nervous.' We arrive back at the tent, and Mariam shakes out her sleeping bag before stepping inside. 'If you want to stick together for the next couple of stages, I think it would be wise.'

'Are you sure? What about Jason's note . . . ?' For a moment I debate telling her about Nabil's poisoning – and my suspicion that it was meant for me. That maybe running with me will put her in danger. Risking my own life is one thing. But putting someone else in harm's way?

I would never forgive myself.

'All the more reason for you not to be alone. Did you learn anything else from those pages?'

I shake my head. 'Nothing. Just a note about Booneshounds – his obsessive fans. It made me wonder if Glenn had been one of them. It would make sense, given how intent he was on cracking the Ampersands.'

'The best thing we can do right now is to get as much rest as possible. Be ready for anything.'

'Of course. Goodnight.' But though Mariam seems to drop off easily, for me it's too difficult to quiet my racing mind.

I focus on visualizing the route ahead. Fifty long, arduous miles tomorrow. And I'll have Matt on my tail, feverish for the win and desperate to prove something. Rupert seems to be hungry for it too, as keen as ever to make his name as the master of the Ampersand races. If he comes first, he'll have won all three.

I just have to keep myself in the game.

And pray that Boones is going to uphold his end of the bargain.

The Ultra Bros Podcast

Hot & Sandy Edition

Mac: Greetings, bro-listeners! I've just heard the news that this is quickly becoming our most listened to race series, and I don't want to let you down despite no longer having a co-host – thinking of you, Jason, keep on getting better!

First of all, apologies if this podcast isn't recorded at the best quality. That's because I'm taping literally live on the road in Morocco, as I'm heading to a top-secret location.

I promised you all an update once we'd heard Boones's next announcement, and here it is: that runner 501, Matteo Poddighe, has been promoted to the elite category. That means he's eligible for the five hundred thousand dollars grand prize. Now wouldn't that be a story!

It's going to be interesting to see how he does. Accompanying me in this tin-can car, I've got Pete Wendell, ultrarunner and Hot & Sandy DNS-er. Most people who DNS aren't that keen for an interview, but Pete is an exception to the rule.

So, Pete, welcome to Ultra Bros!

Pete: Thanks, Mac. Wish it were under better circumstances. But I appreciate you giving me the opportunity to set the story straight. I don't know what happened to my tox screen, but I have never taken any kind of performance-enhancing substances. I took another independent blood test when I got to Ouarzazate the same day I was disqualified. It came back clear.

Mac: For listeners out there, just know I'm looking at those test results now and they seem legitimate.

Pete: That's because they are.

Mac: Of course, of course. You must be gutted not to be out there running.

Pete: The results came back too late for me to rejoin the race, so yeah. It's all I've thought about for six months, ever since I got the invite. And if you count the years I've wanted to run in any Ampersand race, you could say it's been the dream of a decade.

Mac: And Boones has never invited you before?

Pete: Nope.

Mac: What changed?

Pete: I'm not sure. Boones isn't exactly known for explaining himself. I think, though, that this past year I changed up my training, chose races that really pushed me out of my comfort zone. I ran more in North America too – Badwater again, the Yukon Ultra – maybe that put me on his radar. I'll get another shot, I'm sure of it.

Mac: Well, if you could put yourself in the shoes of the runners who are out there, say that fun runner turned elite 501, Matteo Poddighe – what's going through his mind right now?

Pete:	He's not even halfway through the race yet, so you gotta hope he's kept something in the tank. It's really common to peak too soon in this kind of race. For that fun runner in particular, if he's been really pushing his limits to make the cut for the elites, then he's at high risk for burnout. And in these temperatures it's a double whammy. Any fatigue is going to be magnified by the heat.

Then the last stage – the long run – that's going to be the real test. When you start to think about running a hundred miles in one go ... that's serious. On top of all the normal muscle aches and soreness and the battering your limbs take, there's sleep deprivation, extreme digestive issues, cramping, hallucinations – so much fun stuff to deal with. I remember during Badwater, I was so desperate for a burger that I thought I saw one waiting for me at the side of the road. It was wrapped up in paper, like someone had left it for me as a gift. I'd stopped, knelt down, opened it up – it smelled so good, the burger was glistening, the bun was so soft. I took a bite. I damn near ate the whole thing.

Then this runner came up behind me – snapped me out of it. I'd literally been sat at the side of the road eating dirt. That juice I'd tasted? I'd bitten down on the inside of my cheek so hard I was bleeding.

Mac:	And you kept going after that?

Pete: Believe it or not, I felt full! I finished, yeah, but my time sucked. I've heard of people feeling like they're being chased by zombies or the trees around them becoming giants with faces and hands trying to stop them. This is a messed-up sport, but let me tell you, the feeling when you complete something you thought was impossible? It's unmatched. It's pure euphoria. There's nothing like it.

Mac: Aye, but I still think it takes a special breed. I've only done one hundred-miler in my lifetime and never again. I'll stick to my fifty-k ultras, ta very much. And they will have already run a hundred miles by the end of the fourth stage, so it will all be on tired legs.

Pete: Yup. It becomes pure survival at that point.

Mac: How will they do it? How would you do it?

Pete: You know, I hate to say this considering it's your sponsor's strapline – I swear I have nothing to do with them – but for me it becomes about the mantra. Whatever the words are that work for you. I use a different one for each race, but at the end of the day? 'Get it done'. That's what I say to myself. Just get it done.

The irony of that is that even when you are done, your body has still suffered. You can't run these kinds of distances without it taking a real toll on your entire system. You're fucked for weeks, basically. Months sometimes. Talk to anyone who's broken a world record – they're broken themselves, sometimes they even end up in hospital because of it. Your organs start shutting down. Your muscles wasting away.

But without fail you'll be back to chase that feeling all over again. It's a proper trip to finish an ultramarathon. A high unlike any other. That's why the thought that I'd take some sort of performance-enhancing drug before a race like this is just . . . it's ludicrous. I accept my DNS. Fine, it is what it is. But I'm innocent.

Mac: Hmm, speaking of runners on trial – I'm not the investigator Jason is, but I'd be remiss not to ask about the other infamous Wendell. That's your ex-wife out there, right?

Pete: It is. Don't underestimate her. If this was some ordinary foot race, she might struggle to compete after this long out of the game. But this is anything but ordinary. Adri is the most determined, adaptable person I've ever met. When she gets her teeth into something, she doesn't let up. Plus, our son is watching. I wouldn't underestimate what kind of motivation that is.

Mac: I bet. What happened to Nabil shows us the risks all the runners are taking. Aren't you worried about her?

Pete: Of course I am. I'm worried about everyone out there.

Mac: Care to elaborate?

[There's a long silence.]

Pete?

Pete: No, I'm done.

Mac: O-K, well, thanks for that illuminating inter-
          view. I think you've given us plenty for the
          Booneshounds to discuss. And, listeners, I
          can't share much right now, but I promise you
          you're going to want to keep tuning in. I have a
          feeling the next twenty-four hours are going to
          be very interesting.

The Ultra Bros Podcast *is brought to you by Blixt Energy.*
For when 'You won't regret this' just isn't enough.
Blixt. Power for your persistence.

30

Stella

After everyone has gone to bed, Ali and I sneak off to the part of camp where the drivers and local volunteers hang out. Some of them are smoking round a fire, the camels laying close by, basking in the heat. The rich smell of spices rises from pots on the flames, no crappy rehydrated bag meals here.

There's a small table set up in the corner – it looks like it's normally used to stack supplies, water bottles and boxes of permanent markers littering the surface. We push them to the side, so there's space to put down the glass of strong, sweet Moroccan tea I've been offered, spearmint mixed with buds of gunpowder green and a load of sugar. I sip it gratefully, my eyes not leaving the entrance to the tent. Ali tries to engage me in a card game but I can't concentrate on anything right now.

As soon as Pete arrives, I run up and throw my arms round him.

He holds me tight. 'I got here as fast as I could.'

I pull back, my eyes searching his face. 'What did you find out?'

He swallows, glancing behind him.

He's not alone. Another guy enters the tent, wearing a black-and-white-striped shirt and a beanie.

The guy takes one look at me, then steps forward, his

hand extended. 'Stella, isn't it?' He has a strong accent – somewhere from the north of England – a voice I'm sure I've heard before.

'Yeah . . .'

'Stellz, this is Mac. From *The Ultra Bros Podcast*,' explains Pete.

'I flew out here as soon as Jason got injured and when I ran into Pete and he told me he was on his way to the bivouac – well, I had to come with.'

'He's got information you'll want to hear,' Pete adds.

'How is Jason?' I ask, directing them over to the table I've set up, away from listening ears. Most people are heading for bed anyway, the tent emptying out.

Mac chews his lip before answering. 'He's in a bad way. He took a clobbering. In fact, I'd say it doesn't look much like an accident.'

'You think someone did that to him?'

'It's not something I'd say on the podcast but, yes, I do,' says Mac. 'I was telling Pete in the car – Jason didn't only come out here to run. He was chasing a story. The continuation of "The Glenn Affair".'

My throat tightens, my breath shallow. 'And? What does that have to do with Boones?'

'Not Boones. It's who he invited to run. Adrienne . . . she's in danger.'

I breathe a little easier, but my head is still swirling. 'What're you talking about?'

'Look at this.' Mac pulls out a laptop, booting it up on the plastic table.

The electronic glow is overly bright in the dim atmosphere of the tent, and heads swivel to look at us. No one is supposed to have a device in the bivouac. Shit. I reach out and snap the lid shut. 'Not here,' I hiss.

The tent door flings open and someone leaves; I wonder if they've gone to rat us out. I flick the screen back open again, knowing we likely only have minutes before it's going to get taken from us.

'Show me quickly,' I say.

Mac seems to get my urgency. He navigates to a cloud-based storage folder, speaking rapidly. 'Jason's been investigating this case for years. He's got thousands of pages of documents – video clips, interview notes, time-lines. More than the police have, I guarantee it. He's convinced Glenn's death wasn't natural.'

I scan the document names as he scrolls through. He's right; there's so much research gathered in one place. A few of them catch my eye, but Mac keeps talking. 'So, it looks like Jason has been visiting some guy in prison. Multiple times over the past seven years.' He double-clicks on a file. It's a prison record for a Matthew Knight.

My blood turns cold. 'Who is that . . . ?'

'Glenn's son. He's been in prison for manslaughter. Got fourteen years for beating someone to death.'

'I didn't even know Glenn had a son!' I wrack my brains, trying to think if he mentioned it at the Ibiza camp. I'm certain Yasmin would have said something if she knew.

'Me either,' says Pete. 'But it gets worse.'

Mac nods. 'It does. Two nights ago, Jason and I spoke on the phone. He said something that didn't make any sense. That he'd seen a ghost. Then the line went dead. Next thing I hear, he's been nearly brained to death and is in hospital. So I did my own research. Matthew Knight?

He only served half his sentence. He was released from prison a few months ago.'

He lets the words sink in.

'You think Jason saw Matthew . . . in the bivouac?'

'I do,' says Mac.

'But why would he refer to him as a ghost?'

'You know, someone who isn't supposed to exist. I think Matthew confronted Jason in his tent. He wanted him to tell him who killed his father, and when Jason didn't give him the answers he wanted, he whacked him in the head and used the storm as cover. It's why I flew out to Morocco on the first plane I could get. Just bloody annoying it still took me two days to get here.'

'Who did Jason think killed Glenn?' I ask.

'Well, this is the thing. Are you guys ready?'

'This isn't your podcast – get to the point,' snaps Pete.

Mac can hardly sit still. 'No idea how he did it, but it looks like Jason managed to get hold of CCTV from Glenn's neighbour on the day of his death. And it shows *Adrienne* at Glenn's house.'

'What?' Pete's eyes flash, and he grabs the laptop so it faces him. 'You didn't tell me that in the car. Show me.'

Mac reaches over and scrolls to the image file. He clicks on it – even though it's a grainy black-and-white image, it's unmistakably Adrienne. The timestamp reads six a.m. 'Pretty early to be going to his house,' I say. I'm proud of how calm my voice sounds, despite my brain going into overdrive.

'It was the morning of the Yorkshire 100. She must have stopped there before driving to the starting line,' Pete says. I can almost hear the cogs turning in his mind. Piecing things together.

'What do you think she was there to do? Apologize?' Mac asks.

Pete hesitates before eventually shaking his head.

'I don't think so either,' continues Mac. 'All we know is Adrienne was probably the last person to see Glenn alive. And after what she accused him of, she might as well have killed him. Did Adrienne tell the police she'd been there?'

'No,' Pete says in a quiet voice.

'Aha! If it was an innocent visit, she would have told them. But she hid it. Motive, opportunity. I think that was enough for Jason. So it might have been enough for Matthew too.'

'It's fucking absurd,' Pete splutters.

I put my hand on his arm, squeezing it.

'So you think Matthew's here, right now, to avenge his dad? And do what to Adrienne – try to hurt her?' I ask.

'We have to warn her,' says Pete, standing up. 'Get her to safety.'

'Wait a sec,' I say. 'Nabil. Before we go rushing to Adrienne, tell me what you found out at the hospital.' My heart feels tight as a realization sinks in – Pete didn't rush here because I asked. He came because he thinks his ex-wife is in danger.

Pete nods, his eyes dark. 'Well, you were right to ask the question. There was something weird. Traces of sedative were found in his system.'

'And that contributed to his death?'

'Looks like it, combined with his pre-existing heart condition and the brutality of the course.'

Now it's Mac's turn to look shocked. 'We were both keeping things from each other on that car ride then, huh?'

224

'His family insist he would never take drugs like that,' continues Pete.

'So . . . someone did this to him,' I say.

'And that's a terrifying thought,' adds Pete.

'Presumably Boones knows about the sedatives? I can't believe the race is still on,' Mac says, leaning back in his chair.

'That's Boones for you,' I mutter.

'Your dad, right?' Mac says, making me grind my teeth. Whenever someone says "your dad" like that, it makes it sound like they think I'm somehow responsible for his actions. I'm about as responsible for him as I am of a grizzly bear in the woods.

'Hang on, wait. Where was Adri when Nabil went down?' Pete asks. 'Weren't she and Nabil running close together? I was following their GPS tags on the website.'

I pause. 'She arrived before him at the checkpoint. I was there, taking pics. She – she gave him some of her water, then they left more or less at the same time.'

Pete's eyes go wide. 'Wait, *her* water was spiked?'

'I know what you're thinking,' I interrupt him. 'You think it was meant for Adri.'

'It sure fucking looks like it.'

'Or she was the one to give him the dose,' says Mac. 'Gotta admit, the woman has form.'

Pete's on his feet so abruptly his chair hits the ground. It looks like he's about to punch Mac in the face. But I can't let him. We need to work together.

'Guys, come on, we don't know anything for certain yet,' I say, using my arms to keep the two of them apart, and Pete exhales sharply. 'Mac, this Matthew Knight – did Jason have a picture of him anywhere?'

Mac shakes his head. 'There's nothing in his files. I checked. I tried Google but Matthew doesn't have any socials and it doesn't look like the mainstream media followed his trial, so no photographs online.'

'Shit.' I pause. If Glenn's son is here, then I bet my dad knew about it. It couldn't be a coincidence. I think about all the promises he's made. His meticulous planning, as evidenced by the mountains of paper in his trailer. Then it strikes me – that's what was familiar about that photograph I'd see pinned on his wall. 'Wait, a second. What was the Knight Academy logo?'

'A sword, I think.'

I snap my fingers. 'We need to get to Boones's trailer. I think we can figure out who Matthew is from there. Fuck Glenn, hiding the fact he had a son from all of us.'

'Wait, you knew Glenn?' Pete asks me.

'Of course I did. I was with Yasmin and Adrienne in Ibiza. At *that* training camp –'

It's like someone steals the air from the tent. Neither Pete nor Mac breathe – they only look at me. I never planned for that information to come out of my mouth. Not like this. But I also thought Pete had come back for me. Not for her.

'You were there?' Mac asks, his eyes wide. 'I read all Jason's notes and there was no mention of you.'

'Yes, but not as a runner. I was supporting my sister,' I say. I don't look away from Pete. I see the penny dropping in his mind, but there's no time for long conversations, explanations. I have to keep him focused. 'We need to see that photo. There's someone in the bivouac I suspect. Presumably if this Matthew Knight is here, he's using a different identity.' I dip my hand into my bag and pull out the ketamine. 'I found this last night in one of the medic's bags. More than powerful enough to sedate someone – or kill them. I took it to give to the authorities to see if it matched what was given to Nabil.'

'My God, Stella. Which medic?'

'Dr Emilio. The one who took your blood test.'

'Which got me kicked out of the race.' Pete's eye twitches, his fury evident. 'He could be in on it?'

'But if you got hold of these, someone else could have, right?' says Mac.

'I guess.' I clamp my hand back round the drugs and drop them back in my bag. 'The police can figure out if it's connected.'

The door to the tent flies open, and three burly men walk in, wearing Hot & Sandy vests. Part of the security team.

They scan the tent, spotting us with the laptop open. It's too late for us to hide.

Behind them, Henry emerges. 'Over there,' he says, pointing at us. 'Get them out of here.'

3 1

Adrienne

Sleep does eventually dig its claws into me, as sharp as the acacia thorns in the desert. It's the deep, heavy, dreamless sleep of the completely exhausted – another sandstorm could hit and I would have been unaware.

It's why, when I'm shaken from my slumber in the middle of the night, it burns like a thousand scratches. I'm disoriented, groggy, confused. Unwilling to let go of oblivion.

The person doesn't stop, unzipping my sleeping bag and agitating my shoulder until my consciousness finally surfaces. My eyes blink open and I find myself staring at Boones.

'Time to get up, runner thirteen. The real race is about to begin.'

32

Stella

'Boones will fire you,' I say to the security guard standing in front of me, his large arms folded. Maybe he knows my threat is empty, because he doesn't even blink.

Who knew the bivouac had a freaking jail? I didn't. But we'd been frogmarched to a marquee at the far end of the bivouac, the inside of it partitioned into small 'cells' with heavy cloth dividers so I'm kept in a space hardly bigger than one of the toilet tents. Pete and Mac are taken to different segments. Though we can't see each other, I can hear their protests.

I throw my hands up in the air. 'Screw this.' I move to push past him, but he blocks my path. 'Let me go. You don't understand. Boones is my father.'

The guard shifts awkwardly on his feet.

I spot a radio at his side. 'There. Use that. Call Boones right now. If you don't, you could be putting lives in danger. You could be using this jail for a real criminal.'

'And who would that be?' Henry walks into my 'cell' and the former guard sighs with relief. He steps through the curtain to leave the two of us alone.

I clamp my mouth shut.

It doesn't faze Henry. 'Look, by allowing unauthorized people into the bivouac, you've endangered everyone's safety and broken our rules. You'll stay here while we arrange your transport back to Ouarzazate. Hand in your security pass and –'

'Before you go on, I really need to speak to Boones.'

'Because he is your father, I know. I think the whole bivouac's heard you by now. You'll have your chance. But I have a few questions first. Like, why was this in your bag?' He holds up the bottle of ketamine.

'I took that from one of *your* doctors – Emilio. He also had a racer's water bottle in his bag. Have you asked him any questions? Presumably you must know by now that Nabil had traces of that stuff in his blood when he died.'

Henry nods. 'We do know that. We've spoken to the Sûreté Nationale. They're on their way.'

'Good. So Emilio is the one you should be holding in these cells, not us. Pete and Mac have information to give to the police about how Emilio might have poisoned Nabil. We think he was targeting one of the other runners, Adrienne, and Nabil is collateral damage.'

Henry's eyes search my face. He looks exhausted. 'What the actual fuck?'

'Not what you expected for your first time race directing?'

He shakes his head.

'Look, Henry. Take me to Boones now and we can get Emilio into custody and wait for the police.'

'Fine. Come with me.'

It's not what I expect to hear, but I'm glad. I follow him out of my 'cell' – and with a clearer head I see that the private booths must normally be used for medical treatment. I try to see Pete, but he must still be inside.

It's quiet outside the bivouac and it's pitch black.

Thankfully Henry has a heavy-duty torch he uses to light the way.

'What time is it?' I ask him.

'Three a.m.,' Henry answers. 'I've got so much to do. Your father has us working ourselves to the bone to pull off his ultimate race.'

The phrase sets alarm bells off in my mind. Dad had used it with me too, but I hadn't registered it then. I assumed it was his normal hyperbole.

'I thought owning part of the Ampersand races would be such a – well, such a boon for Blixt. Now I'm beginning to think it's a nightmare.'

I agree with him. I pick up speed, darting ahead of Henry and his light. I know the way to the trailer by now. I take the steps two at a time.

The door, to my surprise, isn't locked. It swings open with an ease that makes me scared, not relieved.

Suddenly I don't want to go inside.

I take a deep breath. Step into the darkness. Fumble at the edge of the door for some kind of switch. My fingers find one and the light flickers on.

'Oh shit,' I say.

The trailer is completely empty.

33

Stella

Seven years earlier
Ibiza

'Another glass?'

Kacey – or is it Keri? I can't remember – waves the bottle at me from across the dining table, her black-dyed hair let loose from its ponytail for once. My cheeks already feel like they're on fire and I know there's an unsightly blush spread over my neck and chest, but it always happens to me after a few glasses of champagne. A few more and it goes away again. Better to push through.

'Please.'

She grins and tops me up.

I smile back, clinking her glass. For most of the group this is their last night. They don't know that Glenn has invited Yasmin to stay for extra coaching. They're not the chosen ones. They're not stuck here for a few more days.

Neither am I – not that Yasmin knows that yet. But if she's going to ditch our vacation plans, I'm not going to feel any guilt. My flight leaves early in the morning, but what the hell? I need to do what I want for a change.

I knock back the fizz, then hold out my glass again for a top-up.

Yasmin's sitting across from me between Coach Glenn

and Adrienne. She's glowing in the soft fairy-light flicker of the restaurant terrace. The patio juts out over the water, waves crashing beneath our feet. An idyllic setting.

Glenn leans forward. 'Tell me something, Stella. Has your dad ever spoken about an "ultimate race"?' He uses his fingers to shape air quotes around the phrase. As always, he answers the question himself before waiting for me. 'I heard him in a rare interview saying that's his grand plan. To host the race to end all races – the one to truly test what humans are capable of. Any idea when he's planning it?'

'Where did you hear that? From the Boonesdogs or whatever they call themselves?'

'Well, is it true?' Glenn probes.

'No clue. I'm sceptical. Boones wants every race he hosts to be the greatest test. He always wants to know what people are capable of enduring. Already he's gone too far, and people have been hurt.'

'Not on purpose, though,' Yasmin adds.

I shrug. 'I mean, he's not going to set the trail on fire or anything but he expects people to take responsibility for their own actions and choices. That's important to him. You enter one of his races, that's your choice. You shouldn't expect to be rescued if you need it, like if the weather turns on you or you get lost while navigating.' I take another gulp of champagne.

'So no "ultimate test" then. Big & Dark is as hard as it's going to get.' Glenn's voice is full of scepticism.

'Like I said, you'd have to ask him.'

'Can't you? You're his daughter, after all.'

'Is that supposed to mean something?'

'It should. Children should keep in touch with their parents.'

'How would you know?'

I must have touched a nerve. His eyes glint with anger but he laughs to cover it. 'No matter. Big & Dark is our target. We'll be ready for whatever Boones will throw at us. Right, ladies?' He raises his glass, clinks it against Yasmin's, then reaches across her to the other women.

To my surprise it's only Adrienne who doesn't join in.

Glenn reaches up and wipes a rogue droplet from the corner of Yasmin's lips and Yasmin recoils.

I slam my glass on the table, but Yasmin gives me the smallest shake of her head that tells me to drop it. She shifts slightly out of his reach, acting like nothing happened. Maybe it didn't. I've reached that point where I'm so drunk I can't trust my vision.

I turn to Adrienne. 'Not toasting to defeating Boones then?'

'My focus is on the Yorkshire 100. I won't be entering an Ampersand.'

Glenn snorts, but I keep my eyes on Adrienne. 'And why's that? Too good for my dad?'

'Stella!' In addition to her scolding tone Yasmin shoots me a warning glance.

'What? I think it's interesting.'

'Adrienne doesn't have the stomach for an Ampersand race, do you?' Glenn's tone is laced with disappointment. It even makes me wince, and I'm not the recipient. Gone is the camaraderie between them, the closeness. I feel my curiosity pique. I wonder how the rock goat took such a tumble in Glenn's eyes. 'Races like that require real grit.

Courage to stay the course, strength to adapt to challenges. They are as much mental as they are physical. Not everyone has it. No shame in admitting it.'

'I've had a long day,' says Adrienne. She gets up from the table, throwing down a few euros. 'I'll see you in the morning.'

Some of the others protest at her leaving, but I take another gulp of champagne.

'I think you've had enough,' says Yasmin. She jumps up from her seat, moving to be next to me, and takes my glass away. 'Do you have to be so rude?'

'Come on. She's a big girl.'

'And so are you.' She drapes one of her bronzed arms across my chair, speaking softly so that only I can hear. 'Are you planning on telling her that you're dating her ex?' Yasmin's deep brown eyes burrow into mine.

I sway. 'No. I don't even know if it's going anywhere yet.'

She tuts. 'Now who's afraid?'

'It's not like that.' But Yasmin's right. Maybe it is a bit like that. I don't want to spoil things. Adrienne is intimidating. It's my dumb luck that the first guy to grab my attention in years is her ex-husband – who happens to be the attractive, dependable, loyal-as-fuck man of my dreams. But the ultrarunning world is like that. Shockingly small. Incestuous. Almost everyone is connected somehow.

'So we agree you're in no position to judge,' she says.

'All right, chill. I'll go and apologize.'

She kisses my cheek. 'What would I do without you?'

'Ha ha.' When I stand up from the table, my head swims. I give myself a beat before strolling outside, trying to be casual.

235

Adrienne is outside waiting for her Uber. I debate turning round and going to the bathroom instead, but she looks up at the sound of my heels.

I lurch forward. 'Look, I'm sorry. Actually, I kinda agree with you.'

Her eyes narrow slightly, looking for the barb in my words. 'About what?'

'The Ampersands. I wish Yasmin wouldn't race them.'

'Why is that?'

'He can't be trusted.' Tears well in my eyes. Stupid booze. Brings all my emotions up to the surface. I'm a lightweight and now the floodgates are open. I stumble over the kerb, almost landing flat on my face. So graceful.

Adrienne catches me under the arm. 'Come on, the taxi's here. I'll take you back to the hotel.'

I don't protest. The heat and the alcohol on too little food is a lethal combination for me. I cast a glance back into the restaurant, thinking of Yasmin. I should say goodbye.

Nah. It's too hard. I'll send her some flowers instead.

'Don't let her throw up in my cab,' says the driver, as Adrienne bundles me in.

'She idolizes you, you know,' I say.

Adrienne scoffs.

'She didn't come here for Glenn the legend or whatever. She wanted to learn from you.'

'Shame she won't get the chance.'

'What do you mean?'

'Glenn and I aren't working together any more. He's kicked me off the team. I'm leaving tonight.'

'Oh . . . shit.' Good to know that even drunk my

instincts are correct. I'm dying to know what happened, but my drunken mind is only focused on one thing. 'Does Yasmin know?'

Adrienne shakes her head. 'No one does.'

'So you're not staying for the next few days?'

'No. But I'm glad you are.'

'I'm not either. First thing in the morning, I'm gone.' *To see your ex-husband*, I almost add.

'Yasmin's going to be on her own,' Adri says. There's a tremor in her voice, a hint of fear, that makes me sit up. She turns her back to me, staring out of the window. She doesn't look afraid. It's probably the drink, twisting things in my mind. That and my guilt.

Yasmin's not going to like being left on her own. But I deserve to be happy too. This whole week has been about her.

This time I'm going to think about myself.

34

Stella

Henry steps outside the trailer and gets straight on the radio. I ask him to release Pete and Mac, and moments later they come rushing over.

'Did you find what you were looking for?' Pete asks, as he climbs the stairs.

'See for yourself.' I gesture around at the walls, only the remnants of pins and tape left. I've opened some of the drawers and cupboards but they're empty too. I've only found one thing of substance – a pen. If there's a note to go with it, I can't see it.

'Shit. What do we do now?' Mac asks.

I sigh, leaning against one of the chairs in the trailer. I rub at my eyes. They sting like needles line my eyelids. Too little sleep. Too little water. 'Hang on, the thing I'm looking for – I took a picture of it. On my phone. Henry can give it back to me. Let's go . . .'

'Stella, wait,' says Pete. 'We need to take a beat. The race is due to start again in an hour. Where's Boones?'

The question hadn't even entered my brain. But of course Pete is still focused on the race. He has a point, though.

It seems like we're not the only one with that question. It's already much lighter, making it easier to see the look of concern on Henry's face.

'Find anything?' Henry asks.

'Nope,' I say. 'Cleared out. Except for this.' I show him the pen.

'Crap.' He mutters something into his radio, then listens intently. 'I can't believe this. The elites are gone too.'

'I'm sorry, what?' Pete snaps.

'We're still trying to figure it out. We heard people moving around in the night but we were a little busy dealing with some intruders.' He looks pointedly at us. 'I assumed they were checking the tents in case of another storm. But I guess they must have been collecting the elite runners. They're not here now.'

'So where are they?'

'Hang on. Show me that pen?' Henry asks. I pass it over. 'This is a voice recorder. I've seen Boones use them.'

'Well, play it then!' Pete shouts.

I touch his arm. Being aggressive is not going to get Henry to press the button any faster.

We strain to listen to Boones's soft voice. It's a message for me. He meant for me to find it. Asshole. '*By now, you will see that I have taken the elites for the real Hot & Sandy. Two hundred miles, no support. No GPS tracking. Don't come looking for us. Periodic updates will be sent. Check the forum. The runners have sixty hours. See you at the finishing line – or not, as the case may be.*'

Boones's *real* twist.

He's tricked us all.

Pete knows it too. He releases a deep guttural moan.

Mac is the only one who seems impressed. Excited even. 'Man, I wish Jason were awake to hear about this. He'd go mental. This is exactly what he's been telling me to expect from Boones. You should know that, Pete.'

'I'd be happier about it if there weren't some fucking newly released convict out there hunting my wife,' Pete growls.

'Ex-wife,' I mutter.

Henry's eyes widen with horror. 'Convict?!'

'Now you understand our urgency,' Pete says. 'You must still have a way to access the trackers, though, right? Even if Boones has turned off the public viewing?'

But Henry shakes his head. 'There's only one laptop with tracking capabilities for the elite runners. Boones has it.'

'No, no way,' says Pete. 'This is the Sahara Desert. What if someone gets lost or needs medical aid?'

'I'm sure Boones has a plan,' says Henry, but he doesn't sound confident.

'Henry, I need my phone,' I say, firmly.

He opens his mouth to protest, but I shut him down.

'Didn't you hear that message? Boones is gone. He's taken your elites. Fuck the rules. I need my phone right now. Have you found Dr Emilio?'

'You think this "convict" is the doctor?'

I hesitate. I don't know anything for certain. 'He's our number-one suspect.'

Henry sighs. 'Fine. I'll instruct our security team to find him. When we do, Stella, I'll leave him to you. I'll also take you to your phone. Whatever you need. But I can't deal with this myself. I have responsibilities to Hot & Sandy, to the fun runners. Boones might have abandoned them but people have paid a lot of money to do this race. I've got to do right by them. And I'm not going to let anyone down.'

I bite my tongue – Henry is in way over his head, and he

doesn't even realize, but I don't want to risk him deviating from the plan.

Before I get in the car with Henry, I direct the others. 'Ali, can you take Mac and follow the security team to find the doctor? Don't let him out of your sight until the police get here. Pete and I will get my phone.' To my relief they agree without arguing.

Henry instructs his driver to take us to the administrative area. He drops us outside one of the trailers. 'Your phone is in there. Here, take this radio too,' he says, handing me his. 'I can pick up another one. Then we can be in contact.'

'Thanks.' I slip the radio into my pocket.

'Keep me posted.'

The trailer is stacked with plastic crates, each one filled to the brim with Faraday pouches. Finding mine is going to be a needle in a haystack.

'Looks like these are marked by tent number,' I say to Pete. 'The staff tents were all numbered, starting from two hundred. Look, here!' I find the ones marked with '200' and start lifting lids off the boxes and opening bags.

Pete's radiating anger. It's coming off him in waves. It's not only fear for Adrienne. 'I can't believe you were there.' His voice is calm but his clenched jaw betrays him. 'At least this explains why you never wanted to meet Ethan. It wasn't about protecting him at all, was it? You just didn't want to have to see Adrienne again. It's been seven years, Stella. You're my *fiancée*.'

'I only became your fiancée a few days ago. We always said we'd wait for our relationship to become properly serious before I met Ethan. I was a mess after Yasmin died. You and I were long distance for years, back and forth, will we or won't we? I didn't want to come into his life and then disappear again. You didn't want that either. But now, of course, I want to meet him. As soon as we get back, we'll do it.'

'If *I* want that,' he snaps.

That wounds me. But I let him have it.

Part of why I love Pete is that he's such a steadfast man. A real doer. He'd drop everything to help his son. I didn't get that from my dad. And because of that I didn't know if I could give that kind of parental stability to a child. Now I have to step up, as part of my choice to say 'yes' to Pete. I chew my nails – only to realize they're raw; I've bitten them down to the quick. That sick feeling in my stomach is not going away. *Dammit, Dad. Why do you always have to be such an enigma?*

We go through at least three crates before I find it.

'Here!' Thanks to not being touched for over forty-eight hours, the phone still has some residual charge – hopefully just enough for me to find what I'm looking for. I pull up the photograph, feeling Pete's hot breath on my neck.

'Look.' In the top corner the sword logo that had caught my eye jumps out once again. I zoom in on the words underneath the picture. *KNIGHT ACADEMY*, it reads. There are labels naming each of the people in the photograph. *GLENN KNIGHT* is on the far left. Then, on the bottom right, *MATTHEW KNIGHT*.

'Bottom right, bottom right,' says Pete impatiently.

I pinch across and zoom in on the face. The colour on the image is faded, so it's hard to make out eye colour. One thing is clear: it's very definitely not Emilio. They share a dark mop of hair. But the jaw, the nose – it's all wrong.

'So that clears the doctor.' Pete's shoulders slump. 'Unless they're working together.'

I bite down, hard, on the inside of my cheek to keep from crying out. I recognize that face.

Pete notices the tension in my grip. Probably because the phone is shaking in my hands. Shit. 'You know him?'

'That's runner 501.'

'You mean, the fun runner who was with Adri yesterday, the one who has been promoted to the elites – *he's* Glenn's son?'

'Looks like. Matteo Poddighe, he said his name was. I didn't make the connection . . .'

'Oh my God. That's the surname of Glenn's ex-wife. What's he going to do to Adri? He's got the perfect opportunity now. She's all alone out there. And we have no way to track them.'

Bile rises in my throat. Poor Adrienne. Runner 501 had been one of the people I'd interviewed for the Runners for Hope charity. Hadn't he talked about running for his dad even then?

Matthew is a violent ex-con, who's come out here despite knowing he'll be sent back to prison if he returns to the UK.

He's a man with nothing to lose.

35

Adrienne

In the darkness it's impossible to tell where Boones is taking me. He marches me out of camp, only a narrow beam of light from his torch to follow, until we reach a group of people huddled together, presumably the other elites. Boones threads a thin stretch of rope between our hands, lining us up in single file – I don't know exactly who's in front of me or behind me. I only know that I have to keep moving.

I wonder if the person ahead is Rupert. It's partly the height, which rules out a few of the others. What convinces me is that he seems so calm. His breathing is regular, his shoulders aren't squeezed up by his ears like mine are. I'm so tense I feel like that coiled viper I saw yesterday, unsure whether to strike or hide. If Rupert's relaxed, it can only mean one thing: that he was expecting this. Or something like this. It feels like a real Boones twist now.

When we're further away from the bivouac, I hear before I see how Boones is planning to transport us even further into the desert. Snuffling and snorting, toes pawing at the sand.

Camels.

My first thought is: Ethan is going to love this.

My second is: what the hell is Boones planning?

I glance around at the others, and now that my eyes

have adjusted to the darkness I can make out the expressions on their faces. Most seem as confused as I am. Some are stoic, revealing nothing.

'I'm sure you're all wondering why I've dragged you out of bed in the middle of the night and brought you here. Well, you didn't think I would go easy on you, did you?' He waves his index finger at us, scolding us as if we're his children. 'These camels are going to take you to your individual starting point. At exactly four a.m. you will each set off, navigating only with a map, my directions and your own compasses if you brought them. You'll be running the last two hundred miles of this race in one go. No more bivouacs. No more cosy tent at night. You can sleep when you want to, take what shelter you need, eat when you want to, but remember that everything you take, you must carry with you.'

There are several sharp intakes of breath, including my own. Two hundred miles in one go? This isn't what I trained for.

None of this is.

'What about water?' asks a woman. Mariam.

'On your individual maps you will find water caches, where I've hidden sufficient water bottles for you to resupply. Miss your cache and you won't be able to continue. Simple as that. At the end of the race I'll need to see a bottle cap marked with your race number from each cache to prove you hit them all and ran the correct route. Understood?'

He calls us by our individual race numbers. When mine is called, I step forward and he hands me a map rolled up like a scroll. 'Two hundred miles until you get your answer,' he says.

I don't reply. This is why I never wanted to run in a Boones race. I feel like a mouse in a maze, running for a piece of cheese that, for all I know, could be poisoned.

A man with an intricately wrapped scarf round his head touches my forearm gently, leading me over to one of the camels. With an apologetic frown he ties a blindfold round my eyes. 'Is this really necessary?' I ask Boones.

'You're welcome to quit at any time.'

I'm hoisted up on to the camel's back, blindfolded, gripping on to the reins for dear life. Boones has one last message for us, though. His voice rings in my ears. 'You have sixty hours to complete the race. If you're not back by the cut-off, then you will be disqualified. As always, a camel and rider will mark the back of the pack.' In a slightly quieter voice, though one that still seems just as clear, he says, 'Don't let him catch you.'

My head whips round as his words sink in, but the camel is now moving and I don't have a chance to protest or question.

I have no idea where I'm going – it's too disorienting in the dark, with no sense of direction or of time passing. He could have walked me round in a circle for all I know. Eventually, though, we do come to a stop, and the man in the headscarf helps me from the camel's back and removes my blindfold. Immediately I swing my backpack off and dig around for my head torch. Once I find it, I use it to illuminate the map. It's hand-drawn, the features and caches marked. There are compass bearings and degrees marked at every major intersection. It doesn't seem to turn back on itself at any point – it's just two hundred miles out into the heat and the sand, crossing over the jebel again, before reaching the finishing line.

'One minute,' the man says. 'Then you go.' He's holding a simple digital watch that is counting down.

'OK, OK.' I find my first heading and adjust the compass accordingly. *This is insane* – the thought repeats over and over in my head. And yet I feel that tingle in my fingers. That surge of anticipation. I only have to reach the end. I'm built for this. Made for it. With stage racing Rupert would have had the ability to recover overnight. But with this new format it's all about extreme endurance. Anything can happen over two hundred miles and sixty hours.

I can endure. I can push suffering into the cave, using it as fuel. But I've only done this kind of distance with a support crew and pacers – and the last time was over a decade ago. I haven't attempted anything like it since.

Well, that's not quite true. On weekends when Pete has had Ethan, I'd go for overnight runs deep into the fells, trying to find a way to quiet my mind. I never tracked how many miles I ran, I'd just keep going until I found a spot to camp overnight, then run again in the morning. I know I've covered massive distances on little sleep and food. So strangely I feel like I am trained. Two hundred miles in one stage. It's incredibly daunting. Yet it's actually a change that suits me. Challenging navigation, mega distance, tricky terrain. My specialities.

This is my race to lose.

The watch beeps. A synchronized alarm. I take one more look at the map, and then I set off, running into the night.

Only the small area in front of me is illuminated by my

head torch. It shrinks my world straight down to only a circle. I'm glad. The enormity of the Sahara might overwhelm me otherwise.

I think about the other runners. Are they out there somewhere, as equally disoriented and yet somewhat excited as me? Or are their heads down, powering on, trying to get a jump on the competition?

Eventually, even that thought leaves my mind. Other than occasionally checking my compass to make sure I'm staying on the right bearing, I slip into an almost mediative-like state, so that the first few miles seem to pass with no trouble at all. The sand is gently undulating under my feet, nothing yet too arduous, and I'm able to keep up a good pace despite the darkness.

At the ten-mile mark the first streak of light appears in the sky. I can't stop to appreciate it, however. According to the map, I should be coming across a water cache soon, and I don't want to miss the first one.

It feels like a nigh-on impossible task to find a water cache in the dark. But it turns out Boones isn't totally merciless. There's a small glow stick tied to a bush right around the point I expect the cache to be. I kneel in the dirt and dig for the water. Finding it makes me feel elated, like I've found a pot of gold instead of water. It makes it feel possible. The first step achieved.

I pocket the cap, then tip the water into my bottles, using some of the leftover to wash my face. But I don't linger long. It's quickly going to get hot and I need to move as much as I can in the darkness.

I drop the empty plastic back into the water cache, next to another empty. Then it clicks. There's another empty.

That means someone else has already been to this water cache. Are they far ahead of me? Maybe their route is different. But it gives me a slightly sick, panicked feeling, like I've been going too slow.

It won't do me any good to think about it now. I find the next bearing and move in that direction. When the sun is up, I might be able to join up with another runner. Two hundred miles is a long time to be totally on our own.

My mind is on high alert anyway. So when I hear the sound, I wonder if I'm dreaming. Hallucinating already.

It's a hum. Nothing particularly tuneful, at least not that my running-addled mind can make out. But it doesn't seem like the natural sound of the desert. Not the howl of the wind or the crunch of sand beneath the soles of my trainers. Not the skittering of creatures just outside the purview of my head torch – and, thank God, because I don't need to freak myself out more than I already am.

Someone else is out there.

The hum sounds again. I deviate off my line ever so slightly. There's a big ridge of sand on my left that's blocking my view, and that seems to be the direction the sound is coming from. I know that my sense of perspective in the desert is totally skewed. Objects that seem close can be miles away. Sound can travel, or voices close by can be whipped away by the wind.

I reach the top of the ridge – and that's when I see the source of the sound.

I couldn't be more relieved.

It's Mariam.

36

Adrienne

We stop and embrace, all the tension between us melting away out of sheer delight for finding a familiar face in the middle of the desert.

'You made it. I was worried about you,' Mariam says, as she pulls away. We check our bearings, and for the next two caches they match. Eventually, our routes diverge for a short time, before coming together again at the jebel. In total, we could run together for a hundred miles. It's too overwhelming to think about it like that, though. Only one step at a time. From one water cache to the next. 'When I saw your water bottles in the cache with mine, I decided to see if you might join me.'

'Thank you for waiting. How are you feeling?'

'Out of my depth.' It's hard to tell from beneath Mariam's mirrored sunglasses, whether she's teasing or being serious. Something about the firm set of her lips makes me think the latter. This is way more than anyone could have anticipated. She shakes her map before folding it back into her waist pack. 'What do you make of this?'

'A true Boones-style twist. Although even this seems quite extreme. Did you hear what he said?'

'Which part? The insane time cut-off? The fact we have to collect those stupid bottle tops?'

'When he said, "Don't let him catch you".'

Mariam raises her eyebrows above the line of her shades. 'I missed that. Too distracted by the camel.'

'What if Boones has done something more? What if there's someone out here trying to stop us?'

'What makes you think that?'

'Something the doctor told me. That Nabil had been poisoned.'

She comes to a grinding halt. I stop too. 'You are not serious?'

'I am. I mean, I don't know the details but –'

'Who would do that? Another competitor?'

'I have no idea.'

'If it is, it is down to Boones. That bastard. He would really make us run for our lives out here? Poor Nabil, his family . . . Even if Boones delivers on what he promised me, it is not worth a man's life.'

'He promised you something?'

She nods. 'Money to rebuild my family's village school if I finish.'

'Mariam, look where we are. We're in the middle of absolute nowhere. No official checkpoints. No medical staff along the route. I think we only have one choice.'

She finishes my sentence: 'To keep running.'

I nod.

'Together.'

I nod again.

With two of us navigating, it becomes easier to fall into a rhythm. The sun creeps higher and higher in the sky, unrelenting in its power.

With fifty miles already in our legs from the previous two days, and another ten on top, my muscles ache with every step. I periodically look down to check I'm still wearing my running shoes – my feet feel as if they're engulfed in fire. If it were a single hotspot – the start of a blister, a stone in my shoe, some sand creeping in through the gaiters – I could stop to sort it out. But this isn't one irritant. The laces of my shoes feel like they're being tightened atop my feet, the heat rising through the soles almost unbearable. The ground feels quite literally like lava. But there's nothing to do except quit – or keep going.

I keep going. Mariam's breathing is calm and even, and I try to emulate her. Every now and then I glance over and think *it should be impossible for anyone to be that strong,* but for the most part I stay in my own lane, focusing on my own pain. It's not even just my feet. The rest of me is flagging too. My shoulders throb, tension squeezing my neck in a vice grip, worsened by the weight and constant swing of my backpack. The anti-chafing cream I rubbed on to the sore spots isn't doing the job – they're more like open wounds now, seeping blood on to my filthy shirt that I haven't changed in three days. My legs are covered in grazes – tiny cuts from too close encounters with acacia thorns, bruises from where I've kicked rocks up on to my shins, and every inch of exposed skin is covered in sand and dirt. I don't have to worry about suncream, at least. The dirt is like an extra layer, sometimes cleared by rivulets of sweat, creating mud-brown streaks on my legs – but it never takes long before it's replaced by even more crud.

At the next water cache I swallow painkillers – paracetamol and ibuprofen. Liver function be damned, I need to do something to dull the ache. They stick in my throat, along with the salt tablet. I just can't seem to get hydrated, even though I'm taking in as much water as I physically can. We decide to eat some food too – I shovel calories down my throat, even though my stomach wants to reject everything I put in it. If I don't refuel, then I'm truly toast.

What I absolutely cannot do is think about how far there is to go. Two hundred miles is an unfathomable distance, even though I've run it several times before. If I truly thought about it, my mind would shut down. My body would refuse to do what I ask of it. Instead, the only way I can manage it is to break the impossible down into achievable chunks. Eat the elephant one spoonful at a time. I only have to make it to the next cache of water. Two caches and then I can sleep. Three caches and we will have reached halfway, then go our separate ways. Four caches until I see her again. And then another four caches to the end. Each one I'll mentally tick off, like the countdown to Christmas.

I even plan to give myself rewards. An advent calendar of the race. At the fourth cache, I'll have my protein bar. At the sixth, I can have more paracetamol. At the seventh, I'll stop and cook a warming soup – even some macaroni cheese. To occupy my mind, I recite things. Favourite songs. Poems. Films. I'm able to watch the entirety of *The Lord of the Rings* trilogy in my mind. I picture myself with Legolas's elven skill of running for miles at a time, my feet barely making an indent in the soil. When I feel sluggish, I picture Sam carrying me towards the finish. It can also help to think that I'm running away from a Balrog.

Some people say that to complete this kind of distance, you need to understand your *why*. To have a reason concrete in your mind, some motivation beyond yourself – a cause maybe, a charity, an illness, a difficult situation you've endured and overcome. But this distance is too long for why. Running these impossible distances isn't some kind of need. There's no practical, real-world application for this skill of mine. It can't even pay the bills – well, unless you're like Rupert, or if you win the prize pot.

My real *why* is that running *is* me. Ultrarunning is my art. My body is a lump of clay I've sculpted into becoming an efficient runner – a winning runner. And the same broad spectrum of emotions I've seen conjured by a remarkable piece of music or a moving work of art – tears, elation, devastation – I've also felt in my races. With each race I challenge myself to create something more beautiful. To tweak all the variables in my control and see if I can run something close to a perfect race. To see if I can challenge myself to do better. To be better. It's my version of what Boones wants to do: finding out the limit of human endurance. But while he uses a stick to beat us into greatness, I use a paintbrush to coax my true form to life.

Ultrarunning levels the playing field. It's not really about having the chance to compete equally against men. It's never a question in my mind that ninety-nine per cent of the time, Rupert would beat me in any length of race. He is bigger, stronger, faster, has more endurance, more oxygen at his disposal. But the thing about ultramarathons is that they are rarely run under perfect conditions. And that's when I can come to the fore. While my approach to the physical side of training is more intuitive than most, following my body's lead, when it comes to mentally preparing for the race itself, I am diligent, bordering on fanatical. I research as much as I can about the route, the weather, the terrain – in the hope that I don't get fazed by a change in conditions.

It's the same for most women who enter the most extreme ultras. They *know* the distance is insane, so they don't even enter unless they are capable of finishing. That's what makes it a more level playing field, putting them a step ahead of a man who's just chancing it. Many ultras come down to who makes the fewest mistakes on the day. Often that's a woman.

Years ago, I let myself be a canvas painted by someone else. Glenn held the brush, chose the colours on the palette. He had been almost wholly in charge of my life – he regulated what and when I ate, my training schedule, even what went on in my personal life. Was it a wonder that Pete felt like he and Ethan played second fiddle?

Darkness is beginning to fall in the desert, deepening the hues of orange and red all around me. I glance at Mariam. Somehow we have managed to keep each other going all the way through the first fifty miles together, through the day and into nightfall. The residual heat cooks up from the earth, my legs bathed in warmth as I run.

Our shadows have lengthened, becoming almost like company. My heart rate speeds up, my breaths quicken, as if my brain has forgotten the shadow is attached to me and I suddenly think I'm being overtaken by some unseen foe. Hallucinating this early into the race isn't a good sign.

I glance over my shoulder but of course there's no one there. Yet behind us is the sunset I would have missed if I had only focused on my forward motion. It's so stunning it almost brings me to a halt. I slow to a walk instead, taking the opportunity to pop a salt tablet and swig water. The sun, which has been beating down on us for so long, now hangs low – lingering above the horizon. With the haze of sand in the air, it looks truly golden, almost soft. A falling star. The sky is painted in hues that reflect the desert – burnt orange deepening to crimson. The black of night is quickly encroaching and the contours of the landscape are more starkly apparent.

Mariam hasn't slowed with me – she's in her own zone.

Shit. It really is getting dark quickly. I do stop now, fumbling inside my backpack for my head torch. I try to tell Mariam to do the same, but my voice comes out as barely more than a croak. Another sign the hours of hard running is catching up with me – I've forgotten how to talk. I fix my light to my head, make sure spare batteries are in an accessible pocket and turn it on, flashing it to get Mariam's attention.

A breath of wind tickles my cheek, soft at first, then more firmly. My jaw tenses with fear. I try to calm myself. Wind is fine. Wind is to be expected.

I just don't want it to develop into a storm, like the one we had on the first night.

I can't let Mariam get too far ahead. Night will be the most difficult time to navigate when our brains are addled and an extra pair of eyes will be invaluable. Especially if there is another sandstorm. The wind swirls ominously around my body, warm and yet a little too strong for my liking.

I glance one more time behind me, and I spot something else that gives me pause. On the horizon a figure appears, silhouetted by the dying sun. They're still quite far away, but there's something about their posture that makes me feel like they are staring straight at me.

And I no longer feel like something beautiful. I'm not in control, a predator chasing down the lead.

I'm the prey.

37

Stella

The radio bleeps and Henry calls my name. I fumble in my pocket as Pete continues to stare at the photo of Matthew/Matteo on my phone. 'We've located Dr Emilio,' says Henry over the radio. 'Your friends have him contained in the medical tent.'

'Got it,' I reply. Pete and I exchange a look. 'Just because he's not Glenn's son, doesn't explain why he had the ketamine,' I say to Pete. 'He still might be involved. Matthew's accomplice, like we speculated. We have to be careful.'

We take off at a jog towards the tent. Mac, Ali and Rachid surround the doctor in one of the chairs, whose face is a bright shade of crimson. 'What the fuck is going on?' Emilio shouts, as we arrive.

'Give it up, man – we know you poisoned Nabil!' says Mac with a dramatic flourish of his hand. He's enjoying this too much.

'What?' Emilio splutters. 'I did nothing but try to save that man. Who even are you?'

'Then why did she find ketamine in your bag?' Mac points at me. 'Really, Dr Emilio, explain that to us – or should I call you *Matthew*?'

'Oh, cool it, Mac, you're not Hercule fucking Poirot,' Pete mutters, grabbing Mac by the arm and pulling him back. 'We found a photo of Matthew Knight and it's not him.'

Mac deflates like a balloon. 'What?' He looks at me expectantly, as if I'm going to take his side. 'So he's not involved?'

'I *told* you,' says the doctor, standing up now. This time no one stops him. 'Those drugs are for your father, Stella. That's why I have them with me. But who is this Matthew person and why do you think he poisoned Nabil?'

I swallow. I still don't know who I can trust.

'Tell me now. If there's someone out there endangering the elite runners, then I can help. I might be the only one who can.'

'What do you mean by that?' asks Pete.

'This phone,' Emilio says, grabbing his medical bag and pulling out an old smartphone. 'Boones gave it to me last night. It will ping if an elite sets off their emergency beacon. He instructed me to be in a vehicle, ready to move, in case.'

'So you can contact my dad?' I ask.

'I can't say.'

'Emilio, this is serious. People are in real danger. Including my dad.'

He hesitates, his eyes darting across my face. 'What are you talking about?'

'This man.' I take back my phone from Pete and enlarge the photo. 'Matthew Knight. He's come here to hunt down the person who he thinks killed his dad. He's running under an alias – Matteo Poddighe, race number 501. And now he's got himself promoted to the elites so that he can find his target.'

Pete interrupts. 'That's Adrienne Wendell. You might have examined her?'

Emilio's eyes harden. 'Yes, I know her. This man is after her?'

'And my dad has the only way to track her. So if you have any idea where he is, we have to find him.'

Emilio swears under his breath in Italian, but he nods. Next to me, Pete is twitching with anxious energy.

'Let's go,' I say.

But Emilio doesn't get on his phone straight away. Instead, he walks over to one of the tables. He pulls some of the papers stacked in the corner in front of him, shuffling through them until he finds a map. He unfurls it. 'I only know some of the plan. Boones isn't exactly forthcoming. What I know is that he's taken the ten remaining elites and set them off on different routes. They will lead to the same finishing line, and some intersect more than others. They will all cross this mountain – Jebel Tilelli – at some point during the last half of the race.'

'So the runners are spread out across the desert?' asks Ali.

'Yes. He didn't even share his race routes with the Berbers.'

I turn to Ali. 'Is that a problem?'

He shrugs, but it's not a gesture of nonchalance. It feels more like . . . resignation. Like he knows more about the magnitude of the desert than we can ever imagine. 'If you don't know exactly where the runners are, finding them will be impossible.'

Impossible. I hate that word.

Pete hates it even more. 'Even with the Jeeps?'

'A man was lost in the desert on one of these races. He wandered into Algeria,' continues Ali. 'They didn't find him for a week.'

I'd heard that story. It's one of the legends of the Marathon des Sables. How one person got lost in the dunes after a storm, the desert erasing all traces of his presence.

'But we can use one of the helicopters,' Pete says. 'We can cover so much more ground that way. We know they're going to go to the jebel at some point – we can start there.'

I tap the table. 'Think Henry will let us?'

'We'll force him! We'll remind him that there's a fucking convicted murderer on the loose!'

A loud chirrup of beeps interrupts us all. Emilio digs in his pocket for the phone. He swipes at a few buttons on the screen, then he nods to Ali. 'You've got a car fuelled up and ready?'

'Yes,' Ali replies.

'Great.' Then Emilio looks at me. 'If anything that you're telling me is false, and you've messed up Boones's race for no reason and dragged me into it, I want you to be there to tell him. So, Stella, come with me.'

'That was him? You know where he is?'

'Not Boones. One of the emergency beacons has been activated. Runner eleven. Alexander Schmidt.'

'I'm not letting you go alone,' says Pete.

Emilio shakes his head. 'There's not enough room for everyone – we need space in the car for the patient. If you must, you can follow us.'

Pete glances at Mac and Rachid, who immediately jump up.

'I'll stay back and organize the chopper,' says Mac. 'Henry's a mate – he sponsors our podcast. I'm sure he'll listen to me. I'll contact you on the radio if we find anything.'

'Let's go then,' says Emilio.

Emilio gives coordinates to Ali once we're in the four-by-four. Pete follows in the car behind with Rachid. We swing out of the bivouac just as Henry is gathering the fun runners to start their race. Watching them getting ready to start their third stage as if everything is normal, I feel like I'm having cognitive dissonance. But I can't blame them. They don't know any different. They have no cell phones, no social media, no radio. They're a bubble, cut off from the outside world. They don't know what's going on in their own race even. That Boones has stolen away the elites.

Word will spread. Rumours have a way of flying even in the most remote places. But I have a feeling it will only generate excitement. Our small group is the only one worrying – because of what we know. But for the rest of the world this is the pinnacle of running. This is the ultimate display of human endurance and suffering and triumph over adversity. Boones is enemy and friend, god and devil, trickster and saviour. Father and stranger.

The car bounces as we speed across the dunes, but I'm used to it now. In fact, I urge Ali to go faster. Rachid and Pete can keep up. We need to get to Alex as quickly as possible. Obviously I hope he is all right. But more importantly, I hope he can lead us to my dad.

Dust flies up behind the vehicle as we speed along a dried riverbed – at least here, on hard, compacted earth, it's possible to drive quickly. Ali takes advantage. Until Emilio taps him on the shoulder for him to slow down. He's staring at his phone, at the GPS dot blinking on his screen. 'Somewhere here.'

We slow to a crawl, scouring the riverbank, until we spot footprints in the sand, veering off and away from the path of the ancient river.

Ali swings the car round and we mount the riverbank. On this softer sand it's hard to travel with the same haste. Shards of rock threaten to damage the tyres and Ali needs to carefully navigate round stumpy bushes – like everything in this damn place they're even tougher than they look and can do serious damage.

'Over there,' Ali says, suddenly pulling the steering wheel down to the left, hard.

I brace myself against his headrest, unsure what he has seen. When the car stabilizes, I stare out of the window, scanning the bleak desert landscape. Everything is a shade of brown. Monochrome. It's hard to make anything out. Ali is far more used to it than we are. We have to rely on his instincts.

'There,' he says again, this time pointing. I follow the line of his finger. It takes me a moment – and some movement – to realize what he's pointing at. Someone is sitting on the ground in the meagre shade offered by a shrub. He's weakly waving in our direction.

'My God, how did you see him?' Emilio says. 'That's lucky. A helicopter would have no chance,' he adds.

It's far luckier for him than us. He looks half dead – dehydrated, fatigued – and probably suffering from heatstroke. His race number is dirty, smeared with something that looks like blood.

Emilio is straight out of the car with his bag, water, phone. I follow, not even waiting for Pete in the other vehicle to catch up.

'Alex? Do you know where Boones is?' I ask, once he's had a sip of water.

He looks up at me, but he barely looks human. His skin is grey, his eyes unfocused, and he's staring at me like I've grown three heads. He makes a sound but it's not words.

Emilio frowns. 'I need to get him back to camp. He needs proper rehydration or he's not going to make it.'

I spot a map beside Alex and pick it up. It's hand-drawn, my dad's neat illustrations pointing out the water caches, the jebel climb, the finishing line. It has Alex's starting point marked. It looks roughly thirty miles away. With any luck we can work out where Boones might be.

I walk back towards Pete, who had caught us up, gesturing for him to follow me to the car. Ali is waiting in the driver's seat. I show him the map. 'Can you get us here?' I point to the start. According to the map, it's in front of some sort of rocky structure – another jebel, smaller than Tilelli, or else a cliff of some kind.

'Sure.'

'Pete, get in,' I tell him.

'How's Alex?' He frowns with concern, craning his neck to see.

'Dehydrated. Woozy. Doesn't look like the victim of an attack, though. Emilio can take him back to the bivouac in Rachid's car. Either you come with me or go back with them.'

By way of an answer, he jumps in the car, but I can tell he's agitated.

'Drive,' I say to Ali once I'm in the front seat. I don't have time to coddle Pete right now.

264

Emilio is shouting at us, but it's not like I've abandoned him high and dry. He can get back with Rachid. That was his job, as he was at such pains to point out.

'I don't get it, why are we going backwards?' Pete asks me. 'You saw the map. We should be heading out to the water caches to find Adri.'

'Those were personal to Alex – who knows if Adri is being sent to the same caches. And, remember, my dad is sick. He won't be travelling on foot. He must be in some sort of vehicle. If we go back to where Alex started from, we might be able to follow his tyre tracks. You heard what Ali said – finding these runners will be impossible, like needles in a haystack. Shit, we had Alex's GPS beacon beamed directly to Emilio's phone and we still had trouble finding him.' I glance at Ali, who catches my eye and nods. He's with me. He's not with Pete.

Even I am finding it difficult to be with Pete. It's not his fault. It's mine. I've kept things from him, secrets I've kept our entire relationship. And he's so worried about Adrienne.

Adrienne. The woman who ruined so many lives: Glenn's, my sister's, mine. The anger I'd felt towards her has mellowed over time, becoming more like a simmer. But now that she's back in the game, competing in a race, I feel the familiar heat rising again. That she can get back in the ring, when Yasmin never can.

That she can put the past behind her.

But mostly: that she'd been there when I'd run away. She'd been a sister to Yasmin in the moment of her greatest need. And that fills me with rage and guilt and pain.

'It's going to take us an hour to get to this point, right, Ali?' Pete asks him.

'At least,' he replies.

Pete turns to me. 'Good. We have time. Now you can tell me what really happened in Ibiza.'

38

Stella

Seven years earlier
Ibiza

My alarm goes off at three a.m. Despite my excessive drinking the night before, I feel good – in all likelihood I'm still a bit tipsy. I'm making the right decision. So I'm not going to Barcelona with my sister. That sucks. But I am going to see the new man in my life. And that fills me with excitement.

I don't even care that it's selfish. It's what I want. I promised Yasmin a week, and that's what I gave her.

I stop outside her hotel-room door, my suitcase dragging behind me. I think about knocking. But I know what will happen if she answers. She'll change my mind. So instead, I leave the small posy of wild flowers I'd picked when I'd gotten back from the restaurant with Adrienne. Along with my note.

Gone to see P. Good luck with your training.
I hope it's worth it.

A short flight, train and taxi journey later, and I'm at Pete's door. Thankfully, my surprise works. I grin at his open-mouthed shock at seeing me, toast crumbs round his mouth from breakfast. He picks me up and twirls me round. We kiss, and I forget about everything – everyone – I've left behind in Ibiza. Any second thoughts I had about this plan are swept away, replaced only with lust.

I've timed it exceedingly well. Ethan is with his grand-parents, so we can spend the rest of the day together in bed. He cooks me dinner and even forgoes his evening training run for me – he has no idea how sexy I find that.

I'm tired of being second place to running, after all.

The next morning, while Pete's in the shower, I head downstairs to make coffee. My suitcase is still in the hall, where I'd abandoned it in favour of our kiss. I dig my phone out of my bag, turning it off airplane mode for the first time since I got on the flight in Ibiza. It lights up with missed calls, a voicemail, texts. One from Yasmin is glaring at me: *I need you.*

Guilt gnaws at my stomach, but I squash it down. I'd left a note. Maybe I should have texted her too, but I assumed she'd be too busy training to notice. Obviously not. There's a voicemail from her too. Left in the morning, about the time my plane took off.

At first I don't understand what I'm listening to. It's quiet. Muffled. I'm about to hang up, writing it off as a butt dial. It's not like Yasmin to stay out until six a.m. so maybe she was up early for a run.

Then I hear a sound that sends chills down my spine. A whimper. My fingers grip the phone tight, my knuckles turning white.

Her voice sounds so small. She says my name and it sounds like a prayer. 'Stella. Stella, *s'il te plaît* . . .'

Shit. I should never have left. The voicemail is still run-ning. I listen carefully, trying to hear every word. 'OK, I'm back,' I hear someone say. Another woman. There's a thud, like the phone's been dropped on the floor. It's even harder to hear now. But I recognize that voice. I hear her muttering soothing things to Yasmin, but there's an edge to her voice. An anger. 'Don't tell anyone,' she says. 'Come on. We have to go. The taxi's waiting.'

The message cuts off. What was Adrienne doing putting Yasmin in a taxi?

I call her back immediately, but after a few rings it goes to voicemail. I send her a text, willing her to reply. I check her running app, but no new routes have been added today.

Don't spiral. Everything's fine.

I hear Pete swear loudly from the bedroom. I rush upstairs.

'You OK?' I ask.

He's perched on the edge of his bed, gripping his phone, scrolling with his thumb.

'I'm going to kill him,' he growls.

'What?' I snatch the phone out of his hands, and Pete doesn't protest. He stands up, pacing the room.

'I knew that guy was bad news! I should have told her not to go to that camp.'

My heart pounds in my chest as I stare at the phone. It's a photo of Adri in her racing gear. Her head is down; she's tying her shoe laces. Glenn is standing over her. I know the photo well. I should. I took it. But the image isn't what Pete is angry about. It's the caption underneath.

NOT STAYING QUIET. Last night, I experienced the ultimate betrayal. My coach, a man I trusted without question, attacked me in my hotel room. The police have been notified. He tried to threaten me into silence, but I won't be quiet. He's an abuser. And I won't let him hurt any more women.

269

'Holy crap,' I say, not even meaning to speak out loud. Coach Glenn had always given me the creeps – now this confirms it.

'Right? What is she thinking? She shouldn't be posting.'

'Excuse me?'

'No, no, not like that. Jesus. I mean, because it's a legal thing, right? If what she's saying is true, then –'

'If?'

'Christ, Stella, give me a break. It's a police matter, isn't it? I have to call her.' He takes his phone back. My head is swimming. I need to talk to Yasmin. Was that what she had called me about? Was she trying to get me to help Adrienne? That voicemail must have been left after the attack. Maybe they were together.

I dial her number again, swearing when it doesn't even go to voicemail this time but just rings out. Shit. Is she still in Ibiza?

I'm searching for flights back to that godforsaken island when Pete walks back into the room. He looks ashen.

'Did you get hold of her?'

'Yeah. She's with Spanish police.'

'Did you tell her about us?'

'God no. Not the right time.'

'Did she mention if she was with anyone?'

'She didn't say. Look, I've got to go and pick up Ethan, but if you stay, then we can all have breakfast together . . .'

'Sure,' I say. But I don't look up as he heads through the door. Instead, I text Adrienne. *Where is Yasmin?*

It takes a moment for me to get a response. *She's gone home.*

My heart is pounding, but I don't waste another second.

I grab my suitcase from the hallway, glad now that I never unpacked. If I get the next train, I can be in London in a few hours. I listen to Yasmin's voicemail again. How terrified she sounds. And Adrienne's voice – stronger, more authoritative. Then I read Adrienne's social media post. It doesn't make any sense.

The post has gone viral; the ultrarunning community is up-in-arms, dismayed, outraged. Then I see that Glenn has posted a response on his own page. White font on a black background. He firmly denies all the allegations and is cooperating with Spanish police. He signs off with *THE TRUTH WILL COME OUT.*

It's so messy. Complicated. But I have only one goal in mind: finding Yasmin.

My hope is she has nothing to do with this. My fear is that she's at the very heart.

When I arrive at her flat, I call her name but she doesn't answer.

She's been here, though. Recently. There's an envelope addressed to me sitting on the kitchen counter. I stare at it like it's radioactive. I don't want to open it. I barely want to touch it.

It's heavier than I expect. I take a deep breath, then I rip open the seal. Inside, I find her training journal. Pages and pages of notes documenting her runs. Not the boring metrics, like her distances, pace and heart rate. But beautiful evocative descriptions of the trails – what she saw, how each step made her feel. It's her essence distilled on to the page. Some of it is soaring, other sections more mundane – and then there are parts that I know were for her eyes only. Her private diary. Her innermost thoughts and feelings. The kind of emotions she felt about running that Glenn tried to coach out of her. The elation and the heartbreak. He wanted her to bury all of that and focus on the technique. And when it didn't work, he decided to destroy it another way.

It had started before that night. On the very first night of the training camp. What I'd mistaken for her pushing me away – her hyperfocus on training – had been her retreating from the reality of what Glenn was doing to her.

She wrote about feeling groggy and disoriented after her sessions. How her body never felt right. How she'd wake up the next morning, unable to remember the evening before. She'd find bruises on her limbs and feel sick to her stomach but not know why. She thought it might be a reaction to the recovery drinks Glenn was giving her.

I'm not going to drink it tonight. That's what she'd written the night after I left. The night I'd been living it up with Pete.

She'd emptied it out so he wouldn't know. She thought that would disappoint him. The reality was so much worse. He'd crept into her room in the middle of the night – except this time she was wide awake. He forced himself on her.

She'd screamed. Fought. When he realized she wasn't under the influence of whatever he'd put in her drinks, he begged for her silence with promises of making her a star. When that didn't work, he threatened her with violence and slander. Her word against his. A nobody athlete against a powerful coach to legendary stars.

She must have been so terrified. When I think of how much she must have needed me . . .

I'd left her to fend for herself. With no one to protect her. No one – except Adri. I thought she had gone too. But somehow she'd been there.

The journal entries stop.

It's at that moment that I know I'm too late.

I don't know why, but my first call is to Boones. I tell him everything. I don't know what I expect him to do – certainly not comfort me. It's not in his DNA.

But he comes to her funeral and sits with me as we lay her to rest.

I hold on to that.

I ignore the endless missed calls I have from Pete. I can't bring myself to talk to him, even when I return to the UK to pack Yasmin's things. I'd gone to him, rather than staying with her. The guilt of that will eat at me for the rest of my life.

I ignore all the calls from Adrienne too. I've seen what she's going through online. The fallout from the lie she told – or maybe, more accurately, from the truth she tried to reveal. I know Yasmin's journal would exonerate her. But I'm too angry – with myself, with her, with the world – to care about alleviating her pain.

I have enough of my own now to last a lifetime.

39
Stella

When I finish telling Pete what happened in Ibiza, he leans forward, grabbing my hand.

'I am so sorry, Stella. I had no idea.'

'I know you didn't. After Yasmin died – I didn't want her associated with that man. Her name brought up in the same breath as his. I couldn't tell you, because that would mean it all coming out. That's why I just left.'

'I can't even imagine what you must have been going through. If I had known, I would have . . .' His voice trails off.

I give him a sad smile. 'You would have what? There was nothing you could have done to fix this, Pete. No action to take. Glenn was a monster. But then Glenn died too, and there was no one left to blame but myself.'

'I would have been there for you.'

'I know. Honestly, I really do. And you waited for me. After the way I ghosted you, I assumed you'd never want to see me again.'

'Stella, your sister died. Of course I was going to give you whatever space you needed. It doesn't matter anyway. We're together now.' He lifts my hand to his mouth, kissing my fingers. The he pulls away and sighs. 'So Glenn *was* a predator. Only not to Adri.'

'Yup.'

He frowns. I know what he wants to ask. Why didn't I come to her defence? But he's too afraid of upsetting me.

I take a deep breath, but I can't calm my racing heart. There's another secret that I'm keeping from Pete. Keeping from everyone. If Matthew is hunting his dad's killer, then it isn't Adrienne he's after. Someone else visited Glenn that day, and there's a chance Matthew has found out who.

We need to get to Boones. And fast.

A huge sandstone cliff looms above us. We must be getting close now to the starting point on the map; our eyes are peeled for tyre tracks in the sand.

'The cliff is useful for us,' says Ali. 'It cuts off at least one direction for a car.'

'Good. We're going to need a miracle to find him in the desert,' I say.

'Stellz.' Pete's voice is tight. He taps Ali's shoulder and points at something in front of us, at the bottom of the cliff. A car. Boones's vehicle?

I barely wait for the Jeep to slow before I open the door and run. Pete tries to stop me. He's saying something, but the ringing in my ears blocks it all out. He's freaking out, but I feel calm. Like part of me expected this.

Because I've spotted my dad.

He's slumped at the base of the rock, his head lolling against his chest. Blood splatters the cliff wall behind him, covers his face and drips down his neck, a dried-out pool of it in the sand.

'Dad!' I drop to my knees beside him. I reach out, holding two fingers to his neck.

He groans. He's still alive. But for how long . . . ?

275

'Hang on, we've got you.' I scan the rest of his body. There's a gaping wound at his shoulder, which he's managed to put some sort of pressure on. I gently remove the bloodied strips of shirt he's stuffed against it, then gasp.

It's a bullet wound.

He's been shot.

40

Adrienne

I'm not hallucinating; Mariam sees the person lingering on the horizon too. But if she feels the same fear that I do, she doesn't show it. She stoically carries on running, putting one foot in front of the other, and forces me to follow. I think I spot a bit of tension in her shoulders, a tightening of her running style. But that could be more to do with how far we've run already. I'm sure she's experiencing the same aches and pains that I am, enough to make anyone stiff with discomfort. Of course she wouldn't have the same anxieties as me. She didn't do anything wrong.

She isn't a liar.

And certainly no one thinks she is a murderer.

I match her stride for stride. What else is there to do?

At the fifth water cache, in the pitch black, we stop. We have no choice. At least there will be advance warning of his approach. I'm constantly looking over my shoulder, watching for the bobbing of a head torch. Even runner 501 won't be able to run in the dark without a light.

I am also ravenous, the miles and the fear eating a hole in my insides. The water in my bottles is lukewarm from being out in the sun all day, so I pour some freeze-dried macaroni cheese into my mug and submerge it with water. I wait for it to absorb. In the meantime, I chew on one of the granola bars, although my mouth is so dry, it seems to expend just as much energy to eat one as it does to run. I swap to a gel, allowing the viscous, vaguely raspberry-flavoured goo to melt on my tongue.

I have some chunks of Parmesan cheese and dried sausage, which I cut up into the mac and cheese with my tiny knife. Mariam has a packet of ramen noodles, which she mixes with her warm bottled water and shovels into her mouth with gusto.

My meal is not so palatable. The freeze-dried pasta is still rock hard in places, cracking against my teeth. The cheese is mostly powder and the sausage chunks stick in the back of my throat. The only tasty thing is the odd chunk of Parmesan, but it's so pungent and salty I clamp down so as not to throw the whole concoction up. I need every calorie I can. I close my eyes, force myself to breathe and swallow. Then I take another bite.

Thankfully my body seems to get used to it. I'm able to slow down, enjoy the mouthfuls a bit more. I sense fatigue catching up with me, sleep tugging at the edge of my consciousness. Sometimes I think it has actually taken over parts of me, because all of a sudden I'll realize that my mouth has stopped moving and I've just been slack-jawed and dead-eyed, unchewed food pooling on my tongue. Then I snap out of it and remember I'm supposed to be eating.

Not good, not good at all. We hadn't planned on sleeping at this cache, but I think I'm going to have to get at least a few minutes. Give my brain cells a chance to reboot. Otherwise I'm going to risk serious injury or a mental lapse.

'Mariam, I think I have to sleep.'

She stares down into her half-empty bowl. 'How long?'

'A few minutes. Twenty?'

'I'll be on the move in fifteen.'

I nod. Fifteen minutes is better than nothing. I don't need an alarm; I've trained for this kind of catnap. I lay back, using my backpack as a pillow, and shut my eyes.

My body gives in immediately.

Yet it feels like only a second later that I snap awake. Mariam is still there. I feel remarkably refreshed and jump up to my feet raring to go. I'm amazed that my body has retained the ability to operate on micro-sleeps, my internal alarm still able to go off without fail.

She gestures with her head into the darkness, turning her head torch off. I wait a few seconds for my eyes to adjust, then scan the direction she's looking in. At first I don't see anything. But then I spot the tiniest flicker of artificial light, still some way behind us.

They're still coming.

I shiver. We pack everything up as quickly as we can, confirming our bearings and double-checking the batteries in our head torches. I shed my down jacket layer, despite the surprising coolness of the night. It won't be long until I warm up. I prefer starting cold, knowing my body heat will rise rapidly. With a nod to each other we start running, only turning our lights on again when we're facing forward.

It's so dark, so quiet. The sky is an ocean of stars, pinpricks of light made even brighter by the lack of moon. We don't talk. We don't even look at each other. I keep my focus on my stride, on the small patch of ground illuminated by light. We've got to stay vigilant, watching out for scuttling creatures, cracks in the earth or loose rocks underfoot. At gone four a.m., over twenty-four hours into the stage, I run straight into a thorn bush. Blood seeps into my socks but I keep on running.

There's a silent agreement between us, an urgency that's building.

We need as many miles between us and him as possible.

Slowing down is not an option.

41

Stella

My brain is screaming. Or am I screaming out loud? I can't tell any more.

My dad has been shot.

I'm too late – again.

This can't be happening.

'We've got to get him back to the bivouac,' says Pete. Always a man of action.

But I need answers. 'Who did this to you?'

Boones doesn't reply. He starts shaking, his whole body wracked with convulsions.

Pete places his hand on my shoulder, pushing me back. Then he and Ali take my place, picking Boones up to place him in the back of the Jeep.

While they move him, I rush to the car. 'Pete, his bag is gone. All his stuff.' Now I feel panic rising. 'His laptop's not here.'

'Stella, we need to get him to the medics –'

'Whoever it was took the only way to track the runners. That means Matthew has it. And he has a gun.'

I keep waiting for the sadness to hit me. Fear for my dad's life. But all I feel is wired.

Matthew needs to be stopped.

He can't get away with this.

'Why didn't he take the car?' Pete asks. I've been

wondering the same thing. But the keys are nowhere to be seen. I wonder if Dad tossed them. It was the one thing he might be able to do to give the runners a chance.

But Matthew has the laptop connected to the GPS tracking beacons. We have nothing but Alex's map and the enormity of the Sahara Desert to search. We only have limited amounts of fuel. Our hands are completely tied. All I can do is hope that Adrienne manages to stay one step ahead of him. He still only has his feet to get to her.

If anyone can outrun a killer – it's Adri.

But she doesn't know there's a killer to run from.

Pete calls my name and I walk over to the Jeep in a daze. They lie Boones across my lap in the rear seats and give him water. Then Pete gets in the passenger seat and Ali drives.

There is total silence in the vehicle on the return to the bivouac. Pete keeps glancing over his shoulder at me, and I don't know what to say. There's too much at stake, and we both feel so helpless.

'It's the jebel,' says Pete, once the bivouac comes into view. He's been staring at the map. 'If we have any chance of finding her, we've got to get to the base of Jebel Tilelli. We know she'll be crossing it at some point.'

'We will refuel, then head out again,' says Ali.

I glance outside, not daring to take my eyes off Boones for long. I don't recognize our surroundings. 'Have they moved the bivouac?' I ask.

'Yes, Rachid has sent me the new coordinates. It won't take long.' Ali pauses, then catches my eye in the rear-view mirror. 'I am so very sorry, sister. I hope your father is OK.'

282

'He's still breathing,' I say. He looks on the brink of death. If we had delayed any longer, or made a different decision about where to go . . . I feel my throat start to close, the terror of it choking me. I squeeze his hand, leaning down so close that the edge of his moustache tickles my cheek.

'Is this what you meant by your ultimate race?' I whisper.

I mull that for a moment. All the surviving players from 'The Glenn Affair' have been brought to the desert. Dad lured me here. Invited Adrienne. Invited Jason. Who's to say he didn't somehow get Matthew here too, not knowing he was inviting his own attacker? Was he thinking that we would, what, Battle Royale it out in the desert?

I wouldn't put it past him. It makes me chuckle. Pete looks over at me in alarm, but soon I'm full-on laughing. It's not an appropriate reaction. But fuck it. I'm beyond appropriate.

Bravo, Dad. You're certainly making this Ampersand race one to remember.

My laughter dies as Boones groans, his eyes fluttering open. He's disoriented, scared. I've never seen him like this. So vulnerable. It's shocking to me.

I grab his hand. 'It's OK, Dad. We're almost there.'

He squeezes my fingers back, which I take as a good sign. But then the squeeze turns into a vice grip, and he yanks me close.

'He's gone too far,' he croaks. He licks his lips, his voice as dry as the Sahara. 'I tried to tell him to stop. But he wouldn't listen.'

'Who, Dad? Matthew?'

The car jolts as a wheel crunches against a rock, and I see the pain shoot through my father's body, enough to make him pass out.

It's already getting dark again by the time we reach the new bivouac. It's impossible to believe we've spent a full day out in the desert, and I know Boones doesn't have much time.

In the medical tent Emilio takes over. Boones is taken to the private treatment room to try to keep the news of what has happened to him under wraps. Henry looks floored. But he doesn't want to tell the fun runners, who are still out on the course. 'I don't want to incite panic,' he says. 'What a nightmare.'

'The police – any update?'

'I spoke to Camille, the Hot & Sandy liaison in Ouarzazate. Apparently, they will be here in the morning. They've been caught up with Nabil's autopsy. So much red tape. It's been a disaster. Boones is so slippery; he's ruined everything.'

I wait for him to realize who he's talking to. It does take him a moment. Then he slaps his own forehead with the heel of his hand. 'Oh God, Stella! I am so sorry. I mean, of course I'm praying for his full recovery. If there's anything I or Blixt can do. Anything at all . . .'

'We need the helicopter,' I say without hesitation.

'At first light it's yours. The pilot won't fly at night – it's far too dangerous.'

'You really have no way of tracking where the elite runners are? There's no backup for Boones's laptop?'

Henry blanches, shaking his head. 'We didn't think.

Boones controlled all aspects of the elites' race. He worked directly with the Berbers.'

'So they're the ones who helped him set the route? Maybe one of them knows which way to go?'

'Trust me, I've already asked them. They don't know anything.'

Pete touches my wrist. 'Maybe we should get some sleep? It's been almost two days since either of us rested.'

'Excuse me, but a few hours ago you were out of your mind with worry! Now you think we should sleep?' I turn on him. 'If Adrienne were here instead, I guarantee she wouldn't rest until you were found. I might hate her but at least I respect her.'

He reels back like I've slapped him. 'You hate her?'

I press my lips together. I'm not ready for this all to come out. Yet it will do if we don't find Matthew. *Damn you, Dad.*

It might not be Battle Royale. But if I tell Pete the truth, I can guarantee our relationship will not survive. My chance at happiness, for the family I always wanted, gone. I lightly touch my fingertips to my stomach. Then I look up at him.

'I hate her for being there when I wasn't. I hate her for trying to get justice – even if she failed – while I stayed quiet. But, Pete, there's someone out there with a gun. My dad is almost dead because of him. If we don't do everything in our power to try and stop him, we're going to regret it.'

He nods. 'Stella, you said it. Your father is almost dead. But he's not yet. He's in there, recovering. He needs you right now. There's nothing we can do until morning. Go and be with him. Maybe he will wake up again and give you a clue about where they are.'

I search his face. His eyes. I know it's breaking his heart to be still, to not be out there searching. But he's also making sense. We have to wait.

And in the morning the chase will be on.

42

Adrienne

The first rays of sun catch me by surprise. I sense the warmth first, like steam off a hot bath. Gradually, more shapes emerge on the horizon, into the lavender-hued morning. Soon I'm able to turn my head torch off. We've steadily climbed through the night, and I can see that not too far to our left is a steep drop down to a valley floor. It makes my stomach turn to think we've been running next to that in the dark without realizing. If one of us had drifted from our bearing, we could have had a nasty fall.

Never mind worrying about a man coming after me. I have to worry about not hurting myself.

We will be running down into the valley soon, and I only hope that the path is not too difficult. Mariam runs to the edge of the cliff, stopping for a moment to survey the scene.

'Look,' she says, her voice as hoarse as mine feels.

Once again, the desert has some surprises for us. We can see two runners up ahead, down on the valley floor. The distance is likely miles, but from up here they look close. Catchable.

We're well over halfway now. I suppose soon the remaining elite runners will begin to converge.

'We can get there,' says Mariam, echoing my thoughts.

'And what's that?' She squints, trying to compare the topography in front of us to the map in her hand. Buildings – or the ruins of them anyway, stone structures with roofs crumbling and cracked. An abandoned village? 'We pass quite close to these,' Mariam says, tracing her finger on the map.

I nod. 'Ready?'

She hesitates, looking out into the distance. There's something else there. Far on the horizon. Just a smudge. A place where the line between earth and sky seems slightly blurry, like the artist has rubbed a thumb against the canvas, smearing it. It seems to vibrate, but that could be my vision.

Eventually, she continues jogging. What else can we do? We can only keep moving.

A little further and we find the path down into the valley. It starts with switchbacks, easing our way down the steep cliff. But as the path turns to smooth sand, I try something different. I take a direct line, straight down, almost bouncing off it like a trampoline. My feet slip and slide – but before I fall, I take a leap on to the next patch, gravity working in my favour. The faster I go, the less likely I am to fall – but the harder a potential fall would be. Still, I trust in my feet, throwing my arms out for balance.

I don't dare glance back, but I sense Mariam has followed me. Good, because if she hadn't, I would have put a lot of distance between us. This is much quicker than the more cautious way down. My legs move faster than my conscious mind can process. So I don't try to process. I just let it happen.

I reach the bottom of the valley floor unscathed and

I double-check the bearing – we've come out at the right place. If it was a different sort of race – and we hadn't already run almost a hundred miles – I'd have turned round and high-fived Mariam. But we're already too broken for that. All our energy is channelled towards staying on our feet.

At least it was.

I hear a sound that resonates through me, stinging me as if I've been whipped. A thud, followed by a strangled cry and a sickening crack. At first, selfishly, unbelievably, I feel a spike of gratitude so sharp it almost makes me throw up: that it isn't me, that my limbs are all intact, that I'm still on my feet. Are they? I force myself to do a physical check to be sure. Once, in the middle of the South Downs 100 in the pouring rain, I'd fallen on my face, sliding in the mud, but in my mind I was still running. It took a few seconds for my brain to catch up with the reality. The mud had cushioned the fall, so I hadn't injured anything too badly – only broken my finger it turned out – and I had continued the race. According to the spectators, I'd run into the next checkpoint looking like the creature from the Black Lagoon.

I snap back to the present, spinning round. Mariam is on the ground, her hands wrapped round her ankle, her face screwed up in pain.

'Oh my God.' I kneel next to her. 'What happened?' I lift her backpack where it's twisted round her, and I prop her against it like a cushion. She's trembling. 'Let me take a look.'

I gently prise her fingers from round her ankle, all the while muttering soothing nonsense phrases. 'It's going to be OK, don't worry, I've got you.' Banality is better than panic.

Her foot is wrenched at an awkward angle, and her ankle is beginning to swell. Based on the loudness of the crack, I suspect a break. This is bad. 'OK, Mariam, it looks like you've hurt your ankle.'

She mutters something back, which I imagine is the Arabic version of 'No shit, Sherlock'. She glances over her shoulder, her eyes scanning the offending slope. She must catch the look of guilt on my face, because she shakes her head. 'I chose that way.' She winces in pain, hissing through her teeth.

'I'm activating your emergency beacon, OK?' I depress the two buttons on her shoulder. A red light starts flashing and I hope it won't take too long for help to find us.

It strikes me that our race is now over. Just like that. The prize money. The promised answers. Proving anything to Ethan. Proving anything to myself. It's done.

I wonder if Mariam sees that realization in my expression. 'You go,' she says, swiping me away.

'Enough of that,' I say, sharply. 'I'm not leaving you, no matter what you say, so don't waste energy trying. Now drink this and let me look in your pack. You need painkillers and something to stabilize this ankle.'

My tone convinces her of how serious I am. Or maybe it's what she wants to hear. At any rate she stops protesting, braces herself, and lifts slightly so I can swap her backpack for mine. She takes the bottle of water I hand to her and sips slowly. In addition to the pain, her body will be in shock right now.

I quickly find her first-aid kit, which is shockingly light.

Like me, she's only brought the essentials. I find paracetamol and ibuprofen, so I give those to her first. Something to take the edge off.

'Stupid, so stupid,' she says, as I start to wrap her leg in the sparse remnants of some bandage that I found.

'Don't do that to yourself. It's so easy to lose your footing.' Seeing her in pain, I wish I had chosen the less risky path down. But I take solace in the fact that I know Mariam is just like me. She would have gone for it even if she'd been alone. She's racing too. And she almost made it. It wasn't a lack of skill. Just bad luck.

I look around to see if there's anything I can use to keep Mariam's leg elevated. I stand to move one of the rocks and a gust of wind almost knocks me off my feet. Mariam cries out as I jolt her leg attempting to stabilize myself. 'Sorry!' I exclaim, but it's stolen away by the wind.

It's as strong as the first night of the bivouac.

Another sandstorm.

We exchange a look of panic. I have no idea how long it will take to hit us, but right now we're the most exposed we could be, surrounded by loose sand, rocks and other debris. I think of Jason, being whacked in the head with a rogue tent peg. Anything could happen to us out here. Especially with Mariam injured. I dig out my buff, pulling it over my mouth and nose, then putting my wraparound sunglasses on top, trying to cover as much as possible. I do the same for Mariam, helping her make it comfortable.

I stand up and see what's coming towards us. My stomach drops. It's a wall of dust and wind, approaching like a tsunami. Multitudes bigger than the first night. Tornados of sand – several of them – rise like fingers out of the ground to scrape the sky, heralds of the coming storm. Once the wall hits us, we're going to be completely blind – at the mercy of the wind.

Even the once bright sun has now darkened. The official advice is to stay put and wait for it to pass over. But what if it's like that first night all over again? What if it doesn't last ten minutes but hours?

'It's going to be OK,' I repeat to Mariam, unsure if I'm trying to reassure her or me.

She pulls her bandana down to her chin. 'It's bad, isn't it? Dammit, leave me Adrienne.'

I'm not listening to her. I've had a thought. Those abandoned buildings we saw from the top of the cliff can't be too far away – maybe half a mile.

I lean in close. 'I think we need shelter. If the storm is anything like before, we can't stay exposed. Not with your leg . . .' I drift off.

She shakes her head. 'I don't think I can move.'

'Can you balance on your poles? I will support you.'

She pauses, teetering as the wind buffets our bodies. 'Maybe.' She takes out her telescopic poles, stretching them out to size.

I quickly take a heading for the buildings on my compass, before tucking it in the waistband of my shorts. Accessible in case we need it. In the meantime, Mariam plants one pole firmly into the ground, then wraps her other arm round my neck.

I brace myself so she can use me to push to her feet. She lets out a scream from the base of her belly, a roar to overcome the immense pain. I grip her hand, trying to lend her some of my strength. The first step is more of a hop, her other foot dragging. She grinds her teeth so hard, I can hear it. But we move. I pray that I've made the right decision.

It's a painful shuffle. The storm comes upon us faster than I ever could have imagined, and I feel vindicated in my decision. But it makes moving even harder. Once we stumble, and Mariam cries out in such agony that it brings tears to my eyes. We take extra care, but it means we slow even more.

Mariam grips my hand hard, her nails digging into my skin. I'm struggling to see more than a few feet in front of us through my sunglasses. I focus on following the bearing, and eventually the walls of the building come into view. Weather-beaten and crumbling, broken roof, no door – the desert slowly subsuming the house back into itself – no wonder it was abandoned. Yet any shelter is better than nothing.

I hurry us inside, easing Mariam down so her back is supported by the stone. She leans forward, scrabbling with one hand for a bottle of water. I find it for her, twisting open the cap, tipping some of the liquid into her mouth. 'Thank you,' she says, her voice a croak. The red light on her emergency beacon still pulses. Someone must be coming. Hopefully we'll be easier to find in here than out there.

She looks pale. Clammy. Beads of sweat are forming above her eyebrows. She's warm to touch but shivering, and I fear the shock must really be setting in now that the adrenaline of the move is dying down. I need to find something to cover her, to try to make her more comfortable. I dig my down jacket out of my bag and wrap her up to her neck.

And we're getting uncomfortably close to running out of water.

'I'm going to look around,' I say.

'Be careful.'

'I won't be long.'

She lets out a grunt of frustration as I leave her side. I try to keep my promise to be quick. The storm rages, battering the walls and racing through the empty windows.

There's nothing in this building, but we're close to another. I remember watching a documentary about a man who got lost in the desert and how he had to drink the blood of bats to survive; I seriously hope it doesn't come to that.

I don't stray too far, just in case I can't find my way back. There's nothing. What had I hoped to find, some kind of hidden cache of Coca-Cola? Ridiculous. I stick my head out of the door, trying to see if it's worth running to the next building.

That's when I spot something that gives me pause. A footprint in the sand outside the door. It's clearly defined – a modern running shoe print. It doesn't match mine, a pattern I know intimately. And for it to not be blown away, it has to be fresh.

There's someone else here.

My heart pounds in my ears as I rush back to Mariam.

But someone has beaten me to it.

Runner 501 is kneeling over her slumped form. And in his hands he holds a knife.

43

Stella

The night passes fitfully. Pete, Mac and I set up camp in the administration tent, but I don't sleep much. A couple of hours at most. At four a.m. I've had enough of trying, so I leaf through Jason's notebook, using the documents on his laptop to decode his shorthand, keen to scour for any details that might help us. Jason has a lot of the information but not all of it. I'm not mentioned at all. It's not that surprising; my presence in Ibiza had been a secret, the 'Boones expert' (what a joke that turned out to be) imparting insider knowledge. So he doesn't know Yasmin's connection to me either. That she was my half-sister.

There's more centred around Glenn's death. Jason had been apparently hot on the trail of the story as soon as it had been announced. He'd done more work than the police by the looks of it. Talking to neighbours, gathering CCTV footage, talking to car rental agents, parking attendants – anyone he could think of.

I haven't spoken much to Pete about that time. After we rekindled our relationship, I avoided asking too much about Adrienne and what she had gone through. He was happy to avoid that topic, and so was I. I never expected to fall in love with Pete. Never thought I'd want to get married. Have kids of my own. But Pete showed me how different life could be with a man who could be trusted.

Relied upon. Whether he will still want that life when he finds out what I've hidden from him, I have no idea.

Towards the back of the notebook, a few pages have been torn out. I run my fingers along the edges. Who did this? Jason? One of the volunteers? Curious.

I flip again and something else is circled in red. *BOONESHOUNDS*.

Seeing those words makes me grimace.

'What is it?' asks Pete.

I turn the page round to face him. 'These nutjobs. Boones obsessives.'

'Oh. The superfans?'

'Superfans – that makes them sound benevolent. The guys in that forum are like a cult. They worship my dad and what he's trying to do.' I scan the page. 'Looks like the message boards went a bit mad when Hot & Sandy was announced. All this speculation about whether it's his ultimate race.'

'Damn. Do you think it is?' Pete asks, his eyes wide.

'What the fuck is an ultimate race?' Mac asks, coming over to join us. 'I'm not the Booneshound – that was Jason's domain.'

Pete jumps in to answer. 'There have always been rumours that one day Boones would plan an ultimate race. More than just running. Something that would really put human endurance and capability to the test.'

'And what would that entail?'

'That's the thing – we don't know. It could be anything. Additional obstacles. Maybe a brain task, like code-breaking. Whatever the diabolical mind of Boones could come up with. He's a genius.' He glances at me. 'A horrible father. But an incredible race director.'

I roll my eyes. 'Are you kidding me? He's a man. An ordinary one at that. All he had was an idea for a race in his backyard, which happened to be a big dark forest. It got out of hand from there.'

Pete shrugs, conceding to me. 'No one else could do what he does, that's certain. I don't like the idea of Blixt taking over. The Ampersands shouldn't be corporate.'

'Who would take over then?' Mac asks. He dares a sidelong glance at me, but I wave my hands in front of my face.

'No way. If he dies –' My mouth suddenly feels dry. This is way too real.

'Don't think like that,' says Pete. 'Here's a thing I don't understand, though. Why would Matthew shoot Boones? I thought Adri was the one he wants revenge on.'

My throat tightens. 'My dad was always perceptive. Maybe he was on to him.' I think about what my dad said. *I tried to tell him to stop.*

I should have tried harder.

44

Adrienne

'Stop!' I scream, launching myself forward.

'What?' Matt uses the knife in his hands to slice through the bandage I'd tied round Mariam's ankle, which is now in tatters. 'This is crap. She needs to keep it as compressed as possible.'

'Oh God – I, I saw the knife and . . .'

He frowns, folding the blade into its handle and tucking it back into his backpack. He pulls a roll of bandage from his pocket and rewraps Mariam's ankle with care.

The wind howls through the open roof and I cover my face for a moment to protect it from the blast of sand. When it dies down, I rush to Mariam's side. She's staring at Matt, her eyes watery with pain. I wish I had something stronger to give her.

'I know you,' Mariam says to him.

'Yeah. I'm the one Boones promoted. Some promotion, right? Now I'm stuck here in the middle of a storm.'

Mariam shakes her head. 'No. I know you. You . . . I thought you were in prison.'

Matt's face drains of colour and he snaps his hands away from her ankle as if burned.

'Prison?' I stare at him.

He doesn't deny it, but calmly packs away his things. Then he shifts so he's sitting next to Mariam, leaning back against the stone wall and closing his eyes. Now the edginess I felt is back with a vengeance. I subtly move my body so my hand is on my backpack. It's up to me to keep us safe.

'You don't recognize me, do you?' he asks me, opening his eyes again.

'Should I?' I gaze at his face. That's when it hits me. It's not just the way he runs that is familiar. There's something about his mannerisms and in the amber flecks of his brown eyes, almost a reflection of the desert outside. I've only known one person with eyes like that. 'It's not possible,' I whisper. 'Coach Glenn?'

'It's his son,' says Mariam.

'In the flesh,' he says.

'But . . .'

'But he never told you he had a son? I know. His runners were his children. Forget about the real family he abandoned.'

I still can't believe it. 'So why were you in prison?' I ask, wondering if I even want to know the answer.

He closes his eyes. 'I killed someone.'

I swallow. The casual way he says it sends a shudder down my spine. I've never felt so small.

Matt sees the fear in my eyes and sighs. 'You know what my mama said when your social media post came out? "Finally." *Finally*. As if she had expected it. But my dad was my hero. I couldn't believe it. So when the Spanish police let him go with no charges, I felt vindicated. You had lied. Mama flew into a rage. She couldn't believe he'd got away with it again, and she wouldn't listen to me when I said that the police had no proof. Innocent until proven guilty, right? I couldn't stay in the house with her. I flew back to the UK to be with my dad. I had to tell him I believed him. Except when I showed up at his house, he was already dead. I went out of my mind. I blamed you. I knew you were running in that local race, so I went to the finishing line. I shouted at you. I wanted to hurt you.'

'I heard,' I say, my mouth dry. The anger in his voice is still there, seven years later. 'So then you panicked and stole some guy's car and –'

'Then I went to the pub. Got absolutely bladdered, got aggy with the wrong crowd, punched a guy. Guess I hit him in the wrong place, because he died. One wrong punch and that was it. Got fourteen years for manslaughter.'

Every muscle in my body is still. He's still got the knife in his hand. He's playing with it, opening and closing the blade, like a nervous twitch. I tighten my grip on my backpack.

'Fourteen years. You should still be inside. How did you get out?' Mariam's breathing is heavy, laboured, her voice raspy.

'I served half my sentence, then was released on licence. Broke the conditions by coming to Morocco, of course, and I had to ask some dodgy people for help getting here. But I had to come. God, Dad was obsessed with these races, wasn't he? I mean, you know better than me.'

'I guess . . .'

'He always wanted to coach a winner. You were supposed to be it, Adri. He loved you far more than me.'

I glance down at my watch. We activated Mariam's beacon over an hour ago. It can't be much longer until help arrives. Even with the storm. I need to keep him talking. 'That can't be true.'

'How many times did he mention me then?'

Never. He never mentioned a son. 'Well, we didn't talk much about our personal lives. He was focused on the training . . .'

'And other things,' mutters Mariam.

I glance at Mariam. I catch the edge in her tone. Seems like Matt does too.

Matt jumps on it. 'That. *That.* People worshipped my dad. But then you came out and accused him –' He points at me. 'But he didn't assault you, did he?'

I don't know where to look, what to say. It feels like I've got my foot on a trigger point and that if I say the wrong thing, it all has the potential to explode. But I'm done with lying. 'No, he didn't.'

The air is completely still. 'In fact, he dropped you from his team. So why lie? To get back at him?'

I shake my head. Behind my eyes, I can still hear the sound of her scream. See her distraught face. Feel her tears on my cheek. 'He didn't assault *me.* But he was not innocent,' I say.

'Then tell me: what really happened out there? I've come all this way, run this hard, just to find out. I have to know the truth.' His voice drops to a whisper. 'I have to.'

I think back to that night. Yasmin ended her life because of what happened. My heart is broken all over again. I look into Matt's eyes and I can see that he is searching for answers. I know that feeling.

I take a deep breath. I've never told the whole story. But Matt needs to know who his father was.

'Glenn had been my coach for two years. I'd known about him for a long time – he was local to me. You couldn't be a runner in Yorkshire and *not* know about the Knight Academy, and we'd often train on the same fells. When he asked me to join his roster, it felt like the invitation of a lifetime. And honestly, I trusted him completely. He honed my natural running style and made me a champion. Racing goals I'd thought were out of reach, suddenly became possible. I was standing on more podiums, breaking more records, feeling fitter and stronger than ever. He organized my whole life – my training schedule, my sleep, my nutrition. He even made his own special blends of recovery formula.'

'I remember that! He wanted to market them.'

Mariam shudders.

I catch her eye. She knows. How? But that's a question for later.

'Other runners were begging to join him, but he was so selective. Exclusive even. In the winter he'd station himself at this gorgeous luxury sports hotel in Ibiza and run a training camp. Yet *that* one – the one where it all went wrong – was special. My week there was meant to elevate me to the next level. My goal was the course record of the Yorkshire 100, but Glenn was hyper focused on getting a female runner to win an Ampersand race. It was like the missing trophy on his cabinet. There were five of us – all women – all training with that goal.' I swallow. 'One of the runners was Yasmin El Mehdi. She was nineteen, driven, strong, just absolutely loved running – bursting with raw talent. Her strength was her determination. Nothing could put her off. I noticed

Glenn's extra attention on her, but I didn't think much about it. I didn't think he would act inappropriately. His whole professional reputation was at stake.

'But towards the end of the camp, I knew I wasn't interested in an Ampersand race. He got so angry. I'd never seen him like that before. Told me I'd wasted his time. Called me useless, talentless, nothing without him . . . So you're right: Glenn dropped me – and he was mean about it. But weirdly, I didn't blame him. In his eyes I was quitting and he didn't coach quitters. I was wracked with guilt and shame, begged him to let me stay on. But he refused.

'Then he turned his attention to Yasmin. She was his new golden girl. He'd asked her to stay for private coaching. Everyone else left. Even her sister. I had a bad feeling. Maybe part of me knew something was wrong with him, but I'd never had the guts to admit it to myself. I got to the airport but I couldn't do it. I turned round, went back to the hotel and got my old room back. I stayed out of Glenn's way. I didn't want him to know I was still on the island.

'I spent the whole of the next day berating myself for being paranoid. But the next night, I heard a scream from the room next to mine. I was frantic. At first I thought I'd imagined it. I opened my door, listening. I didn't hear anything more, but I couldn't let it go. I banged on her door until she answered.

'As soon as I saw her, I knew. I wanted to confront Glenn right then and there. But she begged me not to. I told her we should go to the hospital. She didn't want that either. All she wanted was someone to hear her. To listen. She told me what happened: how Glenn had come

303

in in the middle of the night – their rooms had connecting doors. He thought she was passed out – it turns out, he'd been drugging her with his recovery formula. But it had made her feel so nauseous that she hadn't taken it that night. But he raped her anyway.'

I close my eyes, reliving that moment. My body is shaking. 'I wanted to call the police. But she refused. Glenn had threatened her – and taken the spiked bottles with him when he left. I told her that *she* was the evidence, but she didn't want that. She was so afraid. So ashamed. No matter what I said, how I assured her she wouldn't be alone, she refused. All she wanted to do was go home.

'Maybe I could have done more; I could have taken her to the police myself. But she'd already lost so much control. I couldn't take more from her. She just wanted to forget it all and get away. I helped her sort a flight and made sure she got to the airport. By the time I came back, Glenn had gone. He'd checked out in the middle of the night, probably once he heard me go into Yasmin's room.' I sigh.

A curtain had fallen from in front of my eyes that night, and on the other side of it was the truth of who Glenn really was. And I had this awful feeling it wasn't the first time. Other runners had confided in me in the past about nausea, sickness, even weird blackouts in the mornings and pain where there shouldn't be pain. Glenn had attributed it to their female bodies reacting to the extreme, super-intense training he'd put them through, using their own biology against them. Later those women would be dropped from Glenn's roster. He would denigrate them, claiming they didn't have what it takes. But I began to see things differently. Now the wall was down, I realized what had been happening was something far more sinister.

Of course I understood why Yasmin felt she couldn't come forward. The power imbalance between her and Glenn . . . she was too afraid. But the mother inside me had stretched up and roared. I could see the future laid out in front of me – Glenn continuing his camps and assaulting more women. More athletes' lives ruined. I allowed the rage to take hold and got ready to burn everything I'd worked to build. I'd had enough of staying quiet about the things women had to endure just to be in the same space as men. So, like Ethan on the sidelines shouting his outrage at the umpire for a bad call, I did the only thing I felt I could – something so impulsive and stupid and yet, in the moment, so right.

I look up at Matt. 'I couldn't let him get away with it. So I went to the police and I said he'd attacked me. They found him at the ferry port and detained him. I posted on social media to warn other women in his sphere or maybe allow his previous victims to know they weren't alone –'

There's a crash from above us as the wind takes a chunk of the roof and sends it flying into the abyss. I dive over Mariam, sheltering her from the debris. It takes a while for the gust to subside, while Mariam clutches at my arms. She's still shuddering in pain. *Where is the damn medical help?* I want to scream.

'I know why you did it,' she whispers into my ear. 'But without any proof your effort was just wasted.'

'I wanted him to pay,' I say, my voice choking. 'She came to the camp because of me.'

'You couldn't have known what he was doing.'

When it settles, I sit back again.

Matt's eyes are still closed. He shakes his head slowly – but I don't think it's denial. Reality is hitting.

'I never understood why my mother moved us so far away from him,' he said. 'I guess . . . she must have known all along. At least suspected. God. Was it you, then?' Matt's eyes flick to me. 'Did you kill my father?'

I swallow. 'Matt, he died of a heart attack.'

'I don't believe that.'

'I had nothing to do with Glenn's death. The news was as much of a surprise to me as to anyone.'

'But you saw him that day.' He says it calmly.

My stomach clenches. But I quell my initial reaction to say 'no'. No more lying. 'Yes, I did. That morning, as I was packing my bag for the race, I heard that Yasmin had passed away. That broke me all over again. I had to confront him. He had used me – my reputation – to lure Yasmin in. I felt responsible. He had made me complicit in his plans. I had to say my piece. But when I left, he was alive and well.'

Mariam stares at me, looking pale. She's shaking uncontrollably now.

'Your father's death was not my fault,' I repeat to Matt, watching carefully for his reaction. 'Mariam needs help.' I shift my bodyweight towards her.

'Don't move,' he says. He pulls his backpack towards him. 'You know, after the initial checks, they don't bother looking at fun runner packs again. They don't care if we carry extra food or take pills or bring a fucking kitchen sink.'

My breath catches in my throat.

He still wants revenge. That's what Jason's note had said. Now he's got us right where he needs us. He's heard the story. He's got the answers he wants. And we are vulnerable. Weak. With nowhere to go.

He unzips the backpack and puts his hand inside. But what he pulls out is worse than a knife.

He's got a gun.

45

Stella

We look up as Henry runs into the tent. 'Another emergency beacon has gone off.'

Pete leaps to his feet. 'Shit – Adrienne?'

'No, but that woman she often runs with. Mariam. They could be together.'

'Why didn't Emilio come and get us?' I ask Henry.

'After he got Boones off to the hospital, he and Rachid drove straight back out into the desert again. Towards Jebel Tilelli. He wanted to be closer in case of exactly this, another beacon going off – but I insisted he take a radio to let us know.'

'Fuck! It might take us hours to get to them.'

'It's getting lighter now – if you take the helicopter, you might even beat him.'

'Great,' I say.

It takes us minutes to grab our things.

'It might not have anything to do with Matthew,' Pete says, trying to reassure himself more than me. 'Mariam could be pulling out for any number of reasons.'

'Or it could,' I say. I grab Pete's hand, stopping him from leaving the tent. 'Look, there's not going to be much room in the helicopter.'

'Right. Mac can stay behind.'

'No way!' Mac protests.

I wave him off. 'Pete, stay in the bivouac. Coordinate with the police when they get here – show them all this evidence and get them ready to arrest Matthew when we bring him in.'

'Stella, this is insane. There's a mad man with a gun. My ex-wife is out there, Ethan's mother . . .'

'Exactly. That's why you can't go. Ethan needs *both* his parents. You can't take any risks.'

I can see the decision warring on his face. He doesn't like it, but even he can see the logic. He gives me the tiniest, almost imperceptible nod.

I don't know if Mac senses that I would prefer him not to come either, but he's already sprinting to where the helicopter is parked, not giving me a chance to protest. Maybe he has more journalistic instinct than he gives himself credit for. The propeller blades are already in motion, and with a quick glance I see the pilot waving at me, gesturing for me to hurry up.

I duck under the blades and clamber into the seat next to Mac. 'Go, go!' I say to the pilot.

And then we're up in the air.

The door isn't even closed. I'm strapped in but the wind rushes through the helicopter, showing me a view that's both exhilarating and terrifying. Yet quickly I forget about the fear and simply ogle the scale of the bivouac itself, like a tattoo on the skin of the desert. The rolling dunes look almost benign from here, despite the fact I know how menacing they are. Everything bar the sky is in a palette of oranges and browns.

Mac has an iPad on his lap, showing a map of the area; I can see a blue dot on it. 'Are those the coordinates?'

I try to shout, until he points at me to put on a pair of earphones.

Once I do and depress a button I'm able to speak at a normal level so Mac can hear me.

'That where the beacon went off?' I ask

'Yeah!'

'Can I see?' I gesture to take the tablet, but he holds on to it protectively. 'I wanna compare it to the map we got off Alex!' I say. I pull it out of my pocket and unfold it. Mac leans over so that I can see the screen better – still not letting me take control. We try to match the topography of the digital map with the hand-drawn one but it's nearly impossible. It doesn't look to me as though Alex's route intersected with where Mariam's beacon went off. Boones must have sent them off in wildly different directions.

Something that's going to make our jobs even more difficult.

'Holy fuck,' I hear in my ear.

It's not Mac. It's the pilot.

My head jerks up. Those words – and many more like them – are coming at speed out of the pilot's mouth. Not exactly the kind of language you want to hear while in a tin metal box high above the desert.

'Sandstorm,' he says, twisting his head to one side. 'Over there. Moving fast.'

'Didn't that appear on the radar?' I ask.

'These things pop up quickly. We can't fly to those coordinates. I gotta put down.'

'We can't do it here!' I say. 'We're miles from the beacon!'

'No choice.'

'For God's sake, land us!' Mac screams.

The sight of the sandstorm silences any further objections I might have. It's a beast. I think back to the first night, the ferocity we experienced. Like hell I want to be in the air during that. That sand could level a jumbo jet if it was stupid enough to fly in its path.

The pilot agrees. He banks away from the storm, but we can't even fly back to the bivouac. The storm is approaching faster than I could ever imagine. He heads instead towards a flat rocky plain. I think the sunlight winks off something metal there, but I blink and can't find it again. The winds have picked up, chasing us, shaking the body of the chopper. I want to scream in fear but I swallow it down. Keep stoic. The only thing showing my fear are my knuckles, which are white as they grip the edge of my seat.

'OK, everyone, brace, brace! When we land, remove your restraints and leave the helicopter calmly, staying as low as you can until you're out of range of the rotor blades.'

I force myself not to close my eyes but I stare deliberately through the window, trying to focus on the horizon so I don't get the sense of ground rushing towards me. If we can't get to the beacon, then I somehow need to get to the jebel. That's where all the runners will converge.

I see it again – the flashing metal object. Like someone is signalling us.

I can't think about it much more. The helicopter does an almost three-hundred-and-sixty-degree spin that makes me feel ill. My eyes snap shut of their own accord, bile rising in my throat. But then there's a thump as we land on the ground. I wait, holding my breath, but we don't crash or explode. We're safe.

In a split second I'm out of my harness and through the open door. I crouch down until I reach a pile of boulders I can shelter behind.

'Did you see that?' I ask Mac, when he joins me.

'The storm?'

'No – there was someone out there signalling to us. I'm sure of it. Don't the runners have to carry a pocket mirror with them for that purpose?' I'm sure I remember that from Pete's packing list. 'How far are we from the beacon?' I ask Mac.

'Still a few miles. But it's right in the middle of that.'

He points and I follow the direction of his finger. I hadn't realized but we've landed on the edge of a steep drop leading down to a huge crater of dirt and sand. The crater is swirling with the sandstorm – if it wasn't so terrifying, it would be magnificent.

'Jesus.'

'You're telling me. We've got to wait it out.'

'Let's go and see if we can find who signalled us, then,' I say.

Mac shakes his head. 'Are you daft? I'm not leaving the helicopter. What if the storm clears and we can fly again? Or what if it comes this way and we're out in the open?'

I look back out at the massive storm, the wind whipping my hair even here. He's right. Staying with the chopper would be safer. But there's someone else out there. We can't just leave them.

'Fine, you stay here. Do not leave without me. I'm going to see if I can find whoever it was.'

'I don't think you need to.'

'Mac, someone's out there . . .'

'No, I mean, they've found us. Look. Oh shit, I think it's Emilio.' Mac is squinting now, trying to focus.

'What?'

Mac's right. Emilio stumbles towards us, his hand holding a bloody piece of cloth to his head. Mac and I run to his side. He collapses when we reach him, and we prop him up by taking one arm across our shoulders.

'My God! What happened?' I ask.

'Don't . . . know.' He swoons again, teetering on the edge of consciousness. He's got a nasty gash on his temple; I don't know how he made it to us.

'He needs water,' I say to Mac. 'Let's get him to the helicopter.'

The pilot sees us and comes over to help, freeing me to grab water and a small first-aid kit from inside the aircraft. I have so many questions. Where is Rachid? Where is the car?

We prop him up, tipping fresh water into his mouth. The wound on his head is superficial, the blood making it look more alarming than it is.

The doctor seems better now that he's got some fluid in him, colour returning to his face. Now he doesn't look in pain – he looks angry, muttering in what I presume is Italian, before gathering himself. 'We were driving to the beacon but we came across someone on the way. He waved us down and we stopped. When I got out of the car, he jumped me. He had a gun.'

Despite the searing heat, my blood runs cold. 'Runner 501?'

'If it was, he wasn't wearing his bib any more.'

'He doesn't need it. He was never out to win the race. Probably didn't want to be easily identified,' says Mac.

313

'He forced Rachid to drive off,' says Emilio.

'So now he's got a hostage?!' I exclaim.

'And my medical kit. You must have some supplies in the helicopter, right? We have to get to Mariam,' says Emilio, trying to stand up.

I shake my head, and both the pilot and Mac guide Emilio back to seated. 'The storm is still too bad. We have to wait it out. Here, take these.' In the bag I find some painkillers. He pops them dry. 'When the signal is back, we'll send the coordinates to the bivouac and tell them to send as many vehicles as they can spare,' I say.

It's agonizing to wait, but we have no choice. The wind is picking up where we are too, and we're forced to huddle together for protection.

My mind keeps snagging on what Dad said in the car. *He's gone too far.* He's gone too far . . . past what? Boones expected something out of someone, only it's spun out of control.

Is that what's finally happened? Boones has lost control of his own race?

The pilot gets our attention. 'I think we're good to fly,' he says. 'Storm's dying.'

'Great,' says Emilio, wincing. 'Let's get to Mariam. It's been too long already.'

'She's smart,' I say. 'She will have hunkered down somewhere. She would have known we couldn't get to her in that storm. If she had enough wits about her to set off her emergency beacon, she would have known to take shelter.'

'I hope you are right,' says Emilio.

'We should fly him to the biv,' says Mac under his breath to me. 'There won't be room for Mariam in here anyway.'

'Then you can look forward to a long walk back.' Louder, I say, 'Let's get to Mariam.'

We help Emilio into the helicopter, strapping him in – although he seems stronger now. More alert. Once we're all aboard the helicopter, the pilot lifts off.

It doesn't take us long to home in on the emergency beacon. I'm scanning the horizon, trying to see if I can see any sign of life.

'Looks like it's coming from near those buildings,' I say, pointing to a small enclave of abandoned-looking ruins. A smart place to hide out from a storm. I knew Mariam would do it.

Someone emerges from one of the buildings, waving their arms. But it doesn't look anything like Mariam. For one thing it's clearly a man.

'Wait! Don't land!' Mac screams at the pilot, his eyes wide with panic. 'That's the guy with the gun. That's runner 501.'

46

Adrienne

Matt turns the gun over in his hands. It has a bright orange barrel. 'I thought this would come in handy. I found it in Boones's trailer when he invited me in. When the storm dies down, we can send a flare to signal our location.'

I let out a long breath. He doesn't want to hurt us. At least not with *that*.

In fact, his voice cracks with emotion. 'I thought by coming here and running in this race, I could do something for my dad. For his memory.'

'You heard Adrienne's story. Your father was a bad man,' says Mariam through her chattering teeth. 'He did it to my friend too. Drugged and assaulted her. We were waiting to gather proof before going public. We almost had enough.'

I blink at Mariam. 'Really?'

'Yes. But no one would listen to us after what you did.'

I ruined everyone's credibility after lying. 'I'm so very sorry,' I say. I turn back to Matt. 'And it must have been hard for you to lose him. But it *was* a heart attack,' I say.

'No, it wasn't,' says Matt. 'Someone murdered him. I don't care what the coroner said. I've spent the past seven years wondering whether he deserved it. I guess now I know that he did.' He drops the gun in the dirt by Mariam's ankle. I let out a scream, but it's swept away by the wind. Matt drops his head into his hands and starts sobbing.

Mariam and I lock eyes over his head. Matt is unstable, volatile – but also in pain.

Cautiously, I reach out and lay my hand on his arm. 'I'm sorry for your loss, Matt,' I say. 'And I'm sorry the truth is what it is.' I pause. 'Can I ask . . . how did you know I'd been to visit him that morning?'

'That podcast guy. Jason. He visited me inside. I guess he's been doing a big story on the case? He showed me a photograph from a neighbour's CCTV. It shows you arriving at my father's house.'

I nod. I had wondered why the police hadn't bothered to ask the neighbours, but I guess they'd been so convinced he'd died of natural causes that they didn't launch a full-scale investigation. 'And I was the only one?'

To my surprise Matt shakes his head. 'No. Someone else visited him that morning. But their car blocked my view of who it was.'

'What kind of car?' I ask.

'One of those massive black SUVs. A Range Rover or something. I asked Jason about it but he couldn't get any details. Apparently it was rented.'

Now my heart is really pounding. The CCTV camera still that Boones had of the car near my son. That had featured a black Range Rover. It can't be a coincidence.

'Jason had all that information?' I scrabble in the bottom of my backpack as I ask the question.

'He didn't think my father's death was natural either. I could never understand how the police could just accept that he had a heart attack. Not when he was so healthy.'

I pull out the paper I'd torn from Jason's notebook and show Matt. 'Is this the licence plate?'

'That's the one. I couldn't forget it.'

The car had been at Glenn's house that day. The same day my son was almost run over by it. Whoever had visited Glenn must also have tried to hurt Ethan. It was all connected.

'And this.' I point to the words that had given me such fear. *STILL WANTS REVENGE*. 'Is this you?'

He nods, but then his head drops into his hands. 'I wanted you to be wrong.'

'I wanted to be wrong too,' I say.

I still can't believe that Glenn's son is sitting in front of me. Why did Glenn never mention him in the months – years – we spent together? And he's obviously an excellent runner.

He lifts his head up. 'It was Jason who told me about Hot & Sandy. That Boones – the man my father was obsessed with – was organizing another race. I knew I had to come, even if it meant breaking the conditions of my licence. For my dad. I had access to a treadmill and I used it every day, running for as long as they would let me. Guess I'll be doing that again once this is over.'

I swallow. 'So you'll be sent back to prison when you return?'

'I don't care. I'll serve it for him. Some justice for Yasmin. I wanted to know. Meeting you both means I've learned more than I ever thought I would. I hated living in this limbo, the question looming over me about whether my dad was a hero or a villain. I have certainty now.'

Mariam reaches up and pulls the young man into her arms. He sobs against her shoulder, as she stoically endures the pain, patting him on the back. Emotions collide inside

318

me as well, my mind pinballing between fear and sadness and the still overwhelming guilt for what happened to Yasmin. But at least I wasn't related to Glenn. Matt was. And he'd put his body – and his mind – through literal hell to find answers.

'I think Boones expected you to come,' says Mariam, as she releases him from her embrace. He collapses back against the wall of the shelter. 'Why else would it be timed so perfectly for your release? He wanted us all here together in his impossible race. Now none of us has a chance at winning.'

'One of us does,' says Matt. He stands up, staring through the doorway. It might just be wishful thinking, but it does seem like the storm is dying down, ever so slightly. He's come so far; he deserves to see it to the end. His last hours of freedom.

But to my surprise he turns to me. 'If you go now, you could do it. I'm done.' Then he reaches up and turns on his own emergency beacon, depressing the two buttons.

'What? No! I can't leave you here,' I say to Mariam, even though she is nodding along to what Matt is saying.

'You can. You must. I'm not alone. And you need to show Boones that he might have made us pawns in his game, but we won't give up.'

'I don't think he wants anyone to win,' says Matt. 'But you should.'

'Go,' Mariam says again. 'Go and win.'

There are a little over eighty miles left – and an enormous jebel to cross. If I keep a good pace, I could be finished with six hours of buffer to make Boones's cut-off.

You just have to finish, and then you'll get answers. If Boones gives me the unblurred photograph, I can find out not only who tried to hurt my son but who killed Glenn too. Maybe that will help Matt rest.

'OK,' I say. I kneel next to Mariam. 'Don't take any risks with your leg. Get to a hospital as soon as you can.'

'I will,' she says.

Matt stares at the ground and I can almost hear the cogs of his mind working. Processing what he's learned. Knowing he'll soon be back in prison. Atoning for his father's sins. I don't know how I would cope in the same situation. Not well. It doesn't feel like justice to me. Another life Glenn has ruined.

I lift my buff back over my face, fixing my sunglasses over the top. The wind is still strong outside, but not as fierce as it was before.

Giving my shoulders one final shake to make sure my backpack is on comfortably, I take my first step. My muscles scream at me; they've stiffened so much during the break and now they threaten not to play ball. But I force myself to take another step, then another. And then I'm back out on the course. Back on the heading for another eighty miles, towards the next water cache, and the next, and so on until . . . the finishing line.

If I ever make it.

But my why has never been so clear. It's for me – but also for Mariam. For Matt. For Yasmin. And for all Glenn's victims who lost their voice when I lied. I know there are more out there.

And by running maybe I can give them a voice.

47

Adrienne

I appear to be in a deep bowl. The sun is high in the sky – according to my watch, it's gone noon and soon we'll be hitting the hottest part of the day.

I say we. There is no 'we'. There's only me.

I've lost track of the miles. One hundred? One hundred and fifty? I stagger from one water cache to the next, sometimes searching for that tiny glow stick for what feels like hours, hallucinating lights that are popping up all over the place, like moles in the ground, disappearing the moment I get close.

People say that running races is good practice for the challenges life throws at you. But I don't agree. A race has a course to follow: a starting line and a finish. Even if that course takes me through the harshest environments on the planet – through snow and ice in Norway, driving rain and bogs in Yorkshire, or the supreme heat and brutal sandstorms of the Sahara Desert – I know that if I put one foot in front of the other, I'm making progress in the right direction.

If there's anything I've learned about life, it's that it's nothing like that. I've spent years ploughing ahead in a direction I thought was the right one, only to have the ground give way beneath my feet. One foot in front of the other? How can you keep going, keep making progress, when at any point you could hit a dead end through no fault of your own? Every step in life is into the unknown.

It's why sometimes I feel like I can't step forward at all.

Paralysis sets in. I get terrified that I'm going to make a wrong move.

It's why the Ampersand races never held any appeal for me. I understand why Boones does it. To emulate life itself. To make each step unpredictable. To just survive one of his races is to win.

So why? Why are they so popular? Why did I agree to do it, when I know that failure is almost a guarantee, and the only inevitability is suffering?

I think after everything I've been through these last seven years, I understand myself better now. And I understand the Ampersand races better too. The joy is in the expectation of failure. If success is a given, it's no longer interesting. It's not about self-flagellation or a masochistic desire to feel pain. It's about putting myself in the arena. About satisfying that little voice inside that asks can you do a little bit more? A sneaking suspicion that if I truly asked myself that question – really tested it – I would find out that I have no limit.

Ha. Me too.

The arrogance.

Whatever limit there is, I've found it. If there's a precipice, I've tumbled off it. I'm so tired I keep falling asleep on my feet. I want to cry. I want to sleep. I want to curl up into a ball and succumb to oblivion.

My muscles no longer protest every step, but instead they feel like they've turned to molasses. I even glance behind me, to see if someone has strapped an anchor to my back that's dragging in the sand. But there's nothing there except my footprints.

I stare ahead. In front of me I no longer see the route. I see an all-encompassing darkness, the mouth of the pain cave yawning open. I have no choice but to hurtle straight into it. 'Hello, my old friend,' it says to me. 'Welcome home.'

The pain cave. A familiar place for any ultrarunner. Pain is a given in this sport, something I've become intimately acquainted with. To run these distances is to learn to accept that it is going to hurt. The metaphor of the cave is apt – it's a dark place, but it's a shelter. It means that I'm alive. It means I'm moving. It means I'm enduring.

Yet this pain cave is anything but comfortable. There's barely any cushioning in there, my brain colliding against the sharp, jagged edges of things I don't know. How far is left? How many more hours until this is over?

I have a choice now. I can keep the cave this bleak, dark place – only marginally better than letting my mind deal with reality. Or I can pick up a paintbrush and apply it to the walls of the cave, fill it with colour and life, make it an enjoyable place to be. I can make this a place of beauty, not despair.

For a time it works. I distract myself, covering the walls with pictures of my favourite things – of Ethan, of the fells, of dips in shallow mountain pools and the scent of heather in the air. I actually feel my body unfurl and relax as I think of the lakes – diving into the refreshing cool water, glistening in the late-summer evening light – or as I picture curling up with a novel in front of my little wood burner.

But the cave doesn't play fair – and lurking deep inside there are also monsters.

Memories I've tried so hard to bury spring to life, playing in front of my eyes.

'You're my star runner,' Coach Glenn says. In front of him I see a steaming plate of battered fish and salty chips. We're in Poole; we've just done a huge training block along the Jurassic Coast, pounding the cliffs and the relentless changes of elevation. He's put me on a programme designed to harden up SAS soldiers. Despite the fact that I run because I love it, he wants to push me. Annoyingly, my body is responding to it. I'm getting better – running faster, with more endurance, and winning races. Coach Glenn knows me better than I know myself.

I reach out to grab a chip off his plate, but he bats my hand away. Instead, it's a pre-prepared meal out of a Tupperware for me – quinoa and butternut squash providing a surge of carbohydrates, grilled turkey for protein, Greek yoghurt for fat. Every micro- and macronutrient has been calculated to give my body the optimum opportunity for recovery and growth.

But sometimes a girl just wants a chip, you know?

Coach pops one in his mouth and chews, grinning. He knows exactly what he's doing. It's not only the physical side he trains. It's the mental resilience. Sometimes that means putting up with his taunts, dealing with emotions like jealousy and resentment, learning how to channel that into motivation for a better, stronger run.

For some reason now, out in the desert, I can taste that mouthful of grains and cold squash. It makes my stomach queasy. But actually, it's not because of the thought of food. It's because of the memory of what he says next.

'Have you heard of any other prominent young runners coming up in the circuit?' he asks, his tone light. Nonchalant. 'I'm going to hold one of my special Boones training camps again. I don't want another year to go by without an Ampersand race win.'

It's never been enough for him that I win other races – the Yorkshire 100 is my target and he knows it – not an Ampersand race. But he's obsessed with them. He wants to see a woman finish one – maybe even win one.

'There is someone,' I say. 'She ran with me for a time at UTMB. I don't think she has a coach, but she's got a lot of talent and grit. She was telling me about the backyard races she designed for herself. She would've easily made the podium but she bonked a few miles out. Get her nutrition sorted and she'll be flying.'

'What's her name? I'll reach out.'

'Yasmin El Mehdi. I think you'll like her spirit.'

How right I was. And how angry I am that I was the one to lead that bright, beautiful spirit into the lair of an abuser.

I recruited her. It was because of me.

I think back to what Mariam said. *You couldn't have known*. Couldn't I? There had been shades of inappropriate behaviour with me – orange flags, not bright red. The odd touch. A brush of the hand. Lingering looks. But he'd never made a move, never done anything I could really call out or question. Even after Pete and I broke up, he kept a professional distance.

But he obviously hadn't from others. What made me different?

I know now. He needed me. He needed someone the girls would trust to vouch for him. My success was what had sheltered me in this instance.

I'd put Yasmin – and who knows how many others – into Glenn's path.

My body finally quits moving and I drop my hands to my knees, retching into the sand. A drip of saliva oozes from my lips and I spit it out. I close my eyes, pressing my fingers into my eye sockets.

I have to continue. I have to.

I open my eyes again and jerk backwards. Fuck. There's a snake on the ground in front of me. But this one isn't camouflaged with the sand like the other. It's got slick black scales, like polished onyx, curled around like a letter S. I stay stock-still, panic gripping me by the throat. But then it does something I *really* don't expect. It rises up, neck flaring – a cobra. It opens its mouth, its long forked tongue flicking out at me. 'Liar,' it says.

'No!' I reply. I keep running, but the snake matches my pace, so much better adapted to the sand than I am. It seems to slip along the surface, skimming along it like a stone.

'Murderer,' it says.

I blink, shaking my head. 'No, no,' I repeat. 'It wasn't me. I didn't do anything.'

'What about to me?'

When I look back, Yasmin has replaced the snake. Her eyes are bright. She's in running gear, wearing a race number – number thirteen, just like me.

'Not so lucky for us, huh?' she says, sardonically. 'Boones's pick.' She gestures at the number.

I look down at my belly. The number thirteen looks strange from here. Like a backwards letter B. B for Boones's bitch.

'I tried to help.' I offer her my hand but the apparition flickers as soon as my fingers touch the space she'd been occupying, only for her to reappear on my other side.

'It wasn't enough, I know,' I say.

She runs a few paces ahead of me so effortlessly. By contrast, my steps are heavy, as though my shoes are filled with weights. I try harder to keep up with her.

'And then he died,' she says – or I think she says, but I can't quite get level with her to hear.

'Then he died,' I repeat.

'What an asshole,' she says. It's so clear, so surprising, it makes me burst with laughter. Yasmin smiles.

I look down and check my heading. I've drifted. I get back on it.

'You're keeping me on track,' I say. 'Thank you.'

She's running beside me now, matching me. The wind lifts her hair, even though I don't feel a breath of wind. Her skin shimmers; she's not covered in dirt and grime like I am.

'I am so, so sorry.' The words fall out of me in a blubber. Tears stream down my cheeks. I keep repeating it – but to who? To the ghost? To the world? To myself?

'You know the way,' she says. She disappears then. I spin round, searching for her. Willing her to come back. The desert around me is still just a vast emptiness, my trainers leaving imprints in the sand. I blink. Next to mine is a second set of impressions. A different pattern. She had been there. She'd been running with me all along.

I catch a glimpse of something on the horizon. Or do I? Another mirage? It's a peculiar dust cloud speeding towards me. Another storm – or the wake of a vehicle?

I need to keep moving forward. When I turn round, for the first time I see what's in front of me: the jebel. Jebel Tilelli.

I don't know how many miles passed while I was running next to Yasmin. How far she carried me.

My pace picks up. It's a genuine boost. There's not far to go now, and the main obstacle is in my sights.

Yet after a few steps, I feel certain I'm hallucinating again. I see what looks like a white-painted boulder in the middle of the otherwise muted colour palette of oranges and browns.

It's only as I draw closer that I realize what I'm looking at.

It's a body.

48

Stella

Emilio looks over Mac's shoulder. 'That guy?'

'Yes! That's Matthew Knight. You know, the one who has a bloody gun!'

'But that is not the man who attacked me,' says the doctor.

It takes a moment for that to sink in. Both Mac and I look at him, slack-jawed.

'Land the helicopter,' Emilio says to the pilot, who complies.

'Please!' Matthew shouts. 'I have a woman here who needs help. She has a broken ankle.'

Emilio practically leaps out of the helicopter doors. He is full of energy now. I'm right behind him, but when I see the man, I know that Mac is right. That *is* runner 501. That is Matthew Knight.

He even looks like Glenn. I don't know how I didn't see it before. The same eyes. Same stance.

He gestures for Emilio to follow and takes him inside one of the buildings.

I'm hot on their heels. It could be a trap. But then I see Mariam lying on the ground, her features contorted in agony. Emilio goes straight to her side, examining her ankle, and Matthew is staring down at them both with concern. There's not a trace of anger or revenge in his features. There's exhaustion, worry, fear. But it's not the face of a man who shot my father and is hunting the other runners one by one.

I stare straight at him. 'You're Matthew Knight – Glenn's son.'

He recoils. That's not what he expects to hear. 'Who wants to know?' He's cagey, tentative. 'Aren't you that photographer? Are you a journalist too? I'm not talking to anyone.'

He must know who – what – his father was.

It strikes me how similar we are. Both of us raised by our mothers, taking us away from men who had other appetites. Yet this is also a man who was imprisoned for a violent crime. I can't exactly trust him.

'I'm not a journalist. I knew your father. I am Yasmin El Mehdi's half-sister.'

'So I suppose I need to apologize to you too.'

I frown. 'You're not responsible for what he did.'

He grimaces, then he turns back to Emilio. 'Are you able to help her?'

'We need to get back to the bivouac as quickly as possible. Then I can treat her properly. Can you help me carry her to the helicopter?'

I step aside as they lift her to her feet. She winces, unable to put any weight on her bad leg. It's going to be an uncomfortable heli ride for her.

There's a commotion at the front of the building. Several vehicles have pulled up. Pete emerges from the first one, driven by Ali. He runs towards us.

From the other vehicles emerge half a dozen members of the Sûreté Nationale. They must have been driving like madmen to reach us this soon. They start pointing at Emilio, walking towards him.

'What's going on?' Emilio asks. He's still supporting Mariam, his grip on her tightening.

'It's because of the drugs,' Pete explains. 'The ketamine matched what was found in Nabil's system. We tried to explain that we think you're innocent, but they want to talk to you.' Then he gasps. He points at Matthew. 'That's Runner 501, the one who shot Boones,' he says to the closest officer.

'Boones is hurt?' Matthew says, his eyes wide. Even Mariam whips her head around in alarm. 'No, I didn't do anything like that. I've been running for hours – the last I saw Boones was in the middle of the night two days ago when he put me on a fucking camel and sent me off into the wilderness. I didn't shoot him, I swear.'

'He didn't do it,' I tell Pete. 'We can't let the police take them away.'

Pete pulls his arm away from me. 'What do you mean?'

'The person who shot my dad also attacked Emilio. Stole his car and took Rachid hostage. It wasn't Matthew.'

'You're kidding me. Someone *else* is out there? Someone not Glenn's son? Then why would they be after Adrienne? Where is she anyway?'

'We don't know. But he's still out there, whoever it is. We still need to find her – get her off the course and out of his path.'

As Emilio hesitates in the doorway of the ruined building, his phone beeps. 'That's an emergency beacon,' he says. He locks eyes with me. 'Quick, take it,' he says, as the officers approach. 'Get to whoever it is.'

I grab the phone from his hand and step back to look at it, not wanting to interfere with the authorities. Two paramedics take Mariam, helping her on board the helicopter. The officers surround Emilio and Matthew. I have half an eye on them but another on the phone in my hand. I don't know what to focus on.

I trust that they can explain it all, so I focus on Emilio's phone. It's not password-locked – its only use is to alert for emergency beacons so it needs to be accessible by anyone. I'm guessing it's the same with Boones's laptop. I open the alert system, Pete looking over my shoulder.

'Is that . . . ?'

My eyes widen. 'Adrienne's beacon has gone off.'

'Thank God! At least we have her location now,' says Pete. 'No more fucking about. It's been driving me crazy thinking of her out there.'

'We should tell the police.'

'No,' says Pete. 'Let's get her to safety first.'

I hesitate, but watching Emilio try to reason with the authorities, I can see his point. We leave the ruins, trying to remain both inconspicuous and yet move at a fast pace. Emilio's eyes track me. I give him a small nod. I have no idea if he will interpret that correctly or not, and don't have time to worry about it.

I walk straight over to Ali, but he's been waiting by the car, poised and ready to jump into action. He's as invested in this as we are. I turn the phone round and show him the GPS location.

Some of the officers of the Sûreté Nationale are looking in our direction. I lower my voice and lean in towards Ali. 'Can we go to this location?'

He nods, turning the ignition. With any luck the police will be too distracted by Emilio and Matthew to worry about a few people leaving. They'll assume we're heading back to the bivouac.

They let us go and no one follows. As we drive away, I see the helicopter lift off, Mariam being taken to safety. We drive in tense silence, Pete practically trembling with worry in the back seat. I stare at the phone, at the little dot representing Adrienne.

'The emergency beacon is a good thing, right?' Pete says. 'If she pressed it, it means she's alive.'

We can only hope. I plug Emilio's phone in to charge in the car. It's almost out of battery. These devices aren't designed to operate in this heat. Out here signal is intermittent too. That's why it's such a shock to me when I hear a phone ring.

It's not Emilio's, though. It's Pete's. It takes a second for him to register that fact too, patting at his pockets until he finds it. He almost fumbles it on to the floor but gets a hold of himself.

'Hello?'

I shift in my seat, looking at him expectantly.

'Oh, Henry, hi – what's going on?'

I grind my back teeth together, listening to only one side of the conversation. I watch Pete's face.

He frowns. 'OK. Well. Good to know. No, it doesn't mean anything to me. Hang on, I'll ask.'

He looks up at me. 'Henry says he finished their daily headcount of runners and volunteers, and there's someone missing. He wants us to look out for them.'

'Who is it?'

'Someone called Dale Parker.'

'Dale is missing?' asks Ali.

'Wait, you know him?' Pete asks.

'He's the photographer I was partnered with for the first two days of the race. Hang on, let me show you.'

I take out my camera, scrolling back until I come to the photograph I took of Dale on the first day of the race. Standing atop one of the dunes, looking out at the elite runners.

Pete frowns. 'I know that guy. His name's not Dale Parker, though. That's Steve Parsons.' He takes my camera and zooms in on the man's face. 'But it can't be. He's the runner who went missing at Long & Windy. The Steve Parsons I know is dead.'

49

Adrienne

My heart is in my throat as I approach the body. The man's head is slumped against his chin, his shoulders hunched. I recognize his baseball cap. It's Hiroko. For a moment I fear that he might be dead. But when I get close, I realize that he is fast asleep.

I nudge him. This is not the place to rest. He's completely exposed to the sun and other elements. If there's another storm, he will be vulnerable.

'Hiroko, are you OK?'

There's an indistinguishable moan.

'Do you have water?' I search his backpack and try to dribble some from his bottle into his mouth. 'You can't sleep here. You have to keep moving.'

'Let me sleep,' he says, trying to brush me off. 'Just one more minute.'

I hesitate. This is his run, his choice. But he doesn't look good. I glance at my watch and give him sixty seconds exactly. When he doesn't move, I nudge him again. 'Hiroko? Are you getting up?'

'One minute,' he repeats.

His GPS tag is on the shoulder closest to me, but still I don't press it. If I do, his race is over. Do I really want to do that to another competitor, when he hasn't asked me to?

'Hiroko?' He doesn't respond. He's not going to get up again and run. I make the decision to press the buttons. If he blames me, then I will accept that. I will explain it to the race organizers. I take a deep breath, then turn on his emergency beacon.

Except nothing happens. Unlike Mariam's, which started flashing red almost instantly, this one remains off.

I can't leave him here. It's not safe. No one knows where he is. It might be hours before someone comes looking for him. If his emergency beacon isn't working, maybe his whole GPS tag is wonky?

I imagine myself crossing the finishing line and finding out that Hiroko has been left out here to die. It's unconscionable.

At the same time if I stay with him, I'll lose for certain. I know the rules inside and out, but surely they will understand. In every other race I've done, if a runner stops to aid another, they don't get penalized. Especially in such a remote race. Ultrarunners take care of each other. It's part of the ethos.

Whether it's part of *Boones's* ethos, I don't know. Will he grant me that grace? But I realize I don't care. A man's life – that's more important than answers. In this moment it's more important than any risk to my own life. This is imminent. Hiroko needs help *now.*

I swing my backpack off, digging around in the bottom of it for my knife. Then I slice through the cable ties securing my GPS tag to my backpack. Now I really feel like I've lost my mind. But I press the buttons on mine and it flashes. I place it in Hiroko's pocket.

I've done all I can. I need to get to the jebel.

Continuing to run feels like a stupid, irresponsible decision. No one can track me. If I get into trouble, I'll be on my own with no way to summon help. But this is how I love to run. On my own. With only myself to rely on. I've got to see if I am capable.

And I won't stop running until I find out.

The path to the jebel winds its way slowly through increasingly rocky ground, the boulders growing larger as I approach the sheer-looking cliff face. There's just a tiny single-track pass that will allow a runner up over the steep sand, a frayed rope dangling down one side to aid struggling climbers.

Once again, I don't touch the rope but use my hands, clambering up the sand itself on all fours. Maybe they'll change my nickname to 'sand goat'. Better to have faith in my own body right now, rather than depend on an external crutch.

I know I'm moving slowly. I can't ask for more from my muscles right now. What's equally tiring is keeping my mind on high alert for danger. My anxiety is heightened, every nerve ending on edge. Even the hairs on the back of my neck seem at attention.

I'm not hallucinating any more. Some food and drink did the job – but I almost wish I could get the visions back so I could talk more with Yasmin. Have the conversations with her that I never got to. In another world – another lifetime – she would be the woman running this race, under the guidance of someone she could truly trust and who would help her achieve her potential. Hot & Sandy seems designed with her in mind. A tribute.

Maybe it was. Stella was her half-sister, making

Boones a relation too. Maybe not by blood, but by familial ties. He could have set this all up in her honour. If he had, I want to win even more. Another 'why' to add to the pile.

When I get past the sand and on to the jebel itself, on the narrow path cut through the middle, I feel overwhelmed by the silence. No other runner's footsteps echo off the high walls. No snap of cameras. I might even take a snake for company at this point. I have nothing left to focus on but how my entire body is quivering with pain. Every joint is swollen, my feet battered inside my shoes, the sores on my back bleeding, my neck and shoulders tense and knotted. Every few steps my head swoons and I have to grab hold of the wall to steady myself. But still I push up, up, up, refusing to stop. I'm walking half hunched over, pressing my hands against my quadriceps with ever step. The pain is fuel. It's temporary. No matter what, in another day, it will all be over. One more sunset. One more sunrise.

It doesn't matter how much I've endured already. All I know is that the end is coming. It will come whether I like it or not. That's the beauty of a race. Time out, injury or a finish are the three paths ahead of me.

I reach the top, the wind howling around my head. I stay low, pulling up my buff so it covers my hair and ears. The ridge feels familiar to the second day. I know I can move quickly here, confident in my ability to handle loose rocks, scree, precipitous drops. I need to stay alert, stay focused. This technical running is my specialty.

I don't see anyone up here. I take a moment to gauge the wind, but then I start running, leaping from rock to

rock, allowing momentum to propel me faster than cau-
tion could.

Only something *does* cause me to lose my footing, a
stone rocking beneath my running shoes. I throw my arms
out to steady myself, then, once I'm safely down on my
bum, I cover my mouth to stifle a scream.

Someone emerges from the other side of the rock, their
face slick with blood. He lurches towards me, his arms
outstretched like a zombie.

Before I can move, he grabs my shoulders. 'Adrienne.
Thank God.' He hugs me.

'Rupert!'

'I've never been so glad to see anyone in my entire life.'

If it wasn't so horrifying I would laugh. Rupert looks
terrible. His eyes are so wide I can see their whites. Apart
from the blood, his hands are streaked with dirt. 'What
happened?'

He pulls me down low, off the route, so we're hidden by
large boulders. 'There's someone out there,' he says.

'What do you mean?' I start to stand, but he yanks
me again.

'He's got a gun,' he whispers, but his teeth chatter
with fear.

'What?'

'It's my fault. It's my fault.'

'Rupert, calm down. Tell me what you know.'

'This is Boones's ultimate race. The race to end all races.
He must have told you something to bring you here, some
reason you're still running despite all the fucked-up shit
that's happened.'

I blink. 'He did. He promised me answers.'

339

Rupert nods. 'Of course yours would be something good. Not like mine. I'm a bad person. And now I'm going to die because of it.'

I stroke his arm. 'You're not a bad person, Rupert. You're a brilliant runner. You're loved by your fans, your peers, your sponsors. I don't think I've heard anyone say a bad word about you. Whatever Boones has said . . .'

'He has the proof. And he'll release it if I don't finish.'

'Proof of what?'

Rupert leans in. His breath reeks from days without brushing. I'm certain mine smells no better. 'That I am a killer.'

50

Adrienne

'You're not making any sense,' I say. I can't believe that of him. Not Rupert. Not ultrarunning's golden boy.

'It was at Long & Windy. There was another runner. Steve. He was right on my tail. Chasing me, chasing me. Normally I'm good at tuning all that out, focusing on my own race. But this guy – he got under my skin. He was brash, liked to chat on the trail – stuff that drives me nuts. He was obsessed by Boones too. Even had a moustache like him.

'We were running almost side by side on these tight switchbacks. It was so windy. God, the sandstorms here are bad, but this was like gale-force gusts knocking us off our feet. I wanted to stop, but I knew if I did, Steve would overtake me on the flatter sections towards the end. So I kept going. Higher and higher.

'I was so tired. He was taunting me. Calling out my name. I turned round to tell him to shut up. I raised my hand – not to hit him; I'd just had enough. I wanted to shake him off. Then the wind hit and . . . bam. He was gone. Off the side, just like that.'

'Rupert, that doesn't sound like it was your fault. It was the wind. You didn't push him. You didn't kill him.'

'I could have tried to grab him, catch him, do *something*. But it all happened so fast. I thought – I don't even know what I thought. I thought I had hallucinated it. Maybe he hadn't been there at all. Maybe he was taking a rest. I convinced myself he was fine and I *carried on running* and I fucking won. I got all this kudos and sponsorship and all these opportunities. But they never even found Steve's body.'

'Oh, Rupert, it's OK.' I keep repeating his name, hoping he'll come back to himself, but he's lost in his story.

'I didn't know that Boones had hidden cameras everywhere along the course. He's got a recording of what happened. It shows me rounding on Steve, raising my hand, then he falls. It shows me *recoiling*, not reaching out to help him. It shows me continuing as if nothing had happened. If he releases it, that's the end of my career. I'll be – well, I'll be you.'

I swallow. 'But the man with the gun?'

'That's the thing,' says Rupert. 'It's Steve.'

For a moment I'm flooded with relief. Rupert is hallucinating. He's so riddled with guilt, he's conjured a ghost – just like how I saw Yasmin running next to me. I can see how much it haunts him.

He's still talking. '*He* is what makes this Boones's ultimate race. Not the promises. But this – sending Steve after us. Finding out how far we'll go with someone chasing us.'

A shiver runs down my spine. It sounds exactly like something Boones would do. But Steve is dead. Isn't he?

I hear metal scraping against rock. A few taps, slow and deliberate. Then a voice is carried on the wind. 'Ruuupert,' it says, dragging out each syllable.

A chill spreads through my body. That voice. There's so much venom in that tone. So much determination.

Rupert hadn't imagined it. There is someone out there.

There's the sound of water spilling, then a crunch of plastic. A bottle flies off the side of the mountain. I watch it arc in the air. Hit the sand.

He's close. So close. He's going to be on me and Rupert at any moment.

I lean back against the boulder, trying to make myself as small as possible.

Then, without warning, Rupert makes a run for it. He darts along the ridge, trying to get away. Steve is quick too. He chases after him.

It's the first time I get a look at who it is – the bald head, the beard that runs along the edge of his chin to give himself a jawline. He's wearing a Hot & Sandy vest like the volunteers.

That's where I recognize him from. He was one of the photographers. But while he looked benign before, just another cameraman lining the route, now I can see the tension in that jaw, bulging veins in his neck. The rippling muscles in his arms. The hard glint in his eye.

Steve stops, sets his stance and raises a gun. A real one. He aims, shoots and Rupert goes down, all in the span of a second.

I stifle a scream with my hands. Steve still doesn't know I'm up here. He doesn't go and check on Rupert but walks back past where I'm hiding, further along the ridge. With any luck he's leaving the jebel.

I wait until I can no longer hear his footsteps. Then I go to Rupert, keeping as low as possible.

He's alive. He's been shot in the leg, and he needs medical attention. Badly.

You're the only one who can do this, Adrienne. You have to try.

I summon up all my courage and sneak another look. Fate – luck, a fucking prayer answered – means Steve is facing the other way. He's not leaving the jebel. He's waiting, checking something on the ground. A laptop? But why?

A tiny pebble shifts beneath my foot, making the smallest tinkling sound. Steve lifts his head and turns round, and I duck. But he sees me, because his feet spin and he leaps from where he is standing into a sprint towards me.

I explode off my mark, my arms pumping.

He didn't expect that. I hear my name leave his mouth like a bolt of thunder.

'Adrienne!' he roars.

He's no longer shocked; he's angry. He launches after me.

But this is my terrain. I'm fast. Even with the miles I've already run these past few days weighing them down, my legs carry me. I don't have time to marvel at what my body is capable of. All I can do is pray that it lasts a little longer.

I don't know if I can risk a glance back, but I need to. There's a tall rock to navigate on the trail, so when my arms are wrapped round it, I look.

I wish I hadn't. He's fast too. But he's not moving now. He's stopped. That means it's coming.

I dart round the rock and launch myself forward. But I feel a change in the air before I hear any sound. A loud bang, then the boulder behind me explodes into shards. Another bang and then comes pain, a cloudburst of it so intense it's like I've been hit by lightning.

All of a sudden, I am flying.

51

Stella

'It looks so much like him,' says Pete, squinting at the photo on my phone. 'He had a moustache before.'

He takes out his phone and searches on Google Images for Steve Parsons. Sure enough, there's an old race photo from his obituary. We compare the two. It really could be him.

'But how is this possible?' Pete asks. 'And what does it mean?'

'Did they find a body?' I ask.

Pete shakes his head.

'So maybe it is him. Whoever it is, we know they're dangerous, and they're armed.' I lean forward to speak to Ali. 'How long until we reach Adrienne?'

'Not long now. You can see the jebel up ahead.'

The jebel looks dark and foreboding from this angle; it's bigger than the one they climbed before.

My phone rings, making me jump. It's Henry. I ask about Mariam first.

'She's en route to Ouarzazate. She's going to be fine. But I have to tell you something. I just received a disturbing email from your father's solicitors. I've forwarded it to you. Let me know what you make of it.'

'Shit, OK. Any sign of Dale?'

'None. The police are crawling all over the bivouac. I

345

have no idea how we're going to run the last day of the fun run.'

'I think your concern needs to be the fucking killer on the loose,' I say, shutting off the phone.

I take a few deep breaths, then open the email. I frown. 'What is it?' asks Pete.

'It's an email from my dad's lawyers, but it's written in all sorts of legalese. Like a contract. An amendment to a contract,' I clarify.

'Knowing Boones, it's going to be watertight. He's surprisingly on top of those things in his other races.'

'It says that in the event no elite athlete finishes the race, the prize money will be automatically transferred to this bank account.' There are a series of numbers: a long international banking address. But there's no name attached to it. Maybe there's no need. My stomach fills with lead. 'I think I know what's happened. Boones's ultimate race.' I grab Pete's hand. If I'm right, this changes everything. 'Run this through with me. If one of the runners finishes, they get five hundred thousand, right?'

'Right . . .' says Pete.

'And this contract says that if *none* of them finish, the money is transferred to someone else. Some mystery person. What if that's what "Dale" is after? If he can stop people from finishing the race . . .'

'Then he'll get the money,' Pete finishes. He's as white as a sheet.

Suddenly, my dad's words make sense. 'Oh my God. He never suspected Dale would go to *these* lengths to stop the runners from finishing. That's what he meant when he said "He's gone too far". He tried to stop Dale, and that's when Dale shot him.'

'He'd do that for half a million dollars? It's a lot of money, but to actually murder people . . . How can it be worth it?' Pete asks.

'I don't know. But it means whoever is in the race is still in danger.'

'If Adrienne's emergency beacon has gone off, that means she's out of contention. Maybe Dale won't need to do anything to her.'

I bite my lip before speaking, considering Pete's point. 'Maybe. But Rupert is still out there. And Hiroko.'

'Of course.' Pete leans back against the headrest, but I can see a sliver of hope has crept in. That maybe Adrienne is no longer caught up in all this.

Ali slows the car as we reach the vicinity of the flashing GPS marker. We all press so close to the glass, our breath leaves marks on it, scanning the horizon for signs of life.

That's when I see it. A slumped figure in a white shirt. I nudge Ali, who sees it too, pulling the car round in that direction.

Pete is out of the vehicle before it's even stopped. He rushes over, dropping down to help Adrienne.

Except, as I see after a few quick steps of my own, it's not Adrienne. It's Hiroko.

He's fast asleep. He looks shrivelled, dried up like a raisin. He hardly compares to the man who had been on the starting line a few days ago. But he has no injuries that we can see. We attempt to revive him with some water.

'I don't understand,' says Pete. 'His beacon isn't even on.'

There's a red light emanating – flashing – from Hiroko's breast pocket. I reach inside and pull out a different emergency beacon. 'Adrienne's,' I say.

Pete groans.

She must have come across Hiroko in this state and left her beacon with him so he would be picked up. That means it can't have been more than an hour ago that she left.

We both look up at the jebel. She's there – somewhere. Untrackable.

'We have to climb,' Pete says.

'It's not safe. We can take the car and make it round to the other side – it will still be faster than following her. She's already got an hour's head start on us. We can meet her when she comes down the other side.'

'My legs are fresh. I can run.'

We hold each other's gaze for a moment. A turning point. There isn't a decision to be made; that's already happened. It's not permission he's asking for.

I hand him Alex's map. 'Follow this,' I say. 'We'll meet you at the bottom here, where they come out for the final push to the finish. I'll wait for you there. Don't do anything stupid.'

'OK,' he says.

I grip his hand. 'Be careful.'

As we're holding hands, a loud bang makes us both duck. I scream.

We look up.

'Fuck, fuck, fuck,' Pete says. And then he's off.

52

Adrienne

I don't know how I manage it, but I land on the trail. Somehow my feet find purchase and my hands clasp the dirt, even though pain is rattling my skull. I glance down and see a rip in my shirt where the bullet has grazed my upper arm. It burns like my arm's been engulfed in fire. The fact that I've been shot at barely registers – the thought is too ludicrous, too outrageous for my brain to comprehend. But I do know that I am alive. My heart is still beating. My lungs are still sucking in air. And that means my work isn't finished yet.

I'm not dead. But I'm not safe either.

I hear another sound, like a series of clicks, then a roar of frustration. In the next second the gun hits the ground beside me – missing me by inches – and pings off the edge of the drop.

Then he's running after me.

I force myself to stand. The trail is barely wide enough for my foot. I realize my only chance for survival is to force him to slow down, so I rely once again on my balance and comfort with exposure to choose a precarious line on the ridge, where the risk of loose stones and unstable ground is much higher. If he wants me, he's going to have to come after me.

I keep my steps as quick and light as possible, bouncing

from rock to rock. He's following me, not even breaking a sweat. He looks experienced on this terrain as well. Sure-footed. Fearless. And there's a determination in his eyes – a desperation – that is terrifying.

I'm desperate too. The trail is nothing but scree now, sliding and crumbling beneath my weight. I drop down on to a lower section of the jebel, thinking I'll be protected from the wind and can perhaps lose him amongst the boulders. My feet keep moving but my eyes are focused on the path ahead, making a hundred micro decisions in a split second about where to place my feet and my good hand. My other arm is limp.

That's why it doesn't take me long to realize I've made a terrible mistake. There is no more trail. There's nowhere for me to go. I edge out along the cliffside, my body cling-ing to the rock, but there's no escape route.

No holds to grip.

No way to drop safely.

And now I can't turn back.

He laughs as he looks at me, splayed like a fly caught in his web. 'What did you think was going to happen?' He starts to head back the other way.

He's going to leave me to my fate.

I can't let him go and finish the job with Rupert. I have to keep him near me. 'Steve, why are you doing this?' I shout.

He hears me and stops, turning his head a quarter of the way back. 'Oh, so you recognize me?'

'Rupert told me who you are. What you've survived. It's amazing.'

'Nothing you can say will change your fate, Adrienne, but I'll take the compliment.'

'Why are you doing this?'

'You haven't figured it out yet? This is part of Boones's plan. I am his ultimate race! It's me! The prize money is mine if none of you finish, just as it should have been mine for Long & Windy.'

My fingers shift along the cliff wall, my toes cramping up. I don't know if I'm going to be able to cling on for much longer. I have to escape. This can't be it. 'What happened?' I ask, trying to keep my tone light. Keep him talking. I need time to figure this out – and it's the one thing I'm rapidly running out of.

But he doesn't respond.

'What, you knew you couldn't beat him so you faked your death?'

That riles him. 'Fucking Rupert. "King of the Ampersands"? What a joke. I was the original Booneshound. I know everything about these damn races. I was prepared for any surprise, any eventuality. I was set to be the first winner of Long & Windy. All of what he has – the fame, the money, the glory, that place in history – they were supposed to be mine. *Would* have been mine. But then I fell. Destroyed my ankle. Got so much metal in my leg now it might as well be bionic.'

'That's awful.'

'I couldn't take the shame of it. No one remembers a DNF, do they? Might as well be dead. Steve Parsons died that day and Dale Parker was born. That's who I became when I eventually crawled out of Alaska.' He slaps his hands together, and the sound resounds like a crack. It makes me jump, dislodging even more of the path (if you can even call it that) beneath my feet.

I readjust by shimmying even closer to the wall and in doing so nudge my arm, which results in another starry explosion of pain.

'Then Boones gave me another chance. He contacted me through the Booneshound forum. Told me it was time for his ultimate race. He needed someone who would be willing to go the distance. Obviously, I jumped at the chance. If I prevented all of you from finishing, then the money would be mine. Not only that, but the Ampersand races would be mine. I'd be the true King of the Ampersands – because I would be the next Boones. I just needed to find a way to pick you off one by one.'

The realization doesn't dawn – it blasts me in the face with its heat and light. 'Nabil . . . that was you?'

His expression falters, the barest flicker of humanity. Maybe I can play on that.

'That wasn't supposed to happen. They were supposed to discover illegal items in his bag, disqualify him like Farouk. I put the sedatives in *your* water. Just enough to knock you out. You weren't supposed to share it.' He shakes his head, then seems to find his nerve again. 'I thought maybe what happened to Jason would be enough to scare you all off. But Boones brought you all back into his plan. And then definitely after Nabil's death – who would keep on running? I even called in to that damn podcast to try and drum up some fear. But stopping wasn't even a consideration for you, was it? So why should I consider it either? After that, you all fell like fucking dominos. Some of you made it easy, of course. Fucked yourselves up or dropped out of your own volition. When he realized I was responsible for Nabil's death, Boones tried to stop me after he set you all off. Told me I'd gone too far. Can you believe that? He's supposed to be this puppetmaster, the mastermind behind the world's toughest ultramarathons. He didn't even have the stomach to see his own plan through to the end. He tried to shoot me! Stupid old man. So I had to shoot him instead. Good thing I got his conditions in writing from a lawyer. It's watertight. I'll blame all the deaths on that ex-con he brought out here and then the prize money and the races will all be mine.' He pauses then, blinking. 'I did it.' His voice is softer. I don't have to strain to hear, though. The wind carries his every word right to me. 'I won.'

He spins on his heels, walks away.

Right then, my foot plants against ground that feels more solid. Enough to give me the boost I need to nip up the way I came – back to the top of the ridge.

I run now. Faster than I've ever run before.

I hear a roar behind me then, something primal and so dark it sends a bolt of terror through me.

He closes the gap between us in a couple of strides. I jump to the next boulder but he snatches at my bullet-grazed arm and the jolt of pain as his fingers press against my wound makes my knees buckle, my weight colliding with the jebel. He has the sleeve of my shirt in his hand, holding me up awkwardly. I kick my legs out, trying to free myself from his grasp.

This is it.

The moment he kills me. I see it in his eyes.

'Wait!' I cry out, half strangled by the neck of my running shirt. My foot lodges between the boulder and the solid rock of the jebel. 'You don't have to do this.'

He grimaces in response, knowing I'm playing games with him. Trying to get him to talk. He's not going to take the bait.

'Of course I do. If I know anything about you, it's that you don't bloody quit.'

The pressure from my leg is enough. The boulder we're standing on begins to move. It slides. He lets go of me to stabilize himself. But I kick harder. Push with all my might. The rock gathers speed, heading towards the cliff edge – the man with it.

Yet I am sliding too.

We're both going down.

It's my feet that save me. My ability to stay up, to keep moving, to *run*.

Momentum is in my favour. I manage to launch myself forward on to more solid rock. I turn round just in time to see his expression. The realization of what is about to happen to him. He tries to run too, out of instinct. But something happens to him – to his ankle. It folds, crumples, his leg collapsing beneath him.

I think I might be hallucinating, but it's as if I see a thousand expressions cross his face in a single moment. Every permutation of anger, disbelief, sorrow and then – at the very last – fear. He reaches out his hand to me.

He looks like a boy then. Helpless. Small. Terrified.

I throw out my hand.

Our fingers brush. But it's too late. The boulder gains momentum and he's dragged down with it, off the edge and down towards the sand.

I scream.

There's a crack as he lands. I wait there, my breath ragged, my eyes shut. Hoping this is all a terrible dream.

But it isn't. It's real. I creep towards the edge, daring to look over, but he's so small from up here. I can't tell if he's moving. But he is hundreds of feet down and his body is bent at an unnatural angle. Even if he is somehow alive, he's not getting back up here in a hurry.

It's over.

I crawl back to Rupert and, willing my trembling hands to work, tear strips off the bottom of my T-shirt, using them to wrap round the wound on his leg. I press the buttons on his emergency beacon. I need to get him down.

My arm is throbbing, but I support him with my other side.

He moans.

'Rupert, it's Adrienne.' I talk to steady him, to steady myself. 'We're not going to die today. It's not our time. We're going to finish this.'

53

Stella

'There! What is that?' I point to the bottom of the jebel. We're speeding along the road as fast as the Jeep can take us.

Ali leans forward, squinting. 'Looks like . . . people? Runners?'

'Holy shit.' I can't say any more.

He parks, the wheels sending up a spray of dust. The moment the car stops I leap out, running towards the two people.

It's Adrienne and Rupert both soaked in blood. I can't tell whose blood is whose. Rupert has cloth wrapped round his leg, so I'm guessing the majority is his, but Adrienne's face is screwed up in pain. As soon as she sees us, she and Rupert collapse to the ground. She rolls to one side, clutching at her arm.

'What happened?' I ask Adrienne.

She looks at me. Her eyes are wild. Ringed with sweat, dirt and blood. Red with exhaustion. 'He had a gun . . .'

'I know. The man who did it. Where is he?' I glance up at the route they came down from the jebel, wondering if Dale will come stalking out of the mountain at any moment.

'Dead,' she says.

My head snaps back to her as she says it. 'Was it Steve Parsons?'

356

She nods.

'Fell.' She spits each word out, one at a time. 'Rupert. Shot.'

Ali catches up with us now. Adrienne still has her backpack on. She sips at her water as Ali and I tend to Rupert, getting him to sit up. His head lolls – how she managed to get him down the mountain, I have no clue.

'This wound doesn't look good. We need to get him back to the bivouac as quickly as possible. Adrienne, you get in the car first and Ali and I will carry him.'

She takes in a bit more water. 'I have to run,' she says, rolling on to her knees, then pushing herself up to stand. Unbelievably, stupidly, she takes a step forward.

'No you can't,' I say. 'You're in no condition. The race is over.'

'It's not,' she bites back. 'I have to finish. Someone has to finish.'

'At least . . . do you have a bandage for your arm?'

She looks down at her sleeve, at the torn fabric that's bloody at the edges. She blinks as if she didn't even realize she was hurt, even though she'd been holding it limply. She lifts the frayed edge and winces as her fingers brush the open wound. 'I was shot too,' she says. 'Or grazed by the bullet, I suppose.'

'Adri . . .' I shake my head. Surely now she has to come to her senses.

Instead, she rips the sleeve clean off, then ties it round her bicep. I reach out to help but she spins away from my hands.

'Myself,' is all I make out, as she pulls the knot tightly with her teeth. When she's done she waits a beat. Then another. Then she nods.

357

Something breaks inside my chest. A box of emotions I'd locked tight. The sight of her – bloody, dirty, covered in dust and sweat and grime and sand, her cheeks stained with tears. 'I'm sorry, Adri. I'm sorry I left Yasmin. I'm sorry I didn't stand up for you. I'm sorry I let you go through all that alone. I . . .'

She shakes her head. 'Don't.' She takes a deep breath and juts out her chin. 'Let me run.'

Pete's going to throw a fit when he finds out I let her go. But I stand back. I've stood in Adrienne's way too many times.

'What is she doing?' Ali asks me.

'She wants to finish.'

'Should we allow that?'

'Do you want to be the one to stop her?'

Ali stares at her. 'But . . .'

'Ultrarunners are a different breed. I've seen people run with broken bones, severe sleep deprivation, people who have gone completely blind with corneal oedema, people peeing blood. Once I saw a runner come into a check-point with a dislocated hip, had the doctor pop it back in, then continued on. If she's got two legs and they're still moving, she's going. Come on, we need to get Rupert to the hospital.'

'And Pete?'

'I'll send him a message. We'll get another car to pick him up.'

Ali nods as I get out my phone. It's Rupert's safety that's key now. We grab Rupert by the arms and help lift him into the car. His body is limp but his eyes flutter open. 'It's OK, Rupert,' I say. 'We've got you.'

But his fingers dig into mine with force that I'm shocked he can possess given his injury. 'What is it?' I ask. 'What's wrong?'

'Steve. He's up there.' Rupert shuts his eyes tight.

I put my hand over his. 'He's gone now. He can't hurt you any more.'

Boones has a lot to answer for. Steve sits right in the centre of this star map that connects us, the constellation of pain. I stare at Adrienne's back, her slow shuffle towards the finish. If there's anything I know about her, it's that if there's a wrong to right, she'll be on the frontline. She's as stubborn as all hell. As strong and fierce as a Saharan sandstorm.

Against the vastness of the desert, she appears like an ant marching to some unknown destination. Like something insignificant and small.

Easy to be confused out here. She is anything but.

54

Adrienne

'Hi, camel.'

I glance over my shoulder. The beast is right behind me, so close I feel some of its spittle on the back of my neck as it shakes its head. The steps it takes are slow. Ponderous. The man leading it along gives me a sympathetic smile.

I am still one step ahead. I just need to keep it that way.

I'm not really running now. I'm doing the Sahara shuffle. My feet are barely picking up off the ground; my arm is a useless lump on my side. The last of my water dried up about half an hour ago when I used it to wash some of the dust – and blood – from my face.

Soon I can get more.

Soon I'll cross the finishing line.

Or maybe this damn camel will catch me, and then my race will really be over.

'Not today,' I say to it. Shuffle, shuffle.

I look up and I think I must be hallucinating again. Not about approaching the finishing line. That, I know, is real. If it isn't, I've truly lost the plot. I've been seeing it for close to an hour. The flags on top of the tents, signifying the bivouac, fluttering in the hot wind. The inflatable pillars of the finishing zone growing ever larger in my line of sight. People – at first just ones and twos, but then larger groups, standing along the route near their vehicles, watching me. Some of them wearing their race numbers. Others in volunteer vests. Most of them staring. One of them points a camera my way, and it takes everything in my power not to flinch.

That part is real.

But I think I'm hallucinating because of the face I see as I make my final approach. Jumping up and down in a bright yellow T-shirt.

Through the ringing in my ears I think I hear cheering. Maybe? I can't turn my head to look; it's too painful. The only movement I can manage is one foot in front of the other. The entrance to the pain cave is a distant landmark – the whole world is pain for me now.

Ethan.

Ethan is there on the other side of the line.

I've probably dreamed him. Conjured the only image in the world that could keep me sane.

I blink and rub my eyes, but he doesn't go away. What's he doing here? There's a flare of fear but it dissipates almost instantly. I don't care. I've dealt with the threat. I'm glad he's here. So glad. But he can't be real.

Can he?

His dad is holding him back, but then Pete kneels and whispers something in Ethan's ear and releases him. He runs towards me, sprinting as fast as he can.

I scoop him up with my good arm, burying my face into his neck. 'Mum!' he says.

It's that word that breaks me. I want to cry and collapse right there, but I haven't crossed the line yet. I kiss his head, bringing him close. For once he lets me without wincing or cringing, like he's three years old again and I am the centre of his universe. He interlaces his fingers with mine and I clutch at them.

'Ready?' I ask him.

'Let's do it!' he says.

And so, hand in hand, we stagger across the finishing line.

55

Stella

I almost can't bear to watch.

My eyes feel shrivelled inside their sockets; I've cried so many tears that I'm wrung out. Spent. But I force myself to stand in the crowd, shoulder to shoulder with Ali, watching Adri and Ethan. Jason and Mac are next to us, the Ultra Bros together again. Jason's got a bandage on his head, and he's leaning on a cane. He looks like he's dressed for a Halloween party.

'You made it,' I'd said when he first arrived.

'Wouldn't miss it even for a hole in my head,' he says, his lips set in a grim line.

Farouk is here too, witnessing Adrienne fulfil her promise.

We're all spectators to history.

Ali touches my arm. 'You OK?'

I nod but turn away from the tender scene. Mother and son embracing. Pete fist-pumping in the background, a fierce look of pride on his face. His parents had been the ones to bring Ethan out to Morocco. Originally they'd planned the trip as a surprise for Pete so Ethan could watch his dad cross the finishing line – but, as it's turned out, he's witnessing something even more important.

I can't quite believe she's done it. No, scratch that. I can believe it. But the feat is so immense it's hard to wrap my mind round it. Two hundred miles in one go – on top of the fifty miles she'd run the two days before. Battling heat, sandstorms and a man with a gun. Helping runners like Mariam and Hiroko – not to mention Rupert. He's in surgery right now. Rachid, who not-Dale had knocked unconscious, is coming round too.

Applause – cheers, whoops, gasps – explode from the crowd round me. She must have crossed the line. When I look back, I can't see her. Henry blocks my view, stepping forward to congratulate her. Pete envelops her and Ethan in a hug.

The first woman to finish a Boones race.

The first person to win Hot & Sandy.

She's been to hell and back. She's passed the true test of human endurance. I can't help but think my dad would be proud.

'Shame her win isn't valid,' says a voice from behind me.

I glance over my shoulder. It's Boones, sitting in a wheel-chair pushed by Emilio. His skin is grey, his moustache limp, but the sparkle in his eyes has returned.

'What are you doing here? Shouldn't you be in the hospital?'

'And miss this? I don't think so.'

'You let him leave?' I direct the question at Emilio.

'You honestly think I – or any of the doctors and nurses in the hospital – could stop him?'

I shake my head. Of course Boones would drag himself from the brink of death to witness first-hand the conclu-sion of his ultimate race. Not even a bullet could keep him away. That was Boones through and through. He had a deeper, more vast pain cave than anyone on the planet. In the dark hidden corners of the cave were the inspiration for his signature twists. This is just one more surprise to add to the list.

'What do you mean about Adrienne?'

'She used her emergency beacon. That's automatic disqualification.'

I stare at him for a few moments, then I throw my head back and laugh. I can't help it. Adri didn't win. No one won.

I think of the contract. Who's the money going to go to now that Steve is dead? Probably no one. Probably exactly what my dad planned. What an asshole.

'So that's really it for the Ampersand races? You're going to leave them to Henry and Blixt to ruin?'

'Unless *you* want them.'

I stiffen. I never wanted that. Never imagined following in his footsteps. But before I can answer, there is another question I have. 'So if Adri didn't officially finish, does that mean you're not going to show her the footage?'

'You mean this footage?' He digs in his shirt pocket, pulling out a memory stick marked with the number thirteen. He seems to offer it to me, but then snatches it away when I reach out. 'The races?'

'I have to think about it.'

The memory stick goes straight back into his pocket. 'Then this stays with me for now.' He slumps forward in his chair, as if all the energy has leeched out of him. I stare at Emilio in alarm.

'We need to get him back to Ouarzazate.' Emilio grips the handles of the wheelchair, spinning it round. 'Can we go, Boones? Do you agree?'

'I had to see the end of my race. I had to see what she was capable of.' Then Boones looks up at Emilio and nods.

'I'll see you in Ouarzazate, Dad. You're not going anywhere yet. Maybe there's still time for you to have another race.'

'Stranger things have happened, my dear. Thank you for being here. It means more to me than I can say.'

His words of affirmation make me feel uncomfortable, and thankfully Emilio wheels him away. Emotion swells up within me like a tide. I feel on the edge of breaking down, of dropping to my knees and collapsing into a flood of tears. But somehow I remain upright.

'Jesus. This is going to make one hell of a podcast,' says Mac.

Then a commotion comes our way, catching our attention. The crowd divides, revealing a single figure. I frown. It's Adri, staggering towards us.

Towards me.

I jut my chin out. I want to hide, but she doesn't need to know that. Her eyes are fixed on mine, boring into me. I blink, and in that moment it's like I see Yasmin walking towards me instead, though they couldn't be more different in height or build or colouring.

'Atalanta,' I whisper. My hand reaches for my lens.

But she reaches me first.

'Boones promised me answers if I finished.'

'He's going to the hospital,' I say. 'You can convince him later.'

'I know,' she replies. 'But I think you have them.'

56

Adrienne

It's the only thing my mind can think of. I've done it –
through delirium and pain, through literal hell and back,
I've made it. I've crossed his finishing line. I deserve those
answers and I want them now.

Stella shakes her head.

She's really going to deny me now? She's saying something, but I'm not taking it in. Someone grabs me by the
arm – it's Henry. He keeps pushing me towards cameras,
towards people who want to clap me on the back, congratulate me, find out what I've been through. A medic is
on my other side, wanting to take me for a check. I know I
need one. Badly. The bandage round my arm is cemented
to my skin with blood, my joints are swollen and painful,
my lips are tight and my mouth bone dry from dehydration. But I wave them off. I have one target. My vision is
fully tunnelled. I know what I want. And I'm not stopping
until I get it.

'Well?' I ask Stella again.

She won't give me a straight answer. 'Adri, I don't know
what he promised you . . .'

'The footage. I want to know who was driving the car
that almost killed my son. *LK1X XFG.*'

Stella's eyes widen. She knows.

Those podcast guys – Mac and Jason – are behind her.

Jason is looking worse for wear, but he's alive. I reach out a hand to steady myself. My stomach lurches and I feel like I'm going to be sick. I take a deep breath. 'So?' I ask.

'You didn't finish,' says Stella, at least wincing when she says it. She knows how unfair it is.

'I turned on my beacon to save Hiroko. I think I did enough to earn my answers.'

Her silence is deafening.

It's Jason who breaks it. 'Hang on, repeat that number plate again.'

I do what he asks. I don't think I'll forget the number for as long as I live.

He frowns. 'I know who was driving that car. It's the same one that was parked outside Coach Glenn's house the morning he died. It was rented to a Luke Halverson.'

'Luke Halverson.' I say the name like a talisman. But it doesn't mean anything to me. 'Who is that?'

Jason shakes his head. 'I wasn't able to find out anything about him, except that he had an American passport.'

'Right. A tourist. That's what the police said. Although they wouldn't give me his name.' I feel the last of my energy seep from this final pin burst. I deflate like a balloon.

'I know who Luke is,' Stella says.

'You do?'

'It's Dad's real name. Luke Halverson is Boones,' she says.

I blink. *Boones* had been driving the car? Oh my God . . . I'd accepted an invitation from the very man I'd been afraid of these past seven years. The one who'd caused me to give up my career, my passion. I'd walked straight into his domain. I think of the bullet flying towards me. Of the fall that killed Steve. Of the miles I had run, how hard I had pushed my body. When *he* had been the one who had hurt Ethan all along.

He was the threat I feared.

But why?

I have to ask him.

Jason looks as shocked as I feel, his eyes wide. This is a mystery he's been chewing on for so long; he's almost as invested as I am.

Almost.

'Did Boones know Coach Glenn then?' Jason asks Stella.

'No.'

'So why would he go and see him? Why would he kill him?'

I blink. Jason thinks Boones killed Coach Glenn? Then the pieces fall together for me. I suddenly remember my conversation with Matt. Someone else had visited Glenn after me. Boones.

'Because of Yasmin,' Stella answers. 'Yasmin was my half-sister.' She glances at me and I give the smallest nod. 'She was the one Glenn attacked in Ibiza. Not Adrienne. Dad figured it out after she took her own life. He's always been perceptive that way. He was so angry. He flew to the UK to confront him. Or . . . that's what I thought anyway. It turned out to be more than that.'

I stare at Stella. 'Then why would your father go after Ethan?'

'Because he thought you'd been a part of it. Luring Yasmin there, inviting her for him to take advantage of.'

'Never!' I say, fiercely, horrified that Boones would make that assumption.

'We know that, Adri. I think, deep down, he knew that too.' She swallows, her hands trembling as they reach for mine. 'I'm sorry for what he did. For what it almost cost you.'

'It's not your fault. But, Stella, the world is owed the truth. We need to tell them what a monster Glenn was. For Yasmin. For justice.'

To my relief she nods. 'I'm with you.'

I take a deep breath in and count to four, holding it, then exhaling for four. When it settles, I let it go. All of it. I glance at Jason and Mac – it's like I can see their minds working, going into overdrive. The truth will come out and I'm sure they'll play a part in it. I might not like it but I got my answers, like Boones promised. It's what I came for.

And yet what I'm leaving with is so much more. Irrefutable proof that I *can* and I *did*.

Runner 13. A curse for some. But for me?

Time will tell.

The race might be over. But the rest of my life is just beginning.

57

Stella

The rest of the day is a whirlwind. Adrienne is swept away by Henry and taken for medical checks and interviews. She doesn't protest. I'm glad. They insist she goes to hospital in Ouarzazate, and by the time we all get there she's received an offer from Blixt to be a part of their team – a full-time sponsored athlete with a healthy salary attached. She and Pete and Ethan discuss moving closer to Ethan's tennis academy but still close enough to the fells that Adrienne can get her runs in.

My fingers still play with the diamond, twisting it round on the band as I sit in the lobby of our hotel. It's a beautiful building, more used to hosting Hollywood stars shooting desert movies than beaten-up runners with bruised toenails.

I'm not worried about Pete and Adrienne. They've got their shit sorted; they're co-parenting heroes. And besides, I think there's a certain Italian doctor she's intrigued by. If lingering touches and eye contact are anything to go by. But I'm worried for Pete and me. He still doesn't know the full story.

I don't want to lose him. I love him. But I haven't been honest. If we're going to have any opportunity for a future, he needs to know the truth.

He won't forgive me. Adrienne won't forgive me.

Or maybe I'm underestimating her again.

A shadow falls over me, interrupting my train of thought.

'Stella?'

It's Emilio.

His face is lined with sadness, his mouth downturned. He's holding his hands behind his back.

I take a deep breath. I know what he's about to say.

He confirms it. 'I'm so sorry to tell you this but . . .'

'He's dead,' I finish.

Emilio nods. He hands me an envelope. 'He told me to give this to you. If this happened.'

My heart skips a beat as I take it. Emilio gives me a small nod, then walks away. I think about finding Pete, but he's in the pool with Ethan. Besides, this is between me and Boones. Me and my father.

I slip my finger under the seal and remove the papers. Something small rattles inside. I tip it out and a memory stick tumbles into my hands. The number thirteen on the front.

There it is, just like that. Dad is giving me the choice. Reveal the truth – or bury it forever.

I can imagine him watching me, wanting to know what I will do.

I close it in my fist, gripping it tight.

It takes me a while to get through all the papers. Eventually, Pete finds me. I don't know if Emilio has told him about my father, but his expression is solemn. He waits for me to invite him to sit down, giving me that space. That respect.

I reach out my hand and he takes it, then sweeps his other arm round my shoulders, pulling me into a hug. 'I'm so sorry.'

I close my eyes, pressing my face into his shoulder.

When we finally separate enough for me to talk, I take a deep breath and fill him in. 'He left the races and the prize money – all of it – to me. The Ampersand elite races are mine.'

Pete whistles through his teeth.

'All I have to do is sign.'

'So are you going to do it?'

I think of all the good I can do. I could keep the promise Boones made to Mariam to rebuild a school in her village. Work with Blixt and other companies to put on amazing races, preserving the ethos of the Ampersands while keeping runners safe. While allowing them to support themselves through running. Giving them freedom.

And I can give Adrienne the win she deserves.

Decision made. I'm in charge now.

Adrienne refuses the money, of course, when I go to visit her in the hospital. She's recovering well, being given extra fluids and her shoulder has been wrapped and put in a cast. 'Give it to Nabil's family,' she tells me. 'They lost everything.'

Mariam comes in to join us while I'm sitting next to Adrienne, hobbling in on her crutches. She and Adrienne embrace, and I tell her the news about building the school. She hugs me tight.

Then there's the matter of Ibiza. With Mariam's testimony, and Yasmin's diary, we have more than enough to make sure everyone knows the truth about Coach Glenn. I can finally let go of the guilt I didn't do more back then.

I can do it now.

58

Stella

Seven years earlier
Yorkshire

Coach Glenn is dead.

It didn't take much. I had the medication already, taken from my dad's luggage. Digoxin. Works to manage heart failure. Old-school stuff for an old-school guy. Typical Boones.

It worked to slow Glenn's too. Stop it, in fact.

It wasn't hard to administer. Glenn was all too eager to have a coffee with me. Said he loved her. I told him what I'd done – after he'd drunk, of course. He tried to beg for his life – but it was too late.

I made sure to clean up after I was gone.

He wasn't the only one I was angry at. I was furious with myself. That I'd left Yasmin when she'd begged me to stay. That I'd chosen a man over my sister. If I'd stayed, I could have changed everything.

I could have been there for her.

I could have made sure he didn't get away with it.

Adrienne might have tried, but she'd only made things worse. Stupid woman.

I was driving too fast. I wanted to yell at her. Scream. Make her sorry for what she did to Yasmin. She'd brought her into his orbit. Her lies drove my dear beautiful sister to take her own life.

But she wasn't even home. She was out running. Racing! Even after the note I had sent her. *STOP RACING OR SUFFER*. I couldn't believe it. Anger surged through my body, making me feel white hot. My vision was a sea of red.

It was still red when I veered round the corner, losing control. Horrific sounds rang in my ears: the screech of tyres, a high-pitched scream, shouting. A little boy was right in my path. A crunch as the car collides against a stone wall. A man rushing towards the scene. It's Pete. I can't let him see me. He'll recognize me. He'll know.

Fuck. I reverse and I don't see a body. That's enough for me. I speed away without stopping, my heart pounding. The close call clears my mind and my heart rate slows.

I've killed once today. That's enough.

I abandon the car. But when I return to my hotel, Dad is waiting for me. Sitting in the lobby. He probably would have waited there for days. He's patient like that.

'What did you do?' he asks me.

'What I had to,' I say.

He nods. He doesn't ask questions. He'll be back on a plane to the US in a few hours.

If the police figure it out and come for me, so be it. I'll accept my fate.

But somehow I don't think they will.

59

Stella

Back in the hotel, Blixt host a huge race closing party –
simultaneously a celebration of what the runners have
been through and a memorial party for Boones. Huge
firepits are set out beneath strings of festoon lights, plat-
ters of Moroccan tagine and grilled meats served from a
buffet, and champagne galore. The atmosphere is festive
rather than melancholy. That's what he would want. He
would be proud.

He knew this was coming – the bullet only accelerated
his timeline.

I take a moment to drink it in. Not literally, of course.
No alcohol for me. I've got a new family to keep together,
to keep safe. I'll tell Pete the news tonight. I know how
happy he will be to know that I am pregnant.

Boones's final gift to me: taking the blame for what I'd
done, so I never have to reveal the truth. Everyone thinks
he was behind the wheel of that Range Rover. That he
killed Glenn. That he targeted Ethan.

I toss the memory stick in one of the firepits, watching
as the plastic burns, the contents turning to ash.

'This is how far I'll go, Dad,' I whisper.

And I think he would approve.

The Ultra Bros Podcast

Hot & Sandy Redux Edition

Mac:	Well, well, do we have a treat for all you listeners out there. I'm sure by now all of you have watched the Netflix smash documentary *RUNNER 13* covering last year's catastrophic disaster of a race that was Hot & Sandy. We knew we would have drama. We knew we would have pain. We knew we would have DNFs. But deaths? Murder? And maybe most unlikely of all a finisher?

The film covered everything, including the shocking testimony of various female runners who were groomed and mistreated by running coach Glenn Knight for decades. We now know that Adrienne Wendell – the eponymous runner thirteen – lied to protect another runner, Yasmin El Mehdi, who had been drugged and assaulted by Glenn at his training camp in Ibiza. Sadly, Yasmin took her own life in the aftermath of the abuse. When Glenn died of a supposed heart attack, with Adrienne's reputation in ruins, it seemed like the offences would be buried alongside him. But with the collaboration between Adrienne, Stella Mamoud – Yasmin's sister – and Mariam

Hussein, the truth is now out there. It's clear how important that truth is to his victims, more of whom have spoken out since the documentary aired. Glenn's death was not the end of their story.

Then there was the footage from Hot & Sandy itself. Boones's ultimate race – pitting the runners not only against the elements, or themselves, but against a motivated adversary. The ghost from Long & Windy returned. A man so broken by his failure to finish, he faked his own death, and when he came back he wanted everyone else to fail too. But he couldn't bring Adri down. The curse – or cult – of runner thirteen struck again.

What a mind-blowing film. What was it like for you watching it, Jason?

Jason: So weird. Triggering. But I think about Nabil – what a terrible loss the running community suffered – and about Rupert – still not the same after his gunshot wound – and I think that storm might have been the luckiest escape of my life.

Mac: Well, speaking of lucky, we've managed to persuade Adrienne to appear on the podcast to answer all our burning questions. Welcome, Adrienne!

Adrienne: Thanks for having me.

Jason: Truly, it's an honour to have you on the show. I've been moaning to our listeners how it's taken me a year to feel back to normal and I didn't go through half of what you've endured. But you've been smashing races left, right and centre – you're on track to win a UTMB triple crown. It's a joke to ask whether you've recovered but – a year on – how are you feeling?

Adrienne: Physically, I feel much better now. Recovery was brutal. A lot of physio, a lot of much-needed time with my son, a lot of therapy. Mentally, I'm still a work in progress. I'm not sure I'll ever get over what I experienced over those six days – or the past eight years.

Mac: That's totally understandable. You fought in an all-out war. But now you're on the other side and making it as a full-time runner, right?

Adrienne: Yes, I'm very lucky. Blixt are my main sponsors and they give me the support I need to run in the races that I want to, so I can balance training with spending time with my son. I chose the Yorkshire 100 as my first race back. Something a little comforting and familiar.

Jason: Only you would consider one hundred miles in winter 'comforting'! And didn't you break your own record in the process? You're being a little modest here.

Mac: You know, a lot of people wouldn't have blamed you if you never raced again after Hot & Sandy.

Adrienne: I tried giving racing up once. Didn't work. Running is what saves me.

Mac: After watching RUNNER 13, I think I get that. The pile-on you faced in the wake of your

379

accusation eight years ago – that was uncomfortable to watch. I know this podcast and many other media outlets owe you an apology. So we are hand-on-heart sorry, and thank you for coming back to speak to us even after what we said.

Adrienne: Is this a rare moment of sincerity from the Ultra Bros? I'm shocked! But thank you.

Jason: Mac's getting soft! Bound to happen in his old age.

Mac: Har, har. But seriously. You also now offer coaching and support to other runners – is there anything you want to say to young athletes out there, male and female, who are getting into our sport?

Adrienne: I love coaching. I know its importance. Its value. But I also know the power dynamic it creates, the bubble you can find yourself in, and the privilege that comes with being a teacher. For anyone out there listening, trust your gut. Talk to someone if you think something is wrong. Listen if someone comes to you with concerns. There is never an excuse for any form of abuse.

Jason: Exactly. Adrienne, you're an inspiration. I could honestly ask you questions for hours – but I know you're keen to get back out on the fells.

Adrienne: You going to come with me?

Jason: Are you kidding? A chance to run with the GOAT? I'd love it.

Mac: One final question before you go. We polled our listeners to find out the one thing they really wanted to ask. Stella Mamoud is putting on Hot & Sandy again this year. As Boones's daughter, I think she's going to be able to pull off the same diabolical twists as her father, although hopefully with fewer fatalities. Are you going to be on the starting line?

Adrienne: What do you think?

Acknowledgements

There's that old expression – it's a marathon, not a sprint. That certainly rings true when it comes to writing books! Both running and writing are also traditionally solo enterprises, but I couldn't do either without the most amazing teams around me.

First, on the running front. Crossing the finishing line of the 36th Marathon des Sables in 2022 was an experience that changed me forever. Six days of putting myself through the hardest physical experience of my life, running further than I had ever dreamed possible, through the vast and beautiful terrain of the Sahara Desert. It's something I'll never forget. Yet I never would have made it were it not for my incredible companions in tent 74 – Karen, Jon, Dan, Richard, Amelia and Ian. You are all such huge inspirations to me, and you kept me going when I didn't think I could take another step. Thank you for waiting for the 'mint rocket' at the finish line.

I tried to capture as much of my own running experience as I could in this novel, but I also benefited from conversations with amateur and professional ultrarunners, race organisers, course photographers, running coaches, specialist doctors and marathon volunteers, all of whom were so generous with their time. My particular thanks to Ian Corless, Jon Bromley, Dr Savvas Papasavvas, Lauren Gregory and Kerry Sutton. Their stories and expertise helped to shape the plot and fill in the blanks of my knowledge. However, any errors made in the depiction of this fictional race are my own.

For my writing journey, I've been so lucky to be on team Juliet Mushens ever since the beginning. Alongside the rest of the Mushens Entertainment – Alba, Catriona, Den, Emma, Kiya, Liza and Rachel – you make up the best agenting support crew in the business. And huge thanks to Jenny Bent, my US agent, for being my advocate across the pond.

I'm so lucky to have some of the best publishers in the business in my corner – Joel Richardson of Penguin Michael Joseph, Edward Kastenmeier of Doubleday Books and Lara Hinchberger of Penguin Canada. Thank you for your endless patience and invaluable feedback, and for always helping me craft the best book possible.

Behind the publishing scenes, I know there are so many people hard at work. I want to shout out a few: Ellie, Lily, Stella, Grace, Yasmin and Beatrix at Penguin Michael Joseph, Chris at Doubleday, Alanna, Catherine and Chalista at Penguin Canada. Also to Jennie Roman, my eagle-eyed copyeditor, who doesn't let anything slip through her net.

Personally, I'm grateful to my remarkable friends – whether I'm writing books, running ultramarathons, climbing mountains or growing my family, they're always behind me. Kim Curran – for being my incredible first reader – my day doesn't start until we've messaged each other. Saara, Lizzie, El, Juno, James, Amie, thank you for being the best writer friends I could ask for; I look up to you all both personally and professionally. Sarah, Tania, Adam, Maria Felix, Sarah J, Tash, Joanna, Stef, my Tuesday ladies at Tandridge, my NCT pals Abbey, Amreen, Becca,

Fiona, Jagruti, Katy and Stacey – thank you for keeping me upright through challenging times juggling writing and becoming a mum.

I'm blessed with incredible family support, particularly Peter and Tessa, Paul and Clare, Molly, Lily, Anne and Diana. To my amazing sister Sophie (who took over my social media while I was running) and brother-in-law Evan, thank you for flying out to Morocco with me for research and filming. Your combined creativity, passion and vision help me bring my books to life in a way I could never dream possible. Angus and Maria, thank you for always being there when I need you, and for putting up with me while I put myself through yet another tortuous endurance event. You're my biggest and loudest cheerleaders.

And my final thanks go to Chris and Rory, my worlds. I can't wait to see what adventures we go on together.